ECHOES

PlaneTree

ECHOES

by

Ajay Harris

Published 2002
ISBN 1-84294-096-1

Published by PlaneTree

Old Station Offices,
Llanidloes,
Powys SY18 6EB
United Kingdom

© 2002 Ajay Harris

This novel is a work of fiction. Characters and names are the product of the author's imagination. Any resemblance to anybody, living or dead, is entirely coincidental

All rights reserved. No part of this publication may be reproduced, stored in a retrieval system, or transmitted in any form or by any means, electronic, mechanical, recording or otherwise, without the prior written permission of the author.

Manufactured in the United Kingdom

PROLOGUE.

Lightning flashed overhead, illuminating the woodland and highlighting the rope hanging from the bare branches of the oak tree.

Her hands tied behind her back, Rowena Berrysford cursed the three men.

"I swear by all that's holy, you and your descendants will die in the flames of hell fire," she spat, silencing their argument about which of them should rape her next.

Walter Coleman jeered as he pulled his leather poaching sack over her head, muffling her cries as the metallic stench of blood made her stomach heave. Panicking, she tried not to vomit.

His son's, Luke and Seth, lifted her while he put the noose around her neck, tugging it tight before they let her fall. Her breath would not come as she slowly strangled, kicking frantically as her feet sought solid ground.

The last sound Rowena heard was the loud snap as her neck broke. Her slight body jerked involuntarily before it swung limply from the oak tree, twisting slowly in a macabre pirouette.

The dark forest, silent now, held it's breath, waiting...

*****

CHAPTER ONE.

The snap was still reverberating in my ears as my life flashed before me.

I remembered my mother and father at Beaumont Hall. My husband William and Rowena, my beautiful baby. And I remembered the Colemans.

They had dragged me from my home and hanged me. But I had cheated death for I came to my senses hanging almost upside down; still constrained by the rope round my neck, which must have slipped for my weight was supported on my left side, leaving my right arm free.

The thunderstorm...

Lightning! A bolt must have struck the tree, breaking the branch. To the superstitious Coleman's that would be further proof that I was a witch.

The oak tree loomed overhead, its branches looked high as they clawed the dark sky but I was dizzy and my eyes out of focus.

Tentatively I felt my injuries, the worst was my throat, the skin raw and bleeding, aggravated by a fine chain around my neck. But as I combed my fingers through my hair I found a painful lump on my temple, no doubt the reason for my headache. Apart from that I had survived my ordeal without too much damage. More than I could guarantee the Colemans when William had finished with them, I seethed, rejoicing in my anger. Better medicine for humiliation than self pity.

Curses and strange mutterings by my side startled me. Terrified, I feigned death and held my breath as sticky hands groped my face in the darkness, mauling my body and my breast. I prayed silently and miraculously the rope around me was undone.

I was suddenly free but as I landed on the ground it knocked the breath out of me and I lay for a moment gasping for air, trying to regain my senses.

Feeling the earth beneath me I pushed myself to my feet to run. As I touched the tree a bright light lit up the forest like a summer's day and was gone. I feared real witchcraft was afoot this night.

Silence lay like a heavy blanket over Sherwood, except for a strange unsteady roaring in the distance, similar to a storm pounding the sea. The forest smelled of fresh greenery and damp earth after the rain. And of something that I could not quite identify.

Panic drained power from my legs as I tried to lift up my petticoats and run. A scream almost escaped me but I bit my lip and stumbled on in silence. My clothes. Why had the Colemans removed my gown and dressed me in this fashion? What reason could they have for this perversion?

I could only suppose that my gown, torn and bloody, made the truth of what they had done only too clear. I shuddered at the thought of them gloating over me as they pulled on these rough breeches, suitable only for a smithy.

Seth scraped a living digging graves and I prayed that these garments had not been taken from some poor dead soul. The loose shirt was the soft silk of the gentry, obviously stolen. The Justice would hang a man for less, or woman for that matter. Finally I understood. If found, alive or dead, I would be unlawfully dressed in men's clothing. This alone was enough to label me a heretic and witch.

There were sinister mutterings in the village about the hot dry summer and the Elders were looking for a scapegoat for the drought. Walter Coleman's accusation and my strange clothes would be enough to sway them for, always willing to change his allegiance before Parliament or King demanded it, he had become an Elder in Cromwell's church.

Why then had he not taken me for trial? What reason could he have to hang me secretly in the dead of night?

Sounds of pursuit followed me and I was uncertain which way to run. Dressed in this unseemly manner I dare not be seen at Beaumont Hall, which left me without Squire Keeton's or my husband's help, as William is the squire's steward. I turned instead towards my baby's nurse, Mistress Milly Jeacock's house.

It bordered the forest so I could get there without being seen. She would lend me a dress and bonnet and alert my husband whilst I ran home to protect my baby Rowena.

By long tradition my family had always named the first born after the Rowan tree. Rowan for a boy and Rowena for a girl. It was our solemn duty to give the babe the family pendant, one side engraved with the initial R and the other enamelled with Rowan leaves and berries. It was reputed to ensure the safety of the wearer until each new generation was born. I remembered the chain around my neck and I pulled it free of my clothing.

The talisman was still there.

Yet I well remember six months ago I had threaded it onto a silk ribbon and tied it round my daughter's neck when she was new born. I laid her in the cradle which William had carved with the emblem he'd copied from the locket. He had come down the stairs, his eyes shining with love.

"Come," he'd said, taking my hand. "I have something to show you..."

My fingers traced the finely etched initial.

How could I still have it when every morning, every evening, I had reassured myself that the talisman was still there to protect my baby? Anxious for her welfare, I prayed she would be safe without it.

With a stab of fear I remembered what Luke Coleman had said when they had dragged me from my home.

"When we've done with Mistress High and Mighty there will be plenty of time to come back and search for her spells," he'd said, hoisting my bible box onto his shoulder.

"Mayhap the witch keeps 'em in here under lock and key, eh?" he'd snarled into my face.

The bible box was a gift from my father, Sir Rowan Beaumont, on the day of my birth. It too was carved with the emblem of the Rowan but contained naught but the King James' bible. Coleman didn't really believe it held magic spells, did he?

"Witch," he sneered. They all took up the chant, poking me, their ragged black rimmed finger nails digging through my sturdy bombazine gown.

"I am not a witch," I'd argued.

They were only using the accusation to frighten me for a long forgotten slight, weren't they? I had some small gift for prophesy and making things grow but I'd learned to keep it a secret, for such skills were now associated with witchcraft.

"Don't you remember how I did this, *Missie?"* Walter Coleman asked while he was searching for evidence to hang me. He'd shoved his scarred and twisted hand under my nose, making me jerk back from it. "I watched you after you did this," he continued, "every time you were in the woods. You sprung my gins and you didn't use no stick to do it, neither."

"Nor you to open them," I'd replied, probably sealing my fate.

The way he'd said Missie, brought the event back to my mind as if it had happened yesterday.

I was just a child and my father was still the Squire at Beaumont Hall; long before his land had been forfeited for taxes because he'd fought and died on the losing side in Cromwell's civil war.

Mistress Milly had taken me to the king's best wood to pick berries for my favorite syllabub, a special treat for my ninth birthday. We'd heard the fearful crying of what we thought to be a baby, the keening made my blood run cold, such pitiful distress sounded heartbreakingly human. I'd run unerringly to a small clearing where I'd found Coleman, his thin lips pulled back in a grin as he crouched over the screaming hare caught in his trap.

Trembling with anger, I shuddered when he broke its neck and put the hare into his leather poaching sack.

Frustrated as only an impotent child can be, I watched helplessly as he opened the spring and pushed down the plate, re-setting the powerful teeth to catch another poor animal.

"I wish it would trap you!" I'd thought, throwing all the force I could muster at the trap as I'd said it.

He looked up and saw me as it snapped shut, biting his fingers to the bone.

Yelling in anger and pain, he realised what I had done. But he dare not tell anyone for he was stealing the king's game. Cursing, he's tried to prise open the heavy jaws with his other hand but could not. "I'll get you for this *Missie.* Just you wait," he'd said.

Appalled, I backed into the woods preparing to release him and flee but gaped open mouthed when he looked furtively about and thinking himself unobserved, he had stared at the gin trap. The iron frosted over and in an instant it sprang open... He too had the power.

Later that same year my nurse and I were gathering holly and ivy to decorate the Hall for Christmas, when once again we had heard the scream of a hare. I'd run into the best wood to search for it, Milly anxiously beseeching me to take care.

When I'd found the terrified animal, its foreleg was pouring with blood as he struggled to free himself from the gin trap. I'd willed it to open and cradled the wounded hare in my arms, weeping because it was hurt. As I stroked him I held his mangled paw and fervently wished it better. Slowly his leg stopped bleeding and his tiny bones knitted together. When his thudding heart regained a steady, rhythmic beat, I released him and watched him bound away before I walked back to Milly, contented but sleepy.

"It's all right now, Mistress. I found the poor hare," I told her. "It was broken but I mended it."

I remembered what I'd tried so hard to forget, I'd healed the animal without the aid of herbs or potions. I am a witch.

A wave of giddiness overwhelmed me and I fell to the ground retching. I crept into the undergrowth, needing to catch my breath for a moment. To think.

Coleman and I were both witches, yet as different as day and night.

Spontaneous healing was warm and good, the art of a 'wise woman' as white witches were known before Cromwell denounced the blessings of nature. But Coleman's power was cold and evil.

Realising I knew his secret, he'd waited all these years till the time was right before he's tried to hang me. Now one only had to make an accusation of witchcraft and some poor soul would be hung.

I brushed a strand of hair from my bruised face and picked a dew covered dock leaf to cool the rope burns on my neck, the memory of choking as the rope gouged into my throat, took my breath away.

I dismissed the nagging doubt that I was missing a vital point in my reasoning; there would be time to test the errors of my logic when I was back in my William's arms. By now he would be anxious for my welfare but I would comfort him all in good time.

Praying for the safety of my baby I struggled to my feet, desperate to get home. Stumbling though the forest I almost fell over a fallen tree but fortunately managed to climb over it.

Heavy footsteps behind me crashed though the undergrowth and the sound of snapping branches accompanied the dawn chorus.

Closer. They were getting closer.

Day was breaking, lighting my way as I weaved through the trees. Something was dreadfully wrong. Sherwood seemed much sparser than I thought it should be but my mind was hazy, I was probably much closer to the edge of the forest than I thought I was.

In the half light I stared at the bare autumn trees, wondering what strange trick my eyes were playing now. Against the weird coloured sky a green haze seemed to be blooming and the ground underfoot was black and decayed instead of the gold and red layer of fallen leaves. Were my eyes deceiving me? Disorientated, I stopped to catch my breath.

The strange noise which I had heard at the oak tree was louder now and the acrid smoky smell was making my eyes water.

Was it the roar of flames? The smell of my house burning?

What if the Colemans had gone back and set fire to Berrysford House, leaving my daughter trapped?

Veering direction, I ran as fast as my feet would carry me back to my baby. Back towards my pursuers. But the feeling of unease intruded. Something was not right with my reasoning.

I cursed my stupidity. If the Colemans were chasing me, they couldn't have gone back to burn my house. But they must also know that I was not dead and I was running straight to them.

Almost weeping with frustration I moved with legs of stone until I was near the edge of the forest. How I had managed to travel so far in so short a time worried me but the trees were fewer now, giving me less cover and the ground sloped rapidly. Mayhap I would make it to Mistress Milly's and safety.

I looked up, trying to judge the time of day, for there was a strange orange glow in the sky. The world tilted crazily but I fought off my dizziness for fear that all the village was afire.

All of the shire.

But there wasn't any smoke. Nor flames neither.

Rubbing my eyes, I tried to make sense of the peculiar landscape.

Nottingham and its surrounding villages stretched below me for miles, shining with the glow of a million tiny fires.

Bright beams of light were roaring rapidly towards me.

The smell... I could almost put a name to it. The strange noise...

The road below me shimmered and I saw it as it was now and as it used to be. Wavering images distorted as my eyes adjusted to the unfamiliar scene.

Petrol fumes!

I turned wearily to face my pursuers. The pale light was swirling into a grey mist and I fought to stay conscious, after all my suffering I wanted to know my fate, my destiny...

A man came crashing through the trees after me, his face cut and bleeding. 'Rowena,' he gasped. 'Don't run any more please, for pity's sake.'

As soon as he spoke I recognised his voice. But he couldn't be who I thought he was, could he? My husband James Roberts?

'Where is William?' I asked, my voice a hoarse croak. What had become of my husband and my beautiful daughter? 'My baby?' I whispered, realising the answer.

She was dead. They were all dead.

The past shivered around me like echoes in the night and I knew without doubt that the snap I'd heard was the sound of my neck breaking when the Colemans had hanged me.

I had lived Rowena Berrysford's life. And her death.

This was the second Millennium and I would never see William or my baby again.

CHAPTER TWO.

"We were in an accident, remember?' James soothed. 'I drove into the oak tree and you hit your head on the windscreen.'
'No.' It was imperative that he believed me. 'The Colemans took me from my home, tore me away from my baby.' Frantic with grief I tried to shut out the fear of what they might have done to her.

'The idiot Seth raped me and his father, Walter Coleman, hanged me dead on the oak tree, I heard the snap as my neck broke.' I stuttered.

I looked down, puzzled by the blood pouring from the gash on James' thigh. His torn and bloody jeans. And mine. Sobbing, I realised the silk shirt of the gentry was in reality my own and my rough breeches, my denim jeans. The world reeled about me as my brain tried to take everything in too fast, like a downing man gulping air.

Reluctant to let go of the past I saw myself standing before the mirror in Beaumont Hall...

William and Rowena stood in front of the looking glass, his arm draped around her shoulder. He smiled into the eyes of her reflection as he asked her to marry him. Her unruly copper coloured hair was neatly tucked under the finely pleated linen cap, the untied ribbons a mark of her unmarried status, trailing on to the shoulders of her dark green bombasine gown.

I stared at the heart shaped face, green eyes and rather too short nose and mentally superimposed my modern image upon it.

Apart from the fact that after years of jogging and aerobics, I was slimmer and at 5'7", taller than my seventeenth century counterpart, the resemblance was startling.

'It was my fault, I lost control of the car when I thought I saw something on the tree.' James frowned dismissively. 'Someone hanging...'

He rubbed his eyes as though trying to erase the memory. "I must have imagined it.'

Imagined? 'You have never imagined anything in your life, James,' I said with assurance, knowing it was true. Logic ruled his life; it was a prerequisite of his job. I remembered he was a Professor of British Archaeology at Nottingham University.

A flash of fear and confusion crossed his face before he denied his own eyes.

'A trick of the light, sweetheart. Nothing more.'

'But I remember my life. My father, Sir Rowan Beaumont, he was killed at Naseby in 1645. And I can recall every detail of the day I married William Berrysford.'

I tried to block out the sense of William kneeling close beside me at the alter of the small church in the grounds of Beaumont Hall, his long fingered hand surreptitiously reaching for mine. My heart lurched with love as out of the corner of my eye, I saw his blue eyes smiling at me under the deep shadowed veil of his dark lashes.

James was tutting and shaking his head in bewilderment.

'William and I have a six month old daughter, Rowena. Even then the first born was named after the Rowan tree,' I paused as my throat closed up with grief.

They are all long dead and I would never see my baby's smiling face again.

Tears blurred my eyes. My arms ached at their loss. Just this morning I had held my babe and marvelled at her angelic beauty. Her red gold curls and sweet face was dominated by her eyes. Highlighted by flecks of gold, they were already changing into a deep green.

'She is so beautiful.'

James put his arm around me. 'Don't upset yourself, love. You'll be alright soon.'

'William has a twin sister, Sarah,' I stuttered. 'My dearest friend. Her husband, Edward Smithson, owns a brick yard and helped William to build Berrysford House.'

James was looking at me oddly. I had used the present tense. 'I'm sorry, Rowena. But you must realise that it cannot possibly be real,' he said, trying to soothe me. 'You've had a bad knock on the head, love,' he murmured, holding me to his chest. 'It was only a nightmare brought on by concussion.'

I opened my tightly clenched fist and bewildered, stared at the object I was holding. My locket. The locket which my mother had given me when I was born in the twentieth century. It didn't convince me, I could clearly see it around my baby's neck.

'But I remember my childhood in Beaumont Hall. Old friends. My husband and my baby,' I fought back the tears, knowing they wouldn't sway him. 'You can't dream memories, can you?'

He smiled. 'Such delusions are a common symptom of concussion.'

'But it was so real, James. The old man was Walter Coleman, his eldest son Luke was a smithy and his youngest, a burly half wit named Seth, raped me.' I shuddered as I felt Walter and Luke's ragged nails digging into my ankles as they pulled my legs apart. Saw Seth's moon face inches above mine as he tore into me; smelled the rancid stink of his sweat, the stench of his breath.

James held me as I retched at the thought of his seed inside of me.

'It didn't happen, Rowena,' he insisted firmly, 'and even if it did, it could not have happened to you.'

Then how could I remember Luke and his father holding me down; suckling me? I bit my lip to prevent a sob escaping, trying to remain calm and dispassionate.

I was vaguely aware of James holding me gently but I was concentrating on repeating that it hadn't happened to me, Rowena Roberts, Seth's semen was not inside my body.

My stomach churned at the vivid memory and I was violently sick.

There was no doubt in my mind that what I had experienced was a true account of Mistress Berrysford's life and death. If only I could prove it, find her grave and let her rest in peace.

'My poor darling,' James murmured. 'What a terrible nightmare.'

'It wasn't a nightmare. It happened, even if it was in Rowena Berrysford's lifetime.'

'Collective memory?' he asked, obviously trying to quell his natural scepticism.

'No. Not exactly. It was her you saw hanging at the crossroads. The Colemans murdered her. Perhaps she needs my help to prove it,' I whispered.

'The Colemans are just preying on your mind,' James said, sounding exhausted. 'They might be bastards but they wouldn't hang you,' he tried to reassure me.

I gasped with fear and confusion. He knew who I was talking about. The fact rose to the surface and I grasped it tentatively. 'They don't belong in this lifetime, do they?'

I could not imagine Walter wearing anything but the ugly black garb of a so called zealous Puritan.

'Calm down and try to relax,' James insisted. 'You are obviously suffering from shock and concussion.'

'But what about my neck?' I asked, showing him the rope burns. 'I didn't imagine this.'

'Sweetheart,' he said as if talking to a frightened child, 'The seat belt was cutting into your neck when I released it. And if we assume that what you say is true; why after all this time would it be so important for your ancestor to prove who killed her, or why?'

He felt my bruised forehead and kissed it tenderly. 'The last thing you saw was the tree and when the seat belt was throttling you, your mind looked for a reason for your body's pain and "imagined" the rest. Like a dream where the extraneous noises are superimposed into your sleeping state.'

I understood where he was coming from and murmured in half hearted agreement.

'And the snap you heard was probably your neck as it was whip-lashed in the accident.'

'That's possible,' I conceded. 'But I don't like the sound of this at all, James. What are the Colemans doing in my life, after what they did to...' I paused, I was going to say me but to save argument, said, 'Rowena Berrysford?'

He rocked me in his arms and he too was shaking, shock catching up with him.

'They murdered me, James,' I whispered, fighting back the tears threatening behind my eyes. 'Everyone I knew is dead. William, my baby. Everybody,' I sobbed with grief at my inconsolable loss.

William and my daughter had disappeared from my life forever. I had lost everything. My family, friends and my history.

I couldn't expect James to understand my desolation. To him, if it happened at all, it happened centuries ago but to me it was only yesterday.

Feeling him trembling I comforted this stranger, this man I had married, knowing every wrinkle on his intelligent face, every nuance of his educated voice. He, like William, was tall and slim, almost gaunt, his hair was dark too, but receding and sprinkled with grey. I knew he was only 46 years old but he looked older. Distinguished, handsome and charming.

And an inveterate womaniser.

Then, like a punch in the stomach, I remembered that we were no longer married.

I pulled away, trying to control my sobbing as I stared up at him in confusion. 'We are divorced?' I croaked, feeling betrayed and lost.

'But not for long if I have my way, darling,' James murmured in my ear.

'You know I only ever loved you. I'm sorry about Barbara but you know how manipulative she is.'

She was his secretary cum slapper. 'Oh yes, I remember *Barbara*,' I stressed. 'And all the others, James. You love women too much, you just can't help yourself.'

I had stayed with him through his numerous inconsequential affairs because he was such a charmer. But that was only partly true; I loved my stepchildren to distraction and had put up with James' "little indiscretions" as he called them, until the children were old enough to cope on their own. And I couldn't stand his deceit any longer.

Recently however they had joined their father in a three pronged assault to get us back together on a more permanent basis and I must admit that we were getting on better now than we had ever done during our marriage.

'Please don't shut me out, sweetheart. Give me another chance,' he begged, taking hold of my hand as we walked back through the low blanket of mist rising from the earth, the forest alive with bird song.

I couldn't expect James to understand my desolation at losing a man I had loved in the seventeenth century.

'What are the Colemans like?' I asked. Trying to forget their brutish faces. 'Where do they fit in my life?'

'Sebastian Coleman is an eminent industrialist and is standing for Parliament in the local by-election. With his inbred arrogance he'll probably win. But his sons are the bane of his life. Mind you, he will never admit that they are less than perfect.' James said. 'George is overweight which often goes with the mentally disadvantaged, he's like a big child, tantrums and all. Piers, however, is clever enough but he's a spoilt brat. A bully, that's all, ' he said.

Listening attentively as he described the Colemans of today, I just could not remember them, it was as if they didn't belong in this modern world.

'I wish you had never bought that old place on his estate at Beaumont Hall. It has become all mixed up in your illusion.'

I was startled that Beaumont Hall, where Mistress Berrysford had spent her childhood, was now owned by the Colemans.

'I hate to think of you there all on your own.'

This was my ex playing for advantage, I realised, tutting and shaking my head.

'You've got to give me credit for trying,' he said ruefully and changing the subject, continued.

'I don't know how you manage to keep your temper when Piers complains about Buggalugs and Cassidy.'

Warmth flooded into me as I recalled my friendly black and white cat and Cassidy, my little three legged dog. I had found the Welsh border collie cum cocker spaniel, injured by the roadside, obviously run over in a car accident. One of his back legs was hanging by a thin strip of fur, probably caught under the wheel as he ran away.

To my everlasting joy, the vet, bless her heart, had saved his life if not his leg. I'd named him Cassidy after the old silent film star cowboy, Hopalong Cassidy. I just adored old black and white movies.

A cold breeze rustled the tree tops and chilled my spine. I started to shiver, too tired to argue any longer. My life here was coming back to me.

'We'll have to let Justin know what's happened,' James muttered to himself. Then he looked at me anxiously. 'You haven't forgotten Justin and Susan?' he asked. 'My children?'

'No, ' I smiled., 'Justin is sensitive and fiercely protective. He married Debra last year. A bright, lovely, loving girl. They have just moved into their new home in Mapperley.

And Susan, of course.' A clever, cynical but rather selfish teenager who had her father's charm.

Talk about manipulative, Susan could wrap me round her little finger with her sparkling smile. 'She is in her first year at York.'

Through the haze of a thumping headache, I remembered.

After our divorce I had returned to my chosen field, a freelance investigative journalist; mostly but not always, specialising in environmental issues.

James had accompanied me to Upper Berry, a village in Yorkshire, where we'd spent the weekend together, combining a little break with work. I was investigating a cluster of "thalidomide" type birth defects and miscarriages in the area, which, according to medical opinion were Dioxin related. No one knew why such a catastrophe should have centred round this particular beauty spot, a few miles from the University but I was determined to find out.

'We have just spent the day with Susan at Upper Berry. '

Hoping to sell pictures with the article we had taken her out for lunch at an Inn in the picturesque village and I had photographed the beautiful reservoir to give a startling contrast to the suffering within the community.

After taking Susan back to her flat, James and I were on our way home when the car had gone icy cold. Without any logical explanation I knew that something evil had taken control and was forcing the car to the limits of its speed. James had kept pumping the brakes and fighting the steering wheel, which was white with frost. We were hurtling down the narrow road heading for the crossroads, when I had reached for the wheel.

Immediately the frost retreated from the warmth of my hands. I felt as if someone had taken over my mind, forcing me to concentrate. I willed the car to slow down. I was sure that if James had not imagined he'd seen someone hanging and wrenched the wheel from my hands, we would have stopped safely on the grass verge.

I have always been a bit psychic, seen glimpses of the future, especially when my loved ones were in danger, but that was quite commonplace, wasn't it? And I knew who was on the other end of the phone, often before it rang but I had never experienced such a strong psychic force.

'We're nearly there,' James interrupted my reverie, as we neared the road.

The sound of traffic was easily identifiable to me now. In the clear light of dawn we arrived exhausted, at the scene of the accident. My little car was almost vertical, with the right front wheel up against the tree trunk, tilting to the left. The passenger door was hanging off its hinges and it was easy to see how I had fallen out, once James had freed me from the seat belt. The front looked like a concertina. It was a miracle we both weren't killed.

James must have thought the same thing because we collapsed into each others arms, thankful that we were both still alive.

'Well, here's what's left of your car,' he said, sitting down abruptly, his injured leg giving way beneath him. He was ashen and was visibly trembling with shock. 'It's a write off, I'm afraid.'

Sitting close beside him to keep him warm, I stared with little regret at my old car. A decent enough runabout in town but it was hardly suitable anymore for the unexpected amount of travelling I had to do in my job.

'I'll get a better one next time,' I said. 'A Sherman tank, maybe.'

James dutifully tried to grin.

'Cars can be replaced,' he said, squeezing my arm, 'but there is only one of you.'

'You too, James,' I smiled and in a surge of mutual affection we reached for each other and kissed. Not a long sensual kiss of passion but of love nonetheless. Love founded in years of shared memories, good and bad. James had his faults, perhaps more than his fare share but the warmth of his kiss ensured forgiveness.

'Someone will have reported the accident by now, love. You'll soon be home.'

Home? My deadly enemies lived practically next door.

Since moving in to Beaumont Court as it was called now, weird things had happened. Nasty unexplainable things. Underwear, perfume and inexpensive jewellery went missing. My cat had been thrown in the pond. Little things which in the light of day were easy to decry but alone and vulnerable at three o'clock in the morning, they kept me wide eyed and watchful.

Sebastian Coleman, who played the part of a bluff honest farmer to perfection, tried to keep his sons under control but his duties took him away too often. He seemed trustworthy enough; as far as any prospective Parliamentary candidate, could be. His son George, however, who was too much like the half wit Seth for my liking, was always leering at me, more often than not whilst playing with himself. And Piers, the personification of Walter Coleman, with his thick wet lips and glittering black eyes, was insidiously menacing.

Shame I didn't know them before I'd bought one of their conversions at Beaumont Hall. But when the Estate manager's house came up for sale, I'd put in a ridiculously low offer, though more than I could afford, and was surprised when Coleman accepted it.

Why had he sold it to me so cheaply? What did he want from me?

I shuddered uncontrollably, hating them with pathological fury.

'Is your memory OK now?' James asked. 'Can you remember the Colemans?'

'Yes, James,' I whispered, unable to stop shivering at the thought of living so close to my powerful enemies. 'I remember the Colemans.'

And I have the strangest feeling that they remember me.

CHAPTER THREE.

The blare of a police siren drew us wearily to our feet.

'Thank God. Someone saw the wreckage and phoned for help,' James said, sitting down again abruptly, relief draining the strength from him.

The police car stopped.

'The cavalry has arrived in the nick of time,' I cracked, making him smile.

After a few questions one of the policemen radioed for an ambulance whilst the other retrieved our luggage from the back seat and took Justin's name and address, promising to notify him of our accident, assuring me that they would not alarm him.

In the ambulance I asked where we were going, trying not to look as they cut James' jeans and exposed the gaping wound in his thigh.

'Queen's Medical Centre,' the paramedic said.

I groaned but accepted that James needed his leg stitched and hoped the place was clean and we didn't have to wait too long.

When we arrived, the care was sympathetic but long drawn out, as different people wanted information which the Government insisted upon. In triplicate.

James was suffering from shock as well as needing stitches.

When it came to my turn, I told the doctor that I'd been unconscious for a few minutes, James interrupted. ' Tell the doctor everything, Rowena.'

'I'd rather not, the experience was too bizarre.'

'Please,' the doctor said, perching on a stool. 'How did the accident happen? We have to write a report for the police,' he explained.

'That figures,' James muttered.

My memory was hazy but I did my best. 'I'm a reporter…'

'Rowena specialises in environmental issues,' James interrupted proudly.

'We were returning from Upper Berry in Yorkshire where I was investigating Dioxin related incidents,' I paused, suddenly knowing that the "accident" had something to do with that. It may have been my over active intuition but there was something fishy about it. I realised that neither James or the doctor would agree with me so I kept the theory to myself.

'My camera?' I asked James, afraid it was broken.

'In your suitcase.' He patted his jacket on the end of his trolley. 'But I have the films in my pocket.'

I smiled my appreciation and continued. 'James was driving and as we neared Sherwood Forest, the car accelerated at an alarming rate and the brakes wouldn't work.' As I spoke I remembered that every nerve in my body, every brain cell, knew that something was forcing the car to the limits of its speed.

'James pumped the brakes and fought to control it.' I stopped, not wanting to tell the doctor that the steering wheel has frosted over.

'The car went icy cold as I was helplessly hurtling down the road, ' James related the tricky moment. 'I was heading straight for a tree at the crossroad when Rowena reached for the wheel and helped me steer it.'

I'd tried to make the car stop by sheer willpower but... 'I took the key out of the ignition and together we managed to make it slow down before it hit the tree,' I said.

'Thanks to you at least when we crashed we were not going fast enough to kill ourselves,' James added.

'Probably faulty wiring,' the doctor said.

I told him I thought I'd been hanged and he agreed with James.

'Concussion can cause very realistic delusions,' he said.

I didn't want to press the point as I was afraid my sanity would be in question. 'Mmn,' I said. It was no use arguing. Perhaps they were right. But I've always been sort of fey, which I'd dismissed as feminine intuition. Sometimes I'd seen glimpses of what could possibly happen if my nearest and dearest walked blindly into danger, but as I say, that in itself is not particularly rare is it? But I'd never had such a detailed and long lasting vision before.

We were kept in for observation and put in the same side ward. I suppose because no one bothered to check whether we were still married or not, but we were able to talk and comfort each other.

In the evening Justin and Debra came rushing in to see how we were, Justin and I had always whistled the same tune and I found myself telling him about my experience, relieved that he, at least, believed me.

'Rowena Berrysford's father was Sir Rowan Beaumont, squire at Beaumont Hall but when he was killed at Naseby, Cromwell gave the place to Captain Keeton as payment for his support. The captain employed Rowena as under-housekeeper until she married his head steward, William Berrysford.'

Talking about them helped me to come to terms with my grief. Although William was her husband and not mine, the loss closed my throat so I could hardly speak. Trying to pretend it didn't exist in case grieving about my lost husband upset James, had only caused me more suffering. I felt the strange bereavement very keenly and I missed William so much.

'Write it all down, Mum. It will help you to get everything in perspective.'

It seemed like a good idea so I agreed. Perhaps it would purge my pain or convince me that it had all been a dream; an illusion.

Debra went to buy me a note book and a sandwich or something for James. Hospital food, at best merely adequate, was hardly enough for a grown man.

He practically slavered with anticipation when he saw the pizza she brought him.

He offered me half, bless him, but I declined.

Justin asked if we wanted him to notify Susan at the University.

'No!' James and I exclaimed together. 'It isn't worth interrupting her studies,' he said.

'We'll tell her all about it when she comes home this weekend,' I finished for him.

When they had left, the nurse came round with hot cocoa and tucked us up early for the night. We giggled about children being in bed by ten but we were both fast asleep within the hour.

I was woken with a cup of tea at the usual start of a hospital day, the ungodly hour of six a.m. As if awakening from a dream, my life with James came flooding back to me. And it hurt.

Barbara was the last in a long line of affairs. A rather common buxom brunette, widowed and desperate, she didn't give a damn about who got hurt as long as she got what she wanted: in this case my husband. Well, she could have him for now but I bet she couldn't keep him.

Towards the end of our marriage, a friend of mine, Chrissy, the wife of one of James' colleagues, told me that Barbara was in a private hospital having an abortion. I'd never paid much heed to campus gossip but James had a vasectomy shortly after and the rumours about him and his secretary suddenly made sense. He knew how desperately I wanted children of my own and it was the last straw. I cited Barbara for my divorce.

The nurse and I conspired to let James sleep a little longer. I needed to come to terms with his betrayal all over again.

Now I lived alone, allowing James to share my bed whenever I felt like it, relishing the fact that he was now cheating on Barbara with me.

Surely there was more to love than this? Were memories of Mistress Berrysford and William all I had for comparison?

I didn't know whether their love was real or only a dream, an illusion brought on by concussion.

I began to write down everything I knew about Rowena, her family and friends, mini biographies. It helped to keep away the sorrow at living without them..

Stifling a sob I determined to lay Rowena's ghost to rest. I had to find her and know what happened to "our" baby.

Doodling on the pad I noticed with a shock of recognition that I had drawn a picture of my daughter, as clear as a photograph, baby Rowena smiled back at me. I could smell the sweet baby smell of her soft skin, feel the silky curls as I tucked them into the tiny linen cap, see her sparkling green eyes.

'Still writing, Mrs Roberts?' the nurse asked when she returned to take our temperatures.

For a moment the world had seemed a better place because William and my baby were in it. But they were long dead and buried and I didn't even know where. I had to accept that, but it was hard to believe that they had died around three hundred years ago.

I quickly wiped away my tears as the nurse woke James.

'Good morning sleepy head. Rise and shine,' she said, cheerfully sticking a plastic thermometer in his ear.

When she'd gone, James asked what I was doing and was astounded when I told him.

'I thought you'd forget all that nonsense ,' he said, sounding rather annoyed.

'If it had been some sort of dream, it should have faded by now. But it hasn't, James. everything is still very clear,' I snapped, fed up with him belittling me. 'I know who I am but I also know that Rowena Berrysford existed in the seventeenth century and the Coleman's hanged her.'

He struggled over to my bed before I had the chance to protest and got in beside me.

'Let me read your alleged memories then,' he said, as if I were still his student.

When he finished, he muttered, 'Damn the Colemans. I wish we'd listened when old Rowan told us not to trust them.'

I had forgotten about that. Before he died my great grandfather had rambled on quite a bit about the first world war and the Colemans, but not knowing them at the time, I hadn't really paid much attention. Now it all came back to me and I recalled every detail.

'Two of the Colemans were in his regiment,' James said. 'They must have been Sebastian's great uncles.'

Before he had time to say more, an orderly came in with breakfast, a dish of cereal, a slice of warmish toast and a cup of rather weak tea. Fortunately just as I liked it.

My thoughts drifted from Rowan to my mother and father. Great-granddad had set mother up in a little antique business when my father died and I suddenly realised that she had done very well. Ena, as my mother preferred to be called, dropping the "Row" off her given name with, I thought, an unseemly denial of her birthright, had supported me throughout my years at Nottingham University, where I'd met James, who lectured on Archaeology, one of my "extra" courses.

While I was studying for my degree, Ena had taken objet d'art to Canada and made a small fortune. She also made a conquest, Phil Dupont, an art dealer from London, Ontario.

When I'd married James, she accepted Phil's long standing invitation and emigrated there to open an antique shop with him in the cultured Canadian city.

After breakfast we were polished and laid to attention for the doctor to inspect.

He told us we could go home but he would arrange for James to borrow a couple of walking sticks as he'd have to keep the weight off his leg for a few days. As it was stitched from knee to groin, there wasn't much chance of him doing otherwise.

The harassed young registrar examined the bump on my forehead, which gave me a lurid, what we'd call when I was a kid "50 pence" black eye, the money you'd be given not to cry if you were unlucky enough to get one. And the welts on my neck.

'That's funny, it looks more like the marks you'd expect from a noose than a seat belt.'

I kept perfectly still, not daring to contradict or encourage him.

'Friction burns,' he continued. 'Must have been a worn strap.' He unwittingly confirmed James' diagnosis, telling me to take it easy because I was still slightly concussed.

'We'll go back to your place,' James said, too firmly for my liking. 'I can't possibly leave you on your own when you're not well,' he insisted. Then almost as if he read my mind, added. 'If that's alright with you? To tell you the truth, I still feel a bit woozy myself.'

That stopped me from objecting as I suppose it was meant to. I phoned Justin and before we had time to sort ourselves out, he arrived to take us home, telling us proudly, "Debra is making a special lunch for you.'

On the way to Arnold, Justin stopped off at a pharmacists for James' prescription and I took my film to be developed.

As Justin drove into the private estate at Beaumont Hall, ice water ran down my spine when I saw Sebastian Coleman and a builder walking across the courtyard. He was looking over the architect's plans, obviously talking about conversions. They were turning the out buildings into a block of desirable and expensive studio apartments. I suppose if you expected to be elected to Government you could get planning permission for anything.

He scrutinised us closely as we got out of Justin's car. I swear there was a vicious gleam in his eye as he watched James being aided into my house and I was definitely *not* imagining his smug smile when he saw my bruised face.

He saluted us and started to come over but thankfully Justin had helped James indoors and I managed to close the door without appearing to have noticed him.

'May God forgive me but I really do hate that man,' I muttered.

But I soon forgot all about him when I saw the welcome that our lovely daughter-in-law had prepared for us.

Debra had fires lit in the dining room and sitting room. My stripped pine table was set with my best china and a vase of pink roses.

'Darling, you shouldn't have done all this, the flowers are lovely but far too expensive at this time of year.'

They had looked after my rather precocious pets while I was away; Cassidy, my three legged dog, hopped merrily around my feet, licking me to death with his welcome. And Buggalugs, my black and white moggie, greeted me with clinging affection, the stub of his tail which he'd lost in an accident, standing up in salute. Buggalugs had delusions of grandeur, he thought he was a Manx.

'No trouble, Mum,' Debra and Justin said in unison. I loved them calling me that, after all I was only about thirteen years older than Justin and was James' ex-wife.

Debra came through, carrying a platter of salmon, beautifully prepared and presented. She looked at the clock as she set the dish on the table when the front door opened and Susan came in.

'I knew you couldn't resist my cooking,' Debra laughed. 'Honest, Mum, we really did try to convince her that her journey wasn't necessary but she has the typical "Robert's" nose for food.'

Susan, usually quick with the repartee, ignored the remark.

Debra looked disappointed but being of the same generation, she was the first to notice there was something wrong. 'What's the matter, Suze?' she asked.

Susan was shaking, her mouth in a tight line. 'Nothing,' she snapped, dropping her bulging bag, full of dirty laundry, I bet, to the floor.

'How are you? she said, changing the subject and rushing to her father, giving him a quick kiss before she came over to me.

'Oh, your poor face.' She kissed me very gently.

I grabbed her and gave her a strangling bear hug. 'I am pleased you came, love, but there was no need and you should be studying.'

'Debra promised to go over some tricky stuff with me. And I couldn't keep away when Justin told me what had happened.'

She saw the salmon, which was usually only served on special occasions in my house. "Wow! Happy Christmas everyone.'

We all laughed and got on with the serious business of eating.

Afterwards, never ceasing to amaze me, they cleared the dishes for me and stacked them in the dishwasher.

I smiled. There was a lot to be said for living in this century, I thought, glancing at my overfull bookcase. Apart from labour saving appliances, I could read whatever I pleased, pick up the phone and talk to far off friends, watch television and DVD, enjoy stereophonic music on radio, and even CD ROM. I had a car, and air travel brought the world to my doorstep. Unimaginable witchcraft.

Susan brought coffee through to the sitting room.

'Tell us all about it, Mum. Justin said you sort of remembered the life on an ancestor who was hanged as a witch. Awesome!'

I took my notes from my bag and told them everything that had happened to me, in what I believed to be a previous incarnation in the seventeenth century. There was absolute silence as they listened until I told them about Seth.

Susan bristled. 'George made an obscene gesture as I came in.'

She moved over and sat on the floor at my feet. 'He looks just as you described Seth.'

'Right!' James exclaimed, trying to get out of his chair. 'It's time I put a stop to this.'

'Chill, Dad, I can look after myself,' Susan said, not realising that the hackneyed expression served to intensify rather than alleviate parental anxiety.

James tried to calm down, taking my writing pad and studying my notes thoughtfully. "There's a coincidence,' he paused, reading the last page.

'What is?' I asked.

'This curse thing. What old Rowan told me about his experiences in Ypres. It sort of fits in a macabre kind of way.'

'Wasn't there something about him and the Colemans in the first world war?' Susan asked. Then realising she was losing her street cred, shrugged. 'Gramps told me about it when I was in junior school,' she explained sheepishly.

'Rowena's great-grandfather,' James said, emphasising the fact that Rowan had nothing to do with him or his children, I thought uncharitably.

'Captain Rowan Mayhew was in the Sherwood Foresters,' he continued.

Justin interrupted. 'You tell it, Mum,' he said, sliding to the floor beside Susan.

They sat cross legged on the carpet in front of the fire, looking at me expectantly, just as they'd sat listening to my stories when they were children.

Debra joined them and held Justin's hand.

Smiling at them I cleared my throat before I began…

CHAPTER FOUR.

The candle, set in an old boot polish tin, guttered and nearly went out, the oily smoke from the flame rose unsteadily.

Rowan looked up from filling his pipe as the draught caused the papers on his makeshift desk to rustle like dead autumn leaves. The cold gust of damp air was enough to warn him that someone had drawn back the horse blanket which served as a door and entered the dugout. He waited, his hand resting on his pistol, knowing it would take whoever it was, several seconds to descend the twelve foot ladder in the dark.

Sergeant Brook stepped into the pool of flickering yellow light.

"The men are stood down, sir, except for the sentries. And there's a rumour that hot food might reach us before dawn," he said, smiling hopefully.

For four days the men had lived off cold iron rations but now they were consolidated, in what had been until yesterday, Bosche trenches, they could look forward to food supplied by the kitchens at the rear. In the miserable wet and cold of a Belgian October, hot food was a looked forward to luxury.

"I wouldn't hold out much hope, Jack," Rowan said as kindly as he could.

The ground between what had been the British front line and their new position had been turned into a swamp by days of heavy rain and continual bombardment. It was so bad, the tanks, which should have guaranteed rapid victory, had been abandoned, unable to advance through the mud filled shell holes, deep enough to drown a horse. Instead, hundreds of good men had been thrown into the battle to die in the rain for a few feet of mud.

The British Second Army under General Plumer was trying to break out of the Ypres Salient and Rowan's Company, the Sherwood Foresters, were just a small part of that army.

"You're probably right, sir. God help us, it's bloody nigh impossible for a man to cover a hundred yards through the filth, let alone carry dixies for nearly two miles. Still, I'll not give up hope, there's bugger else to look forward to."

Rowan nodded as he offered Jack a fill of tobacco. "Ain't that the truth."

As they smoked, Rowan went through the orders from Battalion HQ. They were mostly requests for casualty lists but there was one that had him puzzled.

He was to report to Headquarters forthwith. No explanation but it was signed by the Brigadier. Jack was right, It would be damn near impossible to cross the open ground in daylight, it was well within the range of too many German guns. Any officer crossing to Polygon was ordered to take a man with him in case he slipped into the mire and needed to be pulled out. If they made it, maybe Jack at least could get some hot food.

"Let's go, Sergeant, the Brigadier calls. We'd better find out what the old man wants," he said, preparing to leave.

When he and the Sergeant emerged from the dug out, the rain had stopped, not that it made much difference. The duckboards at the bottom of the trench were floating on mud, so that at every step it oozed into your boots and soaked your puttees to well above the ankle.

The men who were not on duty huddled into the shallow niches dug into the wall, unfortunately, being a German trench, the firing step and sand bag defences faced the wrong way and those on duty could not use them.

"God. There are so few of us left," Rowan muttered as he passed slowly down the trench to the last sentry.

Nearly two thirds dead or wounded and so many never to be found; lost in the quagmire over which they fought.

How could an officer trained to think of the welfare of his men possibly remain sane when so many had died for a few yards of mud?

He'd steeled himself against insanity, just as he had fought against his own devilish premonitions all his life.

Here in the front line Rowan had slowly begun to appreciate his strange gift.

He was careful not to touch anyone now before they went over the top, preferring to leave the outcome to God. But if he touched them accidentally he did his damnedest to avert their imminent dead, should he 'see' what was about to happen. As most of the hellish deaths he had 'seen' were quite irreversible, the anger and frustration of knowing he could not prevent it, put an added strain on him that was almost impossible to bear.

A burning flare lit up the area, followed by the rattle of machine gun fire as a nervous sentry fired at a real or imaginary danger. Another flare burst directly overhead, flooding the trench with a blinding light.

"Stand to," Rowan ordered as his men stumbled into their positions.

The scene before them was one that no Christian soul should ever have to see. The landscape was straight out of hell.

The ground, torn up and crated by gun fire, was populated by the dead, buried and disinterred in turn by the shells of the advancing troops. And now fat rats which thrived so prolifically, were feasting on the cadavers.

Not two yards from Rowan, one vile creature sat gnawing at the face of a limb-less corpse, whilst the movement of others beneath the blood stained tunic, gave the appearance of macabre life to the rotting remains.

As far as you could see the ground heaved with the vermin as they partook their ghastly feast.

The flare faded with no sign of an attack.

"Shall I order stand down?" Jack, like Rowan pretended to be unaffected by what they had witnessed.

"Yes, please." Rowan turned his back on the carnage. "We'd better get on. Perhaps we can find a drink at HQ. I don't know about you but I could certainly use one."

It took them two hours to cross to Polygon. There were tapes to guide the runners but they were easily missed in the dark, and woe betide anyone who slipped. More often than not anyone who missed their footing drowned without trace in the mud filled shell holes.

HQ was set up in the deep cellars of a derelict farmhouse at Polygon Wood. It was to one of those that Rowan reported, having first made sure that Jack was issued with a decent hot breakfast.

The Brigadier was alone when Rowan entered. He returned his salute and motioned him to a chair.

"Sit down, me boy, you must be all in. I'm damned sorry I had to order you here but I had no choice. You are the most senior officer I can spare and what has to be done must be done by you."

The old boy was nervously shuffling the papers which were piled on his desk. Rowan had never seen the Brigadier so discomfited.

"No sense in beating about the bush as they say; what had to be done is not a pleasant task but I want you to organise a firing squad."

What on earth for? Rowan tried to make sense of what the Brigadier was saying. There must be some mistake, in his exhausted state he had misheard.

"Damn nasty business this, and the sooner it is over so much the better. You'll find all the details in this report." He handed a sheaf of papers to Rowan.

"Dawn tomorrow, there's a good chap. See Colonel Blackshaw about some men, he'll know what to do. Like I said, it's a damn nasty business... Right Captain. Dismissed."

The brief interview was over. Rowan rose, replaced his cap and saluted. The Brigadier barely acknowledged him, already engrossed in the other papers on his desk.

Standing outside the door Rowan read through the orders.

Two brothers had been caught drunk and running the wrong way behind their own lines. And mindful of the mutiny of some French regiments when they were ordered to execute their own men, the Brigadier wanted the deserters shot immediately as a warning to his soldiers. It was supposed to reinforce the expectation of High Command that they would brook no desertion or mutiny from the British Army.

The condemned men were Jessie and Hamn Coleman.

Rowan knew they came from Arnold and had heard of their unsavoury reputation in business but thankfully had never set eyes on them. Be that as it may, did any soldier fighting for his country deserve to be executed for a moment of panic? And a firing squad? Was he supposed to shoot one at a time or both together?

Rowan ensured that Jack had found a comfortable billet before he went to Colonel Blackshaw to learn the correct procedure.

The Colonel was a mine of information and assistance which he offered along with hot food and a bunk in his billet.

"One blank round must be issued, so that no man is sure that he fired the fatal shot. Of course, the officer in command must deliver the coup de grace to the condemned men. Your revolver is loaded, I suppose?" the Colonel asked.

Rowan nodded mutely.

"Had to ask, me boy. Ammunition for side arms is scarce these days."

Rowan found he had little appetite for the cooked breakfast but forced it down, not wanting the Colonel to think he was ungrateful but he told him he wouldn't be able to sleep until he'd attended to his onerous task.

"I understand, Captain," he said. "Hang this Do not disturb notice on the doorknob when you want to rest," he said as he left the billet.

Rowan followed him and went to do his duty.

First he gave instructions to the guards, that the Colemans were to be given a mug of undiluted rum, more if it were needed. He wanted them as near unconscious as possible when the time came.

Then Rowan went to see the men chosen for the firing squad. Twelve men and a Sergeant. He studied their tired faces, young men grown old, he thought. No amount of time would erase the pain behind the eyes of those who had seen so much horror. Boys who should by right be still at school, were ordered to commit a deliberate act of murder. Not in the heat of battle but coldly, in the chill of dawn.

"See that the lads have a stiff drink in the morning, I don't want them so drunk that they can't shoot straight but a generous tot of rum will not be amiss," he told the sergeant. "And make sure they understand that they will be doing the Colemans no favours if they don't shoot to kill. A quick, clean death is a lot more than many poor souls have had in this war."

"Rest assured, sir. We won't let you down."

"Thank you, Sergeant," Rowan said, returning his salute before he went back to Colonel Blackshaw's billet.

Although warm and relatively comfortable, rest did not bring sleep as Rowan's thoughts returned to the drama to take place in the morning. A tragedy which he would have a principle part to play.

He shook his head and thumped the flock pillow. Why, amidst all this carnage did he have to worry about the deaths of two cowards? Thousands of brave men had been sacrificed on the bloody fields of France and Belgium, why should he be concerned about another two?

At daybreak, the firing squad was marched to the orchard where platoons of other soldiers were being paraded to witness the execution.

First Jessie and then Hamn were dragged to the trees, stinking drunk with the surfeit of rum which Rowan had ordered to be issued to them.

Jessie was almost unconscious and apart from his foul language, did not seem aware of being tied to the tree and blindfolded. But Hamn was a different matter. He knew what was happening. And what was about to happen.

He screamed abuse to the men when he was tied to the tree and refused to be blindfolded. He cursed the Army, the men and the Sergeant, using words which would have had him arrested in any town.

"Quiet!" the Sergeant roared. "Or I'll use the blindfold as a gag."

Hamn Coleman glared but held his tongue.

Rowan went over to check that their bonds were tight.

"You!" Hamn stared at him in defiant terror. "Don't think you and your damn Rowans have won. We'll get you in the end."

"Coleman! Apologise," the Sergeant commanded, striding towards him.

"Fuck you."

"Sergeant," Rowan warned, as the man was about to strike the foul mouthed ruffian.

Though red in the face with anger the Sergeant brought the squad to attention, but a high pitched screech overhead warned of another dawn raid.

High explosives burst all around them and gas shells spilled their lethal contents.

"Squad dismissed," Rowan yelled, waving the men to take cover. As they groped for their gas masks and scattered, billowing clouds of mustard gas enveloped the area. Rowan took a few staggering steps towards the Colemans, his eyes streaming as he held his breath.

A pause in the bombardment gave a moment of quiet and the screams of the Colemans also ceased.

Nevertheless Rowan ran to them and drew his pistol to administer the coup de grace. Two shots rang out in the ghostly silence as Captain Rowan Mayhew did his duty for God and the King.

'My great-grandfather also said that in the attack the Colemans looked as if they were dressed in the garb of the Puritans,' I told my family.

'Of course, you must remember that he'd been living in the trenches for months, bombarded day and night. He must have been half out of his mind,' James said. 'The fact that the Colemans died in such a manner must be a coincidence.'

'It sure sounds like hell fire to me.' Justin took the words out of my mouth. 'And it certainly seems to substantiate Rowena Berrysford's curse.'

'But they didn't die in flames,' Debra ventured quietly.

'Mustard gas,' Justin said, putting his arm around her shoulders. 'It burns the skin and scorches the lungs. Like burning to death on the inside.'

He hugged her to him as she shuddered.

I knew that James' reasoning was logical but my throat was parched and my eyes streaming as I coughed and spluttered, feeling as if I had inhaled a whisper of the gas.

I had been where Rowan couldn't go, seen the Colemans roped securely to the trees, helpless and screaming behind the thick yellow curtain of deadly fog. I had watched as the gas burned into their lungs and they choked to death on their own vomit.

This affected me differently from Mistress Berrysford's hanging. This time I was a helpless bystander watching the scene unfold. It sickened and appalled me.

Justin was thoughtful, torn between common sense and loyalty to me.

Susan however, easily dismissed the idea of curses from the dead carrying on through the ages.

'Christopher Lee, eat your heart out,' she grinned.

Why did I feel that the Colemans hated me so forcefully? Even if they knew about my great-grandfather's part in their relatives execution, they could hardly hold it against me, could they? But I knew that whatever the reason, the Colemans were now and always had been, my mortal enemies.

CHAPTER FIVE.

James hobbled up all the stairs with me and although I knew he could never understand, against my better judgement I tried to convince him when we were in bed together. He listened politely then patronised me by dismissing it as my imagination.

'Open your mind a little,' I begged. 'What if the Colemans knew? What if they are born with the guilt of what they did, or that each generation was told about Rowena's curse, or...'

James tried to cover a clearly exasperated sigh.

'What if they believe that Mistress Berrysford was a witch and were trying to get at me for it?' I finished.

'And what if they are right? No one can dispute that you have a gift of some sort, or that your ESP is way above average. If we are going to play "What if," what if your Rowena was like you? She would certainly be called a witch in the seventeenth century.'

'Oh James! Don't be silly, I'm trying to be serious.' What a lovely man he is, sometimes he knows exactly the right thing to say to make me listen to him.

'Don't worry about it, love. Leave it be, it was only a dream.'

And sometimes he didn't, I thought.

'You almost had me there for a moment,' I snapped. 'But "What if" I could prove that Mistress Berrysford existed?'

'Now *you* are being silly,' James tutted. 'You'll never be able to trace back to the seventeenth century with only your family's obsession with Rowan and Rowena Christian names.'

'Other people manage to trace their ancestors without any information at all and they don't have the incentive that I have. I will find her, James. If only to prove you wrong.'

With that I turned over, stiff with anger.

James ran his hand over my waist and caressed my back, kneading the taut muscles until I relaxed against him.

'You are a bastard,' I whispered, trying to turn to face him but he held me fast. As usual he was raring to go, his hardness nudging the cheeks of my bum.

'But I love you,' he said as his hand squeezed under me, fondling my breast and rolling my nipple into a peak of sensation while his other hand circled my stomach, his splayed fingers gently caressing my clitoris.

'Like spoons,' he begged.

I brought my knees up and nestled against him, squeezing my eyes shut as I tried to blot out thoughts of William and concentrate on the man in my bed, here and now.

My libido had not suddenly switched itself off when James and I had parted and although I'd had a couple of part time lovers, James had kept in touch, taking me out to dinner et cetera and had often made love to me.

Perhaps courting me and being unfaithful to Barbara, added spice to our love making. Or maybe spite was the better word. Whatever, I had no need for self gratification when James was so willing and eager to seduce me.

His expertise quickly blotted out all thoughts as his penis probed powerfully. We hadn't often made love on our sides, which lent the experience novelty value as well as allowing him deep inside me while he caressed and teased my sensitive erogenous zones.

I came to a breathless climax seconds before James, wondering for the thousandth time why he needed more than one woman to fulfil his needs.

James was so damned good at making love.

He eased out and snuggled up close but within minutes his breathing deepened into a quiet rhythmic snore.

I was unreasonably annoyed that he should sleep whilst I lay wide awake, my body gratified but feeling as if I'd been unfaithful to William.

Burying my face in my pillow I stifled a sob, remembering the first time he had spoke to me…

William walked in to the ledger room where Mistress Beaumont kept a weekly tally of the household accounts. They had seen each other occasionally of course but he was the squire's steward of the horse and she, the under-mistress of the household; their position seldom brought them into contact.

"Excuse me, mistress" he murmured as he came to the table. Taking her hand he formally introduced himself. "William Berrysford, at your service."

Startled by his touch, she blushed and stared at his long fingers. "Rowena Beaumont," she stuttered, her hand still holding his. "You have nice hands," she said, her wits taking leave of her sense. "Do you play?"

Instead of ridiculing her gauche foolishness, William smiled and told her, "I strum the gittern occasionally for the Master and his good lady."

That very night before the candles had burned low, Mistress Beaumont and William Berrysford had arranged to keep accounts at the same time every week...

The following Monday Susan caught the train back to University and James got signed off from the hospital. On Tuesday he returned to work. And presumably, to Barbara.

James specialised in inner city finds, which were usually discovered during some major traffic scheme or redevelopment plan. Tomorrow, his expertise would take him to London for a few days, where he was being consulted about some artifacts found during excavations for a new shopping precinct.

I fetched my photo's from Boots and sat in the kitchen going through them to find the best ones to illustrate my article, which I'd finished over the weekend. Studying those taken round the reservoir I saw something that hadn't been noticeable when taking the pictures. What looked like two corroded, greenish coloured, chemical drums had been dug into the bank to form seats, either for anglers or kids messing about. Somehow that thought alarmed me.

On the side of the drums, in the middle of some faded initials were two letter's. The filter used for the reservoir shots had minimised the glare and made the water so clear you could see the bottom. My skin went cold. In line with the makeshift seats, at least half a dozen drums had been dumped on the bottom of the reservoir. Though the refraction of the water made it difficult I could also make out letters on them and a logo which looked vaguely familiar.

There was no way that these containers even if empty, should be in the water. And what if they had contained a toxic chemical? All my instincts screamed Dioxin.

My eyes tricked me into seeing skulls and crossbones on them. Nuclear radiation triangles... I pulled myself up sharp, keeping my imagination on a short rein. Before I even thought about the effect of dumping toxic chemicals in the water supply I needed a few hard facts.

First I would take my negatives to the 24 hour professional developers used by the local newspaper and have the pictures enlarged. Then maybe I could identify the manufacturer and find out what chemicals, if any, the drums had been used for.

'Cassidy! Here boy,' I shouted, rattling his lead.

He bounded over, hardly able to believe his luck at two outings in one morning.

'Just a quick walk,' I told him, hoping I'd got time before the builder, Albert Weston, an old friend of the family, arrived.

I was just scribbling a note for him when he tapped on the open door and put his head round.

'Hello Rowena... I'll come back later if it's inconvenient,' he said.

'No, please come in. Don't they say that you must never under any circumstances turn a builder away if you want to see him again? Even if he is a very dear friend,' I joked, filling the percolator with water from the jug in the fridge.

'I know it might be unusual in my trade, duck, but I really will come back.'

'Don't be daft! I'll make you a cup of coffee, ' I smiled, measuring out fresh coffee and plugging in the percolator.

'Thanks,' he smiled, his bright blue eyes contrasting vividly with his shock of silver hair. 'You OK? I heard about your accident,' he said, wedging himself on the pine bench in front of the small refectory table in the kitchen.

We sat side by side going over the plans for the refit. He had the astute mind and imagination to see what was needed and where things should go. I was pleased that he was doing this for me, Weston's had a reputation for quality unheard of amongst builders and I had known and loved 'uncle' Albert for as long as I could remember and trusted him to see the old house was renovated properly.

'I want stripped pine cupboards built in and all the appliances hidden behind pine doors. I would have liked oak really but I have such a lot of antique pine furniture,' I told him.

'Oak would be better though, more fitting to the age of the house,' Albert said. 'My Grandfather was a bugger...Pardon my French,' he grinned sheepishly.

'Don't worry about it; my cat is named Buggalugs so that can't be classed as a swear word!'

He laughed, his eyes sparkling in his weather beaten face. 'Well, Rowena, he was a bugger for picking up what Gran called junk. Beams and doors from the old houses he demolished. As a matter of fact, he used a lot of his old bricks and stuff for our house, long before the yuppies thought of it!'

I smiled. Although half his age I felt we were contemporaries.

'I have a few genuine antique cupboard doors; dark, aged oak. They would look just right with pine. Blend but contrast, if you know what I mean, better than trying to match. And we could rough plaster the walls and leave some of the original beams exposed.'

He winked at me and added as a clincher. 'We could put in some genuine old oak timbers to beam the ceiling too and it wouldn't cost you much extra.'

Suddenly I saw it, my old kitchen, the plaster, the new oak beams which had already turned to a rich buttery gold. My baby Rowena gurgling happily in her beautiful cradle.

The past seemed to vibrate with life, washing away the present...

Rowena sat with her foot on the curved bar rocking her baby, crooning softly to her as she lay sleeping in her polished oak cradle which William had made. Its intricate pattern of Rowan leaves around the initial 'R' on the headpiece, copied from her locket.

She snipped off the green thread with her silver, stork shaped scissors, a gift from William's twin sister Sarah, as she finished embroidering the motif onto the baby's gown.

The golden light from the low rays of sunset mottled the room and reflected on the copper jugs which hung from brass hooks over the mantelpiece.

Slowly she ceased the rocking motion and craned her neck over the cradle, smiling as she tucked the soft woollen coverlet around her first born.

Revelling in the warmth of the sun on her back she proudly surveyed the room. The ceiling was beamed and from the beams hung an assortment of pans. Pewter candlesticks, plates and tankards stood on the mantle shelf under which hung bunches of aromatic herbs. Logs burned and crackled merrily in the brick ingle-nook fireplace...

My head reeled and I had to support it in my trembling hands.

'What's wrong, duck? Are you feeling poorly?' Albert asked, patting my shoulder.

'No. I'm alright. I had a bit of a bump in my car and I dreamt I was back in the seventeenth century. I lived in a house hereabouts and the kitchen was just as you described.'

I shook my head and rubbed my temples vigorously, not knowing whether to tell him everything or not.

'Please go on,' Albert said quietly and I knew he would understand.

'I sort of lived the life of another Rowena. Perhaps I am her reincarnation?' I asked sceptically.

'Several hundred million people in the world believe in reincarnation,' he said, with an air of quiet authority.

He poured me another cup of coffee.

I sipped it gratefully. Perhaps I'd inadvertently hit on the answer. Or part of it.

'My Gran would have loved you, Rowena. She was just the same, she could see an accident before it happened, often it was just common sense really, but sometimes; well, it would have been difficult to explain her gift by logic alone.'

'Gift? That's a nice name for it, Albert. In the past it was called witchcraft.'

'Only by the ignorant, Rowena. Seeing the past or the future for that matter, is no different from being able to "see" a house before the building is completed or knowing how a garden will look before you sow the first seed.'

My old friend was saying what I had always believed but not dared to mention.

'Did you and my mother discuss things like this?' I asked.

'Me and your great-granddad more like! He was the air raid warden round here and when I was still at school we often talked the night away in the shelter.'

'Did he tell you about the Colemans?'

'He told me a lot of things, some of which I'd heard from my grandmother.'

He looked at me carefully. 'That doesn't make it less true.' Albert was persuasive.

'But if anything can't be explained by logic and reason, people often refuse to accept it,' I said, playing the devil's advocate.

'Never mind what other people think, luv. Follow your instincts no matter how illogical they seem.'

I showed him Rowena's talisman. It was heavy and what I'd taken to be tarnished silver, he said looked like a hard white gold. Or a sort of platinum.

I smiled at the kindly old man. ' Now put these plans away and I'll give you a blast from the past that you won't forget for a long while.'

When I had finished recounting my strange experience, Albert's hands were shaking as he picked up his cup to drink his coffee.

'Oh, no, that wasn't a dream. The evidence is right there in your hand,' he said, nodding towards the pendant. 'What's inside it?'

I stared at the intricate pattern, which seemed to have no catch or hinges. Or more likely it had rusted shut.

'I haven't been able to open it. My mother gave it to me when I was born. It's a tradition that its given to the first born to protect them from harm. If only I could prove that it once belonged to my ancestor,' I mused, threading the locket onto the gold chain which I always wore around my neck.

'It must have done,' he said. 'Passed down through each generation. Baby Rowena in the seventeenth century must have passed it on to her own child.'

'Oh, Albert, of course.' I shook my head, why hadn't I thought of that? My Rowena had survived, married and had a baby. That made me feel a lot better. The Colemans hadn't gone back for her.

The talisman nestled in the hollow of my throat as if it belonged there.

'I'll have to have a stab at tracing my family tree; trouble is I don't know where to start,' I said.

'It isn't difficult,' Albert assured me. 'My brother's lad has traced our family back to the seventeenth century,' he said, preparing to leave.

'Anyone I know?' I grinned. Albert came from a large family of brothers and sisters.

'Ken and Vera's lad?' he raised an eyebrow questioningly.

I shook my head, even my mother hadn't been able to keep track of the Weston's, they were the biggest and probably one of the oldest families in Arnold.

'I intend to take out a few books on genealogy and do my damnedest to trace her,' I said, walking him to the door.

He turned to face me. 'I'll be glad to ask my nephew to give you a hand? He could tell you where to start, at least,' he said, obviously not sure how his offer was going to be received.

'Thank you, Albert. I need all the help I can get. I'll gladly pay him if ...'

'No, no need. Our Billy's like my old granddad, he loves rooting round old relics.'

I couldn't help laughing. It just struck me as funny. 'He's going to *love* ME then!'

CHAPTER SIX.

After Albert had left, I phoned a taxi to take me and Cassidy into town. Although the weather was unseasonably warm I was in too much of a hurry to walk nearly three miles into Nottingham.

I took the photographs to be enlarged and went to the Public Records Office to check on companies which produced Dioxin.

A hard faced girl asked a lot of surly questions before leading me to the records of the companies that manufactured fertilisers and weed killers. Amongst them one name jumped out of the page at me.

Colemans Feed and Fertiliser Company.

Instinct told me I had found what I was looking for but I had to convince my editor, Jayne Vincent. And she would want proof.

I walked briskly to the magazine's office. Bracing myself for Jayne's acid tongue I gave her my article.

'Howdy, stranger, she sniped, then abruptly ceased firing when she noticed my fading bruises. 'Jeez! I'm sorry, are you OK?'

'Yes. Sorry the copy's a bit late, James and I had a little accident on the way back from Upper Berry,' I told her. 'My car's a write off and I haven't bought a replacement yet, so I'm a bit stranded at the moment.'

She tutted with either annoyance, sympathy, or both as she walked over to the filing cabinet, on top of which coffee was brewing almost continually. She lifted a mug and an elegant eyebrow.

'Thanks,' I nodded, putting my article on her desk. 'The authorities suspect the outbreak is Dioxin related.'

I told her about the chemical drums in the photographs. 'I'd like to do a follow up on the effects of fly tipping while I check it out, if you're interested?'

She looked at me sharply as she handed me the mug. 'So what are you waiting for? Find out who they belong to and what they contained. This could be a big story.'

'I have a hunch that it's a local firm owned by a highly respected industrialist,' I muttered apologetically, leaving out the fact that I'd bought my house from him and he lived in Beaumont Hall.

'Does that mean that you haven't a shred of evidence?' she sighed. 'Get it before you tread on anybody's toes. Your hunches have usually paid off, so if this one turns out to be hot, I'll give you a hundred percent bonus Go get 'im, gal,' Jayne ordered nicely.

'Have you warned the Health department yet? ' she asked, picking up the telephone as I shook my head. 'They aren't like me, they don't demand proof,' she chided. Asking to be put through she hooked the receiver under her double chin and impatiently drank her coffee while she waited.

Big bold and beautiful, Jayne looked deceptively cuddly and was eyelash flutteringly feminine, but underneath the flowing, cream silk suit she was sharp, efficient and frighteningly intelligent.

'I'm having my kitchen done, ' I told her during the lull. 'And wondered if you'd be interested in a light hearted piece; Living with a gang of navvies?'

'Love the title! If it's in the same vein as "Living like a Lord," I want first option.' (A piece I'd written about showing prospective buyers round my home). She paused while she talked to the Inspector and told him about the drums in the reservoir.

'I could get it syndicated for you. Usual terms?' she continued, hanging up the phone.

Jayne had often sold the First British Serial rights to other, bigger magazines with international markets. She got the article free and I made ten times my usual fee.

'Great.'

I was fairly competent at pencil sketches and promised before and after pictures, cartoon style; drank my coffee, wished her good bye and headed for the door.

After five minutes slowly making my way through the main office, full of Cassidy's ardent admirers, who petted him and fed him titbits, we left, and much to my little superstar's disgust, caught a *bus* to my local library.

Locking Cassidy's lead to a railing I dashed in, promising him I wouldn't be long and an ice cream in the park if he behaved.

I discovered that Colemans company had been sold off years ago, shortly before the scare about Dioxin hit the headlines. It niggled that they were involved. Next step would be to find who bought the company and how they had disposed of the toxic waste before I made allegations of illegal fly tipping.

I wangled permission to borrow the Key British Enterprises, a register of 5000 British Companies, from my friend Chrissy, the head librarian, whom I knew socially because her husband was a lecturer in the same Department as James. I added a Do it Yourself guide to Genealogy and a book on ESP as we chatted about this and that.

Then, telling Chrissy that Cassidy was waiting, we promised to "do" lunch soon and I rushed out into the bright cloudless day.

Cassidy and I walked to Arnot Hill park before going home, where I tried to get my head together. We sat in the sunshine licking our ice creams.

The warm air was full of the sound of bird song and heavy with the scent of wallflowers, tranquil and relaxing. Too relaxing.

Sitting there with Cassidy at my feet I was beginning to think confrontation with the Coleman's was not worth the hassle and I was beginning to nod off.

Cassidy yelped and brought me back to my senses. My little dog was standing, his hackles raised and his lips pulled back into a snarl.

Looking to see what he was growling at I saw Piers Coleman, snogging towards us, making a meal of a blonde with a skirt higher than her IQ.

Recognising the outfit I realised it was the girl from the Public Records office.

An inexplicable arrow of fear brought me to my feet and restored my sanity. I could not just forgive and forget what they had done. If I gave up they would win. And, don't ask me how but I knew that this time I had to fight.

This time it was more than a personal vendetta.

Pulling Cassidy, I quickly walked away. But I couldn't stop looking over my shoulder to see if we were being followed.

Trying to rationalise my fear of Piers I told myself that it was because he looked so much like Walter but I knew it was more than that. I was afraid of him because he was a Coleman.

When we got home I locked the door before taking Cassidy upstairs with me to my office.

My thoughts going round in circles I looked for information on the effects of Dioxin. It was 2pm when I finished and switched off my computer, wanting to get stuck into my library books.

'Ok Cass, let's go down to the kitchen for a snack, eh?'

His ears pricked up and he was down the stairs as if he hadn't eaten for a week.

I paused to pick up Buggalugs from his usual place, basking in the sunshine on the window sill on the landing, but he was not there.

He'd obviously gone to visit one of the local dears who fed him best salmon in return for a cuddle. Buggalugs was an affectionate bugger, if not exactly faithful. Just like James, I thought; but my cat always came back.

I grinned ruefully. So did James. Eventually.

Sitting at the breakfast table under the window, I started reading Extra Sensory Perception and Telekinesis. Engrossed in the book I was startled when James knocked at the door and came strolling in.

'Hello, love,' he said, and walking over to the fridge for the jug of filtered water, he filled the kettle to make a pot of tea. Always the first thing he did.

'I wasn't expecting you,' I said sharply, not wanting him to take it for granted that he could pop in whenever he liked.

'I just came round to see how you were,' he excused, kissing my cheek. 'Coffee?' he asked, still holding the jug. He likes tea but I prefer coffee.

'Please,' I said, exasperated by his assumption that he could treat my home as his own but I wasn't ready to put a stop to his, "let's be nice to Rowena," phase.

I would have to put a stop to it, though. I watched him closely, waiting for a chance to tell him not to come whenever he felt like it.

A prickly tingle made the hairs on the back of my neck stand on end. Dismissively I put it down to anger.

He poured the rest of the water into the percolator and measured out fresh coffee.

'I really must buy you a nice Cafetiere,' he said. 'It'll be quicker than this old thing.'

I saw him through a sickly green pulsing light. The feeling that something was wrong jarred my senses.

'James!' I croaked, not knowing what the danger was, only that it was imminent.

He raised a questioning eyebrow as he plugged in my fairly new but old fashioned stainless steel kettle, which James had bought me when I moved in.

My mouth went dry and panic swept through me.

'Don't!' I yelled, sliding from the stool and rushing towards him.

Startled, James jerked back his hand but my warning came a fraction too late.

There was an almighty bang and a bright blue flash as, with the barest touch of his finger nail, he flipped the switch.

He was thrown backwards across the kitchen, and diving to the table I only just managed to stop his head hitting the edge by fielding it with my body, before we both collapsed to the floor in a heap.

The acrid smell of burning rubber brought me to my feet. Smoke was coiling from the blackened plug in the socket.

Knowing that James was alright by the way he was swearing, I got up and ran to the cellar head, and groping on the shelf found the large box of household matches, lit the emergency candle and to be on the safe side, turned off the mains, plunging the house into darkness.

Lighting all the candles in the dining room I took the candelabra into the kitchen. James had lit a thick vanilla scented candle and was at the sink, running cold water over his fingers and staring at his burned finger and blackened nail.

'Are you alright?' I asked.

'More or less. You'd better phone your builder friend and get him to send an electrician,' he said, eyeing the kettle with suspicion. 'I suppose you had one of your premonitions again?'

Looking up from dialling the phone, I nodded.

'Thank you.'

I was vaguely surprised that he meant it.

Albert sent one of his nephews, Bert, round straight away. He checked the fuses and the wiring.

'Nothing wrong here, ' he said, switching the lights back on.

He examined the kettle. 'Well, I've seen some things in my time,' he said, shaking his head in despair, 'but this just about tops them all!'

He showed the plug to James.

'What the blazes caused that?'

'You've got me there, mate. The plug is a melted lump of plastic and wires. Melted, as in a solid lump.'

He snipped it off. 'It's a wonder you weren't electrocuted,' he commented as he rummaged in his bag for a plug and started screwing in the wires. 'If I didn't know better I'd say someone was out to do you a serious injury. Or some damn amateur electrician has tried welding the plug on!'

My stomach twisted with apprehension. My gut feeling was that the Colemans had done this. But how? And more importantly, why?

'Probably an exhausted kid in Thailand, gone berserk after working twelve hours a day in the factory,' James said. 'I'll take the kettle back to the shop in the morning.'

'If you're not careful, one day your civilised logic will be the death of you,' I told him.

He stared at me blankly. 'You can't seriously believe that Seb Coleman broke in here and deliberately fused the plug on our kettle?'

"Our kettle?" I thought but ignored it for now. 'Not necessarily. But I wouldn't put it past George, trying to emulate the electricians working on the barn conversions.' And that was my reasonable explanation. I actually thought it was more than likely that Piers had done it, not knowing that I only drank coffee and my percolator brought the water to the right temperature. He had intended to electrocute *me*.

'You could be right,' James agreed.

After Bert left, we tried to relax with a glass of Chablis which I sipped whilst making a stir fry with the remainder of the chicken, James doing his bit by chopping the veg.

It seemed churlish to tell him to leave. And I really didn't want to be alone tonight.

Over dinner we chatted about his trip to London in the morning. We were both trying to pretend the "accident" with the kettle hadn't happened. James was already convinced that it was nothing more than an ordinary domestic occurrence. Perhaps he was right but I couldn't forget what had sometimes happened when I'd been alone.

I had found a dead Barn Owl laying on my pillow with its neck broken; with its feathers roughly plucked off the poor thing look obscenely naked. Before that there was a dismembered field mouse in my fridge, singed and trussed up like a chicken. And then there were the lacy thongs missing from my bedroom drawer; not, as James insisted, stolen from my clothes line. And the numerous times my cordless phone had been taken off the charger, leaving me without a life line. Always when I was on my own in the house.

Who else could be harassing me if it wasn't Piers and/or George Coleman? And more importantly, how the hell did they get into my house?

The first thing Justin had done when I'd moved in was put new locks on the doors to supplement the old fashioned keys and put locks on the windows. Not only that but I had bolts on the doors as well.

'Are you sure you won't come with me? You could shop or take in the Galleries.'

It was tempting, if only to give Barbara a taste of her own medicine. But I fought my childish inclination. 'No thanks, James, I've got better things to do than take notes for you. With your laptop and electronic organiser, I fail to see why you need a secretary at all.'

He looked startled at my outburst. 'I don't want you with me just to take notes.'

I sighed and stared him in the eye. That was not the point and he knew it.

'I'm busy, James. I have to check out the drums in the reservoir, I have a feeling they could be the cause of the illnesses in the area. And, don't forget, the builders are starting the kitchen this week. I have to pack everything away.'

Subdued, James nodded, asking if he could stay the night and I deliberated carefully. It wouldn't do for him to know that I was afraid. But I was. The thought of Piers and George living so close gave me the shudders.

'What about Barbara?' I asked offhandedly.

'Barbara?'

'Don't play silly games,' I snapped. 'Won't she miss you?'

'No, of course not, sweetheart. I'm not beholden to her. You know I only love you.'

Maybe she'd chucked him out. Or maybe James was giving her the same run around as he'd given me.

I smiled and took his hand. After all I didn't owe Barbara anything, did I?

CHAPTER SEVEN.

On Wednesday morning I woke as usual with the overwhelming knowledge that William and my baby were not here. Instead of getting easier, it got harder to handle. There seemed no point in getting up. No point in anything. I just wanted William and my beautiful daughter back in my life.

Dragging myself out of bed I performed all the daily rituals to prove that I was alive. I made fresh coffee after James left with Cassidy. He promised to get my photographs on his way to pick up his bag. He was quite good at little things like that. I suppose he liked to think of himself as a New man.

I had decided not to ask if Barbara was going with him to London, not wanting to know how good an actor he was, thank you. But the house was empty without him and my constant companion; Cassidy. Even Buggalugs had deserted me.

James returned, leaving Cass sniffing around the courtyard outside while he popped back to hand me the A4 envelope of my enlargements and give me a quick kiss before he dashed off.

'Try and find yourself a nice car while I'm gone, no older than two years eh? Cheer yourself up a bit, sweetheart,' he said, as he slid behind the wheel of his well past its sell by date, "provided by the University," four wheeled drive. 'I'll give it a thorough check for you when I get back,' he promised as he drove off.

'Thank you, dear,' I said with a saccharine smile as he left. 'I have every intention of finding myself a car and I certainly do not need your permission. Or advice.' Still, no doubt he meant well.

Looking through the prints, I glanced out of the window and saw Piers Coleman striding across the courtyard towards his Porsche. I could hardly bear to look at him, he was so like Walter. All he needed was a black suit and a wide dirty, white collar. His face seemed to age before my eyes and coarsen into the old Puritan. He turned to glare at me, his black eyes glittering coldly.

Hell was not full of fire and brimstone but ice. Black ice. Cold, dark and empty. I saw it all in Piers Coleman's eyes.

Fear gripped me in the sudden chill as his stare rooted me to the spot. I read his intention as if it was written in block letters but before I could shout a warning, he kicked Cassidy. Kicked my poor little dog high into the air.

Cassidy yelped once as he slammed into the pile of brick rubble, landing with a dull thud.

My fear left me and I ran towards Cass, shaking with anger and pointing at the arrogant bastard. My voice resounded in my ears.

'Damn you, Coleman. I'll break every bone in your blasted foot for that!'

My mind skittered to the pile of builders rubble and saw a huge lump of concrete partially hidden under the broken bricks. Running towards Cassidy, through air which seemed to freeze my limbs into slow motion, the concrete upended itself.

The locket round my neck suddenly pressed hard against my throat, choking off the warning I was about to give Coleman.

The heavy lump of masonry smashed unerringly onto his elegant, cream linen boot.

His strangled screams drew me to his side. Sprawled amid the brick rubble and covered in plaster dust, he looked more frightened than frightening. His podgy hand was scratched and bleeding as he held it out to me for help.

I reached for it, even tried to grasp his arm but I couldn't move.

I felt as if someone was holding the chain tight around my neck, pulling me back.

Gasping for air I ran my fingers under the locket, surprised to find it lay loosely in the hollow of my neck as usual.

I tried to shout for help, God knows I did. But I could not utter a sound, struck dumb and unable to make a move to help Piers.

Cassidy yelped behind me and freed me from my momentary lapse of will. I spun round at once and picked him up. He was cut on his belly and was whining fit to melt the heart of a tin soldier.

I held him in my arms, stroking him gently, murmuring sweet nothings. Praying he was alright. Insisting he was alright. He squirmed a little and licked my hand, his tongue cold against my fingers.

Cold? Raising the back of my hand to my face I found it was not exactly hot but as warm as if I'd been sunbathing. I put it down to hot-aches and carried on loving Cassidy better, welcoming the excuse for a cuddle as I stared, horror struck, at the chunk of concrete which pinned Coleman's foot to the ground.

A couple of workmen came out of the barn. 'Is he alright, duck?' one of them nodded to Cassidy.

With great effort I shook my head and managed to croak. 'Please... Help.' They came towards me, more to hear what I'd said than to offer assistance. Trembling with shock and feeling nauseous, I pointed to Piers, who mercifully had passed out.

'Christ!'

As they ran to him they were joined by the rest of the builders. It took two men to lift the heavy slab off Coleman's crushed and bleeding foot. When the other two tried to lift him Piers screamed. The sound was high pitched and shrill, grating on my nerves. It filled me with a queasy mixture of pity and contempt.

I turned away, unable to watch, overwhelmed with the certainty that I had made the cement fall on Coleman's foot. But how?

The world darkened and spun too fast on its axis.

Veering away, I staggered, and held Cassidy tight in my arms as one of the builders led me back to my house. Grateful to get inside, I managed to thank him and after he left I leant against the door until my legs recovered enough strength to carry me to the sink. I laid Cass on a towel before I threw up.

I felt as if I'd physically picked up the slab of concrete and run a mile with it. Without a doubt I knew I had done that to Coleman... Hadn't I?

First I swilled out the sink and sluiced disinfectant around before slurping cold water from my hand to take away the taste of regurgitated coffee. Thank God I hadn't eaten. Then I tended Cassidy.

Gently I ran my hands all over him, terrified in case he had internal injuries, but he didn't even whimper. He was not as badly hurt as I would have supposed. For a second I wondered if I had done that too, perhaps the heat in my hands had helped to heal him? But unable to cope with anything else, I shelved the idea.

Cassidy had a weeping cut under his belly and both of his front legs were scratched but fortunately his back leg was OK. Apart from a bit of antiseptic powder there was nothing to do except make a fuss of him.

I tried to convince myself that it was just a coincidence that the lump of concrete had dropped onto Coleman's foot. It was his own fault, he had kicked Cassidy on to the pile of rubble and the impact had dislodged the concrete. That's what James would have said. But I couldn't accept it.

Feeling the weight of the world on my shoulders I glanced out of the window. Two men were carrying Piers to his car in a "chair" lift. The others bustled about trying to ease him into his low slung Porsche while he called them all 'Clumsy sons of …' his diatribe was abruptly cut off when one of the sons of bitches, accidentally, I'm *sure,* knocked Coleman's foot as he manoeuvred him into the passenger seat.

The builder drove him to the hospital before Coleman's cursing woke the dead.

I hated the feeling of satisfaction which swept over me when, my mind replayed the action as the large piece of masonry lifted itself on end before it literally dived to its mark. A voice, a thought, call it what you will, *something* insisted that I had heaved that concrete on to his foot as surely as if I'd thrown it with my bare hands.

But I couldn't accept that either. That would make me a witch.

Carrying Cassidy with me to the bathroom, I had a quick shower, using my best C K gel to take away the rather metallic smell of the water.

Refreshed, I went back to the kitchen to make myself a sandwich before starting work. I couldn't remember when I'd felt as hungry. Or as tired.

Taking Cass and my photographs upstairs to my office I switched on the lights to brighten the gloomy day, such a stark contrast to the taste of Spring we had yesterday, and studied the enlarged prints.

The first letter on the drums was almost indecipherable but the last one could have been C, although that was probably wishful thinking. However, the two middle letters were definitely F's... As in Coleman's Feed and Fertiliser Company.

It merely confirmed my suspicions though and was not enough evidence against them. Especially as the Company no longer existed.

Phoning around the Government offices I eventually managed to find someone to give me the (to my mind rather naïve) official viewpoint on the legislation, which I deciphered into intelligible English to use in my article on fly-tipping. This would hopefully follow my piece on the alarming cluster of cancer and miscarriages around the reservoir in Upper Berry.

Common sense pointed the finger of blame to an old, ill thought out piece of Conservative legislation against fly tippers which was making it extortionately expensive for legitimate companies to pay for registered contractors. Hence the increased use of fly-tippers. Exactly the opposite of the original intentions. Maybe this Government could find a way to stop this, though don't ask me how.

If I could prove that the Coleman's had knowingly allowed their toxic wastes to be illegally tipped no matter how long ago, then the story would, as Jayne said, be hot. Especially as Seb was odds on favorite to be the next Member of Parliament in this constituency. Not to mention Piers' lucrative sideline which he had taken over when his father decided to stand in the by-election; chairman of a Quango which advised on Agricultural and Environmental issues.

I suddenly became aware of the empty space around me, feeling as if someone was watching me. Something was wrong.

Saving my edit and switching off my computer, apprehension got the better of me. 'Let's go downstairs, eh?' I asked Cass. 'I've got a lot of reading and research to do, might as well make ourselves comfy,' I said, massaging my temples against the threatening headache.

Then the lights went off.

Cassidy started barking, as confused as I was. I stood in the dark wondering what to do, when they flickered on again. A power cut. Thank goodness I'd followed my instincts and switched off the computer.

'We'll go downstairs in a minute, I'll just sort out my notes.'

Cassidy looked at me expectantly, then sighed and settled himself for a snooze. Even he didn't believe in my minutes.

The lights went dim and brightened again.

'It's time to call it a day. I'm starving, how about you?'

It was well past dinner time. Cassidy barked his approval. I picked him up to carry him downstairs. There was still no sign of Buggalugs.

The landing light flickered and went out.

Cautiously groping my way in the dark, mindful of Cassidy's bruised and weeping injury, I opened the door at the bottom of the stairs into the dining room. A small pool of dim light filtered through the window, but only served to emphasise the threatening black shadows beyond.

Holding my breath, I listened. Was that the sound of someone breathing? My eyes searched the dark recesses, sure that we were being watched. I tried to breathe quietly and calm down but I'd always hated walking through a dark room and tonight, the air seemed to crackle with menace. The quietness was oppressive and I strained to identify any alien sound.

Cassidy started growling and squirming in my arms, his hackles rising. Reaching for the light switch I barely managed to resist the temptation to run.

Someone was here, in my house... Watching me.

When I switched on the light there was aloud bang and the bulb blew.

Calming Cassidy, I rushed blindly to the front room and tried the light in there.

Nothing. The mains fuse had blown.

I was on my own and it was dark.

Outside was silent. Threatening. But the danger was not outdoors but here with me. Inside my house.

I put Cass down and searching the sitting room by the light from the street lamp in the courtyard, found the matches and lit the collection of candles on the mantelpiece. By their flickering light I braced myself to open the cellar door and reach for the fuse box at the head of the stairs. A chill crept down my spine as the small circle of light contrasted sharply with the yawning black hole which led to the bowels of the earth beneath me.

My over active imagination painted pictures of Dracula crawling out of his ancient coffin. I felt his red eyes watching me.

I swallowed, trying to overcome my childish fear of the dark as I reached for the fuse box. Cassidy went mad and yelping under my feet, almost made me lose my balance, so I took him through to the front room and put him on the sofa.

Taking a candle in a brass holder to the cellar head, I remembered to switch off the Mains before touching the fuse box and turn it on again afterwards.

The fuse blew with a bang, startling the breath out of me.

It was closer to my neighbours the front way, so I locked the back door, feeling as if I'd locked myself in with Jack the Ripper.

Rushing past the cellar my heart was thumping so rapidly I could scarcely hold the candle and I stood, trying to stop shaking, as I leant against the door.

A creaking board sounded like a pistol shot.

Another thud in my chest. Was that a footstep?

I held my breath but all I could hear was Cassidy whimpering. His terror brought me up sharp; he sensed my fear and was shivering with fright. Letting my breath out slowly, I tried to get a grip, not wanting to finish up a candidate for "Care in the community".

'It's all right, darling. You stay there while I fetch Mel,' I told my little protector, who was scrabbling under the soft cushions.

Running out of the house I was half way across the courtyard before I stopped and looked back uncertainly. I even took a step back, wanting to check that the front door had snicked shut properly.

Standing in the pool of light from Coleman's old fashioned street lamp, everything looked so normal. The soft glow of the candles shining through my window added to the air of Victorian tranquillity.

My friend June Keeton lived opposite and her husband Mel, was a professional Handy man who was always willing to help. It was only as I told them my fuses had blown that I remembered that Jack the Ripper was a Victorian.

CHAPTER EIGHT

'Please hurry!' I gasped before I ran back to my house. Carrying his tool box and a large torch, Mel rushed after me.

There was no light shining through the window. No candles burning.

Panic fumbled my fingers as I tried to unlock the front door, wanting to shoulder it in. When it swung open I rushed inside.

It was unnaturally quiet.

'Cassidy?' I called anxiously. 'Don't you disappear on me too!'

I was worried and scared. Frightened for the safety of my little dog.

Mel flashed his torch around. There was no sign of Cassidy. No sound. The house was empty and cold. What had they done to him?

The acrid smell of candle wax wrinkled my nose. I tried to light them but they had been gutted, the wicks flattened into the melted wax.

We walked to the kitchen. The back door was wide open.

'I locked this before I came out.' I looked at Mel but he was embarrassed, not knowing whether to believe me or not.

'Are you sure? It's easy to make a mistake in the dark,' he said, obviously hoping I would go along with the easy explanation.

'It was on the Yale catch,' I said, trying to convince him. Why were even the nicest men so bloody sceptical?

I nodded towards the old lock. 'And where is the big key?' It was no longer there.

'Didn't you bring it with you?'

'No. I left it in the lock like I always do and came out by the front door.' I held up the Yale, on the ring with my car keys as I closed the back door.

'Yueuk!' the handle was sticky. Rubbing my fingers together I sniffed. They smelled of antiseptic powder and Cassidy's bloody wound.

'Cassidy!' I shouted, yanking open the door and snatching the torch from Mel as I ran into the pitch black garden, frantically searching for my little wounded pal. But he was nowhere to be found.

Instinctively I knew that one of the Colemans had taken him. Piers seeking revenge? Somehow I didn't think he'd be mobile enough tonight.

'God help you if you've hurt him, you bastard,' I swore through clenched teeth. Spinning on my heel I stared into the shadows, knowing someone was listening. Knowing who. After all, it wasn't really Sebastian's style.

The garden was thrown into stark black and white contrast by the torch light as I swung it side to side.

Mel touched my arm. ' Over there, Rowena.'

'Leave him alone!' I shouted, pointing the beam of light at George. 'If you don't want to finish up like your goddamned brother!'

He was kneeling under the weeping willow by the side of the pond, holding Cassidy under the water.

Drowning him.

George let go and Cassidy splashed about as he tried to get out.

Mel ran to the pond, closely followed by me. He took Cass by the scruff of the neck and held him in the safety of his arms.

'You mindless bastard,' I shouted, pointing my finger at George.

He threw his arms in front of his face protectively, backing away from my anger.

'I found 'im, missus, I found ' im,' he sobbed. 'I weren't trying to drown 'im, we were just playing, honest,' he muttered, and when I dropped my arm and reached out for Cassidy, he ran off blubbering.

He was afraid of me, I realised. Afraid of what I could do.

'I'm not warning you again,' Mel shouted after him. 'This time I'm telling your father. Care in the fucking community, my eye,' he said under his breath. 'He should never have been let out.'

I looked at him questioningly as I stroked and petted my little dog, only paying half a mind to what Mel was saying.

'It's time this Government did something about the closure of the special hospitals and letting the so called "educationally disadvantaged" out on the streets. The psychiatrists paid no attention to George's predilection for killing animals. '

Mel shook his head and warned. 'I'd keep your doors locked and Cassidy and Buggalugs indoors when he's about, if I were you. George has no conception of right and wrong. And don't let his big kid act fool you, I saw him wanking off in the loft when I was doing a bit of work for his father. He's no kid in that department, I can tell you.'

My head reeled. Terrifying memories assaulted my brain with vivid reality. I was vaguely aware of my legs collapsing under me and someone holding my arms, of hard fingers digging to the bone...

Walter's hands gripped Mistress Berrysford's arms, which were bound tight behind her back, he shook her so hard she bit her tongue. The pain cleared her vision. He nodded towards his half witted son, Seth.

"He's waiting to play with you. But should it be age before beauty?" he asked, rubbing himself against her before he spun her round to face Seth, who was hurriedly pulling down his breeches. "Or shall we let the biggest go first?" Walter leered, one dirty hand squeezing her face as the other took hold of the neck of her gown and tore it to expose her breasts.

"Aye and we will watch," Luke said. "If the witch can take him we'll know she's been bedded by the devil."

His big hands grabbed her breasts both thumbs roughly squeezing her nipples.

"No milk! I knew it! Sour titties to suckle her master's familiar," he said, gloating over her half clad body.

Walter grinned as he roughly pushed her towards his idiot son.

"Suffer not a witch to live!" Seth kept repeating, too stupid to argue reason as he knelt astride her, rubbing himself.

"Damn you Seth Coleman," she spoke out angrily. "I swear you will never be able to touch another woman again."
If they think I am a witch, so be it. Let them suffer the consequences.
She bit her lip to prevent herself crying out as she watched his grossness stiffen.
"Oh God, please don't let me scream," she prayed silently at the same time she snorted contemptuously at his manhood.
He looked at it uncertainly then rubbed himself harder.
Looking up into the shadows she shuddered as lightning forked across the sky, throwing Walter Coleman into sharp relief. His small black eyes gloating when he saw her watching him throw the rope over a branch of the oak tree.
A chill knotted her stomach when she saw the hanging noose.
"See what this feels like around your precious neck," Coleman snarled. "But first let the lad have his fun."
Forgetting her resolve not to show them her fear, she cried out when Seth pushed and prodded, trying to enter her. His mouth drooling as he struggled to force himself inside her squirming body whilst the others goaded him on. Walter's finger nails dug into the soft flesh of her thighs as he held her down.
"Hurry up, you idiot. But don't forget. I want her conscious," Luke warned, lifting her hips to make it easier for Seth to penetrate her.
Her high pitched scream echoed in the night as Seth's frenzied excitement made him forget his brother's instructions.
"That's better! I like it when you scream," he smirked, tearing into her with such savagery, shock and pain made her lose consciousness when he finally impaled her...

'Rowena!'
Mel was holding me up by my arms as I sagged against him; sickened and humiliated by the memory.
I blinked and stared thankfully at the world about me. Cassidy was yelping at my feet, wet and shivering.
'I'm OK,' I stuttered, coming to my senses.

'Please don't pass out on me,' Mel said, putting a supporting arm round my shoulder. 'I'm sorry if I frightened you. I'll have another word with Seb. He'll make sure George is kept under constant supervision. Piers usually keeps an eye on him but, well, you know what happened today.'

'Oh yes, I know what happened,' I said. And I could imagine Piers keeping an eye on George. Encouraging him more like.

Not thinking about modesty I pulled my jumper over my head and wrapped it around Cassidy, holding him in my arms and crooning sweet nothings over him, trying to dry him and love him better at the same time.

I was out of my mind with relief, hardly aware of Mel talking as he put his arm around my shoulders.

'Come indoors, love.'

I stared at him blankly, not understanding his words.

'Come in, Rowena, please,' he begged. Turning me around, Mel led me back to the house, his calmness reassuring me.

He lit the candles and changed a fuse but as soon as he switched the mains back on, it blew with a loud bang, frightening Cassidy.

'Sorry, there's nothing else I can do, I'm afraid. You'll have to call an electrician in the morning. Meanwhile, come on over to our house and get warm, it's as cold as charity in here. But I'd put another sweater on first, if I were you,' he said, grinning cheekily at my embarrassment.

One of James' gardening jumpers was hanging behind the cellar door and Mel took Cassidy from me while I pulled it on.

Mel carried him across the courtyard, his other arm wrapped round me securely. When we entered his house, he sat me down in front of the fire.

'I'll dry the old fella off, eh?' He took Cass through to the kitchen and I could hear him telling his wife what had happened.

Getting the gist of it, June came rushing in. 'Hello love, how are you?'

'I'm alright thanks, it's Cassidy who's been in the wars.'

Arms akimbo and hands on hips, she tutted and studied me as if she didn't believe a word of it.

'We were just about to have a bit of supper, you'll have some with us won't you? You look all in,' she said, shouting through to the kitchen for Mel to do some more toast.

'I don't want to impose,' I said.

Cassidy trotting at his side, Mel came in carrying a big mug on a plate surrounded by fingers of toast; he put it on the coffee table beside my chair.

'Drink this, it will do you more good than a cup of tea.' He put a mug of Tomato soup into my cold hands.

I hadn't realised how hungry I was until I took the first warming sip.

'Thank you. It's delicious.'

'I gave Cassidy some left over brisket, I hope that's alright?' Mel asked.

'Thank you. Poor Cassidy, I haven't fed him yet. He's like Buggalugs, give him food and he'll be your friend for life. You haven't seen him have you?' I asked. 'My cat's been missing for a couple of days.'

Mel looked rather anxious but June shook her head as she replied. 'No, not lately. He'll turn up, I'm sure. You know how many admirers he's got; he's probably living in the lap of luxury somewhere.'

'I'm sorry I couldn't help with your lights,' Mel said.

'Me too. I thought my fear of the dark had been vanquished long ago but I was wrong.'

'Don't fret, Rowena, Mel will see you safe home,' June said.

The evenings events went through my mind as I was drinking the soup. There was no doubt that I'd locked the kitchen door and left the key in the lock. The door had been opened from the inside. Someone had been there when I'd come downstairs. I thought of George in my house. In my bedroom. Stealing my underwear. Kidnapping my dog.

How could I protect myself when locked doors didn't keep him out? I wasn't superwoman. I hadn't really moved that lump of concrete by will power alone, had I? Surrounded by warm, normal friends, the idea was just too ridiculous.

Doubt and confusion rushed to support logic and reason.

Believing that I had supernatural powers wouldn't help me if George and Piers tried to rob, rape or murder me. For they could, it seems, get into my house anytime they liked. And I had to spend the night there alone.

In the dark.

What could I do? Where could I go?

The clock on the mantelpiece chimed ten.

"I'm sorry, I must be going.' I certainly couldn't stay here. 'James always phones me about this time, if I'm not there he'll be worried sick.'

It was a bit of a fib, James only phoned me if he was alone, but I got up to my feet, thankful that my legs were no longer made of jelly. This was not their problem, I had to deal with the Colemans without their help.

I thanked the Keetons for their hospitality and regretfully left the sanctuary of their warm, cosy home.

Mel insisted on going with me to check out all my rooms. He found nothing amiss.

'Bless you,' I said, as he gave me his big bright torch and made me promise to call if I was frightened or needed anything.

When he left, the house seemed cold and dark. I didn't like it at all.

I carried Cassidy, the torch, candles and a big box of kitchen matches upstairs, set the torch by the telephone and undressed by candlelight.

The flickering flame threw menacing shadows on the wall, like a scene from a Gothic horror movie that I loved to watch on late night TV.

I was a big fan of the old black and white pictures, the witty forties comedies, the weepy melodramas. The horror movies. But telling myself this was like the old Abbott and Costello film about a haunted house did nothing to take away the feeling of being watched.

Standing naked by the bed, goose pimples broke out all over me and I ran over to the chest of drawers and rummaged around for a warm nightie. I could have sworn my clothes were not in the right place. And my nighties were not there. Not one.

Trying not to dwell on the thought of George here in my room, I pulled on a big T-shirt, and climbed into bed, blowing out the candle before diving under the bedclothes and pulling the duvet over my head, admonishing myself for being so childish.

The jangle of the phone made me jump and had me out of bed in an instant. Relief flooded through me and I had the receiver to my ear before I found the torch.

'James? Oh, am I glad you phoned!' But my instincts had let me down in my need to be comforted.

The quietness on the line frightened me.

Standing by the bed, full of foreboding, the only sound was Cassidy snoring but I felt as though I was on exhibition to the worlds worst perverts. Dragging the duvet from the bed I encased myself in its warmth.

'James?' Only the sound of heavy breathing answered me. It was George Coleman. That's why I felt spied upon. Yes, I knew *now* who was on the other end of the line.

I opened the drawer where James had left his old Rugby referees kit, his whistle gleaming like a beacon. I gave a shrill blast down the mouthpiece.

Above it's shriek I heard the yell from the receiver before it clattered back onto the hook.

Cassidy yelped accusingly.

'I'm sorry, love,' I soothed. 'But I reckon I've given your attacker a bit of a headache. With any luck I might have made him temporarily deaf as well.'

Getting back in bed I lay with my arm outstretched, reaching down to stroke Cassidy; I don't know whom was comforting whom. Cold, tense and frightened, I felt that someone was still spying on me. Biding their time.

Was it George or Piers? Or, I realised with a pang of fear, both of them. Or yet again, was I getting paranoid? Letting a couple of blown fuses in a house which desperately needed rewiring and a few mislaid underclothes get me into such a state.

Was it, like James said, all a delusion brought on when the car crashed into the tree? The tree on which I was convinced the Colemans hanged me?

Perhaps I'm going mad. Paranoia with a side helping of delusions of persecution?

No. I think not.

Whatever was the truth, it wouldn't hurt to protect myself.

I didn't fancy going downstairs like the frustratingly stupid heroines in the aforementioned horror movies. And I certainly wasn't going to sleep to be murdered in my bed.

What could I do that would let them know I was watchful and not afraid?

I suddenly knew. Leaping out of bed I grabbed the torch and sprinted across the landing to my workroom, picked up the library books and ran back.

Treating my bedroom as if it were under siege, I moved the bed so the foot was jammed up against the door and the head by the window; opening the drapes the room was bathed in the light from Coleman's street lamp in the courtyard. Finally I put Cassidy's basket beside me and pulled the phone onto the bed and twisted the line round the bars of my brass bedstead, stretching it into a trip wire across the room.

'Right you perverts. You can't sneak up on me now,' I said, sitting propped up against the pillows, with a book resting against my raised knees. 'I'm warning you, I'm not taking any more of this shit. If you so much as look at me cross eyed, I'll show you a few tricks you won't forget in a hurry.'

I had to assume the Colemans were my enemies. If they weren't, none of this would matter but if they believed that Rowena Berrysford was a witch, let them think that I am too. They might not be so keen to attack me if they thought I could defend myself.

A voice from the grave echoed in my ear...

If they think I am a witch; so be it. Let them suffer the consequences.

CHAPTER NINE.

In the light of the early spring morning, everything that happened last night seemed too far fetched, even Cassidy was bright eyed and chipper. But where was Buggalugs? I always thought of them as a twosome.

Splashing about under a cold shower, I tried to convince myself that Coleman fusing the lights was my over active imagination. Fuming at the quality of the water these days, which smelled like a stagnant pond, I hoped it was just another slip in the standard of the water company, rather than having to go to the expense of having a new tank put in.

Dressing quickly I cautiously went downstairs carrying Cassidy. But everything was as it should be; unthreatening. Thank God the menace had fled with the night.

I called Buggalugs, becoming anxious about him. I couldn't bear to think of him injured or dying in a ditch somewhere.

Just after I had moved into Beaumont Court someone had run over his tail, dislocating his spine and damaging his kidneys. Suddenly I wondered if the someone had been Piers. Only by the care and expertise of an excellent vet had Buggalugs managed to survive, albeit without his tail. He looked so unusual, everyone made a fuss of my affectionate cat.

Drinking a glass of tomato juice, I phoned around asking his friends if they had seen him, but no luck. I even phoned the PDSA with the same response. I tried to dismiss my anxiety, knowing my cat was such a charmer, he'd probably found himself another old lady to spoil him.

Thankful that I could at least boil water, I made myself a cup of Instant coffee and phoned Albert; hoping he'd be in the office. The Answer-phone gave me his home number.

'I'll be round in about an hour, as soon as Bert comes in,' he promised.

Looking at the clock, I realised it was still only seven o' clock.

'I'm sorry for disturbing you so early, Albert. I didn't get much sleep.'

'No problem, I've always been an early riser. But you should have called me last night, I'd have come straight away.'

'The last home address I have for you is on Front Street.'

'My goodness, that takes me back a few years. We turned my old house into the office years ago when my wife was still alive,' he paused, no doubt swallowing an unexpected pang of grief.

Remembering William and my baby I knew to my cost that it could sneak up on you.

'I live on the site of the old tannery now,' he continued. 'Anyway, don't worry, we'll soon have your percolator working. '

'Can't get much work done if that is out of action, can we?' I replied, smiling, inordinately pleased that he was coming.

I sat at the breakfast table reading another chapter of my library book. This one dealt with moving objects by telekinesis, which was a well recorded scientific phenomenon. As was healing.

These powers were often referred to as witchcraft but in some Counties in Britain, healers were available on the National Health Service. And even the police had occasionally called upon psychics to help in their investigations, especially where cases involved missing children. It seemed Albert was right, these powers were a gift, no different from being an artist or musician. I remembered that the police had called on a local lady to help them identify the remains of a man murdered in Suffolk during the second world war.

There is no mysterious magic involved in these powers, although there are those of high repute who call themselves white witches. In practising the art of healing, for instance, their energy radiates warmth, while more negative energy turns objects extremely cold. One explanation for this was that positive power sends out energy to the object while the negative draws energy from it. Although black witches (for want of a better name) take in power, they can also send out short blasts of laser like heat, but this is very limited, and thank goodness, rare.

White witches sometimes belong to an ancient religion and believe they are blessed with a slow burning power, the more they use it the stronger it grows. But their power draws from their own physical energy.

Apparently there are many who have this gift which, like any muscle in the body, should be carefully exercised to build up strength. The book cited the case of a Russian lady, who, while practising telekinesis in a scientifically controlled environment, died of extreme exhaustion.

The book was certainly opening my mind, it described my symptoms so well. According to the experts, telekinesis expounds more energy than it takes to physically move things, burning up calorific energy and leaving you hungry and exhausted.

Intrigued, I wanted to...No. I *needed* to try it.

I stared at the empty juice glass and tentatively willed it to move.

Nothing.

I urged it to move, just an inch.

Not a millimetre.

'Please move,' I pleaded out loud, feeling foolish, like a child trying to bend spoons with everyone watching. I concentrated on the glass and "saw" nothing; feeling silly. Getting angry.

'Damn you. Move!'

The glass jumped three or four inches into the air and fell to the floor.

It shattered.

Not believing my own eyes, I stared at the remains of the broken tumbler.

'Lord help me, ' I prayed, completely stunned.

Cassidy looked at me reproachfully for disturbing his nap and moved nearer to the door.

I tried to pick up the pieces of glass but the shards were quite literally, too hot to handle. Hastily fetching a brush and dustpan I meticulously swept up the remains.

Witch or not, I had done it.

There was no question about it. No doubt in my mind. Only a resigned acceptance.

The clatter of Albert's old van intruded into my thoughts. I picked up Cassidy and ran to greet him; hoping he would stop me from feeling like a freak.

Bert went straight to work checking the electricity while I boiled a saucepan of water on the gas stove to make them a pot of instant coffee.

'Something's wrong here, missus,' Bert said from the cellar head.

'I know, that's why I called you!' I joked, relaxed and confident with friends around me.

'No, duck. This isn't ordinary wear and tear. It's been tampered with.'

Albert and I peered at the junction box.

'These wires have been melted like that plug,' Bert told him and turned to me. 'If you had changed the fuse without turning off the electricity supply first, you'd have been a goner, that's for sure.'

I went cold, only Cassidy had prevented me from doing just that. This was not a silly vendetta, nor was it my imagination. This was deadly.

Albert ushered me back to the dining room.

'Call the police before you touch it,' he told Bert.

'Yeah,' he nodded. 'And I'll cancel the other work I've got on and sort this out right now, if you don't mind me using your phone?'

I shook my head, speechless.

'I'll check the circuits, after the police have seen this.'

'Thank you,' I said.

A police sergeant and a young constable came and asked a few questions but because there was nothing missing, they didn't seem very interested in a spot of lethal vandalism.

'It might have been your husband fixing a fuse. God save us all from amateur electricians,' the sergeant said, attempting levity.

'Definitely not! I am divorced and my ex wouldn't mess around with electricity at any price.'

But once the seed was planted in my mind, I remembered that I'd inherited a substantial amount of money from my great-grandfather. And still hadn't changed my will. I pulled myself up sharp, knowing the difference between imagination and reality.

'I've been having a spot of bother with the Colemans,' I said, leading them in the right direction.

'The MP?' He asked sceptically.

'He hasn't been elected yet,' I reminded him. 'And he certainly can't depend on my vote.'

The sergeant looked aghast. 'Even so, madam, I doubt if he'd resort to this sort of thing,' he said frostily. 'I put It down to old wiring and recommend you get it fixed.'

'Just what I was about to do, officer,' Bert said.

He turned away in disgust at the policeman's attitude. 'If you said it was some snafu they'd change their tune,' he told me in a loud aside. 'When you've got Coleman's kind of money you can buy anything, or anybody.'

'My feelings exactly,' I muttered.

'I'll make a note of your complaint, madam,' the sergeant said curtly.

'For your information, sergeant, I believe it was *George* Coleman, not his father. He was playing about with my dog. Trying to drown him.'

There was no point in telling him about my missing underwear. 'Perhaps he was just "playing" with my fuse box.' I added.

Though God knows how he got into my house, I thought, but kept quiet, knowing I'd probably be blamed for leaving the door open.

When they had gone, Bert went down the cellar to start on the wiring and Albert stayed for a chat.

'What do you reckon it's all about?' he asked.

'I reckon George came in here while I was working upstairs, fiddled with my wiring and when I came down, hid in the cellar. When I left to fetch Mel, Cassidy must have been barking like mad, so he carried him outside, leaving by the back door which left the handle all sticky from Cass's wound.'

Everything fell into place. 'He stole my key and tried to drown Cassidy in the pond. That's what I reckon!'

Albert agreed. 'Sounds just the sort of thing he would do. And Seb Coleman could be the bloody King of Siam for all I care, I still wouldn't trust him.'

'There speaks a man who isn't going to vote for him,' I smiled.

'Too right I'm not. The Colemans are all bad lots, born and bred. They seem to know when you are on your own too.'

'I think I'll stay at my stepson's tonight,' I told him thoughtfully. I hadn't fallen asleep until well after dawn.

'I would if I were you, Rowena. Keep as far away from the Colemans as you can, they are up to no good.'

I was surprised by the vehemence in his voice.

'I could tell you a thing or two about them. Mind you, they always come to a bad end; the majority of them anyway.'

Albert told me about the Colemans and I listened carefully, remembering the old adage. "Know your enemy."

'Seb's father was only a babe when his good for nothing uncles were shot for desertion in the first world war.'

He followed me into the kitchen while I made instant coffee and told him what Rowan, my great-grandfather, said about the episode.

'Aye, I can believe that,' Albert said, as I took a cup to Bert.

The cellar ran under the back half of the house, it was damp and some of the bricks were broken.

'This is in a terrible state,' I said, shocked at the musty smell. 'I'll have to get this fixed, later.'

'You could have it tanked and turn it into a den or a workshop,' Bert suggested.

That's what Mel had done to their cellar, but Mel was a carpenter and needed the room to work in. I didn't. 'I'll think about it,' I laughed, thinking instead about the cost.

'My grandmother told tales about the Colemans that were passed down from generations before her,' Albert told me when I returned.

'How long before?' I asked, fascinated by stories of the past.

'Dunno exactly, but it should be easy enough to find out,' he said. 'It was in the days when the tannery was the biggest trade in Arnold. Around 1850 or 60, I suppose.'

'Where was the tannery, Albert?' I asked.

'Why, Tannery Lane of course. Mrs Knight was the lady who owned it at the time and she left the land to my great great-grandmother Emily Smithson, her name was, before she was married.'

He stopped, noticing my shock at hearing the name from Rowena Berrysford's era.

'Smithson? I wonder if she was a descendant of Sarah?' I asked thoughtfully.

'In a small community as old as Arnold it is more than likely,' Albert assured me. 'The original families of the old village are nearly all related by marriage,' he said. 'And I have a niece who inherited the Smithson's old house in Redhill; we've just finished converting it into a restaurant she calls Sarah's, after the first lady who lived in the house.'

I gasped as the world dissolved around me and I remembered my very dear friend...

Rowena was much taken with William's twin sister, Sarah, delighted that they were alike in both looks and temperament.

They got to know one another as they worked together in the herb garden whilst William and Sarah's husband, Edward Smithson, who owned the brick yard in Arnold, worked side by side building their home. Berrysford House.

She and Sarah oftimes sat on the low stone wall which bordered their property, and shared their intimate secrets.

"I remember the day I met Edward," Sarah told her just after she and William were married. "My spirit still soars when I think of it. How did you feel when you first met William?"

Rowena's heart beat faster at the memory.

William was tall, slim and broad of shoulder, with a sensitive face and strong jaw. He had jet black hair, curly and unruly, which was always falling over his forehead. With unconscious charm he tried to blow it away from his face when he was concentrating. But his most striking feature was his bright sea blue eyes.

'My heart beat so loud I'm sure it could be heard in Arnold and I followed him about like a devoted puppy. He could have

teased me but instead soothed my feelings, for he told me later that he was immensely pleased by my attention."

"I can see how much you and William love each other," Sarah said, smoothing her burgundy silk gown.

"But as my mother asked me, do you love him enough to spend the rest of your life with him?"

Rowena's eyes glistened with tears. "Oh yes. But it is not near long enough." She shook her head in despair. "To have less than three score years. It isn't fair."

I blinked away my tears at the onslaught of emotions which the memory evoked. It could have been yesterday. How could I remember thoughts and feelings I had experienced so long ago?

'Anyway,' Albert continued, deciding not to comment on my lapse of attention. 'Our Emily gave the land to her grandson, who was my great-grandfather. He built the house on it, where my nephew lives.'

'What happened to the tannery?' I asked, knowing what he was about to tell me would be significant.

'Two of the Coleman clan burned it down to the ground, but funny thing was, everyone got out of the place except them. It was all very mysterious and caused quite a stir at the time, there was a lot of gossip but no one would speak of what really happened. Rumour has it that the Colemans burned to death on their own pyre.'

I shivered as my imagination conjured up fiery images so vivid I couldn't breathe the fetid air; my nostrils wrinkled at the acrid stench that was making my eyes water.

I fought against the now familiar sensation of drowning in a sea of stars...

'No!' I cried out loud. As if jerking myself out of a nightmare the images disappeared. I had conquered the sickening roller coaster ride into the past.

Who was this woman? What was she to me?

'Mrs Knight?' I asked. 'Was her name Rowena?'

Albert saw the effect his tale had on me and poured me another cup of coffee as he replied. 'I don't know, but again it should be easy to find out; it will be a good start on the search for your ancestors,' he said. 'I'll ask my nephew, I bet he'll know.'

We chatted while he finished his cup of coffee and got up to leave. 'See you tomorrow,' he reminded me. It was the day my kitchen was to be flattened.

Leaving Bert busily chipping hell out of my walls to put in a two way switch, I took Cassidy up to my workroom, the policeman's words revolving round my head. This was dangerous.

The Colemans were not playing childish games. They were trying to kill me.

My mind balked at that; it was too far fetched. There had to be a rational explanation.

I tried to lose myself in my work but my thoughts drifted instead to William and how much I missed him.

I had never known love like that, and now it was too late.

When James and I met he was a handsome lecturer with a twinkle in his eye for the ladies and I was flattered by his attention. Perhaps he represented the father figure I'd never known. Then again, perhaps I had represented the mother figure his children had never known.

His ex wife had just packed up and left. She gave him a clean divorce, no maintenance, no fighting for custody of the children. For the first time I wondered if James had married me just to be a mother to them. But that wasn't fair, he loved me in his own way. I was sure he did. And what about me? Had I married him because he had two wonderful children whom I adored? I had certainly stayed with him because I couldn't bear to leave them.

Needing to get my head together I left Cassidy snoozing and took a taxi to the Land Registry, following my instincts as Albert advised. I was delighted to find the tannery well recorded. Mrs Knight had been made a partner in the business, enabling her to inherit it from her husband Robert.

At that time a woman of property hadn't the right to leave a will but she left it by deed of covenant to be sold to Emily Weston, nee Smithson, for a single penny.

I stared at the beautiful copperplate script, the ink had faded to a golden brown and the writing was spidery and indistinct but there was no mistaking the name.

Mrs Rowena Knight.

I walked out in a daze, my legs feeling as if they were wading through treacle. Shakily I sat on the low wall and try as I might, I couldn't stop the world spinning into the past...

CHAPTER TEN.

After a warming breakfast, Mrs Rowena Knight was ready to face the journey to the tannery.

"We will take the gig this morning, Stanley," she told the young groom.

"Yes, ma'am, I'll be waiting by the door for you."

Putting on her woollen cape and bonnet she was out of the house in a trice.

The lamps on the side of the carriage cast a yellow glow onto the rutted road, lighting the watery grey dawn. She sighed, even after all these years she still missed Robert sitting beside her as they travelled to and from the tannery. She had gone with him every day of her marriage. First because the business he'd inherited took too much of his attention, and secondly, to their mutual delight, she had the knack of buying and selling their leathers which was second to none.

When Robert died she had employed Emily to help in the office not only because she had a good hand and a head for figures but as a chaperone. It wasn't proper to be the only woman amongst so many men.

Emily was a treasure more valuable than gold, providing light hearted conversation and a philosophy far advanced of her years. She had even helped her to ward off the Colemans persistent attempts to buy the tannery for next to nothing, when, after the Children's Act, they instigated riots to force her out. Then for some reason they had tried to close her down.

Mrs Knight shook her head. What had she ever done for them to hate her so?

Reaching the tannery's tall wrought iron gates she was pleased to see them open.

Emily had once again beaten her to work. Through the windows she could see the gas jets had already been lit.

"Come for me at noon and tell cook I will be bringing Emily back for luncheon," she said as she alighted from the gig.

"It's going to rain this afternoon, so bring the carriage, please."

"Yes, ma'am."

She smiled her dismissal and hurried to the new brick office that Weston's had built, abutting the entrance and as far from the stench as possible. Apprehension hastened her feet when she realised the building was still in darkness.

Sparking the tinder box she lit the long wax taper which stood in a rack by the door and went round the rooms lighting the dove tail gas jets.

Where was Emily? A wave of panic swept through her. Something was dreadfully wrong. She just knew it. She had trained herself to ignore these little insights over the years even though her instincts were usually right, she distrusted the ungodly phenomenon. This time however, logic rebelled and instinct took over her senses.

Stealthily she walked through to her office where the gas was already lit. There were papers, orders and receipts strewn all over the floor.

Burglars had broken in, and by the look of it were still on the premises. But how had they got in, there was no sign of forced entry?

No broken windows.

She had the preposterous notion that they (and she also had the idea that it was the Colemans) had opened locked doors and walked in without the benefit of a key.

Emily's cloak and bonnet lay in a heap by the door; perhaps she had run for help. But Mrs Knight knew that this was just wishful thinking. The very air reeked with danger.

Lighting an oil lamp she went to find Emily, shielding the light so as not to betray her presence.

No one was in the cutting room. Entering the dyeing room, she paused. Not a sound.

Following her instincts she silently opened the slatted door to the drying room, which was kept warm and well ventilated, due to the danger of spontaneous combustion.

This room was lit only by daylight, which was weakly illuminating the row of sky lights set in the ceiling.

She scanned the room. Emily must be in here, there was only the liming room left and that held nothing except deep pits where the skins were softened in caustic solutions of lime.

Above the beating of her heart Mrs Knight heard breathing.

Curiously she wondered what her hands were doing as they picked up an oil soaked rag which had been used in the softening process, and watched intrigued as they wrapped it round the end of a stout ponch. The pole was used for pushing the hides into, or out of the lime pits.

It also made an excellent fire brand she discovered, especially with a little help from the lamp oil.

Holding the flaming torch aloft she moved from the cover of the drying racks and stood transfixed, horrified as the scene in front of her eyes, rooted her to the spot.

Two of the Coleman brothers were there, Uriah and Zachary. Where was the other? she wondered anxiously.

Wasn't it rumoured that the younger Coleman had been caught on the premises of Jeacock's? She had dismissed the servants gossip as preposterous. What could Coleman have wanted in the solicitors office? It wasn't as if they needed to steal.

Then what did they want here?

They were kneeling on the hides, mauling Emily's limp body. Zachary was trying to tie her legs to the pallet, while Uriah, trousers around his ankles, was attempting to rape her.

Rowena Knight was immobile, her vision blurred as she felt herself detached from reality. She gasped as strange memories invaded her mind...

She felt her arms tied behind her, and experienced the pain and humiliation as Seth violated her body. The memory as sharp and clear as if it were yesterday.

She forgot to breathe as anger threatened to suffocate her.

It was she who was spread-eagled, and yet she saw superimposed on her retina, that it was Emily who lay unconscious, her clothing torn, her breasts exposed.

Zachary sucked her nipple like a pig. And Uriah was trying to force himself into her...

Mrs Knight shook her head, trying to clear the terror that she knew did not belong to her. Shaken and confused she watched as Emily struggled to regain consciousness while Zachary slapped her face.

"Come on you slattern, wake up and see what you're missing. I want you to know when it's my turn," he sneered.

But Mrs Knight heard the echoes of Walter's voice.

She felt the weight of Seth on top of her, his sweat dripping in her eyes while Walter and his son Luke, held her down.

Bile rose in her throat as Seth managed to penetrate her. Pain and fury forced logic from her mind as he savagely thrust into her.

She stared up at the branches of the oak tree, trying to rise above this humiliation. The orange moon flickered above her.

Flickered?

Puzzled she watched the moon turn into a burning torch that she held in her hand. The memories were from a different time. A different Rowena.

Mrs Knight screamed in anger and confusion. She had felt this invasion, endured the pain and humiliation, tied and helpless. But this time she was free...

Gleefully Rowena gave vent to her rage and ran at them, thrusting the flaming torch at Seth.

'Get off her! I've told you before, Seth Coleman, you will not do that again,' she said.

Uriah scrambled off as Emily, still unmolested, cried hysterically. "Mrs Knight! Thank the Lord you've come."

But Mrs Knight showed no sign of having heard. Holding the burning brand she advanced, her eyes glowing like a tigress.

With far more agility than could be expected for her age, she leapt, thrusting the brand into Zachary's eyes. "And you, Walter Coleman, will not watch!"

His screams echoed through the wooden rafters as he tried to tear out his eyes with his hands. Stumbling, he ran in to the lime room.

Mrs Knight heard the splash, the desperate splutters for help.

The piercing screams renewed as the acid burned into his flesh.

The silence.

"Your turn now, Seth," she said as if she were telling him to read a Sunday School lesson.

Uriah, frightened witless by this uncanny avenger, attempted to pull up his trousers and run at the same time.

"I've got you at last!" Rowena taunted, thrusting the burning pole into his groin.

Desperately Uriah tried to protect himself and push the brand away. His flesh scorched, he doubled over in agony.

"I only did what I was told. It was all his idea!" *he sobbed, as the mad woman waved the torch too close, blistering his skin.*

Emily staggered to her feet, pulling the torn shreds of her blouse together as she ran to Mrs Knight's side.

She quickly swept off her cloak, her eyes never leaving her adversary. "Put this on, dear, and fetch help," *she said.*

When Emily looked doubtful, she added, "Don't worry, I will deal with Seth."

Emily paid no heed to Mrs Knight getting his name wrong as she ran from the room.

"Please, missis, don't!" *Uriah begged as she advanced towards him.*

"Seth Coleman, you will burn in Hell fire with the devil himself." She listened to her powerful voice as it echoed through the woods.

Shaking with fear Uriah tried to slap out the scorching smoke rising from his trousers. As he stumbled backwards he slipped on the wet hides and fell onto his back.
"Oh God! Please missis, I ain't Seth."

Rowena, her hair undone and her face glistening with sweat, stood over him, the glow from the flames reflected in her cat like eyes turned them into red coals as she lifted the torch and aimed it at his lower belly.
"I remember you, Seth," she whispered vengefully.

"I am Not Seth," he screamed in fear and frustration. "My name is Uriah," he begged her to understand. "Uriah Coleman."

She thrust with the strength of two and speared him with the burning stave.
He screeched in agony as flames engulfed him.
The strange Rowena stood, hearing nothing as she looked around in the bright orange moonlight, the branches of the oak tree aflame.

She stared perplexed. It was not the moon but reflections of the fire on the windows in the roof. The woods wavered and disappeared, causing her a moment of dizziness.
Confused she realised it was not the trees but the tannery which was on fire.
Mrs Knight brushed her fingers through her hair, tidying the unruly tendrils as she walked purposefully towards the door.
Then turning to glance at the human torch she whispered absent mindedly as his screams faltered and ceased.
"You Colemans are all the same. Uriah or Seth."
Mrs Knight had no idea where that name had sprung from.
In control of herself once again, she dismissed it from her mind as she calmly left the burning building.

CHAPTER ELEVEN.

Slowly the sounds of the traffic penetrated my consciousness. Arnold and the world returned to the present day.

I walked through the busy shopping precinct in a daze, wondering if it was really Rowena Berrysford who had killed the Colemans. Used Mrs Knight. Not that they hadn't deserved to be punished, but to die like that?

I couldn't help but hope that this whole nightmare was the result of concussion. Where would it end? What was it leading to? And more importantly, why me?

I remembered what the sergeant in the film Zulu said at Rourke's Drift when asked, "Why us?"

"Cause we're here, lad. There ain't no one else, just us."

If I was going to stop them I needed to know just what they were up to.

Pulling myself together I rushed across town to the Public Records office and under the ever watchful eye of Piers' girlfriend, searched through the records to find out who had bought Coleman's Company.

Blinded by Seb Coleman's gentleman farmer image I was still reluctant to believe he could have had anything to do with Dioxin. But I wouldn't put it past Piers.

The work was painstaking and my eyes began to skip through the long list arranged in alphabetical order. Then a name jumped off the page at me. Ernehale Holdings. A holding company, under who's umbrella anyone could hide.

It wasn't listed in the phone book, nor could I find out who owned it, but it was time I listened to my instincts. I knew without a doubt that this was Colemans company. Now all I had to do was prove it.

I arrived home just as Bert was sweeping the floor, all finished bar the cleaning up. He left at 1.00.p.m. precisely, leaving me with safe wiring and a new light switch. I was well pleased.

Plugging in the percolator, I phoned Debra, asking if I could pop round this evening. I was dead on my feet and couldn't bear the thought of spending another sleepless night here on my own. 'I wonder if I could stay over?' I asked, promising a bottle of wine.

'No problem,' she assured me. 'I'll get Justin to pick you up about six. I'll cook spaghetti bolognese if you like?' One of my favourite Italian dishes.

'I can't wait! Shall I bring Cabinet Sauvignon or Chablis?'

'Either as long as it's in a big bottle and you're not driving home.' None of us paid much attention to the white with white meat rule, we drank what we fancied.

Rooting in one of the cardboard boxes packed full of food and things from the kitchen before it was demolished, I found a couple of big bottles of a fruity red Sauvignon, pleased that I didn't have to fetch one from the cellar; staring at its door as if it led straight to hell.

This was ridiculous. I was spending a lot of money to renovate a house which I was no longer comfortable in. The thought of moving as soon as the work was finished flashed through my mind, giving me a crumb of comfort. But it was hardly a good time to sell. It would not be economically viable.

Not wanting to stay in the house on my own, I decided to cheer myself up and look for a new car. Try as I might, I couldn't shake off the loneliness of my life without William.

Dressing in a casual cream linen trouser suit and an apricot silk shirt as befitted the spring like weather, I put on a bit of flash to grab the salesmen's attention. I hated being ignored in a car showroom. Especially when James was with me and I was the one with the money.

'Ok, Cass, wake up. I'm going to treat us both to a nice lunch in town. We can do a bit of shopping and look for a new car,' I told him as he looked at me expectantly.

A *new* car, I thought. Not a second hand one as James so sensibly advised; insisting that with a used car someone else paid the purchase tax. Forgetting that someone else also had all the fun.

Anyway I didn't want sensible; I wanted something sleek and sassy, with a catalytic converter. And safe, I added, remembering what had happened to my other car. Something classy and expensive. After all it was my money. Like the worm, this lady was definitely for turning.

I sprayed on a little Calvin Klein, slung my capacious Gucci over my shoulder and was just about to fasten Cassidy's lead when the doorbell rang.

Rather put out at the untimely interruption, I opened the door.

A shock of recognition electrified me. I stared, open mouthed at the handsome man standing on my doorstep.

He was tall and slim, wearing a beautifully cut pale grey suit which emphasised his broad shoulders, and a dark blue shirt. His navy and emerald patterned silk tie had flecks of turquoise and blue running through the design. Did he know that the blue was exactly the same brilliance as his eyes?

He looked confident and comfortable with himself unaware of the effect he was having on me. His sea blue eyes were startling against his tanned, good looking face. And his curly black hair was still falling over his forehead but there were streaks of silver in it now.

He held out his long fingered hand to shake mine and I realised he was introducing himself to me.

I wanted to hold him. Kiss him, touch the hand he offered me.

Tentatively, I reached out and felt the electricity surge through me as his fingers clasped mine. Taking his hand I held it, loathe to let go, turning it over and studying the pale moons on his well kept nails.

It could not be, could it? Perhaps I was hallucinating? But he was flesh and blood. At least I thought he was. I was not very sure of anything any more.

Hardly daring to believe my eyes, I stared intently.

There on my doorstep, stood William.

'You have nice hands,' I stuttered, walking a fine line between the past and the present. 'Please come in, William,' I whispered, still holding tightly to his hand.

My heart soared like a kite in the wind. William. My William had found me.

'Most people call me Bill,' he said, staring at me.

The resonant timbre of his voice echoed through the years.

I drew a deep breath, trying to retain my fragile hold on reality. This was not the seventeenth century and he could not be William. Could he?

The flicker of hope died and left me bereft.

'I'm sorry. You remind me of... '

What could I say? You remind me of the only man I have ever loved? 'Someone else,' I stammered.

How could I explain without him thinking that I was a stark raving lunatic?

'Didn't Albert tell you I was coming?' he asked, looking confused and embarrassed.

I stared at him blankly, not comprehending. It was my undoing. As if I had been struck by lightning a tingling shock ran through me as we looked at each other in startled recognition.

'My uncle, Albert Weston,' he said hoarsely. 'He must have mentioned me, or how did you know my name?' he asked, his voice cracked.

I tried to look away but my eyes would not listen to reason. 'Perhaps we'd better start again,' I whispered.

I could hear his ragged breathing as if we were locked in an intimate embrace. The mere thought sent my heart racing and lit a fire in my belly as my body burned with the need to cling to him.

The physical impact he had on me was so powerful I had forgotten to breathe and for a moment stars floated behind my eyes as if I was going to faint.

I managed to lower my eyes and stare at my hands. They were gripping his fingers so tight they were shaking with tension. Desperately I willed them to let go, I would not allow them to add to my shame like this.

Hot blood flooded my cheeks and as if in sympathy, tears pricked behind my half closed lids, threatening to overflow.

What cruel fate could have sent him back to me, when conventions would not allow me to touch?

Pride came to my rescue. I lifted my chin and not one to take half measures, smiled directly into his eyes.

'I'm so sorry,' I said, letting him free.

'Albert told me that you might need some help to trace your ancestors? I'm sorry if its inconvenient but I thought we might arrange a mutually convenient time?' he murmured, his face flushed with embarrassment at my behaviour.

I wished the earth would swallow me. He was still being charming but I could see that he was stunned by my weird welcome.

'Your uncle told me he would ask his nephew to come and see me. I expected a youth still at school, not someone of my own age. Please come in.'

We walked through to the dining room, while Cassidy did his ritual dance of welcome.

He sank rather abruptly onto the small settee. Not surprisingly he looked shaken.

'I hope I haven't worried you? It's just that you reminded me of someone I used to know,' I said.

'If you don't mind me asking, who did you think I was?'

He looked up at me and my heart flipped over. His voice was an evocative echo from the past.

Albert must have told him about me but he wouldn't make me out to be a freak. I decided to tell the truth without making a drama out of it.

'I had a car accident and thought I lived in another time.'

He didn't look sceptical or amused so I carried on. 'You look so much like William, the man I married in the seventeenth century, that you could be his twin.' I stopped as it became clear to me. Forgetting my reservations I told him. 'William had a twin sister, Mrs Sarah Smithson, I emphasised. 'You must be one of her descendants.'

'Albert told me about it briefly, he thought we might have been related in another life.'

There was no derision in his voice. 'Smithson was my grandmother's name. You could be right, Mrs Roberts.

He emphasised the Mrs so sadly that I wanted to hold him. Forcing myself to resist the temptation, I acted the part of Bette Davis, my favourite TV movie actress, hiding her broken heart behind the façade of a carefree, sophisticated woman.

I desperately wanted to hear him say my name. 'Please call me Rowena.'

'Thank you.' He coughed, clearing his throat.

Oh God, I've embarrassed him again.

'I have to be back at the office at Two. If you're not in a hurry, perhaps we could use this time to get to know one another before we start on the boring slog of ancestor hunting. I'll be pleased to give you a lift if you're going into town?'

'That is very kind. Thank you.'

I offered coffee, my heart pounding as I rushed into the kitchen, knowing I was acting like a moonstruck school girl.

Running cold water over my wrists I kept telling myself this is not a dream; this is real. Bill is real. He is a living man of flesh and blood.

Without being aware of it, I'd made coffee. When I carried the tray through, Bill was staring blankly into space. Startled, he stood up and took the tray from my hands.

'There is so much to tell you that I don't know where to begin,' I said, sitting down beside him, careful not to touch.

'Yes. Where to begin.' His hands were shaking as he took the cup from me.

I struggled to regain a semblance of sanity. 'Please, tell me about yourself, William. Sorry, Bill. What do you do for a living?' I asked, with an attempt at normality.

What I really wanted to know was if he was married or not. As if that would make any difference to my feelings.

'I am a Civil Engineer with my own, moderately successful, business on Regent Street in Nottingham,' he paused to drink a little coffee.

'Nice,' he smiled, saluting me with the cup.

A gesture I'd seen him do so often since the first time I'd taken my William a cup of rose hip tisane.

'Thank you.'

Bill nodded and continued, 'I live on Tannery Lane with a part time lodger,' he grinned, making him look twenty years younger.

His resemblance to William was uncanny. I clenched my hands together to stop them punching the air with joy, as I accepted that after centuries of waiting, I had found William again.

'Part time lodger?' I repeated stupidly, annoyed that I had lost my brilliant repartee along with my wits.

'Albert. He pops in to keep me company and we take turns to cook and clean. After his wife died, it seemed a sensible arrangement.'

'And your family?' I asked, trying for nonchalance and failing miserably no doubt. But I had to know.

'My wife died three years ago. We had no children.'

'Oh, I'm sorry.' I felt ashamed of myself, as if I had wished her dead.

'No problem. We loved each other very much, if not with a great passion, with deep affection. I think you would have liked my wife, her name was Margaret Keeton.'

'Keeton?' I repeated stupidly. The squire's wife at Beaumont Hall? Then I remembered my friendly neighbours. 'Any relation to Mel and June?'

'Margaret was Mel's cousin. ' Bill said quietly.

'They are my friends, they live in the barn conversion nearest the gates.'

'Yes, I know. Like Margaret, they are descendants of old Squire Keeton, who fought with Cromwell in the Civil War.'

I bit my tongue before I too said, "I know".

We sat drinking coffee and chatting about the people we knew as if we were old friends. We talked about the tannery which, if I was right, had once belonged to my ancestor, Rowena Knight.

'Albert told me the Colemans were burned to death in the fire at the tannery. It's funny that they didn't create a fuss,' I said.

'It's has been said that they broke in to rob the cash box and our Emily disturbed them. There were rumours that they tried to rape her.'

Oh God it was true. I fought to control my rebellious stomach, breathing deeply, knowing that Mrs Knight did what had to be done... With Mistress Berrysford's help.

She had taken control of Rowena Knight and used her. Be damned if I'd let her do the same to me.

'Are you alright, Rowena?' Bill asked, his hand reaching for mine.

I thrilled as he said my name.

'Yes, thank you,' I whispered

'The word was, Rowena Knight saved Emily and locked the Colemans in the burning building.'

I nodded. It was close enough for me. 'I'm sure you are right.'

Looking out of my back window I saw Sebastian Coleman sauntering across the courtyard whistling tunelessly, without a care in the world.

Once again I wondered if they knew about these strange happenings whenever our ancestors came together. And if they did, how did they know?

The kitchen clock chimed half past one. Bill would have to leave soon. Afraid that I would betray my feelings I decided to do my Bette Davis act again and make the first move

'I was going to my favourite Italian restaurant for lunch, would you care to join me?'

'You wouldn't believe how much I'd like that, but I have to get back to the office. I have an appointment with the Council. I don't always dress like this,' he grinned. 'Some other time perhaps?'

'Yes, some other time.' Man speak for next year, never.

Perversely, I gave him an easy option out.

'Are you sure you don't mind giving me a lift to town?'

'Not at all,' he said, sending a tingle down to my toes when he smiled at me.

As we walked out together, I noticed Piers Coleman's red Porsche pulled in behind Bill's black Celica.

Bill, talking quietly to Cassidy, not to alarm him, put his hand on the horn and kept it there until Sebastian came running out to reverse his son's car.

His pale blue eyes glinted like ice when he saw me.

As soon as we were out of the drive I relaxed and we talked so easily together that I hadn't noticed that we were nearly in town.

'Where can I drop you?' Bill asked, his hands resting lightly on the wheel as he confidently eased the sleek sports car through the traffic.

'Just past the next set of lights, please.'

'I didn't know there was an Italian restaurant on this part of the Turnpike.'

'Why did you call it the Turnpike?' I asked. It was straight out of the seventeenth century.

'Just trying to impress you,' he said sheepishly. 'It used to be the old Mansfield Turnpike Road.'

'I know.' I remembered this road when it was a rutted track through the forest. Walter Coleman had slung Rowena Berrysford over his horse and took her to the crossroads. Swallowing the bile rising in my throat I shoved Mistress Berrysford's memory to the back of my mind.

'This is fine,' I said, trying to smile politely. Our meeting was over too quickly; I had to stop myself from touching him. Holding on to him.

'May I come to see you on Monday afternoon?' he asked. 'I have to work this Saturday and when I do I usually take Monday afternoon off,' he said.

Could I wait that long before I saw him again? It would seem like another three hundred and fifty years.

'Please do, I'd love that. Thank you.' I felt like a schoolgirl being asked out on her first date.

He pulled to the curb and reached over me to open the door. The distinctive smell of his after-shave reminded me of green fields after summer rain.

Bill looked at me. He was too close for me to move. Close enough to kiss.

A green double-decker bus rumbled past, jerking me to my senses and I climbed out with as much grace as the low slung car would allow, reached for Cassidy and thanked Bill for the lift.

Feeling like the heroine in Brief Encounter I waved as he drove away. The end of a wonderful romantic interlude. But it wasn't the end, it was the beginning. I had found my William at last.

With the soft sound of Italian ballads in the background I tried to think about food but ordered a mug of Cappuccino instead.

I smiled happily, thanking the kind God who had sent Bill back to me. I wanted him so badly I ached. But I would have to be extremely careful. He was a modern man, not really my William.

When I'd recovered my composure enough to be trusted on the streets, I walked into town to replace my lost nighties. I also treated myself to a couple of outfits for the summer, anticipating Bill's reaction when he saw me in them.

Ambling out of the Flying Horse arcade, the perfume of freesias stopped me in my tracks. A barrow boy offered some to me and I bought half a dozen bunches, to share with Debra. And while I was still solvent, took a taxi to the Insurance Office.

The assessor assured me I'd receive the money for my car within days.

Thinking about Bill, I walked back to Mansfield Road in a dream, wandering along, I suddenly saw it.

The car I wanted. A beautiful, black sweep of powerful elegance. A Volvo C70 coupe was displayed on the forecourt.

The salesman gave me the usual spiel as I took it for a spin, driving in the country to Rufford and back but it was quite unnecessary; the antique leather seat hugged me close and I was hooked.

To me a car had only meant a convenient way to get from A to B as quickly and comfortably as possible so before I could talk myself into a compromise I arranged to buy it on their special interest free deal.

He promised to deliver it on Monday and even gave me a lift home in it.

Well pleased with myself as the salesman pulled up outside my house I noticed, thankfully, that the Coleman's cars were not in the courtyard. But Sebastian had seen me drive off with Bill. An irrational fear that they had recognised him as William Berrysford, shot through me.

Their fight is not with him, I told myself. But the arrival of William in my life had really thrown me. I leant on the door, wondering what on earth would happen next.

Justin arrived. 'Are you alright, Mum?' he asked, with a worried frown.

'Never better.'

Picking up the wine we rushed out of the house in the deepening twilight, almost tripping over each other in our haste to get away.

Debra had the spaghetti ready to serve and while we ate the leisurely meal I told them about the car.

Relaxed after a glass or two I phoned James to tell him about my extravagance but there was no reply. Probably shacked up with Barbara. So much for him wanting me back. If it hadn't been for Justin and Susan I would have stopped toying with the idea long ago. Raising my eyes to heaven, I hung up.

For the first time in ages I watched a bit of telly, but I found it enervating, so excusing myself, I went to bed early.

As I cuddled down, with Cassidy on the thick rug beside the bed, Debra and Justin knocked at my door to say good night and brought me a special bed time treat, guaranteed to send you happily off to dreamland. A mug of hot milk with a large dash of Cherry Brandy.

After the wine and the exciting day I didn't think I'd need much rocking off to sleep but my mind replayed every scene of the short time I'd spent with Bill.

Every time I closed my eyes I saw him looking at me as we sat in the car. And in an agony of wishful thinking I wondered if he might have been about to kiss me.

My mind drifted to a sunlit garden where William whispered just out of earshot.

Contented, I fell to sleep, confusing my seventeenth century husband with Bill, dreaming of him in bright technicolour...

Rowena was happily searching for William in the garden of Berrysford House, knowing he was close by, crouching behind the foxgloves perhaps or hiding behind a tree. She waited expectantly for him to pounce, demanding a kiss in forfeit.

She turned when, tired of waiting for her to find him, William had come to her, resting his hand on her shoulder, he whispered in her ear.

"Come, my lady, the sun is too harsh for you now."

Rowena caressed her rounded belly, six months with child, her heart full of joy.

He took her hand and enclosed it in the crook of his arm, pausing to kiss her.

"You have been to the orchard," he tutted, smiling into her eyes. "And I demand another kiss to prove it."

Sending shivers down her spine, his tongue lightly licked her cherry stained lips...

Rowena Roberts murmured softly in her sleep, confusing William with Bill, unable to distinguish between them.

CHAPTER TWELVE.

I was definitely feeling better in the morning when Justin drove me home in his old MGB. With the top down the invigorating breeze cleared away the cobwebs and made me feel ten years younger; that and the fact that I'd had a good night's sleep.

He touched my arm as I climbed out. 'Give us a call if you need anything, OK?' He shrugged his shoulders at a loss for words. 'Any time,' he stressed, the words conveying his support. No questions asked.

'Thank you,' I leaned over and kissed his cheek. Our affection might seem understated to the casual observer, but it was genuine and immeasurably deep.

Sebastian Coleman watched Justin's roadster pull out of the drive as I turned to unlock my door, realising I was lucky to have such nice step kids.

My house greeted me with an atmosphere cold enough to freeze the halls of hell. Even though it was another warm day the walls seemed to leech out the warmth. Fortunately I had only been home ten minutes when Albert and Bert arrived with a gang of builders.

Feeling safer with them around, I picked up last night's paper and tucking it under my arm, I carried Cassidy and went upstairs to work.

Scanning the Post for items of local interest my eye's fastened on the word Dioxin. The National Rivers Authority had scrapped plans to remove Dioxin contaminated sediment from the river Doe Lee on the Nottingham Derbyshire border. It says it is too dangerous to extract and transport the chemicals.

Too dangerous or too expensive?

Did no one wonder how this carcinogenic defoliant had got there in the first place? Dumping was the least of our problems; what about the chemicals, weed-killers and insecticides which they ladle on the earth; did they think they would just disappear? Or live in hope that nothing untoward would happen in our lifetime? Dioxin was one of the most deadly man made poisons on earth. What a legacy to leave to our children. And it was here right now on my doorstep.

I copied the mind blowing paragraph and looked to see what I could find out about Dioxin in the British Medical Journals. Was this contamination linked with Coleman's or was it just another lethal chemical cocktail seeping into our rivers by the over zealous applications of weed-killers and fertilisers used by our highly competent farmers?

The latter would be almost impossible to stop. Public opinion would do it, but unlike America, in England it would take too long. First one has to overcome the barriers of officialdom, and of course, the influence and money of the biochemical industry.

I spotted an article written by Dr. John Baker, a post graduate at York University whom I'd heard Susan mention. He wrote of the long term effects of Dioxin, which was used in the defoliation of Vietnam.

Next time I saw Susan I would ask her about the doctor's credibility before I made his article the basis for my next project if his facts checked out. But the possible connection to Colemans made me itch to get to the bottom of it. I gathered up my paraphernalia, about to rush to York to interview Dr. Baker when I saw a postscript and sat down with a thump.

A shiver ran down my spine as I read that there was such a furore discrediting his conclusions that he committed suicide just after the article was published. The more I thought about it the more disturbed I became.

Something was wrong here.

Instilled with a sense of urgency, I wanted to interview Dr. Baker's colleagues or anyone who might know something about his work. Making up my mind, I picked up my bag and tape recorder, tucked Cassidy under an arm and was almost out of the door when I remembered.

'Shit!'

Albert popped his head round the dining room door.

'Was that an order?' he grinned.

'Sorry, Albert. I'd forgotten that I don't have a car until Monday. And I need to get somewhere urgently. ' Expenses would not run to a taxi.

Albert picked up his portable telephone and held his hand up to ward off questions. 'Hello. It's me. Rowena has to get to...' He looked at me questioningly.

'York,' I said, 'But...'

Ignoring me he repeated my destination. 'OK. See you in ten minutes.' Albert put down the phone with a grin.

'Our Billy will lend you the company car. An old Range Rover,' he said. 'He uses it to visit the surveyors on site.'

'It's very good of him,' I managed to murmur almost off hand, when you consider my heart was pounding so loud it seemed to have lodged behind my ears.

Shakily I rooted for my handbag, sprayed on my favorite perfume and quickly slicked on a little lip gloss, under the amused gaze of Albert. I grinned sheepishly and gave him a spare key to lock up. It was barely ten minutes before a knock at the front door announced Bill's arrival.

'The weather is so nice this morning I thought I might drive you,' he said. 'If that's alright with you?' he asked, looking over my shoulder at Albert who was watching behind the dining room door.

Unfazed, Albert merely nodded. 'I keep telling him, he should get out more,' he grinned.

Quickly fastening Cassidy's lead and car harness, I followed Bill out to the courtyard and putting Cass and my heavy bag in the space at the back, sank into the Celica.

'This is really good of you,' I said politely, striving to keep the breathlessness out of my voice. 'My editor would probably have lent me a car.'

'No problem. I came because I couldn't wait until Monday to see you again.' He turned his head and briefly looked into my eyes. 'Rowena.'

I was content to sit by his side in the warm cocoon of leather upholstery, the CD playing rhythmic rock. Trying not to look at his long fingers as they competently guided the car through the gears, the leather topped lever perilously close to my thigh, I babbled on about my work.

I told him about my articles on various hot issues; often about ill thought out Government decisions. 'Not that I have a political axe to grind but my work brings me into contact with the mistakes or rather the effects of the mistakes, which those in power inflict upon us all, I'm sorry to say.'

'I should think it's very difficult to be unbiased against those in office at the best of times,' Bill agreed. 'And this is hardly the best of times.'

I remembered too late what great-granddad had said about sex, religion and politics.

'I'm no Pilger but in my small way I'm trying to redress the balance.'

'I read your piece in Focus. It certainly made me think,' Bill mused, glancing at me as we by passed Sheffield. 'The one about irritable bowel syndrome. Was it all true?'

'It's true that over thirty percent of the Western population suffer from bowel disorders or asthma,' I said. 'And medical experts think this is linked with the agricultural chemicals seeping into our rivers, which enter the food chain and pollute our water supply.'

I looked at him and shrugged. 'The increase in vegetarianism has also been linked to the problem but as it hasn't been proven, I didn't put that in the article.'

'Not PC?' he asked astutely.

'Another example of good intentions having a less than good effect. It has its limitations. Vegetarianism is almost de riguer, far be it for me to upset the apple cart.'

I shrugged in apology for the pun.

Bill chuckled. "I didn't get to the top of the food chain to become a vegetarian," he quoted.

'But what about the hormones and antibiotics used in poultry and meat production? That must give power to their case.'

'True. I'm a bit of a closet veggie myself, but my mother is one of the thirty percent that can't eat any fresh fruit, vegetables, whole wheat or pulses. And one person in ten over the age of fifty is the same.'

'An allergic reaction, like asthma?'

'As soon as I find out I'll let you know before you read about it.'

'And Ciproxin?' he persisted, obviously interested.

'Like all the latest drugs, it was developed for humans and is causing great concern because it's being used to prevent diseases in factory farmed chickens. Spanish farmers put these new antibiotics in their poultry's drinking water to keep them disease free. As a result, humans are becoming immune to the only effective antibiotic to treat salmonella and food poisoning,' I replied.

'I saw a programme on TV about the number of fatalities in children and old people from what used to be a minor stomach upset is rising at an alarming rate,' Bill said as if he hoped I would disagree.

'Too true I'm afraid,' I said quietly. 'On the advice of a Quango, the British government allowed Ciproxin to be used here, purportedly only to fight infection in sick animals. But no one is willing to ensure that it isn't being used as a cost effective control of disease.

Did you know that Britain imports meat and poultry from Spain?' I asked.

'Good God! Are you going to investigate this sorry mess? It sounds as catastrophic as putting animal remains in cattle food.'

I nodded, Bill's potential problem analysis was impressive. 'I'm going to investigate this issue amongst others which come under the jurisdiction of the Agricultural Chemicals and Environment committee, which Piers Coleman is on. And what it has to do with Dioxin which his company used to produce.'

Bill slowed the car and pulled up at the turning to the University and Cassidy immediately raised his head expectantly.

'We're not there yet, boy,' Bill said quietly. 'Go back to sleep.'

Needing no encouragement Cass snuggled down again.

Bill looked at me anxiously. 'Don't take the Colemans lightly, Rowena. Be careful; Piers may look like a good time hooray Henry, but he is damn ruthless. And he always manages to get what he wants. Sebastian greases too many palms. And I suspect, eliminates the opposition in ways too sordid to mention; though there are plenty of rumours flying about Arnold.'

'I know,' I said, reaching over to stroke Cassidy, deriving comfort from his warmth. 'But don't worry. I read an article in the BMJ written by a post graduate who killed himself and I only want to find someone here who can check his theory.'

'Do you need to phone anyone for an interview?' he asked, passing me the car phone.

'Not really, but I'd better call Susan. If she sees me roaring round the campus in this, I'll lose my comfortable old shoe image!' I dialled her number and checked the time, trying to remember her schedule. Ten forty.

'Hi,' Susan replied at the first ring.

'Hello, love. It's Rowena. I'm on campus, can I meet you somewhere?'

'Sure, but I have a class at eleven. Is everything OK?'

'Fine. I've conned a lift with Albert's nephew who was coming this way,' I lied. 'I wondered if you can help me with a little research I need to do for an article?'

'OK.'

'See you outside the library in,' I looked at the buildings we were cruising past and pointed for Bill to turn right. 'Five minutes?'

'I'm on my way. See you.'

I said goodbye to an empty line.

Susan was walking to meet me when we arrived. Bill dropped me, said "Hi," smiled at her and drove off looking for a place to park.

'He's rather tasty,' Susan said speculatively. Then her eyes narrowed. 'Albert's nephew, you said?'

'Chill out, sweetheart, he's only a friend.'

'Oh yeah?'

'Believe it,' I grinned. 'Now, what do you think of John Baker. Was he a nutter; prone to exaggeration, or what?'

'John?' Susan stared incredulously. ' He was the best teacher I've ever known. Meticulous, methodical and thorough. He wouldn't say good morning unless he'd double checked the time.' Her eyes sparkled with indignation. 'I don't care what they are saying about him now, I would have trusted him with my life. He never took short cuts or...'

'Whoa!' I put up my hand to halt her tirade. 'I'm not here to do a hatchet job on him, I'm very interested in his paper on Dioxin.'

She looked at me seriously. 'John was honest, reliable and dedicated. And before you jump to the wrong conclusions, I did have a thing about him but he never noticed or at least,' she admitted ruefully, 'he didn't appear to notice.'

'And what exactly are they saying about him now?' I asked.

'Some bigwig tried to discredit his findings and when nobody took any notice, the faculty started spreading the rumour that John was having a nervous breakdown whilst doing the research. Then they said we were to disregard everything he'd taught us.'

'That's what I remember you saying.' Susan had told me about it before the accident.

'The Student Union pressured the faculty to make sure none of us were penalised for the time they said we'd wasted under him. '

'Yes,' I interrupted, 'But why...'

'Oh, don't you start! If anyone else asks "Why did he kill himself if he wasn't having a breakdown", I shall scream. Damn the Coroner who said John had killed himself whilst the balance of his mind was disturbed,' she sighed. 'John's mind was as firm as the rock of Gibraltar.' She looked at me defiantly. 'Ask anyone. Nobody actually believes the crap they're trying to spread about him now.'

She hoisted her bag of books higher onto her shoulder, bored with the conversation.

'Have a word with Mike Meadows at the lab. Number 4a. He hasn't a class till this afternoon. You can't mistake him, he's tall dark and handsome. Alan Rickman ish,' she said, knowing he was my favourite film star.

'Or ask John's mother.' Susan pecked me on the cheek and strode off. 'Got to dash,' she said over her shoulder in answer to my hasty good bye.

The toot brought me spinning round. Bill's window slid down. 'Can't find anywhere to park,' he said.

'I'm going to the labs. There's a pub a few hundred metres on your left as you leave the main gate. I'll meet you there if you like? They do good pub lunches and have a big car park at the back.'

'OK. See you in half an hour ish?'

'Not that long,' I smiled, ' More like ten minutes ish!'

Seeing the lights on in 4a I tapped on the door before I popped my head around.

Susan was right, he did look like Alan Rickman. Tall and rangy with sun streaked hair and hazel eyes surrounded by laughter lines that were far from evident in his chilling appraisal.

I walked in with my hand outstretched. 'Mike Meadows?' I asked.

Before he asked who the hell I was, I introduced myself. 'Rowena Roberts. Susan's step mother.'

He shook my hand. 'Pleased to meet you. Susan isn't in today.'

'I know. Can spare me a few minutes? I'm a journalist...'

He shook his head warning me to stop right there. 'Yes, Susan mentioned that you've written some amusing pieces in ladies glossies.'

He waved towards a door. 'If you go into my office, I'll phone round and see if I can find her.'

'But...'

He took my arm and whispered in my ear. 'These days walls have eyes as well as ears,' he glanced at the security camera as he ushered me in and locked the laboratory door behind us.

Feeling rather foolish I played along with his cloak and dagger charade.

'Thank you,' I said, following him into a cubby hole of an office, hoping whoever he thought was spying hadn't seen us together. 'I should have phoned her before I set out but I wanted to surprise her.'

Mr Meadows closed the office door and perched on the edge of the table-cum desk. He did not motion me to sit down but deliberately ignoring his lack of manners, I moved a pile of books from the one and only chair, passed them to him and sat down.

With a hint of a grin he slid them onto the desk.

'What do you want, Mrs Roberts?' he asked, his face betraying no emotion.

'I read Dr John Baker's paper in a British Medical Journal and hoped someone here could verify his findings.'

'John's findings don't need verifying,' he said. Then realising this sounded too brusque, continued. 'If he went public you can be damn sure every hypothesis was proven above and beyond all doubt.'

'Then why are you so defensive?' I asked.

He stared at me for a long moment before he answered. 'Word is that John trod on somebody's toes and that someone is going all out to belittle his work, ' he said, brushing at an imaginary speck on his chino's as if he were trying to brush me away too.

I waited for him to continue.

'If you aim to do a smear job on John Baker I'm afraid you won't get any help from his colleagues.'

'I assure you that is not my intention, why should I want to blacken his name?'

Mike's loyalty was admirable but his attitude fired my interest.

'The dead make soft targets,' he said. 'What exactly do you want?'

'Any of his papers or something to help me get a handle on all this. My degree was in the Arts,' I explained.

'John's papers were destroyed.' He looked perfectly relaxed, his voice was pleasant and well modulated but I sensed an aggressive rebel under the charming veneer.

'With nothing more than a hunch to go on I think there might be a cover up of Watergate proportions,' I said, deciding to trust him.

'I'm here to follow up an article on fly tipping, trying to link the disposal of Dioxin to a Company which used to be owned by a prominent industrialist. It would help if John had any evidence I could use.'

'I wouldn't go round the campus asking those sort of questions if I were you. After John died they took every scrap of his work. They even stopped the government investigation into the link between pesticides and breast cancer.'

'The work which Leicester University is now carrying out?'

'That's right,' he said, looking at me appraisingly. 'John's mother has his notes on the deadly additions to pesticides.'

'Sorry?'

'John expanded his investigation into the long term effects of Weed-killers and was deeply concerned that the chemicals had a life expectancy of X. They remain active for an incalculable number of years,' he explained.

'A million? Billion?' I asked.

'Forever. They remain active forever. Dioxin is nothing compared to the stuff they are experimenting with now.'

'Experimenting with as in lab tests?'

'Ha!' he snorted. 'Experimenting as in spraying crops here in England with a poisonous chemical. And I'm not talking about DDT either.'

I asked if he knew Mrs Baker's phone number. After reading John's article I have a gut feeling that there is more to this than meets the eye.

'John's mother is ex directory and will not speak to the press.' He stood up and unlocked the door. 'If you'll excuse me.'

'You have an appointment,' I guessed, rushing out of the laboratory.

This story was so hot it was almost unprintable. How could anyone manufacture a weed-killer that was a bigger threat to mankind than Dioxin?

CHAPTER THIRTEEN.

I met Bill in the lounge bar and ordered a light lunch and a pot of coffee.

'They wouldn't let Cassidy in but I ordered a cold chicken baguette for him, minus the bread,' Bill said, with a smile that sent my pulses racing.

I tried to concentrate on the salmon pasta but it was more than difficult, the table was so small our knees were touching. Funny how erotic that can be, and when our fingers accidentally reached for the coffee pot together, I could almost see the sparks.

Bill grabbed my hand. 'Rowena...' Without words we were both suddenly aware that this was a hotel.

'Mrs Roberts!' Mike Meadows broke the spell.

He was being ushered past our table, a pretty doe eyed woman in her early forties turned to look at me and scuttled after the waitress.

Bill got up, his hand outstretched. 'Bill Weston.'

I waved my hand towards Mike. 'May I introduce Dr. Meadows.'

They shook hands as Mike apologised for having to join his friend.

When the waitress brought the bill we nodded politely at Dr. Meadows and his companion before we left.

'I wonder if she's his wife?'

'More likely someone else's!' Bill quipped.

Giggling, I climbed into the car.

During our rather subdued journey home I couldn't help thinking that I had missed a rare opportunity to make love to my seventeenth century husband. Would Bill have booked us into a room if we had not been interrupted? Gnawing my lips I glanced at him.

Wearing a Paul Smith business suit, he had removed the jacket when we came out of the restaurant and was driving in his shirt sleeves, a white cotton shirt and no tie, he looked so much the modern man. Without a doubt I would have gone to bed with him had he asked.

I sat up straight and stared out of the side window, embarrassed by my own sexuality. This was not William. I didn't know this man. Didn't love him. I couldn't, could I? We had only just met.

My head rung with echoes of laughter and I'm sure I heard Mistress Berrysford ask, *"What has time got to do with love?"* Or maybe it was me. Whatever, I knew it was true. You could fall in love in a heartbeat.

Bill dropped me off in the courtyard as Coleman's builders unloaded pallets of bricks and put them in the building adjoining mine. My house was semidetached, but the other half, which was a stable in the seventeenth century, was now used to store the building materials.

Coleman had promised me first refusal when the work was finished; and I'd intended to convert it into a garage and granny flat.

It was barely three o'clock when I climbed out of the Celica, lifting Cassidy into my arms. But Bill was out of the car, taking Cass from me and waiting while I unlocked the front door. I turned and looked up into his eyes. His head drew closer but as I raised my lips to be kissed, Cassidy yelped and squirmed out of his grasp. Blinking, I grabbed his harness before he had the chance to chase Piers Coleman, who was leaning against the builder's van, watching us with a sardonic grin.

'See you Monday?' Bill shouted over the din, and thanking me for a lovely day, he left.

I couldn't bear to watch him go, so picking up Cass I went upstairs to my office to write everything I had learned on to the computer.

After the Ciproxin scare in meat and poultry this threat to vegetables from pesticides, brought home the inherent dangers of poisoning the land and water supply.

We could all die of toxin related diseases. And if there was nothing left for us to eat we would all die of starvation.

I shivered, feeling bone aching cold; my fingers numb. My breath fogged the air, rising in drifting patterns to the ceiling. It hung like a cloud above my head, ever changing as I exhaled. Swirling.. Fascinating. Hypnotic...

My eyelids were so heavy it took all my will power to keep my eyes open. I stared at the words on my screen. They could have been written in ancient hieroglyphics. I barely managed to save it to disk and switch off the computer.

Cassidy's yelping drew my attention, he was running round in circles making a fuss but I just couldn't raise the energy to tell him to be quiet. And there was an irritating ringing preventing me from going to sleep.

A familiar voice in my ear urged me to move. Quickly. To get out of the room. Out of the house. I knew it was Rowena Berrysford. Nagging me. Frightening Cassidy in her attempt to get through to me. But I was unable to move. My limbs would not obey my brain.

As if from a long way off I heard someone shouting. Someone real.

The voice reverberated through my brain as I struggled to identify it.

'Rowena! Are you alright? Do you want me to answer the door?' Albert yelled, startling me out of the trance like stupor.

I vaguely identified the persistent ringing of the door bell and desperately wanted it to stop so I could sleep.

I tried to answer but the effort was too much, I couldn't keep my eyes open.

I half lifted my head, fighting the exhaustion as I tried to flap away the noise of someone pounding up the stairs, the cold air making my fingers tingle. With a great effort I opened my eyes as someone crashed into the room.

Bill.

Cassidy ran to him, barking madly, anxious to be gone.

'Dear God, what's going on here?'

With a sense of relief I closed my eyes as Bill's warmth enfolded me. He carried me out of the room.

Feeling safe I laid my head against his shoulder and clasped my hands round his neck, inhaling the scent of his aftershave as he carried me down the stairs, Cassidy hopping in front of us.

I could feel Bill's heart beating hard against my breast. Fast and strong with exertion.

I came to my senses. What on earth was I doing behaving like a swooning virgin?

'Put me down now, please,' I said as we reached the first floor landing. 'I don't know what came over me.'

'Neither do I, but thank God I listened to my instincts,' he said as he lowered me to the floor. 'I've been worried sick.'

'Instincts?' I asked, wondering if he too had the so called gift.

'What Albert calls my gypsy blood, sometimes it's too strong to ignore. Way back in the seventeenth century an ancestor of mine married a gypsy,' he said with an apologetic shrug.

Still holding me in his arms he ignored Albert's questions as he rushed up the stairs. He stopped and looked at us uncertainly.

'Are you alright?' he asked.

'I am now,' I said. 'Thank you, Albert,' I said as he turned to go.

Fortunately, Bill was gripping my shoulders tight, because we were so close my knees threatened to let me down.

'I'm sorry,' my voice sounded weak. I felt giddy and on the verge of tears.

Stepping back, I tried to control the surge of emotion but Bill's eyes melted my resolve.

He rocked me in his arms.

'Rowena, my love, I thought something dreadful had happened to you,' he said, holding me tighter.

'This place gives me the creeps, you've got to get out of here, I don't like it at all.'

I couldn't concentrate on what he was saying, I just wanted to stay in his arms forever.

'I'll be alright, Bill, you don't have to worry about me.'

'Maybe not, but you must know that I do worry about you,' he ran his finger down my cheek and tilted up my chin to look at him. 'I care about you very much, Rowena.'

His blue eyes darkened and I arched towards him, crying out for his kiss but before our lips touched there was an almighty crash; tearing us apart.

We rushed back to my office, followed by Cassidy and Albert.

Cold billowed out of the room in a cloud of icy fog. It had a faintly sulphuric smell. Cassidy stood on the threshold refusing to enter, his breath misting the air.

Holding Bill's hand we slowly walked in together, glass crunching under our feet.

'I don't suppose the air conditioning's gone berserk?' Bill asked, blowing on his fingers.

I made a sound half way between a laugh and a sob. We all knew I didn't have air conditioning.

My room was a wreck. Paper, books and notes were floating in the air like confetti. The window had shattered; imploded by the look of it. Frosty splinters of glass were embedded in the desk and the back of my chair.

I squeezed my eyes shut as the room started spinning, I hadn't been out of that chair for more two minutes.

'Jeez!' Albert hissed through his teeth. 'You can smell the evil in here,' he said, his words leaving white trails.

Remembering the ennui I had experienced, I nodded, feeling I'd been bewitched.

In that ice cold room which felt as if all warmth and humanity had been sucked out of the air, Albert's statement did not seem as melodramatic as it sounded.

Maybe Piers was getting his revenge for what I had done to his foot? Then again, his girlfriend in the Public Records office had no doubt warned him of my investigation into Colemans Feed and Fertiliser Company and their involvement with Dioxin. He certainly had reason enough to frighten me. And he'd made a damn good job of it.

How could I fight him if he had such strong supernatural powers. Fight fire with fire? I was an inept amateur, how could I compete?

My computer had been flung across the room, the monitor smashed to smithereens. The dent where my tape recorder had hit the wall had left a hole in the plaster deep enough to show the slats underneath. The black plastic casing was fern scrolled with a coating of rapidly melting ice.

Bill picked up the keyboard and dropped it on the desk. 'It looks as if someone has taken exception to your articles,' he said, only half joking.

'Or my investigation.' Damn Coleman, I'll give him a run for his money. Compete? He'll wish he'd never been born.

'But this is unnatural,' Bill said, gesturing at the wreckage. 'You can't stay here.'

Realising it was true, I stuffed my notes in the drawer and put the computer disc in my bag. If need be Jayne Vincent would let me work in the office.

'You can borrow my old typewriter if you need it,' Albert said, ushering me out.

'No thank you, Albert.' I opened the door to the large built in cupboard with a flourish; it contained all my stationary, cameras and equipment. On the bottom shelf was my old portable Olivetti which I used when away on an assignment. I picked it up and a folder of A4 paper as well.

'"Ve halve thee technology," as they say in the Guardian,' I quipped, relief making me giggle.

Taking a last look round I wondered how James' logic would explain the damage, and laughed out loud, grinning when Bill looked at me askance.

'I was just wondering what to put on the Insurance claim,' I told him. 'I doubt if they'll believe it was caused by witchcraft!'

'It looks like a whirlwind has struck but I don't think they'd buy natural disaster either,' Bill said, hugging my shoulders.

We all trooped in to the dining room and I had just set my typewriter on the table when the doorbell rang. We answered it together.

Sebastian stood on my doorstep and I could have sworn that for a moment he looked furious to see me with two strong men at my side. But his expression changed so quickly I could have imagined it, after all why should he care who I entertained in my own home?

'Are you alright, Mrs Roberts?' he asked, putting on his "concern for the peasants" look.

'Yes?' I said, leaving the answer a question.

I let the silence stretch between us. No doubt he knows what Piers has done and has come round here trying to hush it up. He's probably had a lot of practice at that.

He cleared his throat. 'We... er, it seems we've had a freak hurricane,' he stuttered, looking at me with murder in his eyes. Then he smiled quickly and continued as if he was addressing a Tory conference. 'The wind uprooted a tree and rattled windows at the Manor. And I noticed your upstairs window was blown in.'

I raised a sceptical eyebrow. 'I hope my insurers will accept your explanation.'

'Well, I'm sure mine will,' he smiled. 'And my builders will be pleased to glaze your window, my dear.'

Albert interjected before I could scratch Sebastian's condescending eyes out.

'I am going to get the glass cut now; we'll carry out the repairs, Mrs Roberts wants the work done properly but I'll send you the bill if you insist,' he added.

Albert left Coleman no choice but to agree.

'Of course, of course. Well...'

If he's waiting for me to say thank you he'll have a long wait. Then straightening my shoulders I nodded. 'Why thank you.' I almost said kind sir, but stopped myself in time, employing the subtleties of exaggerated politeness. 'So kind,' I said instead, closing the door and sinking back into Bill's arms.

'Phew!'

'You can say that again,' Bill said, pausing for Albert's repeat.

'Phew!'

We collapsed in a huddle, laughing hysterically, relieving the tension.

'I'll get the measurements for the glass,' Albert said, discreetly leaving us alone.

I closed my eyes as he bent to kiss me.

The touch of his lips was light but the tingle curled my toes. Leaning towards him, I caressed his neck, my fingers revelling in the feel of his crisp silky hair. His kiss deepened and our bodies melded together as if they had never been apart.

We swayed drunkenly, trying to press closer to each other with a desperate need.

My hands, of their own accord, had pulled up his shirt and slid beneath to caress the smooth skin of his back, his muscles flexing under my fingers; steel covered with satin.

Bill was holding me so close I could feel the hard evidence of his desire.

The surge of joy at being in his arms again was so sweet I was nearly in tears.

'Rowena,' Bill mouthed in my ear. 'Not here, my love.' he said, gently pushing me away. 'And not now.'

He kissed the tip of my nose and a flood of memories overwhelmed me. William had done that so often.

'I love you too much to make love in a rush. Will you come away with me for the weekend? I'll book us into a nice hotel...'

"I'd love to,' I nodded.

'Will you be alright if I leave now?'

'No. I'll never be alright without you,' I whispered.

Summoning all my strength I managed to move away from him, holding on to the door knob for dear life.

'I'm only a phone call away,' he whispered as he left.

Seeing Bill walk away was unbelievably painful but I could not take my eyes off him, not even blinking less I missed seeing a turn of his head or the line of his thigh as he climbed into the Celica.

When his car disappeared from view I was bereft.

CHAPTER FOURTEEN.

I must have moved, breathed, done something but I have no memory of anything except Bill's graceful stride as he walked away.

Albert returned with the pane of glass and I know I must have made him and the rest of the workers coffee because after they'd left. All my Denby mugs were dirty and stacked in the dishwasher. Like an automaton I started to prepare dinner for James who had promised to call in to see me; I was trying to make an effort and not think about Bill. And William.

James walked by the dining room window. 'James! I'm so glad you've come,' I said, jumping up to give him a kiss but he walked past me and went straight to the sink to fill up the kettle. He plugged it in before he turned and looked at me, stony faced.

'What's been going on here while I've been away?' he asked, glaring at me as if we were still married. So much for his be nice to Rowena period. I didn't have to take this crap any more.

Before I had a chance to reply, Cassidy, hearing his masters voice, waddled in from the sitting room.

James ignored him.

'Apart from Piers kicking Cassidy into a pile of rubble so hard a chunk of masonry fell off and crushed the bastard's foot?' I asked, my voice coming out in a deadly quiet whisper. 'Or that someone did the same to my fuse box as they did to the kettle, leaving it to electrocute me had I been foolish enough to touch it?'

Before he could interrupt I continued. 'Now let me see, what else has been going on while you were safely ensconced in London with Barbara?' I mused. 'While I was fetching help to fix my fuses George kidnapped Cassidy and tried to drown him in the pond. And this afternoon for a little light entertainment, a so called "freak hurricane" blew in my office widow, shredding my work and smashing my computer, spearing knife like splinters of glass into my chair... Where, if it had happened thirty seconds earlier, it would have killed me.'

'You don't seriously believe the Colemans did all that?' James said. 'I suppose you think they were using magic spells as well?'

For a moment I actually believed that James really could have something to do with all this. Maybe he was paying Piers to kill me to get my insurance... I still hadn't changed my will. But I would now, that's for sure.

'After everything that's happened while you were away, I am not in the mood to tolerate your churlishness any longer. So chill out or get out.'

'What did you say?' he gasped, astounded by my outburst.

'You heard. Cool it,' I said, taking the meat out of the oven.

'Justin and Debra are coming for dinner,' I told him in a lighter tone. 'I've cooked your favorite, leg of lamb sprinkled with garlic. But, *if* you're staying, I trust you will be in a better mood when they get here?'

James hurrumped and took his case upstairs. 'Don't turn on the tap,' he ordered. 'I'm going to have a shower.'

I was tempted to run the water full blast but common sense prevailed. Just.

'By all means, help yourself,' I shouted to let him know it was no longer his right to do as he pleased in my house. He didn't seem unduly upset by my outburst. Surprised maybe but definitely not upset.

Justin and Debra arrived at seven, presenting me with a couple of bottles of Bulgarian Cabinet Sauvignon while I was piling the vegetables into warm dishes.

The atmosphere wasn't very pleasant but the wine was delicious.

Even after he'd drank the lions share, James was still subdued so I didn't mention the Volvo or my lift to York with Bill.

'Did you try phoning me while you were away?' I asked, thinking that was the reason for his bad mood.

'And if I did, where were you? Out with your boy friend?'

'Dad!' Justin exclaimed, shocked at the uncalled for suggestion.

'What?' James snapped.

Guilt stabbed me in the stomach. How did he know about Bill, had he spoken to Susan?

Embarrassed, Debra smiled too brightly. 'Shall I make coffee?' she asked.

'Yes please, love. At least we can enjoy a decent cup since Bert fixed everything.'

'Is he another of your fancy men?'

My temper, usually kept under strict control, erupted. 'My God, James, that is quite enough, I will not be insulted by you in my own house.' My voice trailed away...*"It could have been your husband, fixing a fuse..."* Or fixing me perhaps. But James wasn't capable of that sort of treachery. Was he?

I had to know. Had to think.

'If you will excuse me, I'm going to bed,' I told all and sundry. 'I've got a bit of a headache.'

'I bet you have,' James muttered.

'Lock the back door before you leave please, Justin and make sure the Yale's on the front. Goodnight,' I said, rushing out of the room.

I went upstairs leaving Cassidy asleep in his basket. It wasn't necessary to tell James to bugger off, he must know there was no chance of him getting into my bed tonight.

Let him try to justify his aggressive behaviour to his son. Trying to get us back together indeed.

I was going to have a shower but it would keep till morning, the water still smelled fusty and visions of Psycho flashed through my mind.

In my room I undressed, missing Cassidy's company. It was too quiet without his snoring.

The old house settled into its ritual creaking, making me nervous. I rushed round in my bra and thong, looking for my new nighties, yelping at the soft tap on the door.

'Sorry. It's only me,' Debra said, coming in carrying two cups of coffee. 'I thought I'd have mine with you, while Justin tries to find out what's the matter with his father. '

She shivered. 'God, it's freezing in here,' she looked at me appraisingly.

'You two will soon get back together if that's all you wear in bed,' she grinned as she passed me the coffee.

'I'm not interested in getting back with James.' I said and realising how stuffy it sounded, added with a shrug. 'I just haven't got a thing to wear. ' I opened and closed the drawers systematically. 'All my nighties are missing!' I said, trying to make light of it. 'And my silk undies.'

'I don't understand.'

'Neither do I, but I appear to have been the victim of the phantom nightie nicker.' I liked the description, it put the mystery into perspective. 'And his twin, the naughty knicker nicker!'

'What you're really saying is you haven't done any washing for a fortnight,' she grinned, hugging my shoulders. 'It's a good excuse, I'll have to remember that one.'

We sat on the edge of the bed giggling like schoolgirls.

'It's true, honest.'

'Weird. Not to mention your bedroom. It's a bit creepy in here, isn't it? do you keep real live skeletons in your wardrobe?' she said, rubbing the goose pimples on her arms. 'Or should I say, real *dead* ones?'

I grinned. 'Do you feel it too? It wasn't always like this.' But it was like this on Tuesday night before the phone rang.

'I'm cold,' she said. 'And you must be too in that get up. Come downstairs with me. Please?' she pouted prettily.

'OK. Just for you.'

'Good. Mission accomplished. Justin will be pleased.'

'Meaning James won't be?' With my hands on my hips and humming "The stripper," I sashayed round the room.

'Perhaps he's jealous,' Debra offered.

'Good! It's time he knew what it feels like,' I replied, shrugging into my bathrobe as we went down stairs.

We talked for a while, keeping to safe subjects until Justin pleaded the need to be up early in the morning and he and Debra said their goodnights.

James sat watching my every move, obviously not intent on going anywhere.

I thought about leaving him in the dining room and going up to bed but he would only take that as an invitation.

Pouring myself a small glass of Tia Maria I sat at the opposite end of the table. This was as good a time as any to find out what James really felt about me. Did he love me? Or was he trying to get rid of me, permanently?

Common sense told me that neither was true. He may not love me in the Mills and Boon sense of the word but our relationship was civilised. He was a friend. At least he tried to give that impression. Maybe I was wrong?

He caught me looking at him and we both started talking at once.

'Sorry,' I gestured for him to speak first.

'I heard that you had a man around here,' he said.

'That's no longer any of your business.'

James got up and came towards me, arms outstretched. 'I know, but I just can't bear to think of someone taking advantage of you. We were married ten years, love, it must give me some rights?' he murmured, pulling me to my feet.

'I have never stopped loving you,' he whispered, taking me in his arms, his hands going under my dressing gown.

Moaning low in his throat he caressed my half naked body. James was always ready to make love, his high sex drive was probably at the root of our problems.

'I never refused you, James. Why did you feel it was necessary to play the field?'

He shrugged and looked me in the eye. 'I managed to turn away all but the most determined.' His hands were perfectly still around my waist.

I thought back to my human behaviour course. Did that mean he was telling the truth or lying? I couldn't remember.

'But some of the students offer sex as readily as you offer a cup of coffee and they collect scalps.'

Chrissy had said the same thing about some of her husband's students.

'But not all of the lecturers take them up on the offers.'

James chuckled. 'Most of them can't get it up with their wives!'

Chrissy had said that too.
'I've only ever loved you.'
Maybe it was true.
'Guess what?' I whispered.
'Mmn?' he murmured, concentrating on kissing my neck.
Whatever James did he gave it his full attention and right now he was making me feel as if I were the only woman in the world.

'Someone has nicked all my night gowns. Who do you suppose would do a thing like that?' I asked softly, pulling up his shirt and running my fingernails round his bare back. He loved his back scratched.

He sucked his breath through his teeth and unzipped his fly.
'Rowena, I heard the Coleman's talking when I got back...'
Covering his lips with my hand. I kissed his ears.
'No, James, this isn't the time for gossip.'

I began unbuttoning his shirt as his erection pulsed against me. Teasing his nipples I untied the belt on my dressing gown. 'Come to bed,' I whispered feeling like a slut.

But James was turned on and as I moved to go upstairs he deliberately peeled my bath robe off my shoulders. It fell to the floor.

I was startled, we'd only ever made love in the bedroom before, usually in the dark.

Standing naked in the dining room with James almost fully clothed was surprisingly sensual in the glow of the myriad of candles.

He pulled me to him, grinding his manhood against me, letting me feel the hardness of his erection. Heat shivered down to my centre of pleasure.

'No, Rowena. A little excitement. That's what you want isn't it?' he pleaded, pushing me back to the pine table. 'The kids are always telling me that I don't show you how much I love you. Spontaneous romance and passion, Justin said.'

He was babbling, kissing my breasts as he lifted my bare bottom onto the smooth pine. And pulling my legs apart, he pressed me back onto the table.

The curtains were not closed. From my position I could see the lights on in Beaumont Hall. Shadows standing against their windows.

'Please, James, this is not a good idea.' I protested, trying to back away.

But his penis was hard and demanding, impatient to enter.

My stomach quivered with anticipation.

'You don't have to find a bit of rough to give you passionate sex,' he said, licking my nipples as his penis pushed against my pubes.

Aroused, I pushed aside thoughts of the Colemans watching and tried to concentrate on my ex husband. I might have succeeded had he not tried to kiss me.

Quickly moving my head aside I avoided his lips and nibbled his ear lobes. Making love was indeed a good way of measuring if a person was in love with you or not, but it worked both ways. A kiss was an intimate expression of love and I balked at that.

He held my face and I struggled as he kissed me. His tongue probed deep against the sensitive roof of my mouth and I was annoyed that it aroused me.

As if he knew he'd been rejected, James thrust into me. Hard. The table under my buttocks made it impossible for me to squirm away as he grabbed my hips and thumped away, not quite hurting me.

Putting my hands flat on his chest I tried to escape but the more I squirmed, the more he liked it.

Drops splashed on my cheeks and looking up I saw his face was wet with tears.

'Don't leave me. I can give you what ever he can.' He accentuated his words with rhythmic thrusts and my body automatically responded.

Wrapping my legs round his back we clung to each other, gasps and grunts blending into a frenzied harmony. Harder and faster, James took me to the edge. Before my limbs had a chance to relax, he came in a shuddering release.

We lay for a moment in embarrassed silence. As soon as he withdrew I slipped from the table, rubbing my bum as I blew out the candles.

'Good night, James,' I said as I picked up my robe and hugged it tightly round me.

'Rowena, we have to talk,' he said.

'Some other time. I'm tired.'

'Tomorrow, then. We'll go for a meal somewhere, OK?'

'OK,' I agreed.

Slowly he walked to the front door, his arm around my waist. 'You'd tell me if you found someone else?'

'You don't tell me about your conquests,' I parried. 'And you gave up the right to interrogate me when you took Barbara to Bradford.'

With that I shut the door, locked it and ran upstairs, Cassidy following me.

Laying in bed I re-hashed James' strange behaviour and hated myself for enjoying his lovemaking.

My only excuse was that he'd been my first experienced lover and after our divorce I only had a couple men to compare him with, so my experience was almost virginal.

Was that why I tossed and turned all night, remembering the breathtaking ways that William had made love to Mistress Berrysford?

Would Bill make love to me like that?

Longing for his arms around me I slept fitfully.

CHAPTER FIFTEEN.

I got up as soon as it was not too obscenely early and had a shower; making a mental note to ask Albert to have a look at the tank, the water still smelled rank.

I manhandled three packing cases of pots, pans and food stuff into the dining room and had just finished when Albert, young Bert and a crew of three strong men arrived. They moved my appliances into my overcrowded dining room.

Almost before I'd read my mail the crashing and banging started as they demolished my kitchen. The noise and dust drove me to distraction.

'Come on Cass, let's get the hell out of here,' I said in my best John Wayne drawl. 'We'll have coffee in Arnold, eh?'

Cassidy wagged his tail approvingly. The girls in the coffee shop always managed to find a broken sausage roll or pie to give my "Look at me, I'm a loveable, half starved, three legged dog."

Clipping on his lead I reached over and picked up the telephone before it rang, a gift taken for granted for so long, I thought nothing of it.

The health officer from Upper Berry told me the drums in the reservoir contained traces of Dioxin and assured me the amount was so insignificant it wasn't cause for concern but there would of course be a full investigation.

Recognising a snow job, I thanked him nicely and hung up.

If Coleman's old company was to blame for dumping the Dioxin, how could I prove it after all these years.

Remembering the anxiety of the people I'd interviewed; the heartbroken young woman who'd just had yet another miscarriage and the parents of the children suffering from leukaemia, officially classed as a statistical aberration, I was determined to have a damn good try.

Putting my cinnamon coloured blazer over a chino shirt and skirt, I took Cassidy out of the oppressive atmosphere into the crisp air of a bright but chilly spring day.

We took a leisurely stroll into Arnold, stopping off at most of Buggalugs's haunts but no one had seen him for days. I even enquired at the police station but mercifully no accidents involving cats had been reported. The RSPCA said they hadn't heard of a black and white cat with no tail, either. All I could do was hope he'd come home in his own good time.

'While we're here we might as well pop in to the library, eh?'

Cassidy was not impressed but looking at me resignedly, he allowed me to fasten him to the railing outside.

It had just occurred to me that Chrissy, Arnold born and bred, might know something about Colemans Feed and Fertiliser Company. However, when I walked in to her office, I found myself asking casually. 'Do you know anything of a place hereabouts called Berrysford House?'

Chrissy nodded. 'They don't call me the brainy bird of Britain for nothing,' she grinned. 'Or is it...?'

'Bird brain?' I prompted.

'Something like that!' she giggled. 'I'm sure Berrysford House is on the old maps,' she said, going to the rack of Ordnance Survey maps.

Overly sensitive about her slightly pear shaped figure, Chrissy bent her knees and pulled out the shallow drawers, her maroon and cream flared skirt falling gracefully over her hips as she bent to study the old maps.

I looked over her shoulder as she pulled out a rack and searched until she came to one dated 1932.

'Here's the last time it was recorded,' she said, her hazel eyes sparkling. 'And this is the oldest map we've got of the area,' she said, checking the one at the bottom and nodding as she laid it on the top of the rack. Her long maroon painted finger nail tapped the area of Daybrook.

I stared at the evidence before me. Nestled beside the brook was an L shaped outline clearly marked Berrysford House. I had not imagined my ordeal as Rowena Berrysford. My memories of her life were not figments of my imagination nor the manifestation of concussion.

If Rowena Berrysford was real so was Walter Coleman. And I lived under the close surveillance of his descendants.

'Are you alright?' Chrissy asked anxiously. 'You've gone a bit pale.'

'Yes, thank you. ' I tried to smile, 'That's what you get when you go rushing out without any breakfast. The builders are re-modelling my kitchen.' I explained.

She scrutinised me with concern. 'Coffee and cake are on me,' she said, looking up at the library clock, 'In five minutes. OK?'

'OK, Mum,' I grinned.

With the long Victorian style skirt and blouse and her nut brown hair woven into a plait, Chrissy looked all of sixteen.

'What I really came to ask was what you know about Colemans Company which used to have a lab around here.'

'They went out of business years ago,' she said. 'I believe the lab is used for research, now.' Her eyes glazed as she delved into her memory's databank.

'When I was a kid their vans used to drive past our house. They were sky blue, with a soaring eagle on the sides,' she said, her words sending me flashing pictures of the chemical drums in the reservoir with their eagle logo.

'Why an eagle?' I asked, my voice a strangled croak.

'Arnold,' she stressed, surprised I didn't know. 'The name is derived from Erne hale; soft E as in Derby.'

It was not something I had learned but what I remembered...

"See the eagles soaring over King Hal's best wood," Rowena's father, Squire Beaumont, told her as he swept her up onto the crook of his arm. Her hands clasped around his neck, she gazed out of the great window at Beaumont Hall.

Beyond the gardens and cherry orchard, birds were circling against the clear blue sky, swooping into the dark green carpet of the tree tops.

"They are building their nests where the best wood abuts the forest," Squire Beaumont told his five year old daughter. "In the Domesday Book, Arnold was known as Ernehale," he said. "Where eagles nest..."

Aware of my surroundings once more I stared at Chrissy as she repeated slowly. 'Ernehale means...'

'Eagles nest,' I whispered with her.

I remembered where I'd seen the eagle logo. On the drums in the reservoir; it was also on the drums used for storage in the barn adjoining my house.

Working on the premise that if he took so much trouble to cover his tracks Coleman must have something to hide, I decided to confront my illustrious neighbour and see what he had to say for himself. Getting an interview with him would be a feather in my cap, credibility wise.

Chrissy had a word with her colleague before we left, unfastened Cassidy from the railing and marched us to the supermarket.

'Be a good boy for Auntie Chrissy and I'll bring you a sausage roll,' she promised him as she fastened him outside the shop.

Hearing his favorite word, sausage, he yelped once and sat prettily, waiting for his treat.

In the coffee shop. She sat me under a fan wafting cool air and fetched a carafe of coffee, cakes and a giant roll for Cass.

Taking a bite from a chocolate éclair Chrissy poured me a cup of coffee.

'You can have the Elephant's foot,' she said, licking the cream from her elegant fingers.

'Thanks.' I said. 'I know you're an expert on local history but I didn't realise you knew so much. I owe you one,' I said.

By the time we had finished I felt cheerful enough to face the builder's mess back home. At least James had promised to take me out for a meal tonight.

Dropping my shopping off at home I picked up my notebook and dragged a protesting Cassidy to the oak door of Beaumont Hall.

My hand automatically reached for the bell pull, where it used to be in the seventeenth century, but it had been replaced by a modern intercom system.

'Mrs Roberts!' Sebastian said as I rang the buzzer. 'What can I do for you?'

Startled that he should know who was at his door, I stepped back in alarm before I realised that there was a hidden camera.

'Could you possibly grant me an interview vis a vis Coleman's Feed and Fertiliser Company?' I asked.

'Whatever for? We sold the company years ago,' he sounded genuinely puzzled. 'No matter, my dear. Come in, come in.'

The doors clicked open as a cynical voice whispered in my head. "*Said the spider to the fly."* But I didn't need any warning. Only the thought that this interview might win me a few kudos with the right wing press, made me walk inside.

Who knows, I might find out if our gentleman farmer was aware that his chemicals had been dumped at the bottom of a reservoir. But Cassidy would not come with me.

Short of dragging him along on his backside I took off his lead and told him to wait for me.

Even as I went in I knew his judgement was better than mine. This was not one of my better ideas.

Walking through Beaumont Hall was like walking into a dream which is hovering on the edge of a nightmare. Weak sunlight struggled to cast dusty beams through the high, stained glass windows, accentuating the deep shadowed corners beyond.

Like ghosts; voices, smells and images of my past life whispered seductively. The air was redolent with memories of burning pine and the perfume of pot pourri.

The Great Hall, which I remembered being panelled in light oak when Squire Keeton had taken over, was dark with age. The stone fireplace in the corner was the same though...

Through a mist of tears I saw from the perspective of a child, Rowena's father standing with his back to the crackling log fire, wearing a black velvet doublet and breeches, a colour he had worn since the death of her mother in childbirth, and soft sheepskin leather boots draping over his knees.

He stood in his favourite position, his right foot resting on the rump of one of the reclining lions which flanked the hearth. Suddenly he squatted in front of her, wagging an admonishing finger.

His words echoed in my head.

"Promise me that you will not run off on your own again, sweeting," he beseeched her. 'Best wood is frequented by poachers and blackguards who would do you harm..."

The hairs on the back of my neck stiffened at the timely warning but before I could turn round and leave, Sebastian greeted me jovially. 'Come in, my dear.'

He escorted me into the library, the one place where as a child, Rowena had not been allowed to enter; for which I was grateful as the room held no memories for me.

'Would you like tea?' he held the telephone intercom at the ready.

'No thank you, Mr Coleman,' I said, unwilling to call him sir.

'Seb,' he insisted with a "Blair" smile.

But I didn't want to be familiar either.

As he motioned me to a chair angled in front of the massive cherry wood desk I noticed Piers was sprawled in an over stuffed armchair.

Coarse featured, his skin was blotchy with broken veins and already dark pouches puffed beneath the dull black eyes; evidence of his excessive drinking. Watching my progress across the room Piers broke wind as he lifted his bandaged foot onto the pouffe.

'Piers, please! Ladies present,' Coleman reprimanded.

His son replied by letting off another, his eyelids drooping as he feigned sleep. He appeared to be in a drunken stupor except for the fact that I could literally feel his clammy hands on my flesh. I pulled down my skirt and smiled brightly at the industrialist, pen at the ready. After all, what could Piers do with his father watching?

My stomach lurched as I remembered what Seth had done whilst his father watched.

But Sebastian looked so different from his sons; tall and thin, his sparse grey hair was close cropped and his watery blue eyes stared at me with bored inquiry. He could not be aware of what his son was doing to me. Could he?

Wanting to get out of there as quickly as possible I cut out the preliminaries and went straight for the throat.

Switching on my mini tape recorder I said briskly. 'I've discovered some of Colemans old drums which contain traces of Dioxin, in the reservoir at Upper Berry. Can you tell me why you allowed them to be dumped there?'

'How do you know they are mine? I sold the place years ago,' he said, still smiling.

'They have been positively identified,' I gave him an equally false smile.

Treading warily I tried not to show my shock when I felt the pressure of Piers' fingers on my inner thighs. My skin crawled as he squeezed my flesh, his unseen fingers probing my pubes.

I squirmed in the chair and crossed my legs, resting the notebook on my knees. The invasion stopped.

Sebastian was politeness personified, showing the right amount of horror and concern when I told him the devastating effects Dioxin was having on the Yorkshire community.

He unlocked the file drawer at the bottom of his desk and pulled out a bulging folder.

'We always paid a properly licensed company to dispose of our unwanted chemicals,' he said, as he rifled through it. 'Here you are, one of my last receipts.' He gave it to me as though that was the end of the matter.

I made a note of the invoice number as well as the name and address of the company. Arnold Hauliers.

I dropped my pen as cold fingers squeezed my nipples. It was like being molested by a ghost.

'I must stress, Mrs Roberts, that I do understand the importance of disposing of chemicals in an environmentally friendly manner,' Coleman murmured in a scratching for votes patronising tone. 'I'm only a farmer, my dear,' he gave a self depreciating shrug. 'And know nothing of the technical side of the Plant. As I said, the Company was sold before the effects of Dioxin were known.'

Crossing my arms I leant forward and threw a fiery glance at Piers' hands; he stood up and yelped, his eyes opening wide.

I could have sworn I'd woken him.

He stuck his fingers in his mouth and struggled to his feet glancing at the fire screen in front of the low fire.

Did he really think a spark had burned him? I was tempted to let him know what he was up against but discretion stilled my tongue.

Sebastian flicked a glance at me as his son rushed from the room like the proverbial scalded cat. Then he smiled and escorted me to the door, giving me his word that all Colemans drums had been safely disposed of.

'You may rest assured, Mrs Roberts, although as I'm sure you are aware, it is no longer my responsibility, I will nonetheless accept the duty of care and investigate this matter,' he said, looking at his watch as walked me through the hall.

'Fair enough,' I muttered, desperate to get out of there.

'Please assure your readers that I will work with the County Council on this to ensure such illegal dumping will not occur again. Indeed, should I be elected,' he smiled at the unlikely possibility that he would lose the by-election.

'I propose that fly tipping be made illegal and anyone caught desecrating the environment in this way will be subjected to imprisonment or heavy fines; the money raised to be used to clean up the pollution.'

I did not ask how the unlicensed hauliers responsible for fly tipping would be caught. They were hardly going to be seen dumping toxic waste in daylight.

Cassidy greeted me as if he hadn't seen me for days. Thankfully, I managed to walk across the courtyard without my knees letting me down.

As soon as I got home I made a dash for the bathroom, stripping off as I climbed the stairs. Turning the power on full blast I stood under the shower, letting needles of hot water pelt my skin as I tried to scrub myself clean after Piers foul intrusion, but the rank water didn't help at all.

Soaping myself with perfumed shower gel I realised that James would never believe what Piers had done to me; I could hardly believe it myself. Perhaps James was right and the knock on the head was causing these weird delusions.

Already the feel of Piers fingers invading me was rapidly fading from my mind.

CHAPTER SIXTEEN.

By the time James arrived I was showered and freshly made up, wishing that it was Bill who was taking me out. But he was a good looking bachelor, he must have his pick of gorgeous young girls. Why couldn't I accept that?

I tried to concentrate on James, after all he was doing his best, trying so hard. Too hard. That was the trouble, James had to try so damned hard and Bill had only to smile.

I glanced out of the dining room window at the Hall. For the life of me I couldn't remember why I had been so worked up about going there, Seb Coleman was really nice, the interview had gone well and I was pleased to have given him a chance to clear his name.

Niggling at the back of my mind was the thought that something was not quite right but it could hardly be life threatening if it had slipped my mind. Even so, I massaged my temples, hoping to clear the fuzziness out of my brain.

James took me to the Moat House for dinner. Over the second bottle of wine I told him about the car.

'Darling, I saw the car of my dreams the other day. A Volvo.'

'Mmn?' he murmured, his mouth full of Stilton. 'Nice car,' he said. Sensible was what he meant.

'The new sports model.'

'Well, I'm not so sure about that, you want a good second hand one. A Volvo Estate might be useful, though,' he conceded.

'I don't *want* a second hand car.' I said firmly. 'I want this convertible.'

'The C70?'

'Yep. I've ordered it,' I said, tensing for an argument, 'It will be delivered on Monday.'

'What brought this on?' he asked; I think the expression is gob smacked.

'I need a reliable car when I'm travelling to assignments and it presents a successful image, career wise.' I quoted the salesman's unnecessary sales talk. 'And,' I added with new found confidence, 'I can afford it. But how do you think I should pay for it? I'd get a discount for cash, or I could buy it interest free over three years.' I gave him the illusion of choice.

Naturally he plumped for the interest free deal, convincing himself that he had a say in the matter. I didn't tell him that I'd already arranged the deal.

When the taxi came to take us home, James was so relaxed he almost poured into it. I thought about sending him back to Barbara but I noticed shadows at the window of the Hall and suddenly I didn't want to be on my own tonight.

James' attention was flattering and made me feel good. But as we undressed his manner changed abruptly.

'How did you get those bruises on your thighs?' he asked, staring at me through shuttered eyes as I searched for a sexy night gown.

I looked at my legs. 'I've no idea.'

'And your breasts? Walked into somebody's fingers did you? Who was it?'

'I really don't know what you're talking about.'

'Have you forgotten who left those love bites too?' his voice was quiet and clipped.

Puzzled, I looked at the bruises around my nipples and glanced up into his startlingly cold eyes as I walked towards the bed, stark naked. My breasts were tender, swollen and covered in small dark bruises that looked for all the world like finger prints.

'I don't know. I probably bumped into something.'

'I bet you did. Who was it, one of the bloody builders? Like a bit of rough do you?'

'James! I don't know what you're talking ab...' My words were abruptly cut off as his arm snaked out and pulled me onto the bed, pinning me down as he kissed me with angry ferocity, his tongue forcing my mouth open whilst his knee did the same to my legs.

He entered me so quickly it hurt. I pressed my buttocks down in an attempt to force him out, and desperately tried to escape the bruising pressure of his mouth.

I struggled to breathe; hating this, hating to be held down. Hating him.

My head swam and I saw not James but Seth Coleman on top of me.

James must have sensed something of my distress because he tore his lips from mine and asked. 'Is this the way you like it?'

'No, James. Please,' I cried, his unexpected assault taking me by surprise.

He kissed me hard and long as if to prove he did not need my permission or consent. It was not desire but anger because he thought I'd allowed someone else this privilege. But that only proved that he cared. Didn't it?

I lay unmoved and un-aroused, watching him through half closed lids as he rode the waves, making appreciative noises in his throat. It sickened me.

Throughout our long marriage, James had always taken me for granted, he had never been forced to prove that he loved me. Never had to compete. Perhaps that was why he hadn't placed too high a value on me as a person, wife or lover. I had always been there for him and what's more, self righteously thought that was enough for any man. I had allowed myself to be taken advantage of. James was no more to blame than I was.

Even so, I was disgusted by his show of macho virility. And when he came, I felt defiled. No matter how hard I tried, how illogical it seemed, I couldn't help feeling that I'd been unfaithful to William.

There was a sharp noise from the attic. A creaking floor board.

Startled, we both looked up at the ceiling.

James jumped up buck naked and strode to the open window completely confident and unconcerned about who might see him.

'It isn't outside,' I told him, 'it's in the attic.'

He closed the window, leaving the curtains open, the soft light from the outside lamp made the room as clear as day.

'You don't seriously believe that do you?' he said, in his 'reasonable' voice. Which, I might add, sent me straight up the wall these days.

'Draw the curtains,' I snapped, desperate for the room to be dark so no one could spy on me. I realised I had spoken too sharply and tried to explain as I pulled the duvet over me. 'Someone is watching us.'

'You're just letting your imagination get the better of you, Rowena.'

When another sound came from overhead, it seemed ominous and threatening.

'Are you going to tell me I imagined that?'

I could "see" a dark and lustreless eye staring down at me as if through a telescope. George Coleman's eye.

'Sod off, you pervert,' I yelled, mentally thrusting my finger nail into his eye in fury. The high pitched screech sounded like an owl in the room, but it was easy to distinguish what was to me, terrified but smothered, swearing.

'It's probably a bat. Son of Dracula, no doubt,' James said, oozing sarcasm.

He sat on the bed and pulled on his underpants and socks. Now he'd had his way he was going back to Barbara.

'I'm sure you're right, dear,' I replied too sweetly, 'Who would want to break in to my attic when they could just walk in through the hole where the back door used to be?'

'You're not suggesting I go up there at this time of night are you?'

"I'll tell you what I do suggest, Roberts,' I said, knowing how he hated being called by his surname. 'One of the bastards will be blind as a bat in the morning.'

'Rowena! I don't know what's got into you lately, you sound like a common fish wife.'

He was certainly right about that. Rowena Berrysford would have the vapours if she could hear me. Or would she? I had never considered myself a wimp but was half convinced that my new found assertiveness was at her instigation.

'And you sound like a pompous, patronising, school marm,' I lashed out at him.

'I can't understand how a so called intelligent man could possibly ignore what has been going on under your nose.'

'There has been one or two things going on under my nose which I have so far chosen to ignore,' he said, pulling on his trousers.

God knows what he meant by that.

'Just who do you think tried to kill me with the lights and the kettle? And do you think Cassidy tried to drown himself?' I asked. If I was going to be argumentative I might as well go all out to win. 'What do you want me to do to prove who is behind all this. Take a bloody photograph?'

'Rowena, that's enough, you know I don't like you swearing,' James admonished.

'Tough,' I said, tuning my back on him.

I was shaking. Not with anger but exhaustion, every muscle in my body aching from the effect of my psychic attack on the pervert in the attic. And James' physical onslaught.

Once again I wondered if it was him who was trying to kill me and Piers Coleman was just a red herring. James was devious enough. But did he really hate me that much? Or need my money so badly?

'By the way, I've changed my will. I've left the bulk of my estate to be shared by the kids,' I said, determined to see John Jeacock about it as soon as possible.

'Fine. I shall do the same,' James said as he tied his shoelaces.

Picking up his jacket he slammed out.

'Goodnight,' he said as I quickly followed him, pulling on my bathrobe as I ran down the stairs.

'Get a taxi in Arnold,' I said, noticing the lights were still on in Beaumont Hall as I locked the door.

My house was suddenly empty and frightening.

On the spur of the moment I ran upstairs, got dressed in my jeans and a sweater and pulling the duvet around my shoulders, picked up Cassidy's basket.

He awoke as I carried him downstairs.

'It's OK, Cass. I thought we'd have a change tonight, eh?' I settled him under the dining room window, wedged the table in front of the cellar and pulled the chaise longue across the door, hoping I'd feel safer. But as Cassidy started snoring again I couldn't take my eyes off the glass door leading to the front room.

I lay till early morning, too exhausted to sleep, the events of the day replaying in my head. Did James suspect my feelings for Bill? Was he jealous? What had been achieved by my cursing an imaginary eye in the ceiling? Was I quite literally mad?

And why were my breast so sore and covered in bruises?

With dawn courage I ridiculed my fear and went upstairs to prepare for a new day. If I couldn't shake this silly nervousness I'd have to take a loss and sell up. Buy a little flat somewhere. Somewhere where the natives were friendly. Then it struck me. Perhaps that was what it was all about. Maybe Coleman had realised his mistake in accepting my offer and wanted me out so he could sell at a juicy profit.

But right now I had other things to worry about. The hole where the kitchen wall used to be for instance. It left me feeling decidedly vulnerable.

Taking off the clothes I had slept in or tried to sleep in, I showered and dressed in stone coloured jeans with my pale green shirt and shrugged my blazer on top.

I decided to go into Arnold and buy a padlock and a couple of strong bolts for the dining room door.

'Walkies?' I asked, but Cass opened one eye and snuggled back into his basket, obviously he didn't think much of the idea.

When I got into town it was quiet and deserted in the mist, all the shops were still closed. The pealing church bells gave the early morning a dreamlike quality, relaxing and peaceful.

Then I remembered. It was Sunday. That's what happens when you don't get enough sleep.

Taking a stroll down Tannery Lane to see if Albert had a padlock to spare, pleased that although I didn't know exactly where he lived, there were only two houses, and the lights were on in the big old looking house. I was just going to ring the bell when the front door opened.

'Rowena! What a pleasant surprise. Are you alright, duck?'

Albert picked up a thick wad of Sunday papers from the old fashioned outdoor mailbox and ushered me inside, a mile wide smile of welcome on his face.

'Anything wrong?' he asked.

'No. I couldn't sleep, I felt so exposed. I was going to go to the shops but I've just remembered what day it is.'

'What are you after that's so urgent?' he asked, as I followed him through the beautiful oak panelled hall.

Walking past the ornate newel post I stopped and fondled the old oak, warm and familiar in my hand. As if it were welcoming me home.

'A stout padlock for the dining room door,' I answered.

'No problem, we're bound to have one somewhere. I'm sorry, I should have thought of it myself,' Albert said. 'We store all our building materials in the tannery's old office at the bottom of the orchard. I'll just pop out and see what I can find.'

'Put the coffee on. We've got company,' he shouted.

Bill came through from the kitchen, his arms open in welcome. He was saying something but the words didn't register, my mind was elsewhere, completely overawed by an uncanny sense of deja vu.

'Rowena!' I heard Bill's voice as if from a long distance. Half a dozen lifetimes away.

I studied my William's handiwork on the newel post. The Rowan leaves and berries which he had carved especially for me.

My fingers ran over the pattern as memories flooded back, tears running down my cheeks unheeded as I caressed the old wood, grieving for William and my baby.

'Do you recognise this?' he whispered, holding me gently.

When I had recovered enough to speak, we were in the kitchen. 'Have breakfast with us,' Bill pleaded, pulling out the captains chair at the head of the table.

I sat down gratefully. A large red Aga fitted snugly in a brick alcove and a modern ceramic hob and electric oven were inset into the fitted stressed oak units.

The sun streamed in through the two windows which overlooked the orchard, highlighting the bright brass fittings.

'Sorry,' Albert said, coming in through the back door, 'I can't find one. I'll check to see if I've got one at home.'

'But I thought you lived here? '

Bill grinned. 'Not quite. This is my house, Albert owns the bungalow next door.'

'I'm sorry, I didn't know,' I said.

'After my wife died Bill gave me a room here, to keep each other company sometimes. He needs me to cook him a decent meal now and then,' Albert whispered behind his hand, pretending not to notice Bill's raised eyebrows.

'Did I tell you that I am an excellent cook, Rowena?'

'If she doesn't know, you will be sure to tell her, won't you?' Bill said, winking at me.

I relaxed as I listened to their friendly banter.

'Just coffee, if you don't mind,' I said as Albert was about to set another place at the table.

He tutted disapprovingly.

'I'm sorry, Albert, I couldn't face food so early in the day. But I'd love to wander round the garden while you eat,' I looked at Bill. 'May I?'

'Now your talking my language,' Bill murmured. He opened the door and ushered me into the long walled garden.

The only sound was the peeling church bells in the distance, even the birds seemed to be holding their breaths. Inhaling the heady perfume the world stopped. It was I that was spinning, spinning...

Rowena was conscious of her elegant damask gown trailing through the pink carpet of fallen cherry blossom.

A warm breeze swirled the blossoms into the air, and the baby's happy gurgles filled the Sabbath morning as she reached out her chubby hand to catch them.

"Come, rest a while, sweeting. Rowena has found a new toy."

His wife on one arm and his daughter cradled in the other, William led them to the stone bench beneath the arbour.

Tinker, their jet black cat, tail high in the air, nuzzled and purred round their legs as they sat watching their baby try to capture the blossom as it drifted down from the trees.

William turned towards her, his eyes glowing with love as Rowena kissed the tips of her fingers and pressed them against his lips. "Consider yourself kissed," she smiled.
He took hold of her hand, raising it to his lips. 'You too my lady.'

'Penny for them, Rowena?'
It was William's voice. No, Bill's I was confused, shaking my head, I held on to his hand tightly. Bill was looking at me, his eyes full of concern.
'Sorry. The past is very close here,' I stammered, withdrawing my hand.
'No need to apologise.'
Bill smiled and tucked my hand into the crook of his elbow like William used to do. I couldn't speak in case I broke the fragile spell as we walked back indoors.
Albert went next door to look for a padlock for me and Bill and I had coffee and toast. We talked about his family's old house and our ancestors. It was comforting to know that there was still a few remnants of William and Rowena's house around. It gave me a sense of continuum.
Bill told me that Berrysford House had been built by William Berrysford.
'My William,' I whispered.
'He bequeathed it to his nephew, Edward Smithson and down the line to Emily Weston nee Smithson,' he said.
'I will take you to the site in Daybrook if you would like to see where it used to be. A lot of this house was built from what was salvaged from there.'
'That would be wonderful. Thank you.'
I wondered if Bill had as much trouble keeping his voice under control as I did.
He mentioned taking me to Sarah's, a restaurant which belonged to his cousin who, as Albert had told me, had renovated the seventeenth century manor on Brickyard Lane.
Bill, with his interest and knowledge of the architecture of the period, had acted as a consultant.

We talked about our shared heritage and the coincidences and friends which bound our lives together. Bill was convinced, as I was, that there were no coincidences in life that didn't occur for a reason, and that good friends accompany us through different lives... as did our enemies.

'It's obvious when you think about it,' Bill said, his eyes shining with enthusiasm. 'How else can you account for the shock of recognition when you meet someone you have never met before, to whom you take an instant dislike? Or strike up a deep rapport with a stranger?'

'We are like pebbles thrown in a pool, the circles are people we love or who have influenced our past lives. They often overlap and return time and time again, gravitating towards each other for comfort, ' I said, without fear of ridicule.

'Or to repay old debts,' he agreed.

I told him about Sarah Smithson, nee Berrysford and Emily Weston nee Smithson. And he told me about his wife Margaret Keeton and her ancestor, Squire Keeton, Cromwell's captain who had taken Beaumont Hall from Rowena's father. Which led me to tell him of my need to find Rowena Berrysford and "our" daughter.

I even told him about my strange powers.

'I think almost everyone has more mental abilities than they give themselves credit for,' he said.

The more I discovered about Bill the more I realised that in looks, temperament and character he was exactly how William would be in today's world.

'And religion has a lot to answer for too,' I said, warming to the subject. 'The inquisition made male and female witches afraid, although they only hunted women, fostering the misconception that only females were witches. But it became a matter of survival to suppress their gifts and I suppose in time, their powers just withered away.'

'But you shouldn't use the power unless it is absolutely necessary, Rowena, ESP can be dangerous. There is a reported case of a woman who moved objects but it left her so weak that during the tests, she had a heart attack and died.'

Albert came in. 'I've found what you need.' He held up a strong bolt and a padlock. 'Would you like me to put them on for you? I could give you a lift home if you like?'

'I wasn't going home just yet. I wanted to go round the churchyard to look for the graves of my ancestors.'

Bill stood behind me and rested his arm on my shoulder. His touch sent a thrill down my spine. As if he understood what was happening to me, his grip tightened reassuringly.

Shakily I let out my breath and concentrated on breathing regularly.

'May I come with you?' he murmured in my ear, undoing all my efforts of normality.

Albert looked at me and winked. 'You be careful or he'll take you round all the church yards, junk shops and...'

Bill interrupted, laughing. 'Don't you dare mention it. I solemnly swear I will not drag Rowena round an Auction room.'

'Oh, and why not?' I asked, the cheerful camaraderie had restored my equilibrium. 'I've spent holidays in exotic places and only seen the inside of Auction rooms and Antique shops.'

'My idea of heaven!' We both said together and burst out laughing.

Albert shook his head, grinning ruefully. 'You've met your match here, lad!'

'If you think I'm mad, you should meet my mother,' I said, remembering the happy hours we'd spent wandering round auctions and rummaging through junk in the hope of some undiscovered treasure. We were often rewarded for our efforts too.

I gave Albert the keys to my front door and he promised to hang on until either James or I returned.

Bill still had his hand on my shoulder. 'James?' he asked quietly. 'Where does your ex husband stand in your life, Rowena?'

'We're friends,' I said, rather ashamed of the truth. 'I suppose I have used James lately. Afraid to make a clean break,' I told him.

'And Susan?'

'She and Justin are conspiring to get us back together.'

'Is that what you want, Rowena?' he asked as if my answer was the most important thing in the world.

'No,' I said firmly. 'I've just been drifting with the tide, waiting for the right time to tell him that it's over.'

'Is it still OK for tomorrow?'

'Of course. I'm looking forward to it.'

That was putting it mildly, I thought as we all left the house together. What a wonderful world.

Bill and I wandered around St Mary's churchyard but we didn't find a Rowan or Rowena. The Vicar came out but there was a service starting so I couldn't speak to him. Bill casually put his arm around my waist and pulled me towards another ancient head stone.

'Rowena?' he whispered, putting both hands on my shoulders he turned me to face him and I stood on tiptoes lifting my face to be kissed.

Then Sebastian's car pulled up outside the church gates.

I didn't want him to see how much I loved Bill. 'I'll have to go, I didn't get any sleep last night,' I said, taking him to the side of the church, out of Coleman's line of sight.

'I'll walk you back home,' Bill said, putting my arm through his and squeezing my hand as we strolled through the churchyard.

We stopped under the ivy covered lich-gate and tilting my face up, his lips brushed mine.

My eyes closed as I leaned toward him, but he gripped my shoulders and held me back. I opened my eyes and realised what I was doing with the parishioners watching.

Before I could apologise his finger touched my lips. 'Please don't say anything, Rowena. It isn't necessary, we both know how we feel.'

Walking back, we held hands like star crossed lovers. Were we destined to be star crossed forever?

Reluctantly we parted outside the gates of Beaumont Court.

I remembered to thank him for bringing me home and Bill promised to call me but parting was not easy.

Walking towards my house I spun round at the sound of a car on the gravelled drive, filled with apprehension.

An ambulance pulled up outside the Hall. The driver climbed out and whistling tunelessly, strolled round to open the ambulance door.

I stood watching like a ghoul as he helped an injured man shrouded in a red blanket, out of the back.

A big man. A man with his head swathed in bandages. And when he looked up and saw me, he flinched.

George Coleman stared at me out of one eye.

And I knew without a doubt that I had done that.

CHAPTER SEVENTEEN.

I rushed inside as the implications of what I had done, dawned on me.

'Good morning, my dear, are you alright? You look a bit pale,' James said, putting his arm around me as I entered the dining room.

'I came to apologise about last night.' He took me in his arms, 'I was well out of order.'

My mind in a whirl I let him lead me to a chair.

'I was worried about you until Albert told me where you'd been. Sit down, dear. I've just made a pot of tea, would you like a cup?' he asked. It was his answer to everything, a panacea for all ills.

'Yes please,' I stammered, trying to keep the picture of the bandaged eye out of my mind.

'I've had a word with Albert about the funny noises. He said it could be subsidence, or pigeons. And whatever the cause it would be made worse by all the banging about that has been going on in the kitchen.'

James was being his reasonable self again, thank God. I was honestly trying to concentrate on what he was saying but all I could think of was George Coleman staring at me.

'Albert said he will have a look in the loft tomorrow and meanwhile you'll be safe.'

I nodded, looking at the padlock and chain and the two strong bolts on the door to the demolished kitchen. My only defence against intruders.

'You will be alright tonight, love,' he said, as though he'd thought of it.

'I can't stay here tonight, James!' The thought made me feel sick.

'Alright, whatever you say. Shall I give Justin a ring?' He didn't offer to take me to his flat, I noticed.

'No, I'll go to York and stay overnight with Susan,' I said, making up my mind to try to see John Baker's mother. I had the feeling that all this was tied in to the Coleman's and their chemical company. And my interview with Seb did not seem right. I must have missed something.

I sipped the tea James made and noticed him glancing at his watch.

'If you pack a few things while I wash these,' he said, picking up the tea cups, 'We can be at the University in time for lunch. I'll give Susan a ring and let her know we're coming.'

I was ready before he hung up.

The strain of living near the Colemans washed away from me as James drove to York. The next thing I knew, he was shaking me awake.

'Rowena, wake up, dear, we're here.'

Cassidy, asleep in his box strapped on the back seat, yawned and yelped to remind us not to forget him.

We walked up to Susan's studio flat but she had seen us coming and before we rang the doorbell she had thrown herself into her father's arms with whoops of glee. Almost immediately she rushed over to hug me affectionately while Cassidy danced for her attention, his tail going like a metronome.

In the kitchenette she had a cafetiere all ready for coffee and plugged in the kettle while James took my bag into the lounge area.

'Don' t bother with that, sweetheart, we'll go to The Carvery for Sunday lunch.'

If our previous visits were anything to go by I knew lunch would stretch to an afternoon by the river and I wouldn't get any work done.

'I'll have a cup, if you don't mind, love. And may I scrounge beans on toast or something while you two go out for lunch? I want to check a few things for an article.'

James made to protest but Susan, who understood my dedication to my job better than her father, nodded and opened her refrigerator.

'No need to be so Spartan, Mum,' she said. 'I've made a salad and there's cheese and eggs. And I've got soup and stuff.'

She must have someone special in her life, I'd never seen her fridge so full. Or her flat so tidy. I smiled, she would tell me about him in her own good time.

'Cheese salad will be fine. Thanks, love.'

'That's OK,' she said, brushing her long hair.

'Come along, dear, or all the beef will be gone.'

'Please! You can court mad cow disease if you want to but I've turned vegetarian.'

Probably the boyfriend's influence; so there was no point in my telling her the dangers in vegetables grown with liberal dousings of weed-killer and pesticides but I had a go anyway.

'I know it's more expensive but try to buy organic, love.'

She lifted an eyebrow, just like her father. 'Of course.'

'Good.'

'Are you sure you won't come with us, Rowena?' James asked.

'No thanks. I'll have a quick bite here before I try to find Mike Meadows.'

'Oh, he'll be in the lab,' Susan said airily. 'Naked chorus girls couldn't drag him from his work.'

Another thwarted conquest? I wondered. Susan was so pretty she tended to think she could have anyone she set her cap at, and I was not about to disillusion her.

'You're not expecting me to take you out in that, are you?' James said, glancing at Susan's hi tech Nikes just about visible under her long denim pinafore dress. 'Can't you wear something a little less aggressive? You look like a lesbian milk maid.'

'OK,' she said, giving me a crafty wink as she went into the bedroom.

I waited with baited breath.

Susan emerged wearing a skin tight black lycra mini skirt and one shoulder top, showing her belly button. She still wore her trainers. She looked, as they say, absolutely fabulous; but them I've never professed to be unbiased where my step kids are concerned.

I burst out laughing. 'You asked for it.'

'I should have known better. I don't suppose you would change back into Grandma Moses?'

Susan shook her head slowly and walked to the door giggling like a ten year old.

While James took Susan and Cassidy out for lunch, I had a salad sandwich and rushed over to the laboratories hoping to find someone willing to talk to me about John Baker's research.

Once again I found Dr Meadows and we went through the M I 5 procedure. I asked to meet John Baker's mother, determined not to take no for an answer.

'I had a word with her about you. Are you in a car?'

'No.'

'Never mind, I'll drop you near her house but be discreet. The faculty seem to be under orders to forget John ever existed. Dr Baker has a few influential friends of her own but she's hanging on by the skin of her teeth. And, having no one up there who gives a damn about Mike Meadows, I'm considered suspect as well as dispensable.'

I nodded. 'Mike who?'

He gave me the first warm smile of our acquaintance as we walked to his car. It was worth waiting for.

Mike stopped at the corner of the street which intersected with Susan's.

'Third house on the right. Tell Alice to call me on the car phone if she wants to check you out,' he said, as he drove away.

If Dr Baker was out or refused to see me I could find my way back to Susan's flat.

She kept the chain on her door when I told her who I was and that my intentions were honourable.

It was the same lady I'd seen with Mike at the restaurant. Dr Baker was less suspicious than Dr Meadows and let me in without too much preamble.

'Come in,' she said in a soft Yorkshire accent. Down to earth friendly. But I had the impression that if she didn't like you she'd slam the door in your face, no messing.

Her lounge at the back of the house was decorated in warm tones of terracotta and cream with contrasting touches of blue. French windows overlooked the south facing garden, overgrown with narcissi and bluebells.

She offered me coffee and seemed surprised when I accepted and followed her into the kitchen while she made it. There the scientist in her dominated the decor. Sparkling white and steel. It was saved from looking like a laboratory by the masses of greenery hanging from the ceiling in baskets and rampaging across the window sill.

Perching on a steel stool by the breakfast bar I explained what I wanted to know and why, while she prepared coffee.

Dr Baker was an attractive woman in her forties, plumpish, with warm brown eyes and curly brown hair showing grey at the roots. Her son had only been dead three months and hairdressing was not likely to be on her list of priorities.

Reaching out I touched her arm. 'I'm so sorry about John. I don't know what I would do if I were faced with such a tragedy.' I wanted her to know she had my support and sympathy but everything sounded so trite. 'Such a waste of a brilliant mind.'

She spun on her heel and faced me, spitting fury. 'You don't believe the crap that he killed himself, do you? I thought you knew what was going on around here.'

I opened my hands in surrender. 'What do *you* think happened to your son?'

She didn't seem deranged but it was hard enough to cope with sudden death without the guilt of having a loved one commit suicide.

'John had no reason to kill himself, that's for sure.'

She stared me in the eye. 'Do you think he didn't expect opposition from the establishment over his findings?' she snorted derisively.

'May I?' I asked, taking out my tape recorder.

Dr Baker nodded and switching on the machine I listened quietly.

"He wasn't a moody teenager, he was brilliant but down to earth. And apart from the fact that he had accepted a sabbatical at BYU and was looking forward to going to Utah, he certainly wouldn't have killed himself in that manner. John of all people knew the effects if the attempt didn't succeed. Paralysis. Brain damage. And the pain would have been excruciating.

Poison? I wondered, waiting for Dr Baker to continue but her face drained of colour and I led her to one of the chairs and poured her a glass of water.

'No thank you,' she said, waving it away impatiently. 'But if you'd do the honours.' She nodded to the percolator.

'I'm sorry. I can't bear to think of his agony. The skin was burned off his lips and the inside of his mouth.'

She grabbed my arm as I picked up the coffee pot and I quickly put it down as she shook it, demanding my attention.

'He wouldn't have done that, don't you see? John was a scientist, he knew the effects of the weed-killer.'

The picture she painted startled me. Suicide by such a method was unlikely but who would murder a young graduate? And why?

'There must be easier methods of killing yourself,' I whispered handing her a cup of coffee.

'Exactly!' Dr Baker nodded. She sat back and sipped the strong brew. 'My son was murdered. Someone forced that poison down his throat.'

'He must have put up a hell of a struggle. Why wasn't it mentioned at the inquest? '

There must have been bruising and possibly a broken bone or two, I thought.

'The Coroner didn't find anything suspicious. Or he was bribed,' she said defiantly.

I nodded, suppressing a sigh of disappointment. If it assuaged her guilt I would leave her with her delusion. 'It has been known.' I said, but she knew I didn't believe it.

'John was not a radical but he'd upset too many important people. Benefactors and Government advisors, amongst others, ' she said.

'Before his paper was published on Dioxin he was offered a high paying job in Africa if he withdrew it. He received a few threats as well but I can't prove it,' she said, holding her head in her hands. 'But I do know he was frightened,' she took a ragged breath. 'Scared to death,' she said, in control of herself once more.

Dr Baker took a swallow of coffee before she continued. 'As for his work on the Scorpion virus, he was so incensed when the Advisory Committee on Agricultural Chemicals and the Environment approved random testing of the new insecticide in Cambridgeshire, he leaked the information to Friends of the Earth.'

'I'm sorry, you've lost me. How did he find out about the quango's recommendation? And I've only just heard of this scorpion thing.'

'Alice,' she insisted, the barriers finally down. 'John tested all kinds of pesticides and weed-killers as well as Dioxin. And I happen to be on the Committee. Quango, call it what you will.' She cut off my apology with a raised hand. 'I've tried to instil a sense of reason and responsibility into the proceedings but as most of the members are in the Chemical industry, it's difficult to control their enthusiasm.'

'Like Piers Coleman,' I said flatly.

'Especially Piers Coleman,' she emphasised.

'Let me get this straight. You are on the same committee as him?'

'That's right. He took his father's place when Seb stood down to fight in a by election somewhere,' she said, looking at me questioningly.

My stomach clenched knowing the Colemans were involved.

'The Advisory committee were each given a sample of the product, which was supposed to kill cabbage caterpillars and slugs. It was to be sprayed on to greens and carrots but John wouldn't let me use it until he'd done a few routine tests. He found it to be a highly toxic chemical cocktail containing a deadly, genetically engineered virus from scorpions.'

The very thought made me shiver.

'What appalled John was that he'd only done the preliminary tests that a second year student would use and he found that the virus was carcinogenic, did not break down in the food chain and had a life expectancy of X. In other words it could not be cleaned from the ground in the foreseeable future.'

I nodded, 'Mike explained the term.'

'The virus passes on to whatever is planted there. Vegetables, cattle food, et cetera.'

I went cold. 'Do you have his notes? If I could photo copy them?' I managed to croak out of my suddenly dry mouth, Susan's words resounding in my head... "I've turned vegetarian."

'Yes. And I've got plenty of copies. One is in my bank along with my will and a letter to my solicitor.' Alice stared at me coolly. 'You might think I'm paranoid but I assure you too many people have disappeared in one way or another. Been promoted. Seconded. Gone to Africa. Sacked or discredited, that I'm taking no chances,' she said. 'And I've made sure that everybody knows it.'

She took a bag containing a bulky folder from the freezer and gave it to me as she spoke. 'They're hidden all over the place just in case I am accidentally run over,' she said, without a trace of drama.

'The week before John died I confronted my colleagues on the Advisory Committee. But they went ahead and arranged for the pesticide to be sprayed in Cambridgeshire. That's when John blew the whistle by informing his girl friend who is a secretary at Friends of the Earth.'

'Do you know who manufactures this pesticide?' I asked.

'I don't remember; it's a company I've never heard of before but the name is in John's notes,' she said.

Alice looked at me earnestly. 'More than likely it was the product of a post graduate, abandoned when the probable consequences became evident.'

'Then why would a company produce it?' In my job it pays to be sceptical.

'Research is expensive. Every year industry combs the universities for their brightest students and graduates, along with their work.'

'I know all about puppy hunting.'

'The legitimate companies offer places to the cream of the crop, of course,' Alice said. 'But during the last decade, as cut backs have become the creed of the day, the leeches crept from under the stones. These get rich quick entrepreneurs come not to employ the hopefuls but to buy their research. After years of scrimping on inadequate grants and student loans the gullible pups are willing victims of industry's cost effective ethos.'

'This would make a good story,' I said, making a mental note to look into the allegation.

'Trouble is, the only evidence is word of mouth. Those who accept the money are not going to talk and those who don't, at best have had their research grants cut off and those, like John, who tried to stir up trouble, have mysteriously disappeared. Some, as I said, were offered jobs in far off places. Others were not so fortunate.'

'Can you prove any of this?'

'Only by proving what happened to my son. You probably think I'm a deranged mother who can't accept the allegation that her son killed himself, but if you had known him you'd agree. John would not, could not and did not commit suicide. That is a statement of fact. He was sadistically murdered to keep him quiet. And I intend to prove it.'

I nodded thoughtfully as I turned off the tape recorder. I might have been inclined to believe her but for the fact that the Coroner found no bruises on John's body.

No one could have forced him to drink the corrosive chemical without leaving some evidence of a struggle...Could they?

CHAPTER EIGHTEEN.

After a rather uncomfortable but peaceful night on Susan's bed settee; no sex involved, we drove home on Monday morning. Over the blaring inanity of early morning radio which James could not live without, I ruminated on the mystery of John Baker's death.

How did it tie in with these largely ignored findings on the misuse of pesticides and weed-killers?

As a closet veggie, the militant section of vegetarians, unlike the Food without Cruelty organisation, managed to put me right off. My mother was just one of a dozen people I know who, try as they might, could not eat fresh fruit, pulses or green vegetables without chronic diarrhoea and all the danger and inconvenience that goes with it. I wondered if vegetarians would actually live longer, most of them didn't have much to shout about in the skin department but they made people listen and I wished them luck.

The irony was that if this latest scare got out, they would be hardest hit. Carrots were already suspect and cabbages and beans were definitely to be taken off the menu if the Government didn't try a cover up of BSE proportions.

God save Friends of the Earth. Which brought me back to John Baker. And regardless of his mother's plausibility, I just couldn't accept that he had been forced to swallow something that burned the skin on contact, without being forcibly held down.

James dropped me off at home just as the builders arrived. To escape the noise and dust I took Cass upstairs with me and had just started to check through my exclusive interview with Sebastian before I took it to Jayne, when the telephone rang.

'Bill?' Could it really be him? My heart fluttered at the caress in his voice but all I could say was... 'How nice of you to call. What can I do for you?'

I tried not to sound like a breathless teenager but my throat had suddenly gone dry. A frisson of joy ran through me. At the same time I was full of dread in case he was going to cancel our date.

'I wonder if you'd like to meet me a bit earlier? I've re-organised my schedule and I thought we might have lunch together?'

I answered as calmly as I could. It was ten forty five. 'I'd love to. What time?'

'Is now too soon?'

In my minds eye I could picture his smile.

'Well, I have to see my editor but if I left this instant I could meet you about quarter to twelve. Will that suit you?' I could hardly believe it, Bill was impatient to see me too, maybe not for the same reason though, I reminded myself.

'Great! Come to my office on Regent street. See you as soon as you can make it. Rowena?'

'Yes?' I whispered.

'I've missed you.'

I blinked away tears of joy. 'Me too.' I said as I put down the receiver.

I phoned a taxi, sprayed a little C K on my erratic pulse and powdered my nose before changing in to my new cream suit and emerald green sweater, which hopefully flattered my copper coloured hair and green eyes. Then I put on a slick of lip gloss while I waited for the car to arrive.

I even remembered to pop a note pad into my bag; reminding myself that I was only going to trace my ancestors.

Bert whistled cheekily when he saw me through the open plan kitchen. 'You look a bit of alright, duck,' he said approvingly, causing Albert to stop slapping cement onto the layer of new wall.

'I'm off to see my editor.' And to shame the devil added, 'Then Bill's taking me to the Archive Department. Come on, Cassidy,' I said, waving his lead. 'Promise to behave.'

'Leave him with us. You don't want to be stuck in Bill's car on a lovely day like this, do you?' Albert asked my little dog. Cassidy thumped his tail and moved towards Albert.

'Especially when I've got some nice corned beef sandwiches,' he grinned.

'You're getting more like Buggalugs every day. Cupboard love is so unworthy of you.' I admonished. 'I don't suppose we'll see him till all this is over, Buggalugs gets very upset if there's a cushion out of place; no wonder he's keeping well away from here.'

The taxi hooted in the courtyard and waving cheerily, I rushed to get away.

As I walked in the office the girls were concerned about Cass and upset that I'd left him at home. Even Jayne enquired about his health before she scanned through my interview with Coleman, her eyebrows getting higher with each page.

'What's this?' she asked, flapping the manuscript at me. 'Taken up decorating?'

'Sorry?'

'You've been a bit heavy handed with the whitewash.'

I suddenly remembered swallowing the crap Coleman had fed me. Why had I believed him?

'I'm sorry, I don't know what came over me. He is such a smarmy son of a bitch.'

'No sweat. I'll print it of course; it will lull him into a false sense of security while you investigate the bastard. This is written as if you were in a bloody trance but if you read behind the lines you can tell he's definitely got something to hide. It's not your usual style but an air of incredulity comes through. And at least he can't sue us for libel.'

I still couldn't remember writing it but I saw myself typing away in my office by the light of the moon. A shiver of distaste ran through me, as if I had been used. Manipulated. Hypnotised.

Jayne waved a cheque under my nose. 'Payment for your last article,' she said.

To keep up to date I told her what John Baker had discovered and that Friends of the Earth had prevented a virulent insecticide, approved by an autonomous Quango, from being sprayed on crops in Cambridgeshire. The same Quango on which Piers Coleman was a leading member of the board.

'That's more like it. Find out who, what and where, and I'll buy it. And Rowena,' she grinned as I waited expectantly.

'Leave the paint brush at home.'

I saluted in acquiescence and rushed out to meet Bill.

His eyes lit up when he saw me. 'Hello, Rowena. I was waiting for a call…'

'Does that mean we can't go out for lunch?' I asked, my spirits sinking.

'Not likely! But I've got to phone my office at 2.30,' he said, picking up his car keys.

"Take notes when he calls, please,' he called over his shoulder to his receptionist. 'Phone me on the mobile if anything urgent crops up, Jean. And I mean urgent!' he said as we left.

He drove to the Castle Marina for lunch and sitting in the sunshine at a picnic table by the canal, we watched a narrow boat chug by. The daffodils nodded their heads approvingly as we sat, hips and thighs almost touching. My muscles tingled with excitement at being so close to him.

What would it be like to be on a boat with him, away from prying eyes, I wondered, my heart over riding common sense in my dream world.

'I wish I could sail away with you,' Bill whispered as if he too dreamt the same dream.

'But I don't think your ex would approve.'

The words brought me down to earth. 'Or my stepchildren.'

Sneaking a sideways look at him to be sure he wasn't rejecting me, I saw the desire in his eyes. I had not imagined that he could feel the same way.

Conscious of the world around us we "spoke of ships and sealing wax," and mutual friends and acquaintances. I also told him about my strange experience when interviewing Coleman and that I felt they were at the dark centre of things.

'Never ignore your instincts,' he said, taking my hand protectively. 'The Colemans go back a long way and as much as our PPC likes to ignore it, his family have always had a very unsavoury reputation.

I don't suppose you'd consider moving? The incident the other day was far from natural.' He shrugged and looked at me earnestly, 'I'm half inclined to believe they're in league with the devil.'

I shook my head. 'I would lose so much financially.'

'But don't you realise you are in danger? Surely...'

'I know but there is James to consider. He put up half of the money for he house and he says it will be at least three years before I should sell.'

'Your safety is more important than money,' Bill insisted. 'And what does he know about the housing market? Anything could happen.'

'It's his training I suppose. Part of his job at the University is to investigate every new find, thoroughly checking every fact before he can present it as evidence.'

Bill was quiet, as if he were holding his breath. 'Bill?' I asked anxiously.

'What exactly does he do?' he asked quietly.

'He's a professor at Nottingham University; lecturing on British Archaeology.'

'JR.'

'That's what he likes to be called, yes.'

'James Roberts; of course. We've met, in fact it's his call I'm waiting for,' he said, leaning away from me and loosening his tie. 'I am often asked to verify buildings and such which could be of national importance. James and I worked at Bradford together.' Bill's voice went quieter.

'Bradford?' It was there that James had a little rendezvous with Barbara. I'd found out about it when I'd phoned his room late one night and she'd answered. I felt my colour rise with embarrassment that he might know of James' indiscretions. Somehow it made me realise that I was deliberately flirting with Bill because he looked like a man I had loved in another life.

He reached out and touched my face, as if he couldn't help himself.

I closed my eyes waiting for the kiss that was in his eyes.

His lips touched mine. The sort of kiss that should last no longer than a second or two. But his lips stayed on mine, tingling, deepening. He pulled me closer, awakening a hunger I remembered sharing with Rowena Berrysford.

Breathlessly he pulled away, his long eyelashes shadowing his eyes.

'Sorry,' he said, reaching for his glass and draining it in one swallow. 'I don't know what came over me.'

How could he reciprocate my feelings? He didn't have memories of another life to influence his judgement.

I reached for the wine but even my hands betrayed me; shaking, they splashed my drink over the table. Bill jumped up and mopped it with a paper napkin before the puddle dripped onto my new suit.

'Thank you.' It came out too quiet.

He smiled and pecked the tip of my nose. 'My pleasure, madam,' he said, but he remained standing over me, making me aware of his masculinity.

I fidgeted nervously with my pendant.

'That is very beautiful. And unusual, is it very old?'

Relieved that he had sat down again, I relaxed. 'Ancient. I believe it belonged to Rowena Berrysford, but I can't prove it.'

'May I see?'

'Of course, ' I said, trying to unfasten the safety clasp.

He moved behind me I felt the shock as his fingers brushed mine as he helped me to remove the pendant. He studied it closely, turning it over and over in his hand.

'The design is very familiar. I'm sure I've seen something similar before,' he mused. 'Sorry, I can't remember,' Bill said as he passed it back to me, deliberately avoiding contact.

I fastened it around my neck.

'Why don't you show it to an assayer friend of mine, who's reckoned to be an expert on antique jewellery?'

It seemed like a good idea, so I agreed.

After lunch we went to the Archive Department and looked though a lot of Thorotons; Parish records, et cetera, writing down all the relevant names and dates to check on the microfiche.

'Who is the oldest member of your family whom you know the date of death or birth?'

'My great grandfather, Rowan Mayhew; born April 17th 1898, died February 21st 1998.'

'Good innings,' Bill said. 'We'll start with him.'

'His ambition was to live to be a hundred,' I said, smiling at the warm memory. 'He used to say he'd sue Kaiser Wilhelm if he didn't make it.'

Bill grinned, 'Sounds like my kind of man.'

Old Rowan was easy to find as was his parents and their parents too.

'This is where it starts to get a bit tricky,' Bill said. 'Sometimes it's more luck than judgement.'

'Are you sure you have time for all this?' I asked.

'Of course, I'm in my element. Let me show off a little. Please?'

He sounded so much like my William, I had difficulty stopping myself from hugging him. Instead I smiled and nodded, happy just to look at him.

In less than an hour Bill had found Rowena Knight of the tannery, proving she really was my ancestor. He put his hand on my shoulder while we looked into the magnifying screen. People were jostling around us but we were in a world of our own. He must feel the same way as I did... Or was I imagining it because I wanted him so much?

'I've found it best to keep going when you're on a winning streak,' he said. 'What do you say, are you in a hurry to get back?'

'No. Wild horses couldn't drag me away,' I said truthfully.

In less than thirty minutes he exclaimed. 'Darling! Look what I've found!' He pointed to the name on the screen. Rowena Knight's father had married Anne Beaumont, a high born lady from Arnold.

I gasped. He had called me darling!

'Another link of my ancestors to the original owners of Beaumont Hall.' I murmured.

Bill and I read his name, aloud.

'Sergeant Rowan Harris of the 45th Regiment of Foot.'

The screen swirled before my eyes as the room filled with smoke and noise...

CHAPTER NINETEEN.

Sergeant Rowan Harris walked over to his bedraggled men with a heavy heart, remembering how spruce they had been when they had first arrived in their new red uniforms, proudly bearing the forest green facings of Nottingham's 45th Regiment of Foot. Now, their scarlet tunics had faded, and covered in grey dust the green facings were barely discernible.

After months of campaigning, Wellington's troops were beginning to look very ragged. But, dishevelled and unkempt as they appeared, this small army was slowly pushing the might of Napoleon out of the Iberian peninsular.

The men were resting now, taking advantage of the shade from the few sparse trees. The barrels of their Brown Bess muskets, leaning together in tight circles, resembled the cook's bonfires ready to light.

"We go tonight, lads," Rowan said as cheerily as he could. "At night fall. It will be bayonets all the way, so get them honed. You will be issued with sixty cartridges of ammunition but God help the man who dares to load."

Muttered protests and objections came from a smattering of the men.

"Like it or lump it, Wellington wants s action to be swift and silent. A man with just his bayonet to fight with, will not delay in getting to close grips with the enemy."

Wellington also didn't the looting which was commonplace in his army. But Rowan would ensure his Company behaved with honour.

The sun burned the back of his neck and the glare reflected from the white rocks, hurt his eyes. He shifted his position and leant on his halberd as he studied the walls of the besieged city for the thousandth time. Badajoz.

Just one more fortress town to be captured. One more bloody battle to be fought.

"We are to attack over the Mill Dam. The charges to go first, to blow a breach in the wall and the ladders to follow. We are to *form the right column with a detachment of the 88th. But Badajoz is ours, eh lads?"*

He had a score to settle with a sergeant in the 88th Company, a man of his own village, Coleman was responsible for the deaths of two of Rowan's best men when he had "mislaid" an order warning of an ambush. Not only that, but the man had been promoted on very dubious grounds after the regular sergeant had been shot in the back, allegedly by a sniper but there wasn't an attack and no witnesses either.

Rowan's Company, worked up with thoughts of glory, cheered.

"That's the spirit! Now eat and get some rest. Sleep if you can, there's a long night's work ahead of us."

The 45th were given the honour of leading the assault on the walls of Badajoz. He had been in enough battles to have no illusions about this one. There would be death and pain and fear, that above all, fear. No matter how often you overcame it, fear always returned to belittle your courage.

He was not afraid of death itself, but that it took him with the long drawn out agony that reduced a man's dignity. He prayed that when his time came he would die quickly, without the suffering which had accompanied so many on their last journey. But enough of these maudlin thoughts. He had just heard that he had become a father and was determined to go home after this battle was won.

His wife, Ann, had given birth to a baby girl, who would be christened, as was the custom in his family, Rowena. When he got back to his bivouac, as usual before a battle, he wrote to his loved ones. A brief letter to his mother then a long one to his wife, thanking her for his new born babe, enclosing his talisman to be given to keep the child safe. He also dashed of a note to welcome his daughter into the world, promising, God willing, to see her soon.

Then, taking his own advice, he settled down to rest, knowing that sleep would be impossible before the uncertainty of battle. If only that were true. For Rowan, life held few uncertainties.

He had always been a solitary creature, man and boy. He'd had to be, for he had learned early in life that not everyone had his power.

It had been quite simple at first, a knowledge of the outcome of events before they happened but as he'd grown older so the power had increased, until he could sometimes alter the outcome. To his horror, he'd discovered that by touching a man he knew if their death was imminent. But more often than not, their deaths were inevitable. So now, he avoided close contact with anyone. To know who would die and how, would drive a man mad.

After an hour he ate a little hard bread, washed down with some watered down wine and meticulously checked his weapons before going to assemble the men.

As the sun sank in the fiery sky, the vast army stirred. The fact that they were moving again brought an undertow of excitement and a sharp awareness of the senses that Rowan liked.

Dust and flies rose from the ground, mingling with the smoke of the camp fires. The air was filled with the sounds of men and horses; coarse laughter interspersed with the rhythmic beat of tramping feet as Company after Company formed up.

The men of the 45th were shuffling into line, hiding their nervous apprehension behind masks of bravado. Their muskets glowed with a dull sheen, whilst bayonets shone red, reflecting the final rays of the sun as if they were already dipped in blood.

"We lead the attack across the Mill Dam from Picurina Fort to scale the walls of the citadel, whilst the other divisions advance through the breeches we have made," Rowan said, oozing confidence. If only it were that easy! They had, after all, been bombarding those walls for twelve days.

"The charges are to go first," Rowan repeated the orders, "and four ladders to follow..."

He was interrupted by a ripple of laughter from the ranks and turned to see what was amusing the men.

A small figure, heavily laden with kit and drum was running towards him. Davy Keeton, the drummer boy, twelve years old and hardly bigger than his drum, came rushing up with all the speed that his short legs could muster.

His uniform was in the Regiments reversed colours to signify his vocation. The dark green jacket with scarlet facings contrasted vividly with the rest of the Company's red coats. It was lavishly decorated with braided chevrons running down the sleeves, the lacings arranged in bastion shaped pairs which fastened the rows of pewter buttons.

Well brushed and polished the drummer looked quite splendid even though his uniform was as faded as the rest of the Light Company's.

As he arrived abreast of Rowan, the weight of the drum coupled with his momentum caused him to over balance and he fell in a tangle, losing his Shako, which rolled away, disappearing in the half light.

Automatically, Rowan reached down and grasped the lad's elbow to help him up. A violent shock ran through his hands and up his arms, draining the colour from his sun burned face. With a sharp intake of breath he staggered back a step, only vaguely aware of the appreciative guffaws from the men, who thankfully thought he was clowning.

In his minds eye Rowan saw Davy stumble over a grenade the French had lobbed over the wall. The young drummer boy lay dying at his feet, the blast had taken off his leg and most of his arm. Blood was spreading in a wide pool around the boy's head like a halo from hell.

"Drummer Keeton reporting, Sergeant Harris."

Rowan took a deep breath and frowned sternly at him.

Davy looked a little sheepish, aware of the amusement his undignified arrival had caused.

Still unnerved by his vision, Rowan tut tutted and shook his head, giving himself time to think. He forced his face into a wide grin and winked at the men, who roared with laughter, releasing their pre battle tension.

"You are late, Drummer Keeton," he said, smiling as he knew how he could save the lad. "But no mind, you shouldn't be here at all. This is supposed to be a surprise attack and we don't want you warning every Frenchman in Badajoz with your awful drumming!"

He sauntered in the direction of the lad's Shako and with great display, picked it up and twirled it around his fingers as he marched back to the red faced boy, feeling guilty at adding to his embarrassment.

Better to suffer humiliation at the hands of a friend than death at the hands of an enemy, Rowan thought as he planted the hat, with it's bent and bedraggled green plume, firmly on Drummer Keeton's head.

"Be off with you," he ordered, straight faced and pointed towards the tent. Tapping the top of Davy's Shako with a marching beat, he deliberately grasped him by the shoulder and propelled the lad in the direction of his bivouac, saying a thankful prayer that the spectre of death had left the young drummer boy.

He breathed a sigh of relief; the power of second sight could sometimes be of great benefit.

"You can guard my traps until I return, and use the time to practice the drum roll for our victory march!" he said.

The men laughed and made noises of approval, cheered by the sergeant's confidence.

Davy left, dragging his feet like a reluctant martyr as he struggled with the heavy drum. When he looked back in dog eyed appeal, Rowan winked and jerked his thumb for him to be off.

Straightening his shoulders the lad nodded and marched back to the tents beating a perfect victory roll.

Sergeant Harris marched his men in quick time, four running steps and four strides.

They passed the 88th with practised ease, not through any great act of heroism on their part; as veterans of this campaign they knew that being either first or last in a battle was always safest. The enemy were either caught off guard and unprepared, or were depleted and low on ammunition.

The newly promoted sergeant of the 88th stood aside and waved them on. As he passed, Rowan felt the hairs on the back of his neck rise as if Sergeant Coleman had him in the sights of his rifle.

"Light company, be ready," Rowan ordered. "Remember, do not load your muskets, Wellington wants no shooting until you are inside the citadel."

A muttered growl came from the men, signifying acknowledgement but not necessary approval of Wellington's order.

"Forward the 45th!"

Firmly grasping his halberd, Rowan started the advance.

Behind him, his company, bayonets fixed, clattered across the uneven cobbles on the road.

As they came within twenty yards of the walls, they were met by a hail of musket fire. The balls made a strange high pitched buzz like a million angry wasps as they flew overhead.

Above the thunder of the weapons, Rowan heard the screams of the dying as the musket balls struck their targets.

The noise and smoke gave the scene a hell like quality. Men moved through the pall of smoke like ghosts the faint red haze of their jackets, lightened and dulled by wear and dust, added to the wraith like spectre as they faded in and out of his vision.

Ahead of him, his men were lighting the fuse to the charges they'd placed against the base of the fortress's high wall, impeded by the Frenchies throwing grenades over the parapet. Fortunately the long spluttering fuses often went out as they spun clumsily from the great height but the heavy powder filled balls could do serious damage if they landed on your head.

Almost immediately the world erupted into a flash of bright light as with a deafening roar the charges exploded.

The men with the scaling ladders ignored the explosions and methodically placed them against the tower; scrambling up like monkeys, only to fall back as they reached the top, shot or bayoneted by the defenders.

The air reeked with the acrid stench of gun powder and the metallic smell of blood.

The 45th were caught like rabbits in the range of fire as the 88th came up behind them. Once more Coleman seemed to be deliberately using the 45th for cover as he dithered, reluctant to give his men the order to scale the walls to support Rowan's Company.

Encouraging his men up the ladders Rowan stepped over a dud grenade, waving the 88th on.

Coleman stared at him with icy hatred

In an instant Rowan knew.

He saw again young Davy Keeton stumble over a grenade the French had lobbed over the wall.

The drummer had not stumbled, he'd dived over it.

Rowan looked down in horror as the blackened burnt out fuse ignited and fizzled instantly to the lead casing.

Young Davy had been going to save his life.

Coleman grinned as the explosion blasted Rowan into a blood red pulp.

"The last of the bloody Rowans!" he sneered triumphantly.

According to eye witnesses Sergeant Rowan Harris died in a freak accident when what appeared to be a dud grenade suddenly exploded on the dusty battle field of Badajoz...

CHAPTER TWENTY.

I sat in the quiet room of the records office, the sight, sound and smell of the battle surrounding me; trying to get my head round the fact that I had not died at Badajoz...

Bill hunched down by my chair and wiped away the tears that were coursing down my cheeks.

'What happened, love? Are you alright?'

'Coleman killed him. That bastard lit the fuse on an unexploded grenade... And he didn't use no matches to do it neither!' It was as if someone else was speaking for me.

Bill looked at me oddly, switched off the screen and picked up my bag, swinging it over his shoulder as he helped me to my feet.

I walked unsteadily out of the building, over the patterned bricks towards the Celica, taking deep gulps of the sweet scented air to erase the smell of Rowan's blood from my memory.

Once sitting in the safety of the luxurious car, I relaxed. Before he drove off, Bill phoned his office and pressing a button, the sun roof slid back, revealing a patch of painfully bright sky.

'After finding Rowan Harris, the next step might not be so easy,' he told me. 'If Rowan's mother was a Rowena, we'll have a lot of searching to do and the further back we go, the murkier and more casual the records become,' he said, as he competently eased the Celica into Wilford Street.

'Would you like me to take you home? This has been far more traumatic for you than I thought.'

I wasn't very enamoured with the idea of parting so soon.

'Or is there anything else you'd like to do?' he continued. 'A drive in the country? I'm completely at your disposal, my love.'

Thrilled by his offer, it nonetheless reminded me. 'Would you mind dropping me off to pick up my car? It's at the showroom on Mansfield Road. '

'No problem. As long as you agree to see me again,' he said, not looking at me.

I almost blurted out that I wanted to see him, touch him and be near to him all the time, but stopped myself just in time.

Bill mistook my hesitation for uncertainty. 'If I promise to behave like a gentleman?' he begged. 'Where's the harm in it?'

The tension between us; his shaking hands and my desperate need was proof of where the harm lay.

He reminded me too much of William for our friendship to be platonic. But the thought of not seeing him again was too much to bear. As for James trying his best to win me back. I didn't care. This was Bill.

'Of course. Where's the harm indeed?' I said.

We drove to town on a bright, busy, afternoon. But I wanted to... Well, Bill knew what I wanted to do.

Instead, I sucked my fingertip and touched it to his lips.

He gasped as if I'd electrocuted him and swerved the Celica into a club's car park near the showroom.

Almost before the car had stopped his arm was around my shoulders pulling me towards him. His lips found mine and we kissed with the certain knowledge that we belonged together and nothing would ever be the same again.

When we could tear ourselves apart we stared at each other. I was trying to imprint his image in my heart. As if I would ever forget.

But we must wait a little longer for it to be right. I unfastened my seat belt.

'Not here,' I whispered as I opened the door. 'And not now, darling.'

'I've searched for you all my life, Rowena. You will see me again, won't you?' He caught my hand and pressed my palm to his lips.

I stiffened as the shock of recognition ran through me. William had done that so many times. I ran from him whilst my legs were still obeying my will.

'Yes.'

'May I phone you tomorrow?'

Not daring to look back I slowed my steps and waved my hand in assent. 'Please.'

Then before my legs rebelled and carried me back to him, I walked to the car showroom, full of wonder that destiny had brought us together at last.

My new car was ready and waiting for me, shiny bright and full petrol. I deliberately pushed aside the reason that I needed a new car. And the crash into the tree where Mistress Berrysford was hanged. Life was good and I was in love.

On my way home I drove past my solicitors and abruptly pulled in to his forecourt. How could I have forgotten Douglas Jeacock? He could probably throw some light on the mystery surrounding my ancestors and the Colemans.

'Do you think I could speak to your father?' I asked John Jeacock. 'I'm trying to trace my ancestors and just remembered that Mr Douglas (as they called him in the office) was my mothers solicitor and it's most likely that our family have used this firm for generations. Do you know if he's kept the records very far back?'

'Not only that but he can probably quote you chapter and verse on most of them!' John chuckled.

'Putting the old documents into some sort of order has been a labour of love since he retired.'

We fixed a time for me to see him and John assured me the old man would be delighted to help me. I knew Bill would be pleased by my initiative.

'And I want to change my will,' I told him. 'Take James out except for the house. He can still have the property he helped me to buy but I want the rest to be divided between my step children, Justin and Susan but I'd like Debra to have my car.' I filled in the names and addresses, glanced through his notes and signed them. John promised it was legal but he'd have a proper document typed up for me when I came to see his father.

That taken care of I drove home in my gleaming black and tan charger.

The builders had my kitchen wall almost up to window height. I was amazed at the speed which the work was progressing.

'Hi!' I smiled at Albert who was taking a tea break, sitting on the rockery by the fish pond, keeping an eye on Cassidy in the garden.

The air was redolent with the scent of lilac and apart from the slap of cement on bricks the only sound was the sleepy buzzing of the bees.

'Bring a cup and come and share my coffee, it's lovely out here.'

'Alright, I'll nip up and change out of my glad rags and join you in a moment!'

Bill; finding my kinship with Rowena Knight, even discovering the death of Rowan at the hands of a murdering Coleman, all combined to infuse my senses with joie de vivre. But Of course I was kidding myself. It was all down to Bill.

Every step back into the past took me closer to William and Rowena Berrysford and their beautiful baby daughter. And, I reminded myself as I slipped into a pair of jeans and a T-shirt, I was now the proud owner of a sleek new car.

Rushing back and sitting beside Albert on the rockery, I admired the unique tranquillity of an English garden. There had never been so many blossoms as there were this Spring; a sure sign of a long hot summer to come. It seemed to shimmer with expectancy.

My heart ached for Bill yet soared with the certainty that he loved me.

'It's been a wonderful day,' I whispered, hugging myself.

Albert smiled, filling my cup from his flask. 'Good! We can all do with a day like that now and then.

I told him about our finding records of Rowan Harris. 'The father of Rowena Knight of the tannery. Genealogy is fascinating isn't it? I could easily become addicted.'

'You're as bad as our Bill,' he paused and looked me in the eyes. 'You do know he's smitten with you?'

I felt the blush rising with the glow his words brought to me. 'Albert! I don't know what you mean.'

He looked away sadly. 'I'm not a fool, Rowena. I am very fond of you. Too fond, considering you're not really family. But

I wouldn't like to see either of you get hurt,' he said quietly, as he sat drinking his coffee.

He was right of course. There was James who was not to be dismissed lightly. And there was something else to consider. Something I had to do. Something which would place all my loved ones in jeopardy. It was one of those things I knew without question. There was a fight ahead of such proportions that nothing should stand in my way.

With a mood swing more typical of a lovesick teenager, tears threatened to overflow.

'I wouldn't hurt him for the world, Albert,' I whispered.

'Yes, love, I know that. But it is too late now, isn't it? It was always too late.'

Idly, I started pulling out some of the overgrown water lilies which were smothering all the other plants in the pond. Yes, it was too late, someone was going to be dreadfully hurt.

A chill coursed through me as the sun disappeared behind a cloud and the first premonition that something was wrong inched into my brain.

I called Cassidy, needing a cuddle. But he wouldn't come near me. Since the episode with George, he avoided the pond like the plague.

Convincing myself that it was nothing more than a change in the wind direction, I rubbed the goose bumps on my arms, determined that nothing should spoil my day in the sun.

Seeing something glistening on the bottom of the pond I delved up to my elbows in water and pulled the object out.

'My back door key. Of course. George must have thrown it in here with Cassidy.'

I looked at my demolished kitchen and laughed. The sound was hollow in my ears.

'It isn't much good to anyone now. But how did he get in without it?' I asked.

'How could anyone get into a locked house without leaving signs of a break in?' I was half convinced that the Colemans had supernatural powers.

Albert looked at me and I could see a light dawning in his eyes. 'It might be easy in an old building like this,' he said.

Cassidy and I followed him inside, Cass trotting to his basket in the front room while Albert found a couple of torches.

'We're going up to the loft, I promised Mr Roberts I'd check out the water cistern,' he told Bert.

I went with him to the top floor and gave him the thingamajig that opened the access door to the roof and the ladder automatically folded down.

I watched Albert disappear into the loft and with a sense of foreboding, I followed.

He was shining the torch about, but it was lighter than I expected because of the daylight coming in from under the eaves.

'Is it supposed to be as open as this?' I asked.

'Yes. It needs a through draft. All these old houses are the same. But do you notice anything else, Rowena?' he sounded well pleased with himself.

The attic was huge and surprisingly long.

'I had no idea that it was so big,' I said, whispering. 'But the stink is awful!' I was coughing with the stench and dust.

'It smells as if a pigeon has died up here,' Albert said, shining his torch around the eaves.

The thick grey fibreglass insulation was littered with rags and I walked over to a lump where the padding had been rolled back. A large ashtray full of cigarette ends was sitting on top of the lagging with a familiar looking rag at the side of it.

Picking it up, I stared at it blankly, hardly able to believe what I was seeing. It was peach silk and trimmed with lace.

A thin finger of light poked up from the attic floor where it had lain.

Albert came over to me, 'Someone has drilled a hole through your ceiling,' he muttered.

We both bent over to check it out and peered into my bedroom.

Looking at the lace trimmed silk again I recognised it for what it was; one of my stolen nighties. Dirty and stiff with semen

Albert realised it at the same time.

'George! Filthy peeping Tom!' he said, picking up another wrinkled piece of my expensive lingerie and putting it in his pocket. 'In case you need evidence,' he said.

George had stolen my clothes so he could watch me wander around my bedroom naked. And wank himself off into my underwear. I hung my head, hot with embarrassment and found myself staring at the ash tray.

'George doesn't smoke,' I croaked. 'They were both up here. George and Piers, egging each other on. '

Somehow that made the obscenity ten times worse.

'We'll plaster that up for you right now, Rowena, and I'll brick up the communal access.'

The awful stench was fogging my brain. 'What are you talking about?'

'The roof space is shared, love. All the Colemans have to do is go up through the access in their storage barn and come down into your house through yours.'

'Oh my God!' I shivered in the humid air. 'Can you fix it now? Please, Albert?'

I felt like weeping with humiliation at the thought of them gloating over me, knowing they could get in and rape or murder me in my bed, any time they wanted to. It must have added spice to their masturbation.

'Don't fret, duck, I'll see its bricked up if I have to stay here all night,' he said, walking over to check the water tank.

Like a lost lamb, I followed him.

'Sweet Jesus!'

Albert had lifted the loose wooden cover from the tank and stood staring into it. He turned away and gasped. 'Don't look, Rowena!'

But, too late, I saw him floating there...

Buggalugs.

'Oh, God.' Automatically I reached out for my lovely cat, wanting to cuddle him better even as my mind registered his mutilation.

Why didn't I "see" him in time to save him? He didn't deserve to be tortured to death. Swallowing hard to prevent myself from being sick I noticed that Albert too, was retching as he put his arm into the water and pulled out my once beautiful cat.

Stiff and bloated, Buggalugs' neck was almost sawn through and his stomach was split open, the once white fur on his underbelly was watered down red and matted with gore.

Rigid, I was unable to turn away from the dreadful sight even as I fought the waves of nausea which churned my stomach. Blinded by tears my mind replayed the vision of the child Rowena, watching Coleman bend over the trapped hare and twist the poor things neck.

Albert took the nightie from me and wrapped it round the sodden corpse of my beloved cat.

'Come on, Rowena, enough is enough!' he said, as he led me to the ladder.

The attic bucked beneath my feet but he restrained me before I fell headlong down the gaping hole. Glad of his strong arm, I reached the safety of the landing and rushed into my office, where in the privacy of my room I could hold back my grief no longer.

Swearing and mutterings came from the builders as Albert told them what we had found.

'I'd swing for the stupid "do gooder" that let the bugger out,' Bert said, identifying George as the culprit.

'Don't give any of them the satisfaction of knowing Rowena is upset,' Albert told them. 'I'll take Buggalugs home with me and give him a decent burial in my garden.

One of the lads said he wished he could bury the sick bastard that did it.

I couldn't get over the fact that all the while I'd been searching for him, Buggalugs was dead. Mutilated and thrown into my water tank. No wonder the water smelled awful. They probably thought it was the drinking water, I realised, my grief hardening into furious anger.

Albert tapped on my door and came in. 'I took the liberty of bringing you this,' he said, giving me a large glass of Brandy. 'I hope you don't mind, I poured one for myself too.'

He raised his glass. 'Drink it, duck. It'll do you good.'

I tried to smile before I took a deep swallow.

'About Buggalugs,' he cleared his throat.

'I heard you talking to Bert,' I said, sipping the warming spirit. Then I remembered Mistress Berrysford's cat, Tinker, playing under the cherry trees in the garden, so long ago.

'I'd like you to bury him in the orchard, if you wouldn't mind,' I asked, trying not to think of my lovely Buggalugs as dead, but rather as if he was going to sleep underneath the beautiful cherry blossoms. 'I mean Bill's orchard,' I said, 'If he wouldn't mind?'

'Of course he won't, love. And Buggalugs would like it there. I'll see to it for you, I promise. He was such a friendly fellow.'

Albert took a sip of the brandy. Like me, he was trying not to think of the way we had just seen him.

'Bert has gone to fetch some breeze blocks, you won't need facing bricks or anything fancy for the roof space.' He was at a loss for words and trying to bring me back to normality.

'Thank you, Albert,' I said and held out my arms.

He came over and held me, patting my back, while I cried for Buggalugs, Bill, "my" baby, William and Rowena, and for James and myself.

We stood comforting each other until we heard Bert come clomping upstairs carrying the building materials.

'I'll be back in a short while,' Albert said as he went to the door. 'Don't worry about the attic, not even a fly will be able to get in by the time we've finished.'

'Thank you Albert,' I said.

Taking another sip of Brandy I tried to force my life back into it's normal routine. I needed to work this out so Bill would not be hurt. As for me. Well, so be it.

To get away from the noise of the builders up in the loft, I checked the kitchen and dining room. There was a lot of mess to clean up; at least it would keep me busy, thank God; I felt as restless as a caged tiger.

The thought of the Colemans watching me, kept coming into my mind. Piers and George gloating together. I saw him glaring at me out of one eye, knew he had been spying on us when James and I made love. Him and Piers. They probably told the titbits to their father too. Damn them all. Jerking themselves off into my lingerie, with the dreadful sickly sweet smell of my cat decomposing beside them.

I replenished my glass and took another sip to calm my queasy stomach. My poor little Buggalugs.

I picked up Cassidy and staring out of the window cuddling him, I was incensed with anger when Sebastian and Piers walked across the courtyard, George shambling behind them.

'You murdering perverts!' I whispered, glaring at Piers through narrowed eyes.

His bandaged foot reminded me of what he had done to Cassidy.

You will not harm me or mine so easily again, I thought. Hard.

As if they had heard, Piers and his father looked up at me simultaneously.

I hated Sebastian for breeding the likes of his sons. Drawing together all my inner strength I mentally thrust my hand against his chest and thumped him with my mind, knocking him backwards.

He fell heavily onto the gravelled path and lay there struggling for breath.

'What the blazes did you do that for?' he bellowed at his son.

'Do what? I didn't do anything,' Piers said, looking down at his father with a puzzled frown.

'You pushed me. I felt your hand on my chest.'

I watched the process as his brain struggled to come to terms with its input. Piers was walking beside him, how could he have shoved him? His eyes locked with mine and I saw the fear as he realised what had happened.

My mind kicked Piers crutches away and he fell on his backside, sprawling on top of his father.

'She did it!'

George was blubbering, frightened when he saw me at my dining room window.

They held on to each other and pointed at me with shaking fingers.

'Witch!' they whispered.

'It takes one to know one,' I grinned, feeling like Arnie in the Terminator. 'This is not the seventeenth century. You can accuse me of witchcraft if you want to be laughed out of office. This time I am not an innocent like Rowena Berrysford. Not only have I the power but I have the freedom to use it.' I said, knowing they heard every word.

But as the rush of adrenaline depleted, I felt cold and clammy; my ears were buzzing and black spots massed together behind my eyes. I drained the Brandy before I passed out.

They knew. The Colemans had recognised my power and were afraid of me.

Then they too possessed the art, I reasoned. The Black art. There would be no holds barred now. I was in more danger than ever, but then... So were they.

I narrowed my eyes and watched the three of them rush in to Beaumont Hall. Resting my forehead on the cool glass of the window, I realised that I could have killed them. Could have stopped their hearts.

I shied away from the thought of what I could do. The power must be used only in life threatening situations or... Or I would become like them.

'Sweet Lord protect me,' I whispered. 'Lead me not into temptation.'

For I knew such hatred would not be denied. And I was only human.

CHAPTER TWENTY ONE.

I watched James walk past the dining room window and come breezing in, full of the joys of spring. It didn't seem fair to upset him.
'What do you want?' I asked. I really must get back my door key.
'I've come to tell you some good news.' He put the kettle on and noticed my brandy glass.
'It's a bit early for the hard stuff, isn't it?' he asked. 'I don't suppose you want a cup of tea?'
Our conversations had developed into an art of communication on two levels, the civilised words and the unspoken criticism which lay hidden beneath.
'No thank you,' I replied abruptly, too tired to continue playing games.
He didn't offer coffee, and I decided to cut through this crap. 'But I would like my door keys back please. This is my house and I'll thank you not to come without an invitation.'
I heard my voice but to be honest, didn't sound at all like me. Was this a symptom of extreme exhaustion? I'd hardly the strength to stand up. "Mental energy takes ten times more effort than the same physical activity," I remembered. And I felt as if I'd just done a Basho with a Sumo wrestler.
James looked surprised at my outburst; give him his due, he also looked a little sheepish.
'I'm sorry, dear, I only popped in to tell you the news. Is anything wrong? You don't usually drink this early. Would you like to get out of this bomb site and come out to dinner with me?'
He was making himself a cup of tea when he noticed the noise.
'What on earth are the builders doing here at this time of night?'
'I'm sorry, James, there isn't an easy way to tell you this.' I swallowed the lump in my throat. 'Buggalugs is dead. Albert and

I found him mutilated in the water tank with his neck broken.' I spared him the gory details.

'Oh, Rowena.'

James rushed over to my side and put his arm around me, obviously upset and close to tears. I wondered for a moment what he thought he was doing, it seemed so strange, like an embrace from a complete stranger.

'I'm so sorry, darling. Please forgive me, I've been acting like an idiot. My only defence is that I was jealous.'

He led me into the comparative comfort of the lounge. 'Sit down dear, I'll make you a cup of coffee.' He picked up the brandy bottle and noted the contents. 'Or would you prefer another glass of this?'

He was trying not to sound sarcastic, so I shook my head. 'Coffee would be nice.'

'Will Instant be OK? It's quicker...'

'Fine, thank you.'

James smiled and went to the kitchen.

'Why *are* the builders still here?' he asked when he returned with my coffee. 'It's a bit late for them isn't it?' he asked, looking at the clock.

He went pale as I recited as calmly as I could, what they were doing and why. By the time I had finished he was shaking with anger.

'Bastard! I'll kill him! Spying on me.' He strode round the cluttered room leaving clouds of plaster dust in his wake. 'The simpleton ought to be locked up.'

'There was an ashtray full of cigarette butts up there, James. George doesn't smoke. If it was him he wasn't alone.'

'Oh God, that makes me feel unclean. They must have been watching us every time we... I'm sorry, Rowena, I should have listened to you but I was so angry.'

James was holding my hand trying to make me understand. I knew that what he was trying to tell me was important but I couldn't work up much enthusiasm.

'Why, dear, what had I done to annoy you?'

'I tried to tell you when I came back from London last week.'

'Last week?' I asked lamely. Was it only a week ago when James had come round in such a foul mood?

Wondering what James was trying to explain, I pushed the image of my cat floating in the water tank out of my mind and concentrated on what he was saying.

'I parked the car by the side of the barn and overheard the Colemans talking about you.'

'Well?' I demanded, losing my patience. 'What on earth could they possibly say that you believed about me?'

'They said they had seen you in the garden with a man. They called him your bit of rough. And you were whispering sweet nothings.'

'So?' I asked, but it didn't really matter.

'They saw you take off your jumper and he...'

'Held me in his arms?' I interrupted.

'They said you were clinging to him half dressed in the garden and he carried you indoors like a bloody caveman.'

James was trying to be reasonable and I could see what he was accusing me of but I could not pretend righteous indignation. If it had been Bill.

'Yes. That's true, every word of it.'

I was tempted to leave it at that, but James looked so hurt and stricken, it would not be fair.

Raising his hand to my lips I kissed it, sorry for my callous thought.

'Only it was not a bit of rough, it was Mel, and we had just found Cassidy in the pond. I forgot about proprieties and wrapped my half drowned dog in my sweater. The sweet nothings they overheard were meant for Cassidy. I was distraught and Mel was kind enough to help me back into the house.'

James said he was sorry and I was too, because it was, as Albert had said, too late.

I kissed his cheek, 'It doesn't matter, dear.' And it really didn't.

'I should have known there was a logical explanation.'

I couldn't help grinning, 'Yes, you of all people should have known that.'

'But you needn't worry about the Colemans any more, Rowena. Everything will be alright, just you wait and see.' James said, being macho and chivalrous.

Albert popped his head round the door. 'We're going now, everything is finished, duck. Good night, Rowena, you'll be safe now.'

He nodded to James. 'We've bricked up the attic on your dividing line and put a couple of bolts outside the trap door too.'

He turned to me, 'See you in the morning. Try and get some rest, love.'

Looking at the kind old man I noticed that his face had lost it's healthy glow and he looked his age. It had been an upsetting experience for him too.

'I will, Albert and you do the same.'

I went over and hugged him, not caring what James thought about my over familiarity. To me Albert was a dear friend.

'Thank you for everything you've done for me today. Good night and God bless you.'

When the builders had left, James locked the doors and sat on his haunches in front of me, looking at me earnestly. 'I've had the offer of a year's sabbatical in Toronto, giving lecture tours all over Ontario. It is just what you need to get away from all this. You need a break, sweetheart.'

He paused for breath, then added as a clincher, 'And you would be near to your mother.'

I was appalled, I didn't want to go to Canada, I wanted to be near Bill. I wanted to find Rowena. Had to find her! And I couldn't leave Bill, not know. Not ever.

The thoughts surged into my head in a split second along with the knowledge that I had to have a damn good reason for refusing, what was on the face of it the perfect solution to my problems with the Colemans. I must not forget the Colemans.

'I can't go with you, James. I've got far too much to do I can't leave the house in this state.'

'But, Rowena, look at yourself, you look quite ill! It's a wonderful opportunity for us to make a fresh start. You can rent this place easily, I could probably get it taken by a visiting lecturer, and you can freelance anywhere, if you're worried about your work?'

'I'm in the middle of this investigation.'

'Give your findings to Jayne Vincent, she'll sort out another reporter, come to that, with fax machines and e-mail, she'll hardly know you've gone.'

'But what about Susan and Justin?'

'I'll call to see Justin first thing in the morning if you'll give Susan a ring?'

'She'll take the news better from you.'

'I know but tell her I'll come to see her or perhaps she can come here for a few days?'

James and I had parted after Justin married Debra and moved into a flat but Susan always came home to me.

'That's impossible, with the place in such a mess,' I said, casting for a lifeline. 'And where would we live in Canada? You know my mother hasn't got room for us to stay with her for long.'

'That's the beauty of it. I am being given a rent free, fully furnished, four bedroom detached house in Mississauga, a few miles outside Toronto. Your mother could come and visit, she will be company for you while I'm on tour.'

James was right, it should have been a dream come true. If only this had happened two weeks ago. But going with him would not only keep me away from the Colemans but away from Bill. I could not leave him now. It was unthinkable.

James went on about the fantastic money and standard of living we would enjoy, and I couldn't think of a valid argument against it.

'The only snag is...'

I paid close attention to " The Snag."

'The problem is, this post was originally offered to a friend of mine from Leeds. His wife has just discovered she is pregnant with their first child and there are complications so he declined the offer at the last minute. What I mean to say is...'

'Yes?'

'I would have to leave almost immediately.'

I tried not to show my relief. He had said "I" not we.

'But I can't possibly leave with the builders half finished and there's no way I could rent it to anyone while it's in this mess.'

'I know, darling, I thought we might find an agent to make proper arrangements,' he smiled ruefully, 'but it doesn't matter, I won't go. In the circumstances I can't leave you like this.'

'Nonsense!' The last thing I wanted was for him to change his mind. 'I'll manage.'

The thought of being on my own in this house curdled my stomach. Maybe it wasn't such a good idea to stay here after all.

James put his arm around my shoulder and squeezed reassuringly. 'I know you will, dear. You could join me later, though.'

Funny, but I suddenly felt that I had been conned. 'It won't be easy,' I told him, not letting him off the hook so lightly. 'Anyway, I'm still not sure that I want to go to Canada with you.' I stared into his eyes without flinching at the surprised anger there. I was definitely burning my boats.

'I'm not a fool, James. Maybe we should use this opportunity to make a clean break.'

'If that's what you want, it's your decision. Perhaps you will come to your senses before I go,' he snapped.

I couldn't believe my ears. James didn't want me to go with him at all.

'I've made up my mind. You go, I can certainly manage without you,' I said, scarcely able to believe the abrupt about turn our conversation had taken.

Putting out my hand I opened the door. 'My keys.'

'Rowena, there is no need for this.'

'Please,' I said, wiggling my fingers impatiently.

James dug out a large bunch of keys from his pocket and took off a small key ring, which we had bought in Niagara Falls. I blinked the tears from my eyes as I took it from him. 'Thank you.'

I closed and bolted the door, not wanting to see him stalk away. Then running upstairs I closeted myself in my office, upset that James had given in so quickly.

Then I picked up the folder Alice had given me and John Baker's dissertation put everything else from my mind.

I read his notes with growing horror. He discovered the virus insecticide was being produced by a company called Arland. After searching through the Register of Key British Companies I found it wasn't listed. Even so, after all his research I couldn't believe that John would deliberately mislead so I tried A R Land but still nothing.

Even if it was under a holding company the name at least would be registered. My cynical nature insisted that I checked the Colemans investments in their holding company. And discovered Arnold Hauliers were a subsidiary of Ernehale Holdings. Coleman had used his own company to dispose of the toxic waste.

I sat back and massaged my aching neck. No doubt Sebastian would plead ignorance and twist it to his advantage. Glancing at the window I saw my reflection mirrored by the darkness outside. For a moment I felt lonely and vulnerable, knowing that the Colemans could see my light burning like a beacon. And I was alone in the house.

Drawing the curtains, I shouted Cassidy, wanting him by my side. He came gallumping up the stairs on his three little legs, making me smile at his agility and awkward grace. We had a good cuddle before he settled at my feet while I read the International Index, which by necessity only listed the largest companies of each country, but I looked anyway, to no avail.

If Arland was American or based in the far east I'd have no chance of fulfilling the reporters creed... Who owned the company. What they were doing. Where they were doing it, and when.

According to John Baker, Arland set about selling the deadly Scorpion virus product to the third world for direct consumer testing. Thank God, Dr. Baker could use her influence to stop this company inflicting this madness on mankind.

I started typing the article, leaving out the crucial information such as who was behind this diabolical marketing promotion. At least that couldn't be laid at Coleman's door.

When I had finished typing, the silence of the darkest hours crept up on me and carrying Cass, I rushed to my bedroom, put him in his basket and undressed in the dark.

Feeling a bit foolish I walked round my room reciting the spell I'd read of, which promised protection from evil spirits.

Physical danger was taken care of now the Colemans no longer had access via my loft, but if they could reach out mentally, I needed all the protection I could muster.

The spell must have helped because I fell asleep as if I hadn't a care in the world.

CHAPTER TWENTY TWO.

Early in the morning I phoned my mother, forgetting that it was two a.m. in Ontario. Fortunately, being a bit of an insomniac, she had just gone to bed. I told her of James' imminent arrival and she was delighted but began to pressure me to go over with him. I needed her here, not the other way round. I found myself almost begging her to come home. At least for a holiday.

'I can't babe,' she used her pet endearment to soften the blow. 'Phil's asked me to marry him and I've accepted.'

Before I had time to digest this news, she carried on blithely. 'But I promise we will come for a visit before the wedding. We might even spend our honeymoon in England.'

I could only splutter my congratulations. After all, it was not exactly unexpected.

'You should pack up and come to Canada with James. I have been a lot happier since I left the old country with all its superstitions and hatreds. You would too, dear.'

This was the closest we had ever come to discussing our strange heritage.

'I can't, I'm researching our ancestors. I want to trace back to Rowena Berrysford in the seventeenth century.'

He reaction surprised me.

'Stop it at once! You'll only bring trouble to yourself, poking about in the past. It's too bad old Rowan isn't alive, he'd tell you the same. No good will come of it.'

I stood looking at the rubble of my demolished kitchen while she bulldozed my deepest need into the ground.

'You should come to Canada with your husband; get away from the Colemans.'

'Why did you say that? I haven't mentioned them.'

'Sebastian owns the place doesn't he? Old Rowan was worried about them living in Arnold and now you live in the same complex. They are evil, Rowena. All of them. I wish you'd listen to me for a change and get away from them.'

'I'm sorry Mother, I can't just sell up and move, I wouldn't even cover my expenses.'

'Some things are worth more that money, babe, your safety is paramount. I worry about you, especially now you're living there all on your own.'

'I'll be Ok, you don't have to worry about me, Mum. But if it makes you feel better I'll come over after you're married, I promise.'

'Why wait? It's isn't as if you've got to give in your notice, you can write anywhere.'

'I know, that's what James said but I'm in the middle of some important research and I want to get to on with our genealogy.'

She sighed and told me to speak to old Mr Jeacock.

'He will be able to help you. Maybe if you go back far enough it will all make sense. I wish you luck, babe. I didn't have the time or, I'm afraid, the courage. I only got as far as Rowena Knight. You know what happened at the tannery?'

I nodded mutely before I realised she couldn't see me. 'Yes, thank you Mum. I've already made an appointment to see Douglas Jeacock.'

Promising to give him her regards and let her know which flight James will be on so she could "surprise" him and meet his plane, I hung up.

Then I phoned Susan and told her that her father was going to Canada for a year and would be leaving shortly. After the usual babble of questions she said she would come home straight away so I checked with Justin and Debra to see if they minded putting her up, as my house was in such a mess; only to find that they didn't know what I was talking about. James hadn't arrived there yet. God knows where he's got to.

Albert and the builders had the new wall up to the top of the door frame by the time James returned three hours later.

I asked him casually where he's been, but he was evasive and angry.

'I've been to see Justin,' he insisted.

'But you weren't there when I phoned them about Susan.'

'What is this? I can go where I like without your permission.'

The truth hit me in an instant. 'Does that include your clandestine meetings with Barbara?'

He blustered and turned on me angrily. 'And how do you know about that? Feminine intuition or your so called powers?'

Before I had a chance to reply Susan came breezing in, putting the argument on hold.

She flew to her father.

He looked disapprovingly at her grey micro skirt, thick tights and trainers.

I grinned at her street wise image; which was only the protective façade of youth. Hugging her, I gave her a kiss.

She smiled and turned back to James. 'Oh Dad, I'm so pleased for you. I'll miss you both of course but it will be great to come and see you in the holidays.'

'Your father's going on his own, ' I told her. 'But no doubt we'll have visiting rights?'

I was deliberately goading him to see how far he would go to perpetuate this charade.

'Mum! You can't let him go on his own.'

Susan was shocked, bless her. It would never enter her head that he might not want me to go with him.

'It's his decision, darling. Anyway, I have to stay here till the house is finished.'

'That's not fair, Rowena. You know I asked you to go with me.'

'Asked, dear, not wanted. And only *after* I've sorted out the house. And the Colemans.'

'What have they been up to now?' Susan asked, breaking the tension that was building up between us again.

'Oh it's just Rowena's imagination, sweetheart. Nothing for you to worry your pretty little head about.'

Susan rolled her eyes to heaven at his patronising cliché.

'Is that your new car outside, Mum?' she asked, going back to open the door for another look. 'The black convertible?'

'Yes,' I grinned, jangling the keys. Then seeing the lecherous look in Piers eyes, I pulled her indoors.

'Wow. May I take it for a drive?'

I hated to come on like the stereotypical step-mother but I really didn't want her to drive my car, especially with Piers watching.

'Why? Where have you got to dash off too, young lady? I'll give you a lift, I have to go to the University first though,' James interjected. 'I have to sort out my salary and arrange for some time off before I leave,' he explained.

Susan pulled a face. 'I've forgotten to bring my laundry and I have nothing to wear,' she said, panic stricken at the thought of going around naked.

'Here.' James took out four or five twenty's. 'Buy yourself something. And make sure it covers more of you than that outfit.'

'You're so old fashioned,' she gave him a hug and a loud kiss on the top of his head as she took the money. 'But sweet. Thank you.'

'It's cheaper in the long run than letting her drive all round the country in your new car,' James told me. For all his thrifty ways he seldom refused Susan anything.

She raised her eyebrow at me. 'Any chance of a ride later?'

'Only with me driving,' I smiled.

'Rowena hasn't had her fussy out with it yet,' James said.

I nodded. 'I must dash, I've got an appointment with old man Jeacock,' I said, and giving Susan a quick kiss I opened the door.

Piers and Sebastian stood watching as I strode to the Volvo, unlocking it with the flicker beam. 'Here, Cass,' I said, hitting my thigh with his lead to capture his attention. 'Let's go for a drive in my nice new car.'

He wagged his tail and lolloped after me, eagerly jumping onto the front seat to keep me company. I quickly fastened him into his car basket and anxious to be away from the Colemans inquisitive eyes, drove off. But not before I heard Piers say to his father, 'I wish the car would drive the witch straight to hell.'

Driving through the gates I felt as though someone had poured ice water all over me.

Cassidy rested his head in my lap, comforting me with his warmth.

Heading for the city I fiddled with the air-conditioning and the heater. The car rapidly built up speed.

189

'What the hell?' I whispered, my breath frosting the air. I took my foot off the accelerator but the speedometer kept moving higher as it got colder.

70... I flicked a switch to open all the windows but nothing happened.

75... 'Sod this,' I spun the wheel and hung a left onto a quieter road, snatching the automatic gears down into one as I turned left again, heading out of town.

80... Cassidy whined and burrowed his head under my thighs.

Frantic, I hit the gears into two, bracing myself as I hit the brakes. The car carried on increasing speed.

85... Desperate now, I pumped the brakes and wrenched on the hand brake. Nothing happened. The car kept going faster and I couldn't stop it.

Going for broke I slammed it into Park, wincing as the gears crunched.

90... I tried to rationalise what was happening but I didn't think it was a mechanical failure.

The air inside the car was flowing and swirling like sulphurous fog. My hands were so cold I could hardly hold the wheel. Then I remembered the heated seat and switched it on.

'Thank you, my beauty,' I murmured, feeling the warmth easing my limbs.

95... 'Oh God!' I swerved round corners praying there was nothing coming in the opposite direction. The needle hovered around 100 miles an hour as I careered down the winding lane.

Scraping ice from the inside of my windscreen I saw that without being aware of my destination, I was heading for the crossroads.

"I wish the car would drive the witch straight to hell," Piers had said. My Volvo wasn't at fault, it was him.

This could have been happening to Susan, I realised. Thank God I hadn't let her take my car. She hadn't the experience to cope.

Fear left me as anger scorched my blood. He had tried this trick before.

Concentrating, I willed the car to slow down. I too had done this before.

97... My vision narrowed, like looking through the wrong end of a telescope as I focused on the road in front of me.

Slow down, I commanded.

The speed dropped to 90... 85... 80.

The ice was melting, running down the windscreen. Slower, I urged.

My hands were gripping the steering wheel so tightly, blue veins stood out against my bone white knuckles but the needle swung down through the seventies and sixties. In the distance I saw the outline of the oak tree and had the crazy compulsion to make Mistress Berrysford understand that this vendetta had gone on long enough.

It was as if, like Bill said, they couldn't stop themselves. All because of her curse.

The Volvo shuddered to a halt as I pulled it onto the grass verge and switched off the engine before I reached for a handful of Kleenex and mopped the windscreen.

Cassidy yelped, scrabbling to be let out. Needing fresh air I unfastened him and followed him to the oak tree.

The rustle of leaves and the massed chorus of bird song greeted me. There was a tangible feeling of mystery about the place. The misty blue of the bluebells as far as the eye could see, was a shocking contrast to the horror which had happened here.

'Your power, Rowena,' I whispered, 'was so strong, yet you hardly ever used it.' I truly believed she was listening.

'If you had not died with the curse of revenge in your heart, you might have learned that you were a powerful witch in the true sense of the word. Witch means wise, Rowena. Where is your wisdom now?'

A loud creak jerked my head up.

I saw myself hanging by the neck. My hair hidden under a starched linen cap. The slight body convulsed as it swung to face me.

My scream rent the air as my eyes, green and lifeless, stared into my soul...

Rowena Berrysford's eyes.

"You are the one who must see clearly."

Her voice was not only in my head but all around me.

"As those of our kin ignored their gift when they encountered the Colemans, our powers fell into disuse while theirs grew stronger. If you fail, Colemans greed will poison the world..."

"But why me?" I managed to ask.

"Because you must. If he wins you will be the last Rowena. The last of our line..."

I became aware of the grass all around me. I had fallen to my knees and Cassidy was licking my hand. I hugged him to me, not a little frightened, Mistress Berrysford's words echoing in my head.

With the practised smarm of a politician Sebastian Coleman had managed to turn his company's responsibility for the dumped Dioxin to his advantage but if Piers was marketing an untested systemic weed killer based on an uncontrollable virus, it would indeed poison the world. And his greed was legendary.

Stiffly, I hauled myself up. Basically I was quite fit for a thirty something but even with my new found psychic ability I could hardly be mistaken for Sigourney Weaver's, Ripley.

"If he wins you will be the last Rowena..."

What could I do?

I'd do as always, give it my best shot. Scrutinise all the Colemans dealings, gather evidence against them and broadcast it from the rooftops; I had enough contacts in the media.

Feeling a little more confident I called Cassidy who was scratching around under the tree. He was too busy to pay attention, so much to his dismay, I walked over, picked him up and carried him to the car.

Slowly and very carefully I drove to keep my appointment with Douglas Jeacock.

John took me through to his father's old office and Mr Douglas and I went down into the basement together. Where, he told me, all the old documents and files were kept.

The room was brightly lit, rather warm and smelled of dry paper. A faint throbbing came through the walls.

'The boiler,' he said. 'That's what keeps the place so cosy down here.'

'It's very good of you to help me like this,' I said, shaking his hand.

'Not at all, I'm only to pleased to talk about my hobby.'

I nodded. 'My mother sends her regards.'

'It's nice that she remembers me, tell her I appreciate it.'

He smiled and led me through piles of box files to a small desk and removing a stack of yellowed folders from a chair, motioned me to sit down.

Mr Douglas was tall, wiry and tanned. He looked fit and agile for his age. Any age, I corrected myself as he picked up a huge pile of books from another chair and sat facing me. He was very good looking too, with a neat moustache, thick silver hair and twinkling blue eyes. He reminded me of an old, true British, film star.

'What do you think of my little retreat?' he waved his hand, encompassing the orderly confusion. Neatly labelled cardboard box files lined the walls and took up most of the floor space. He pointed to the corner by my chair.

'Those are some of the first Jeacock's cases and go back to the seventeenth century.'

Mr Douglas showed me. 'They are all cross referenced to the various clients kin.'

It would take a madman to devise such a system and a genius to unravel it.

'I have gone back as far as 1792, the year Rowan Harris was born. Can you tell me anything about his parents? He married Anne Beaumont.'

'Ah, yes.' Mr Douglas bent down and examined dates and names on a few box files and in thirty seconds he pulled out a file and started rifling though it. The parchments kept in the dry heat were yellowed with age but remarkably pristine.

'Here we are.' He untied the faded tape and flattened the roll of parchment on the desk. 'The last Will and Testament of Rowan's father. Edward Harris. He left the property in Redhill to his son with the proviso that his wife, Rowena Harris, could remain in residence unto death; quite usual in those days when women didn't have the right to make a will.'

'Rowena Harris, nee Monteque. Born 1770, survived her son.'

It was as easy as that.

'I don't suppose you can tell me anything about her parents?' I asked.

'Funny, I seem to recall the name. I'm sure there was some sort of notoriety in your family around that time. Something interesting...'

I knew this old gentleman from my dealings with him over old Rowan's Will and his memory was as sharp as a razor blade.

He scanned a few files and unerringly pulled out a box, the label well worn and long past deciphering. Nodding to himself, he took out some musty papers and read the faded ink on the old parchment.

In great trepidation I held my breath while I waited for enlightenment.

'Here it is!' he said triumphantly. 'Interesting case, it caused quite a stir at the time.'

I commenced breathing again.

'Whom did it concern?' I asked, proud of the normality in my voice.

'Mrs Harris's mother, Lady Rowena Montegue,' Mr Douglas informed me.

Giving me the parchment, he pointed to the top of the page. 'She appeared at Nottingham Assizes in 1740 to testify to the accidental death of a blacksmith.'

I tried to read the faded copperplate but my eyes were jolting in and out of focus.

The room dimmed and brightened around me like a power surge in the electricity supply. I squeezed my finger nails into the palms of my hands trying to keep control of my physical body while the onslaught of emotions overwhelmed me.

Echoes of a different time and place invaded my mind.

I knew the answer but couldn't stop myself from asking. 'Does it give his name?'

'Of course, this is the transcript of the case.' He peered over my shoulder at the extravagant script. 'The blacksmith's name was...'

'Coleman,' we said together.

Fortunately I was forewarned and held on to consciousness even as I watched...

Riding home on a late afternoon in February, Lady Rowena Montegue's horse had lost a shoe and she had been forced to the nearest blacksmith, Coleman. He was feared in the village, not only because of his ruthless father and brothers but because he was a violent blackguard whom it was rumoured, beat his wife to death.

Whether this was true or not did not concern Lady Montegue, she was anxious to be out of the smithy as soon as he had shod her horse well enough for her to ride home as quickly as possible. However, the blacksmith assumed that a lady with only a young groom for protection was sent for his pleasure.

He had grabbed hold of her and kissed her. Knocking the boy away when he tried to protect her.

The stench of his rancid breath made her gag, reminding her of a time before...

Memories of another time, another Rowena, flooded her mind and lent her the courage born of anger.

Suddenly Lady Montegue knew what to do.

As if following instructions she pushed her thumbs into his eyes and when he let go of her, she ran. But unseen shutters barred the smithy. Memories of unseen hands molested her.

Her groom lay dazed, and alone she faced her attacker.

She pushed Coleman away, as surprised as he was when he fell backwards and landed with a crunch atop the wall of the forge.

A sheet of blue flames whooshed up with a roar, setting light to his clothing.

He ran screaming round the smithy, burning like a beacon.

Beating at himself to put out the fire, he bumped into her horse, who reared in terror.

For a moment everything went deathly quiet.

As Lady Montegue watched she blushed with shame at the elation she felt when, panicked beyond control, her horse trampled Coleman into the ground...

'Would you like a glass of water. Rowena?' someone was asking me.

I blinked, rubbing my hands over my face, scorched from the heat of the human torch. My throat too dry to speak, I nodded and tried to compose myself as Mr Douglas fetched me a drink.

Shamefaced, I muttered something about a bug going round as I sipped.

Gentleman that he is, he accepted my lie without demur.

It seemed that something dreadful happened whenever the Colemans and my ancestors came into close proximity. Thank goodness they didn't cross swords every lifetime. It was becoming increasingly evident that when they did there were horrific consequences. For one or the other.

I felt a profound sense of relief that they didn't always come out on top.

Somehow that gave me confidence, if Lady Rowena Montegue could beat them, please God, maybe I could too.

CHAPTER TWENTY THREE.

Promising to call and see him again, I made my way out of Jeacock's office and was fastening Cass into his car seat when a horn hooted for my attention.

Bill was getting out of his Celica.

Curious, John Jeacock was looking out of the window while we, wanting to kiss, made do with shaking each other's hands.

'Bill! How did you know I was here?'

'I phoned Albert on the mobile. At the risk of you thinking I'm a bloody fool, I was worried about you. Is everything OK?' His blue eyes searched my face anxiously.

'I'm fine... now. I had a bit of an argument with the car though, the brakes went, amongst other things. At least that's what I'm going to tell the garage.'

'What happened? No bull, tell it to me straight.'

I grinned ruefully. 'Piers Coleman happened. He wished the car to hell and I had a heck of a job keeping it from going there.'

His mouth hardened into an angry line. 'Give me your keys.' He put out his hand, waving his car keys. 'Take my car. I'll drive yours back to the showroom.'

'The Celica?' Much as I'd love to drive Bill's car I shook my head, refusing to put him in danger.

As if he read my mind he whispered, 'Rowena?'

I looked into his eyes and was lost.

'Toss you for them?'

He patted his pockets searching for change and pulled out a large silver coin.

Taking it from his fingers and making sure the silver dollar was not the same both sides, I tossed it into the air.

'Heads,' Bill called.

It landed on my palm, head up. And I drove his Celica.

The garage promised a thorough overhaul and said they would bring it back to me tomorrow. Bill gave them his Access number and told them to put in a car phone as well.

'You can call me if anything like that happens again. And we can keep in touch,' he said as he opened the Celica's door for me.

In the cocooned privacy I told him of John Baker's allegations about Arland. And my gut feeling was that the Colemans were involved.

'My wife used to work at Colemans when it was just the Feed and Fertiliser Company. Margaret did laboratory tests on weed killers before Dioxin was found to be so deadly. Of course it's too late to prove anything now but I've had my suspicions about the cause of her lung cancer,' he said quietly. 'Neither of us have ever smoked or even worked in a tobacco smoking environment.'

Bill slowed down at the traffic lights; although deep in conversation his attention was still focused on driving.

"The Colemans did only perfunctory tests and their safety precautions were non existent. I even bought Margaret surgical masks to prevent her breathing in the spray chemicals, but...' He sighed and shook his head as we cruised down Plains Road. 'Seb was a Councillor at the time, before he sold Colemans to Ernehale Holdings,' he said, the subject of Margaret's death too painful to dwell on.

'I see.' I could no longer give Sebastian the benefit of a doubt. 'The Colemans own Ernehale Holdings. Who in turn own Arnold research laboratories and natural development.'

'Really?'

'Definitely,' I said. 'I just wish I could get in there and check their records.'

'That might be arranged,' Bill said quietly. 'Margaret was worried about opportunists breaking in because Seb only has the inside office alarmed. Of course that's where the safe is. And the files,' he looked at me appraisingly.

'I quite fancy a spot of breaking and entering,' I grinned, only half joking.

'Don't even think about it. If you try it on your own you'll have Coleman and the police round in five minutes,' Bill said. 'Whereas *I* know the layout... Are you on?'

'Of course, When?'

'It will have to be in the middle of the night. No sense in advertising ourselves to the local bobbies.'

'Which one?' I asked, having investigated the Community Policing con. 'There's only one policeman on duty at night and all he does is answer the telephone and if you're lucky, pass on the details to Central.'

'We'll do it the night James flies to Canada. Next weekend. OK?'

'Ok, I said, feeling my colour rise at the double entendre.

'There's one thing that puzzles me about all this,' he said, slowing the car near the entrance to Beaumont Court. 'If the Colemans bought the lab back, why did they make all the biochemists redundant? He only kept a caretaker staff.'

'Research is expensive,' I said, remembering Alice.

'Tight bastards.' Bill nodded.

'Should I drive you to your door?' he asked, knowing I didn't like them jumping to conclusions.

'Yes, please. We've done nothing to be ashamed of.'

Bill pulled to a stop. 'Given half a chance,' he murmured, reaching for my hand. 'Marry me. Or come and live with me, whichever you want. We could go somewhere nice, away from all this. Please, my love, just get away from the Colemans.'

His words made all my dreams come true. 'Marry you?' I gasped.

I'd die for him. But that would make him a target. 'Oh Bill.' I couldn't do that. Couldn't put him in danger. 'I...'

His eyes darkened with pain as he sensed rejection.

Trying to be flippant I quipped. 'There's no future in living together, tempting as it might be.'

Seeing the pain in his eyes I stuttered truthfully. 'I love you, Bill. I've always loved you. But I need more time. A week, days even. We can wait a little longer can't we?'

I had to settle this thing with the Colemans first. Just being seen with Bill put him in danger and as for him breaking and entering with me...

Bill gave me a wooden smile. ' I don't know, my love. Every day without you is too long.' He brought my hand to his lips. 'But I can wait.'

Reaching over he opened the door and with leaden feet I walked away from him.

All my senses told me the inevitable confrontation with Piers Coleman was going to be bloody and I was determined that Bill would not caught in the crossfire.

James and Susan were already home when I got in, helping the builders put the window frames in.

'We should be ready to start on the roof tomorrow,' Albert told me cheerfully.

'Then they will lay the concrete floor,' James chipped in.

'Thank God!' I was fed up with going outside to get water, and it was even worse scrambling up into the dining room carrying it.

They had the inside breeze blocks up to roof height and outside the old, red facing bricks looked good and was almost finished too.

Susan had vacuumed up the thickest of the dust, not realising it would be just as bad in an hour or so, I didn't like to disillusion her for her thoughtfulness.

'I've had a spot of trouble with the car,' I told no one in particular. 'I couldn't turn the air conditioning off, it was so cold it frosted the windows,' I said, trying to make light of it.

Albert searched my face, reading more into the statement than the words suggested.

I frowned as he opened his mouth to say something.

'That's the trouble with new cars,' James said in his best I told you so tradition. 'There can be so many teething problems. Did you take it back to the garage?'

'Yes, dear.'

Susan surprised me by asking. 'How did you get home; you didn't walk all that way did you?'

I smiled. 'No, love. Albert's nephew gave me a lift.'

Once again Albert's eyebrows shot up but he didn't speak.

'I thought we could take all the kids out for a meal tonight eh?' James said eagerly, obviously trying to make amends. 'To celebrate my promotion and because you really can't cook in these conditions.'

'That will be nice, I'll wear my new soft suit and we'll go posh.' It always pleased him when we put on a bit of a show.

As I got dressed for the evening out I couldn't stop thinking that I had somehow got to stop the Colemans from (a) poisoning the earth and (b) prevent them from killing me. Neither of which I could tell James or even Justin.

It was funny though, I knew that nothing was going to happen until James had gone to Canada; as if the Colemans knew my plans... Or Sebastian came back from London, where he was campaigning for party support in an important vote.

Instead of appreciating the breathing space I was anxious to get it over with. Wanting James to be gone. Wanting to live my life with Bill in safety.

We picked up Justin and Debra and drove to the Royal Moat House. James had booked a table there; it was very nice but my mind was elsewhere. I remember sipping a nice chilled Vin d'Alsace. So I probably ate chicken but I can't be sure. I only know the taxi dropped everyone at Justin's and drove me home alone.

The wine helped me to sleep straight away but I woke up at first light. No matter how much I tossed and turned I couldn't get back to sleep so I got up at an uncivilised hour, had a long shower, did my hair and nails et cetera to pass the time. Dressed in chino's and a faded navy silk shirt, I felt ready to face the world.

I was drinking my second cup of coffee in the morning, enjoying the peace before the builders arrived, when the tranquillity was shattered and Susan came bouncing in.

Radio on (loudly) she tuned in to the pop music station and spent an hour on the phone, talking to the man in her life. I didn't nag her because I would have liked to have done the same thing. My mind was full of Bill.

Munching toast she told me she'd decided to go back to York in the morning, mainly because she wanted to see her boy friend, I thought but she said she had an impending mock exam.

By the time James came to take Susan out for lunch, the house was full of builders so I borrowed his car and dropped them off in town so I could do a bit of research into Wills.

I found Lady Montegue's father, Sir Rowan Trent, born 1708, died 1795. His father was a Rowan too, born in 1678. Being landed gentry they must have led sheltered lives without coming into contact with the Colemans because I sensed nothing extraordinary.

Picking up James and Susan we drove home and I was delighted to see that the Garage had delivered my car. It looked a picture. Even James approved of the car phone but I wondered what he'd say if he knew who had paid for it.

Mel Keeton drove up in his old van and I was gleefully showing him all the features on the Volvo when Piers Coleman came hobbling towards his Porsche, glaring at me. I could almost see his mind whirring as he dismissed any claims about my power as superstitious nonsense.

'If I were you, I would find a safe place to park this or he will be scratching your paint work. Isn't there anyone who has space in a garage, till he gets over his jealousy?' Mel asked.

"That's a very sensible idea. Perhaps Bill Weston has room at Tannery Lane. I'll ask Albert. Chalk up another one I owe you, Mel,' I told him.

His face crinkled into a cheeky grin that reminded me of Davy Keeton, the drummer boy.

'All part of the service, madam,' he said.

Gravel sprayed as Piers started the engine, reversing the Porsche to face the gate.

'Christ!' Mel swore.

Glancing round I saw Piers hurtling toward me.

Mel grabbed my arm to pull me out of the path of the speeding car but I shook him off and ran towards it instead, paying no attention to Mel's shouted warning.

I had an overwhelming compulsion to get to the entry at the side of Mel's house. Fast.

Time seemed to go into slow motion as if in a dream, I ran through air which had the sluggish consistency of cement.

The Porsche sped relentlessly towards me.

Piers was blank faced, his eyes popping out of his head as he gripped the wheel with white knuckled concentration. Driving at me.

I spotted a large pebble on the ground and willed it sharply into the windscreen.

Almost at Mel's house, the car swerved as the glass frosted with cracks, but continued to track me.

My heart pounding with fear, the roaring in my ears was deafening.

Without thinking about it I used all the power I possessed to wrench his steering wheel to the left, away from the covered entry.

Gasping for breath I managed to scoop Mel's daughter from her tricycle a split second before the car scraped past us, the mirror tore my shirt and the car smashed Lizabeth's trike to smithereens as the wheels crunched over it.

Thank God it wasn't the toddler's head.

The Porsche went crashing into the Victorian lamp-post in the centre of the courtyard.

Lizabeth screamed with fright and anger at seeing her tricycle destroyed and holding her tight, my legs let me down and with my back against the entry wall, I slid to the ground rocking Mel's daughter in my arms.

The crash and the screams brought the neighbours out, and Mel reached me only moments before June.

The clattering of her platform soles on the cobblestones echoed in my ears as she ran towards us.

James and Albert rushed over to my side and Sebastian and George went to help Piers.

When he heard their raised voices, light gleamed in Mel's eyes. He shoved the Sebastian and George aside to get at Piers.

I watched him, too exhausted to move, as June took Lizabeth from me and swooped her into the safety of her arms.

'It's alright, baby. Daddy will buy you a new bike. A two wheeler with stabilisers, eh?'

Mel dragged Piers, cut and bleeding, out of the car, one fist clenched around Pier's neck as the other was about to punch his face.

June yelled at him to stop. He looked astonished at her interference.

'This bastard deliberately tried to run over Rowena and nearly killed our Lizabeth,' he told her, giving Piers a thump. 'If Rowena hadn't saved her, Lizabeth would have been under his wheels as well as her bike.'

June looked at Mel as if she couldn't believe her ears and turned to me for confirmation.

I nodded, thinking she only wanted to know the truth. But June calmly put Lizabeth back into my arms and walked into the fracas. She waved Mel aside.

'You bastard!' she hissed quietly but with each word she kicked Piers hard on the shin and as he bent over screaming, she kneed him in the groin.

George tried to push her away but Mel swung a right uppercut and knocked him out.

'I couldn't help it, the accelerator stuck. The damn car wouldn't stop!' Piers sobbed.

'What a coincidence,' I snapped. 'How do you like it?' He didn't really expect me, of all people to believe him, did he?

Arms out spread placatingly, Sebastian Coleman tried to calm the volatile situation.

'Now, now, I'm sure it was only an accident,' he said, doing his rally the peasants to the polling booth, bit.

'I'll have the Police on you for this. Assault and Battery in front of all these witnesses,' Piers yelled, spitting blood.

'What witnesses?' I asked.

Everyone turned away and started to walk back to their homes, moving to the perimeter so as not to miss anything.

'All I saw was you speeding across the courtyard trying to run over Rowena,' Mel said. 'Not to mention my daughter.'

'If I were you, I'd say your brakes failed,' Albert told Piers.

'And any injuries you sustained were caused by the accident,' James said, surprising me with his support.

'Otherwise I wouldn't give a penny for your chances around here,' Mel added, poking his finger into Piers chest for emphasis.

He turned his attention to Sebastian. 'You might think you're the fucking king of the castle round here but God help you if either of your bastard sons try anything like this again.'

Lizabeth was sobbing for her mangled tricycle. The sound was heart rending.

'I'll have the money for a new bike. Now. Sixty quid will do it,' June said, with her hand out.

'Don't be ridiculous, a kid's bike doesn't cost that much,' Coleman argued.

'Are you calling my wife a liar?' Mel said, with a glint of hope in his eye.

'No, no of course not,' Coleman stammered, backing away from Mel's aggressive anger. He pulled out a tooled leather wallet and counted out three twenties. 'Here you are, my dear,' he said.

'Thank you.' June took the money gingerly between thumb and forefinger as if it was a piece of dung and held it to the light to check it's authenticity.

Although it was a common enough practice in these days of laser printed forgeries, I applauded her silent insult.

'And don't ever call me "my dear" again,' she said.

Turning on her heel, she walked over and took Lizabeth from me.

'Thank you,' she said softly, giving me a hand up before she carried her daughter home.

'How did you know Lizabeth was in danger?' Sebastian asked, too smugly not to know the answer.

For a moment I was nonplussed, used to my family accepting these things. I straightened my back and looked him in the eye. 'I heard her,' I replied icily.

'Rowena has fantastic hearing,' James said, unexpectedly coming to my rescue, though he didn't know it.

'Yes,' I said, thankful for the logical explanation. 'I heard the tricycle while Mel and I were talking. When I saw the car, I figured that if I didn't stop her, Lizabeth would come out of the entry, right in the path of Piers speeding car.'

'Congratulations, Mrs Roberts. Your swift action was commendable.' He bared his teeth in a saccharine semblance of a smile. 'If your hearing was less acute things might have been a lot worse.'

He shook my hand before I had the chance to withdraw it and walked away, knowing that neither of us believed a word of it.

Mel took me by the arm and tilted his head at James to follow him into his house.

I went in smiling but shaking like a leaf.

White faced, June and Mel declared their gratitude for ever while she set to and made us all a cup of coffee.

Mel added a tot of Brandy to mine before he passed me the cup and looked at me, puzzled.

'Did you really hear Lizabeth on her trike?'

'Of course,' I smiled. 'How else could I have known she was coming?'

'I don't care if you're in league with old Nick himself, love. I'll always be indebted to you.' June said, hugging me.

Lizabeth gave me a sloppy, sticky kiss, knowing that I'd done something special for her. Fank you, auntie Wona,'

I swung her gleefully into the air. She screamed with delight and we all laughed uncontrollably, overcome with relief.

Still giggling, James and I went home arm in arm.

CHAPTER TWENTY FOUR.

When I had recovered my composure I mentioned Mel's idea of garaging my car at Bill's house, to Albert.

'I'm sure he'll be delighted, he has two double garages at the back,' Albert said.

'That's a cracking idea,' James agreed. 'It would be a relief to know that your car couldn't be tampered with again. Tell your nephew we will be pleased to pay him rental.'

This was the time to tell him the truth, or part of it, about Bill.

'James, Albert's nephew is William Weston. The Civil Engineer, I believe you two know each other.'

'Bill? He's a fine chap, Albert. Greatly respected,' James looked at me smugly, 'It will be alright, Rowena,' he said, turning to Albert. 'Please, mention my name. Tell Bill I'll owe him one if he will do this favour for Rowena,' James said.

Albert agreed.

'Isn't he helping you with your genealogy?' James asked but carried on talking before I had the chance to answer. 'You must not take up too much of his time, dear. Bill is a very busy man.'

I told him I appreciated that and we only met when it was convenient for him.

'Why don't you bring the car round later?' Albert asked. 'I'll make sure it's alright with Bill.'

Preparing dinner was reminiscent of camping out but with Susan's help and a tin of condensed soup I managed to make a half decent pasta before I left, as sedately as possible and rushed to see Bill.

He gave me the keys to his old garage and we had a pleasant hour alone together.

Albert had discreetly "remembered" that he had to write a few cheques and he's left his cheque book at his own house.

Bill showed me where he'd buried Buggalugs in the cherry orchard and we sat in his lovely garden watching the sunset while I told him what had happened to Lizabeth.

He was so easy to talk to that I told him things I'd never dare mention to anyone before. I even told him what James had said about him.

'I'll phone him to put his mind at rest about the garage and tell him you can "bother" me any time you care to.'

'Bother as in hot and?' I grinned. It was so good to be alive when I was close to him.

He kissed the top of my head, put one arm round my waist and led me indoors.

'I'll drive you home,' he said, picking up his car keys.

'Couldn't we walk? It's such a beautiful evening.'

As we strolled through Arnold he tucked my hand under his arm. 'Not quite as conspicuous as holding hands,' he whispered in my ear. 'And I can hold you closer to my side. '

My blood pounded in my ears thinking of the implications of his innocent remark. When we arrived he waited by the gates until I was safely indoors.

James berated me for not asking him in for coffee, but I couldn't handle the thought of Bill and James sitting side by side at my table.

Concerned about the near miss accident, Susan decided to stay another day, trying to convince me to go to Canada with James.

'I think you should get away for a while, Mum. There's something fishy about the Colemans and I won't be able to concentrate on my studies if I'm worrying about you here on your own.'

The subtle mixture of blackmail and genuine concern impressed me.

'Then you must talk to your father; but don't concern yourself about me, love.' I said.

"If the going gets tough I'll go to Justin's.'

She tried her wiles on James but all she got for her trouble was a promise to drive her back to University and a shopping trip in town first.

I went upstairs to my office, after they left for Justin and Debra's.

Trying not to listen to the silence in the empty house I concentrated on writing everything I'd learned about the Scorpion virus. If I could link the Colemans with this it could not only bring Sebastian down but might even shake the complacency of this rather patronising, government.

When I'd finished the article, bar names and dates, I phoned Bill. He promised to take me to meet his cousins the Smithsons, tomorrow, to have lunch at Sarah's; their restaurant on Brickyard Lane. I looked forward to the visit with mixed feelings; wanting to see the place that held so many dear memories for Rowena Berrysford, yet apprehensive in case I made a fool of myself.

I spent the rest of the night dreaming of Bill and worrying about his safety, wanting to be with him every minute and at the same time steeling myself into not seeing him again until the business with the Colemans was over.

In the morning James asked if he could take Cassidy with him to York.

'Go ahead, I know you hate driving without company,' I'd told him.

I had always put his carry on with Barbara down to that simple fact until the extent of his infidelities became all too evident.

'Just make sure he has a drink et cetera before you go, and take him for a good long walk before you drive back.'

As I kissed Susan goodbye she whispered, 'I'll keep plugging away at Dad.'

I knew she would be wasting her time but her heart was in the right place so I merely smiled and slipped her a couple of twenties. James would probably give her double that, but God knows it's no fun being a student if you're constantly skint.

She kissed my cheek and was off, leaving behind a perfumed waft of my C.K.

As soon as James drove out of the courtyard I started getting ready for what was really my first real date with Bill, trying on and discarding all my nicest outfits before I settled on my old stand by, a cream trouser suit, updated with a gold satin top, tan leather belt and matching high heeled, pointed toe ankle boots. I sprayed on a little perfume, slicked on peachy lip gloss and before I could change my mind and start all over again, Bill arrived.

I rushed to the door, throwing it open just as his finger reached for the bell.

'Hello,' Bill gave me a shame faced grin. 'I'm a bit early, I'm afraid.'

'So am I,' I smiled, slipping my tan bag over my shoulder. 'Ready and waiting.' I almost said "willing" but stopped myself just in time.

I floated to his car on cloud nine.

His long fingered hands resting lightly on the steering wheel reminded me so much of William that I reached out and touched the back of them.

'You have nice hands.' I whispered.

Bill smiled. How I loved his smile.

'There's nothing to worry about, Rowena, I'll be with you all the time.'

I tried to keep my eyes off him as he drove to Brickyard Lane, but couldn't of course. Smiling, laughing, talking, touching, we couldn't keep our eyes or hands off each other.

When we drove up the gravelled drive to the restaurant, I looked for a recognisable landmark. The tall cedar trees were impressive with age, but new to me. Daffodils covered the high banks which I remembered as a flat rose walk. Turning to mention these discrepancies I saw the house through the trees and my breath caught in my throat.

The sky darkened, becoming chill, as a crescent moon replaced the warm sun...

"Mistress Rowena Berrysford." She repeated her new title as they drove from the wedding breakfast trying to get used to the sound.

Rowena inhaled the heady perfume of gilly flowers when William opened the door of the carriage.

Nervous and slightly vexed at her trepidation, she held out her hand, thrilled when his long fingers clasped her waist and lifted her to the ground.

No matter what gossip she had heard of the dreadful things that lay in store for her on this first night of marriage, she knew that William would never hurt her.

To prove her implicit faith in him, she gave him a dazzling smile and ran up the wide stone steps to the front entrance of Sarah and Edward's home, which was to be theirs alone for this very special night...

His hands gripped her shoulders firmly. 'Rowena?'

I rubbed my eyes as William dissolved and became Bill.

'Sorry,' I stammered, embarrassed, 'I remembered the first time we... I mean Mistress Berrysford, came here.'

'Does it look the same?' Bill asked.

'The house does but not the garden.' I stared at the wide timber framed Manor, the open porch, the small windows with leaded quarries.

He held my hand and we went inside.

Keeping a tight grip on myself I looked round the hall with its half landing staircase leading to the minstrels gallery. The ornate Victorian furniture looked alright. It would have been horrendously expensive to furnish in any other period but of course, Sarah's house used to have a mixture of old and the new of the time.

I looked behind the door. The carved oak coffer which William had made for his sister's wedding gift was noticeable by it's absence.

'They've made a good job of the restoration but I'm glad it isn't too recognisable,' I said.

As we entered the restaurant through the glass panelled double doors into what used to be the dining hall, a good looking man in his late thirties with neat dark hair and wide smile, ran towards us, his arms outstretched in welcome, closely followed by an extremely pretty redhead, slim and full of joie de vivre.

Bill introduced me to Shane and Andrea Smithson.

They gave me a grand tour and I was impressed how well they had kept true to the basic structure of the old house. Some rooms still carried the aura of Sarah.

Knowing how traumatic this was for me, Bill kept hold of my hand to give me his support. I didn't know how much I needed it until Andrea opened one of the bedroom doors.

Closing my eyes as the room swam before me and their chattering voices faded, I heard only the giggles of the young ladies maid who had shown me into the guest chamber...

William removed Rowena's cloak and led her over to warm herself after their moonlit journey from the celebrations in their honour held at Beaumont Hall. The fire crackled in the huge brick fire place, filling the room with warmth and soft light.

"Would you care for a glass of Madeira, my sweeting" William whispered in her ear as he stood behind her, his hands resting lightly on her shoulders...

'May I get you a drink, Rowena?'

'Sorry?' I whispered, scraping my hands through my hair as I tried to disappear into the woodwork.

But Bill had his arm round my shoulders, hugging me, his warmth sweeping away the cold centuries as he led me to the four poster bed.

'No... Please, Bill. I'm alright.' God knows what would happen if I lay on that bed. 'This room is too right. The bed...'

'Yes. It's what was called the best bed, being used just for special guests, it was in excellent condition. It only needed a new mattress. We had the draperies copied as close to the originals as we could,' Shane told me, putting a glass of Port into my shaking hands.

'I often wonder who might have slept in that bed,' Andrea mused.

'Honeymooners,' I whispered, but only Bill heard.

On closer inspection, I noticed the superficial differences, the fitted carpet, the new draperies and chairs. But the fireplace in the corner of the room had very similar furnishings and as I inhaled, the room even had the same perfume of gilly flowers.

Andrea smiled. 'Do you like my pot pourri?' she asked. 'I made it myself from a recipe I found in an old book in the library.'

'It's very authentic.' I said, sipping the fortified wine and blinking away the tears.

Perfume brought back the emotions as well as memories. I missed everyone so very much.

'I'll write you the recipe if you'd like?' she offered.

'Thank you, that's very kind of you.'

Some people liked to keep these little treasures to themselves. But although I appreciated the gesture, there was no way I could live with that evocative scent.

I remembered my first night with William in this room. On that bed...

'I think we should take Rowena out of here, what she needs is some of our recipes of a culinary kind,' Shane said.

'I'll second that. Come on, my love.' Bill held my arm and led me out of the room.

It took all of my self control not to look back.

We all had lunch together, talking about what the house used to be like. Somehow these wonderful people accepted me for what I was, no scepticism. No ridicule. It was easy to forget my natural reserve and open up in such warmth.

After lunch, Bill and I left, relaxed and happy. I was a little tired perhaps, but I was getting used to the enervating effect of my journeys to the past.

Holding hands we strolled through the wild daffodils which grew under the trees. I realised how exciting, how intimate holding hands could be. It gave me a feeling of warmth and comradeship that it was him and me against the world. I was head over heels in love and like cool water when you're thirsty, I couldn't drink it fast enough.

'I've got to pick up a couple of reports at my office, do you mind?' Bill asked, as we were driving home.

'Not at all. I have the afternoon free.'

'I was impatient to see you and left before Jean had finished typing.'

He picked up the reports and we were just leaving Bill's office when a tall fellow with a boyish grin and crinkled fair hair bumped into us in the foyer.

Bill introduced me to his friend Joe, the assayer and jewellery expert who had an office on the second floor. Before I knew it we were following him upstairs so he could look at my pendant.

Joe was very knowledgeable and completely fascinated by the enamelling and workmanship. He did a few tests.

'It is very ancient. Possibly Saxon,' he said.

I was amazed. 'It can't be.'

'Without doing further tests it's only a guesstimate, but I'd say it was close,' he told me, turning my family heirloom over and over. 'The metal has me stymied though, it must have been treated by some special process. It isn't platinum.' He shrugged his shoulders in annoyance. 'Nor is it white gold. I've never come across anything like it before,' he shook his head frowning. 'I can't think of anything that would account for it's age with no sign of wear.'

The scepticism must have showed on my face because Bill said quietly. 'Joe is one of the most respected experts in this field.'

'And it isn't a pendant, it's a locket with a secret clasp. God knows how you would open it now, it's probably well and truly stuck with age.'

I looked at Joe, not comprehending.

'Look, you can see, there's a tiny spot of gold sealing it together.'

He moved aside so I could peer through his powerful jeweller's microscope.

I gasped at the fine workmanship. A pinhead of gold covered the catch where the interweaving branch of the Rowan formed part of the holes for a chain to go through. Part of the pinnate leaves disguised the hinge. It was definitely a locket. I wondered what secrets it held.

'Can you break the seal without damaging the locket?' I asked.

'Yes but it seems to have been deliberately disguised as though for a good reason,' Joe said, carefully chipping off the gold. With an optician's screwdriver he pressed and fiddled with the catch.

'I'm sorry, it's impossible to open, it's probably been stuck for centuries.' He shrugged and gave the locket back to me.

It lay in my open palm and as I fingered the engraving, wondering what magician had wrought such beauty, I closed my eyes and automatically pressed the clasp just so.

Momentarily it pulsed with life and the strange metal grew warm. The gold seemed to turn to putty as the locket sprung open in my hand.

I felt light headed and not quite solid. There appeared to be an intricate pattern engraved inside both halves of it.

'This could be an inscription,' I said.

I held Bill's hand as Joe put the locket under the microscope. If it was only legible through the powerful magnification, how could anyone have engraved it without modern technology?

'The words are easily decipherable. Have you had this engraved yourself?' Joe asked in an aggressive tone of disbelief.

'No, of course not! I didn't even know it could open. Why?' I asked, wondering what had made him so angry.

'It has ruined the value of it. I can't understand how anyone would do such a thing, it is nothing short of sacrilege!' he spluttered, rebuking me.

'What is?' I asked, puzzled by his manner.

'It's written in Modern English,' he said accusingly.

That could only mean he was wrong about it's antiquity, I thought.

Joe read my mind. 'If it hasn't been engraved by you, or one of your parents, it would still make it only a couple of hundred years old. There is no way I could be that far out, even in the simplest of tests,' he told me earnestly.

Knowing for certain that it hadn't opened when it belonged to Rowena Berrysford, I wondered who had sealed it and for what reason.

Her memories invaded me and I recalled the talisman was reputed to have magic properties to protect each first born child until the new generation was born.

The locket had probably been sealed to protect the innocent, perhaps during the witch hunts of the seventeenth century;

around the time of Rowena Berrysford's father. That made sense.

'It's an enigma. I reckon it's at least a thousand years old yet we can understand the writing,' Joe said. 'Shame though. It's lost all the value of antiquity.'

'But what does it say?' I was far more curious about the message it contained than it's monetary value.

Joe wrote down the words and them to me. 'It might not be Shakespeare but it's interesting.'

'Thank you, I can't tell you how much this means to me,' I said, putting it back around my neck.

Bill promised him a pint and I kissed him lightly on the cheek, holding the paper until we were safe in Bill's car.

My surroundings dimmed as I stared at the verse, trying to hold on to reality but the pull was too strong...

Rowena sat on a stool in front of the lectern which held the bible box. Made of oak it was beautifully carved with Rowan leaves and berries and clasped with a brass lock. A fitting container for their precious King James bible.

With her foot, she absent mindedly rocked her baby in the carved cradle which William had made, running her fingers over the inscription written on the bible's frontispiece.

"On the birth of my first born, Rowena. To keep her forever on the path of righteousness. Sir Richard Beaumont, dated in the year of our Lord, 1630."

Mistress Berrysford read the rhyme written in her father's finely penned script.

> *All my descendants remembered shall be*
> *For they shall be named from the Rowan tree*
> *In a duel to the death my chosen must know*
> *You will not survive lest you strike the first blow.*
>
> *Deny not the power on which your life does depend*
> *Or they who are cursed will bring our line to an end*
> *But if you see clearly the world will be free*
> *We of the Rowan give our powers to thee.*

Her father's marriage was recorded on the first line of the blank pages, as was the date of her parents birth and death. And her own date of birth, her marriage to William, and now her baby Rowena's birth was recorded there for posterity.

Mistress Berrysford stood up quickly as heavy footsteps echoed in the hall.

She locked the Bible box and hid the key in the secret compartment as the Colemans burst into the room.

Bending over her daughter she slipped the talisman under the baby's gown for fear the Colemans might use it as evidence against her innocent child.

Walter knocked her away from the cradle, striking her so forcibly she almost lost her senses, unable to struggle when Luke bound her arms tight behind her back.

"Shall we burn her, eh, fa'ther?" Seth asked excitedly. "Burn the witch, burn the witch," he sang tunelessly.

"And have the Squire and all his men come running to our bon fire?" his father answered scornfully.

She realised their intent and demanded to be taken to the elders to stand trial.

"And give you the chance to accuse me, Missie?" Walter sneered. "Tell them what you saw in the woods? Oh no, you won't get me and mine hung for witchcraft..."

'May I see?' William asked calmly.

I looked at him and realised it was not my husband but Bill. I handed him the paper.

'Does this mean anything to you?' he asked as he gave it back.

I nodded, reading Sir Richard Beaumont's words which I had once known by heart.

The verse instilled me with a terrifying fear. Fear, the basic instinct to ensure survival. For I knew without a doubt that the directive was meant for me.

CHAPTER TWENTY FIVE.

The next week passed without giving me a minute to myself. I spent so much time checking everything that might be a danger to me and mine that I scarcely had time to sleep. Every corner of the house seemed to hold a hidden menace.

Fuses kept blowing inexplicably. James put it down to the "bloody builders," of course. I found a nail hammered into the tyres of both mine and James' car.

'Vandals,' he said.

And getting up in the middle of the night, warned by instinct alone, I discovered one of the packing cases was on fire without a sign of entry or any evidence of arson. In less than a minute it would have set fire to the couch and the noxious fumes might have killed us.

'It was an accident,' James said, and told me to make sure that none of the builders smoked on the premises. He refused to listen when I told him that none of them were smokers.

Sometimes, in the bright sunlight of day, I could almost believe his logical explanations, if the accidents had not come too thick and fast to defy rationalisation. But how did they get in my house now the attic was secure?

"There's no such thing as coincidence," I remembered Bill saying. Even so, sometimes I found it hard to believe that the Colemans could be so determined to harm me for no logical reason. Unless they knew about Rowena Berrysford's curse or the feud that stretched back in time. But that was impossible, I argued with myself. Wasn't it?

Whenever I managed to speak to Bill he tried to talk me into living with him, no strings attached; his anxiety for my safety evident in every word. But I daren't commit myself until I was sure the Colemans would not try to get to me through him.

He knew there was more to it than I made out but all I could do was pray he didn't suspect the truth. I only hoped he understood when James drove me to Tannery Lane to pick up my car before he took the old Land Rover back to the University.

I didn't get an opportunity to say more than 'Hello' and 'Goodbye' to Bill.

Trying to appear aloof was more than difficult, I loved him, couldn't even think of living without him. We were meant to be together but when and how, I had no idea. I wanted to see his smile, feel his breath on my cheek, make love to him.

Susan couldn't bear to see her father leave so James had spent his last day with her in York. Justin and Debra were driving to the airport in the MG and planned to spend the weekend in London.

James and I spent our last night together in my lounge, talking about my mother, the children, the house and his job till the sun came up. He made no attempt to make love to me nor did he touch on the subject of if or when I should join him in Canada. But when we got to Heathrow it was a different matter. The man I had married and once loved was leaving and we both knew that nothing would be the same again.

He hugged me tight before he went into the departure lounge, his voice husky as he said 'Goodbye, my dear.'

I saw the tears, as too late to hide them, he tried to turn away. Holding his face between my hands I forced him to look at me.

'Don't be ashamed, your tears show that you love me. Perhaps not enough but we've had a lot more than most,' I said truthfully. 'You are a very special man and I will always love you dearly.'

I kissed him goodbye in public and he forgot protocol and kissed me back.

Cassidy yelped for a cuddle too.

'Cheerio, old fella,' James said, crouching down to fondle his ears.

My little three legged dog balanced precariously to lick his master's face and James jerked to his feet, swallowing noisily, his eyes glistening as he strode away.

Cassidy barked and pulled on his lead to follow. Only the presence of Justin and Debra prevented the scene from becoming too maudlin; I hadn't expected it to be so distressing.

'Take care,' James shouted, his eyes red with unshed tears, and with a final wave, he disappeared through the swinging doors.

Justin and Debra said their farewells and drove off for their weekend break and I rushed to the Ladies, feeling weepy and unreasonably upset at my abandonment.

Sitting in my car watching James' plane take off I felt as if my comfortable "nine to five" life had ended and the future stretched before me like no man's land in the Somme.

I cuddled Cass and phoned Bill for reassurance. The mere sound of his voice restored my confidence.

Driving back to Nottingham, I pulled off the M1 at Luton, stopped for lunch at the Forte House rest and, as Bill had advised, booked myself a room for a few hours, wanting to be alert for the planned spot of breaking and entering that night.

Albert looked after Cassidy whilst Bill and I borrowed his van to drive to the lab, hoping it's anonymity (and dirty number plates) would shield our identity if anyone spotted us loitering with intent.

We drove in to the almost derelict industrial estate, a product of the hopeful seventies and victim of three decades of high taxes, low investment and never ending cut backs.

Bill parked in a dock at the back of a disused Road Haulage Company, hoping the old van would look like it had been left there. Before we got out he took hold of my hand.

'Are you sure you want to do this, Rowena? If we get caught, even if you don't go to jail you'll have a criminal record.'

'I'm sure. If we get caught by the Colemans, we'll have a damn sight more than a criminal record to worry about.'

He nodded. 'Then take the spare key to the van,' he put it in my hand, squeezing it reassuringly. 'If anything happens, get the hell out of here without me. I'll have a better chance if it comes to a fight. Promise?' he demanded. 'Or we can call the whole thing off right now.'

'I promise, but no one's going to catch us, I doubt if there's been a night watchman here for years.'

Climbing out I was surprised to find my throat dry and my knees not quite steady as I tucked my hair in a baseball cap and shrugged into Albert's old navy duffel coat. With Jeans and trainers I could be mistaken for a youth dressed for the job in hand, if there happened to be video surveillance.

We crept away, leaving the van doors wide open; not only to add to the general air of abandonment but to ensure a quick get away, I told myself in the vernacular of old, Hollywood gangster movies, in an attempt to steady my nerves.

The night was overcast, there was no moon and the low clouds obscured the stars. The fine drizzle in the air was enough to chill the blood without wetting the skin.

Bill and I threaded our way through two foot high weeds which grew through the cracked tarmac where traffic had long since ceased to travel.

'Why would the Colemans continue to use this as a base if they didn't have something to hide?' I whispered.

'They own the site. And there's talk of a road extension cutting through here.'

'I see... Greed.'

Bill nodded. 'And a large helping of arrogance,' he whispered.

As we got closer, the squat concrete block took on an air of menace, its deep shadows waiting to swallow us.

It looked the sort of place one might find a corpse which had laid undiscovered for years, I thought as I followed Bill's footsteps. I moved cautiously to the back of the building, hoping he couldn't hear the beating of my heart above the background drone of distant traffic. The whooping of an owl added to the tense atmosphere.

Our precautions were unnecessary, Bill tapped a window with his elbow and it squeaked open on its rusty hinge.

'The ladies,' he whispered, feeling round the edge of the frame and searching it with the pencil torch while I stood there like a redundant gangster's moll.

'Just as I thought. No alarm.' Bill quietly moved a large wheelie bin under the window and popped the torch in the inside pocket of my duffel coat. He linked his fingers to give me a leg up and I froze, terrified. What if I got stuck half way?

He took me in his arms and held me close. We stood like that for what seemed an age, till my fear evaporated in the warmth of his love.

'You don't have to do this,' he murmured.

'I know,' I said, moving away and sizing up the window.

His strong hands waited to boost me up. Without a qualm I stepped into them and clambered onto the wheelie bin. My feet found the window sill and I wiggled my head and shoulders through the aperture, wondering what on earth I should do next.

Beneath me was a sink. I reached for its rim and slid over, my hands supporting my weight in the porcelain bowl as my trainers bumped against the window frame. In the blink of an eye I was inside. But I would never make a criminal, my nerves were stretched so tight my heart would have given out if anyone so much as coughed.

Standing there, trying to regain my composure, I watched Bill ease his shoulders through the window and when his hands found the sink his legs came down in a crouch and he was miraculously beside me, as if he had been doing this all his life.

He opened the door and flicking on the flash light, we were inside the lab.

There was a dusty chill in the air suggesting a place not lived in. Only the faint drift of chemicals overlaying the musty odour of damp, distinguished it from an empty warehouse. It smelled like an old crypt.

He aimed the torch towards the windowed partition at the back of the long room, careful to keep the narrow beam on the floor.

Edging along the side bench I recognised some of the equipment but got the impression that the lab hadn't been used for a very long time. It had a residue of dust just thin enough to assume that the cleaners came in occasionally.

Bill stopped and examined a heavy wooden door. Colemans office. The inner sanctum. He swung the beam, stopping to highlight a wire running from the top of the door frame to the outer wall.

The alarm.

Illuminating the wiring we noticed that one wire also ran to the inside of Coleman's office.

'There's probably video surveillance in there too,' he whispered.

I remembered the security camera instead of a door bell outside Beaumont Hall.

'No doubt the whole lot rings an alarm in his house,' I said quietly.

'Or the Police Station,' Bill nodded, motioning me to search the filing cabinet while he methodically went through the desk drawers, from the bottom to the top. Very professional, I thought.

'Amazing what you learn watching old gangster movies on Cable,' he whispered.

I grinned. He was a fan too!

Trying to concentrate on the job in hand I looked in the filing drawers. If their secretary kept records they should be here but the cabinet was empty except for receipts; petrol coupons, electricity and water bills. I shook my head as Bill came over to my side.

He pointed to the computer.

Sitting down I stared at it amazed. An old Amstrad, not exactly big business technology. The large floppy discs were stored in a plastic box on the desk top.

I plugged in and ran the programmes. They were in early Locoscript which was old fashioned enough to deter a modern thief but I had used the system long before Word.

I looked through Invoices without finding anything unusual and even studied the Wage sheets. Unfortunately I found nothing incriminating, apart from the fact that the secretary was under worked and suspiciously overpaid. To keep her mouth shut? I wondered. God knows what she had to keep quiet about when the lab seemed to be nothing more than a front. Perhaps that was what they didn't want anyone to know...

Research is expensive.

Alice Baker had said that some Companies bought their research. Was that illegal or merely unethical?

I was getting jumpy, panic mounting as the time sped on. And we'd found nothing to use against them.

Bill shrugged and motioned me to leave but leaning over to switch off the computer I noticed a poorly printed letter on the printer's out tray, and read it in sheer desperation. Scrawled across the sheet in Seb's spidery hand, was written; Reprint.

It was to an Import Agent in Zambia, acknowledging the arrival of a consignment of Sting, giving details of quantities and shipping dates etc. I suppose even Colemans had their legitimate customers.

Before we left, Bill tried the door of the storage room and we were both surprised that it opened. We entered stealthily, the beams of our torches searching every corner.

It was empty apart from a couple of discarded drums with the same Eagle logo as Colemans Feed and Fertiliser Company. By the light of the narrow beam I saw that printed on the sides was the name Arnold research laboratories and natural developments.

It jogged my memory; I had seen the logo in the storage barn adjoining my house. But it only strengthened their link in the chain, what I needed was indisputable evidence that through them, Piers was selling the virus insecticide. Evidence which even our stalwart political candidate couldn't cover up. Perhaps Dr Baker had something I could use.

Bill helped me onto the basin in the Ladies and I slid gratefully out of the window and waited for him.

Trying not to run, we made our way back to the van. Stripping off the baseball cap and gloves I reached over and squeezed Bill's hand. A surge of love swept through me when I felt the faint tremor in his fingers. He too had been nervous and he had done it all for me.

'We'll never be Bonnie and Clyde, my love,' I smiled.

'That's good. I'd hate to come to their sticky end,' he paused as he cautiously drove out of the estate. 'I just wish we had something to show for our pains.'

'I'm impressed by your competence as Burglar Bill but I'm itching to know how you acquired the skill.'

I had forgotten how good it was to hear him laugh. We were both hyper on adrenaline.

'Sign of a misspent youth,' Bill winked and continued conspiratorially. 'Sneaking into cinema's through toilet windows.'

'Ah aah! What's all this then?' I asked, imitating the stereotypical policeman.

'I refuse to answer on the grounds that it might incriminate me,' he grinned.

'You can't plead the fifth amendment in England!'

We were still giggling when he parked the van at the back of the house.

Albert came rushing out to meet us, Cassidy at his heels. Picking him up I nuzzled him joyfully and before Bill could protest I headed for my car.

'I won't stop,' I told them, 'I've promised to stay with Susan tonight. She's a bit upset about her father leaving,' I lied convincingly, my gut urging me to hurry to York.

To Alice, not Susan.

Something was wrong. Dr Baker was in terrible danger.

'I'll phone you first thing tomorrow morning,' I told Bill.

'Are you sure you wouldn't like me to drive you?' he asked, hopefully.

'Quite sure, you've done enough for me tonight. Love you,' I whispered, pulling away and getting in to my car while I still had the strength to resist him.

CHAPTER TWENTY SIX.

Driving to York I became more and more anxious about Alice. If Piers Coleman was trying to keep a multi million pound deal quiet, he could well have murdered her son. I could almost see the bastard making John write his own suicide note before forcing the weed killer down his throat.

Giving my imagination full reign turned the simple 90 minute journey into an hour of hell as I drove, pushing the car to its limit in my haste to get to Dr Baker's home.

When I arrived, cold with apprehension, it was three o' clock in the morning and her lights were still on. Subconsciously I'd hoped to find her safely tucked up in bed, annoyed at being disturbed by a neurotic journalist.

Cassidy was fast asleep in his special basket on the back seat, regretfully, I decided to leave him there.

The front door of course was locked. I hoped I didn't have to put my new found burglary skills to the test. I crept stealthily to the small office cum workroom at the back of the house. The fluorescent lights glared, spilling their light onto the lawn. The patio door was wide open.

Alice sat on a stool at the work bench, glassy eyed, the veins in her neck standing out as she strained against putting a bottle of weed killer to her tightly clamped mouth.

A shock of relieved recognition shone in her eyes as she struggled, in a macabre replay of my intuition. But thank goodness, she was alone. No one was there except Alice.

I rushed towards her, my breath rising like smoke in the frigid atmosphere.

Then I "saw" him. His image stood behind her, almost transparent, one hand on her forehead forcing her head back, the other grasping her hand over the weed killer, trying to raise it to her lips. Her knuckles white against the strain she desperately tried to keep the bottle from her mouth.

'Let go of her, you bastard,' I yelled, breaking his spectral concentration.

The out of the body manifestation wavered and became translucent. He glared at me with naked hatred. The feeling was mutual. But it was not Piers. It was Sebastian.

His eyes glittered as he jerked back Alice's head, forcing her mouth open. But I lashed into him with my mind, snapping back his fingers, the snaps echoing like rifle shots.

Immediately she threw the bottle at the wall, breaking it.

Coleman glared at me, then shrugged. 'I have all the time in the world,' he whispered as he disappeared, leaving only the echo of his laughter in the ice cold room.

'Murderer!' Alice accused, taking a note from her pocket and tearing it to shreds.

Her suicide note.

Taking off Albert's warm coat I draped it round her shoulders before I locked the patio doors. Coming back to her I helped her out of the room.

'Do you have money, credit cards?' I asked.

She nodded. 'In my handbag in the kitchen,' she said, through chattering teeth.

I sat her down and switched the kettle on.

'I think you should get as far away from here as you can. OK?'

'OK,' she murmured, still in shock.

The kettle started to boil and opening the cupboards I saw a large tin of drinking chocolate. I made her a cup, adding plenty of milk and a little extra sugar.

'Drink this while I pack a few things for you. Is there anything you can't live without?'

She shook her head, sipping the comforting chocolate. 'First on the left,' she told me. 'But what are you doing here? How did you know what Coleman was doing to me?'

'I didn't,' I shrugged. 'I've just broken into his lab but couldn't fine anything and came to see if you might have overlooked something?'

'Not that I can think of.' She made to get up.

'Relax. I'll have another look when I've finished packing for you,' I said, rushing upstairs before she recovered her senses enough to ask when I'd started visiting before dawn.

227

I found a hang up suitcase on the top shelf of the wardrobe. Inside was a matching overnight bag. I threw three pairs of shoes, an assortment of undies, jumpers and jeans into the bag. Then tucked in her jewellery box, perfume and make up and put in the book on the bedside table.

I carefully hung a couple of skirt and trouser suits in the case and added a posh dress and a few silk shirts. Pulling out drawers I found an old flat sweet tin and opening it, took out her passport. I kept all my important documents in a similar tin in the bottom drawer too.

I was downstairs just as Alice was draining the mug.

'Anything I've forgotten, you'll have to buy,' I said, putting the cases on the work top. 'Before we go is there anything here to prove why Sebastian Coleman murdered your son?'

'Not that a jury would believe. He literally forced me to write a suicide note saying I wanted to die in the same manner as John. Our only chance is to expose his discreditable business practices, ruin his reputation and force him to resign the Parliamentary candidacy before he becomes another example of Government sleaze,' she said.

'I have just come from Coleman's lab but I couldn't find anything to link him to Arland, which John mentioned.'

Alice stood up and clutching Albert's coat around her, she walked back to the workroom, and taking a portable fan's plug from a wall socket, she flipped the plate up on its hidden hinge to reveal a document safe.

'Not very sophisticated but it fooled that bastard,' she said, taking out a tin and opening it with a decorative silver key which she wore like a pendant around her neck.

She laid the stack of papers on the work bench and rifled through them.

'Will this help?' she asked, taking out a couple of sheets and handing them to me.

The first was a photocopy of the Advisory Committee's report to the government, stating that Arland's insecticide, Sting, was proving invaluable to Malawi .

Apparently Sting increased their production and the money raised selling their crops was helping to pay off their national debt.

The second was a photo copy of Arland's bill. They had sold the product to our government who used it as part of their Aid to Africa. Help the starving millions by poisoning their earth!

Out of habit I turned the page over. On the back of the report John had scribbled that in order to pay their National debts, Zambia, who had also been given the product, was exporting their vegetables back to Britain.

Zambia?

Oh my God, how could I have been so dense? So bloody stupid? I asked myself as I put the papers back in their safe hiding place.

'If you're ready, Alice, I'll drop you at Donnington Airport on my way back to Coleman's lab,' I said, picking up her cases and ushering her out.

'There was a discarded letter on the printer, signed by him,' I told her, taking the keys from her and locking the door.

'Arland is Arnold Research Laboratory And Natural Development.'

'Capital A, capital R.' Alice murmured.

'Spells, Arland,' I said. 'We've got him!'

I switched on the electric heater in the front seat, the cocoa and the comforting warmth quickly lulled Alice into a well needed sleep as I drove to East Midlands Airport. I phoned ahead and booked her a ticket on the first plane out.

'Lay low and relax. Don't tell anyone where you are staying or when you'll be back.' I scribbled my telephone numbers on the back of an old petrol receipt. 'Give me a ring if you are worried about anything,' I told her as she tucked the paper into her purse.

'Thank you,' she said, kissing my cheek before she ran to the departure gates.

Deciding to follow my own advice I went home to pack a few things and lay low until I could expose Coleman... After I'd got a few tools to break into their lab again, before dawn.

Cassidy, bless him, was still snoring when I got back to my car.

The closer I got to my house the lower my spirits dropped. It was like travelling into a cold damp fog.

A faint greyness was lighting the horizon when I parked my car outside the gates for fear of alerting the Colemans.

'Please Cassidy, don't make a sound,' I begged. 'Quiet boy.'

His soft brown eyes reproached me even as his wagging tail signified he understood. It was still dark. No self respecting dog would bark in the middle of the night.

Squaring my shoulders, I tiptoed around the edge of the courtyard walking as far as possible on the grass verge. But as we came to my house Cassidy pulled back, his three little legs locked as he refused to move and growled low in his throat.

I unlocked the front door and bent to pick him up but Cassidy drew away from me. Afraid that he was going to start barking I whispered, 'Suit yourself. Wait there for me, then.' But as I went into my house, Cassidy was off like a shot to Mel's, running to the back door at the side of their house.

I was at a loss, wondering what he was playing at.

Leaving the door open for him to follow me when he was ready, I walked into the lounge and immediately knew that Cassidy was right and I had got it very wrong.

The sweet smell of Sebastian's expensive aftershave wrinkled my nose just before the weight of the world smashed onto the top of my head...

I came to my senses in the dark with a splitting headache, nausea wrenching my stomach and a strangely familiar sound in my ears.

Where I was or what had happened to me I could not recall. My mind was a void.

It was cold, damp, and dark.

Squeezing my eyes shut and blinking them rapidly I tried to get accustomed to the oppressive blackness. I was lying on a musty floor, my hands tied behind my back.

I strained at the rope but it was too tight. The bastards had tied it too tight.

The Colemans.

They had done this to me. But that was all my pounding head could remember. And that they were nearby. Watching and waiting.

My scalp prickled with fear when the idiot giggled. Terror and sheer panic turned my blood to ice water.

Thoughts of the damp woods, of Seth.

Seth! Oh God, I had been raped by that monster.

I barely managed to prevent myself crying out at the dreadful memory of what they had done to me... To Rowena Berrysford.

My first thoughts were confused as my brain struggled to retain its fragile hold on reality.

Had all the rest, James, Justin and Susan been a dream?

And Bill? Had he always been William? I could not tell which of my memories were real and which were nightmares.

I closed my eyes as the struggle to make sense of the tangled complexity of my memories became unbearable.

A candle was waved in front of my face, it's hot wax spilled, burning my cheek.

Seth's one eye stared at me. Why had he got a patch over the other? The question puzzled me but I couldn't think; did not know. It was not important.

'She's conscious!' he yelled gleefully. 'Go on Piers, give it to her like you said.'   Piers?

'Put that candle down and get out of my way. This, madam, is what I think of you.'

By the flickering light I recognised Walter, and screamed. But his hand clamped over my mouth, cutting off my cry and my breath.

Walter Coleman opened his trousers and knelt beside me. I stared at his arrogant face. What witchcraft was this? He was too young.

Piers. This was Piers, not Walter.

I must stop him, I thought, but how?

From a distance someone seemed to whisper...

"Squeeze his heart. You can do it."

I was bewitched! 'Sweet Lord have mercy on my soul,' I mumbled.

Pulling my head into his groin, Coleman pushed his foulness into my face.

Involuntarily I gagged and as I retched he forced his penis into my mouth.

'Eat this,' he sneered. 'I swore I'd make you choke on it before you died.'

'Then it's my turn to play,' Seth whispered, his words filling me with horror.

"Use your powers," the voice in my head told me.

'Oh God, help me...'

My head swam as Coleman held my head hard into his groin, squashing my nose into his hairy flesh; obstructing my air passage as he jerked in and out. I could not breathe.

I tried to bite his penis as I realised what he was doing but he was almost snapping my neck with his hold and the more I struggled the tighter the other two held me down.

Sebastian and George were holding my legs.

Why were they unlacing my Reeboks, pulling them off? They were not going to...

Rape. They were going to rape me in turn. Oh God.

I fought to stay conscious. Stay alive.

Bright colours swirled in time with my thumping heart. My lungs screamed for air.

'Please help me,' I prayed to whichever God might be listening. 'Please,' I begged silently, unable to make a sound.

"Be still and sleep now, I will not let them hurt you," the familiar voice promised.

It was accompanied by a thousand spinning lights...

Mistress Berrysford bucked and heaved to throw Coleman off, thrashing her head to dislodge this unspeakable invasion, but with her neck pulled back by her hair she was pressed so tight against his groin she could not stop him thrusting past her tongue, unable to bite as her jaw was forced open.

She heaved as Piers pushed hard into her throat and when she swallowed he stiffened.

"Yes. Yes," he groaned. "Do that again."

He jerked faster. "Again," he demanded, grinding his hips into her face.
Her lungs were screaming for air, her ears pounding. Retching, unable to breathe, the friction burning her throat.
He pushed deeper as she gagged.
She flayed helplessly against the restraining hold on her legs, fighting to stay conscious. Stay alive.
Through the ringing in her ears she heard Seth laughing and jerked back from the edge of darkness.
She must remember it was not Seth it was George. And Sebastian was helping him. They were both mauling Rowena eagerly, pulling down her rough breeches, ready to...
Mistress Berrysford fought to survive, weakly stabbing fire into Piers' hands. As his grip loosened she threw back her head and drew in air through her nose, trying to regain her strength. But her power was being used to keep physical control of Rowena Roberts.
She was desperately trying not to let the novice suffer.
Sebastian gripped her ankles and wrenched her legs apart as George straddled her hips, his fingers invading her. Impatient, he was going to rape her before Piers had finished.
Remembering what Seth had done, Mistress Berrysford was unable to endure it all again.
"Forgive me, Rowena. I can help you no longer..."

My vision cleared and the blackness turned a throbbing blood red as I regained control of myself again.
This was only a nightmare, it couldn't possibly be happening to me, they were doing this to Mistress Berrysford, not me. But the blow to my head was making me confused, they had already killed her, hadn't they?
Yet my throat constricted as Piers frantically jerked so deep, I couldn't breathe. At the same time, George was on top of me, stretching my thong as he tried to enter me. Not Mistress Berrysford. Me.
I yelled with revulsion. And when I did, Piers climaxed.
His foulness choked me. Filled my mouth.

Then I saw his fist clench and he hit me so hard I was startled by the venom. He thumped my breasts, my face.

'Don't knock her out, you stupid bastard.'

Sebastian let go of my legs and tried to pull him off but one of the punches hit my jaw...

My head was swimming, my jaw throbbing and my throat sore but I lay quiet, fearing I would vomit. Trying not to breathe as I tried to assess my situation.

My arms were bound behind my back but the Colemans were no longer holding me down. I was laying on my side with my back against a damp wall.

I closed my mind to the aches and pains and cautiously opened my eyes but there was only darkness.

Echoes of a nightmare scratched at my brain, irritating me as I tried to recall it.

Scrape. Splosh. Scrape.

The strangely familiar noise pervaded my mind. An ordinary noise which had somehow become menacing.

I struggled to identify the sound. I had heard it so often.

Scrape, splosh, scrape.

They were laying bricks!

For a moment I thought it was Albert, but gradually it dawned on me and I had to face the facts. The Colemans were bricking me in.

Bastards.

Sebastian sat on a chemical drum watching Piers and George slap cement onto the bricks by the light of the guttering candle. Where was I that they dared not show a light?

I bit my lip hard to stop myself from fainting. No one knew where I was or when I would be back. No way was I going to take any more of this shit.

Taking a deep breath I let anger take over and I suddenly knew my power.

With my mind I twisted my nails into Piers' testicles and pulled as far as they would go and then some. He squealed and dropped the brick he was laying level with my face, thinking I had bit him. It seemed like a good idea, so I did.

Forcing my teeth into his penis, I bit through skin and gristle, deep into it's nerves and veins, while my fingers clawed and twisted his balls. His sucked intake of breath burst into a thin scream at the same time as his testicles split open.

She let go abruptly and he slumped to the ground, unconscious.
The confines of the brick wall in front of her shimmered and became the open air.
Her memories were of the woods, of Seth...

Confused, I tried to remember who I was.
Panic threatened me momentarily as I tried to remember my name.
A voice in my head whispered. *"You are Rowena Roberts and this is not the woods. You can escape."*
I am Rowena Roberts.
Rowena Roberts. I can speak and breathe. I am not dead yet.
I struggled to my feet, unable to balance properly with my hands tied behind my back. I stumbled into a mound of cement, my knees banging into a low wall, which toppled over.
The sharp pain brought tears to my eyes and I fought to keep my balance.
George leered at me, looking like a demon from hell by the light of the candle he held in his hand.
'Untie me now and I might let you live,' I hissed.
His smirk faded.
'I said, NOW!'
With the power of my mind, I clawed his good eye.
He yelped and stumbled over his brother in his hurry to help me.
'Don't be a bloody fool!' someone yelled.
I was confused, not knowing whether it was Walter or Sebastian. It didn't matter.
'She can't get out of the cellar. We've got her trapped, leave her be.'
The cellar?

"That's enough, Coleman. Be quiet," a familiar voice said softly and mentally thumped her fist into his chest.
His voice went squeaky and he started to choke on his vomit.
"That's better! Nice and quiet..."
Seth or someone like him, cut through her bonds and ran.

I followed slowly but managed to climb the cellar steps, emerging in the barn, full of pallets of bricks and bags of cement. Daylight squeezed in through the cracks in the door frame.
George stood with his back to the door watching me fearfully.
I strolled over, reaching out to open the door as he sidled away.
It was locked.

"Seth? Unlock this door at once," Mistress Berrysford asked politely, sounding like a school mistress.
He did as she asked.
"Me name's not Seth," he chanted. "It's George."
His sing song tone annoyed her, the discordant notes grating on her nerves.
A flash of fitting retribution lit up her mind and she twanged all the nerves of his rotting teeth.
He screeched as they haemorrhaged, filling his mouth with blood.
"It doesn't matter what your name is, you Colemans are all the same," she said.
Why hadn't this power helped her before? Mistress Berrysford wondered. She had been as innocent as a new born babe. Then.

I wondered what I was doing in the courtyard, half dressed..
Cassidy was yelping somewhere and I swayed across the yard to find him.
Mel opened his door to investigate and shouting over his shoulder, he ran towards me.
I struggled to remember one very important fact.

My name is Rowena... Rowena Roberts.

Nothing else mattered as long as I remembered my name.

'Rowena Roberts,' I muttered, holding on to the lamp post, trembling with shock when I saw William.

His long strides passed Mel with ease.

'Thank God!' he said, reaching out for me.

I wondered which century I was in as the world spun into a black tunnel.

He caught me as I collapsed.

CHAPTER TWENTY SEVEN.

I opened my eyes to find Bill washing the grime and caked grey mud from my hands with a soapy face cloth.

Taking note of my surroundings I realised I was on Mel and June's sofa, covered with a duvet but I couldn't stop shivering.

'What happened, Rowena? Where were you?' Bill asked, drying my hands.

No picture came into my mind. No memory. Nothing.

'I don't know. I can't remember.'

My head was empty, I could hardly remember my own name.

'I am Rowena Roberts... Aren't I?'

Bill's looked stricken as he stared down at me.

'It's shock,' June whispered. 'She must have had some sort of accident and lost her memory. It's the body's defence mechanism, she'll remember when she's recovered from the shock.'

Exhausted, I hadn't the energy to remember. Closing my eyes I was ready to sink back into the darkness.

'Come on, darling, don't pass out on me again, please. Don't give in, open your eyes.'

It seemed important to him, so I did as I was told.

Bill was washing the sludge from my feet. 'What happened to your shoes?' he asked. 'And your jeans?'

I shook my head and winced as the pain exploded behind my eyes.

'She's covered with wet cement,' Mel said, bringing in a laden tray and setting it on the coffee table.

"The Colemans were going to brick you up in their cellar," The voice in my head, startled me but somehow I knew it was true.

June was staring at a wet blood stain on Bill's sleeve and gently turned my head.

'Christ! Who did this to you?' he asked, examining the wound on the side of my head. 'You look as if you've gone ten rounds with Tyson.'

'I don't know, I seem to remember someone named Walter,' I stammered.

'Walter? Who's Walter?' Bill asked, turning to June.

'I've never heard of anyone by that name. But Rowena's concussed and doesn't know what she's saying,' she whispered.

'What are you doing here, with Mel and June?' I asked Bill.

'Cassidy started barking very early this morning,' Mel said, handing me a cup of tea.

'We got up to see what was wrong and we discovered your front door was wide open.'

I took a sip of the too sweet tea and pulled a face.

'Drink it up, love, it's supposed to be good for shock,' Bill instructed.

I dutifully drank the milky liquid, while Mel carried on.

'When we couldn't find you we phoned Bill.'

By the time he had cleaned the wound on my scalp, the doctor arrived, put in a couple of butterfly stitches and gave me an injection to help me sleep.

I spent the rest of the morning on June's couch with Bill holding my hand and reassuring me as sleep came in snatches of nightmares which made me dread closing my eyes.

Half of my conscious mind thought I was Rowena Berrysford while I struggled to remain Rowena Roberts.

'I'm taking you home with me,' Bill said when I was feeling more steady. 'I won't take no for an answer so save your arguments.'

'I see! You are just a chauvinist at heart, eh?' I tried to grin but winced as my swollen face hurt. 'Thank you, Bill. Just for a couple of days.'

It would be good to take a break from whatever was looming on the horizon. If only I could remember what it was.

We went to my house to pack a few things but Cassidy refused to enter and that nudged the empty spaces in my brain.

'Why did you come back?' Bill asked. 'You said you were going to see Susan?'

'Probably needed a change of clothes. I seem to remember packing.'

But that wasn't right. I was almost sure that I'd packed for someone else, was it Susan?

Shaking my head to clear the cobwebs sent the room spinning and I held on to Bill's arm while he made soothing noises. I had a vague recollection of driving to York, but I couldn't remember seeing my step-daughter.

The builders had been and gone, leaving the house secure but it had an eerie feel to it, as though it had slipped out of it's proper time and place.

After changing my clothes I threw a few essentials into an overnight bag but heading for my office to pick up my notes, Bill put his hand on my arm and shook his head.

'No work, love. You need to rest.'

I made to protest but my head was aching so I acquiesced; I could always pick them up later.

As he took me to his car, Bill asked Mel if he'd mind following us in my Volvo, and getting no argument, we all drove to Tannery Lane.

I felt fine except for a headache, a sore throat and the nagging worry that I had lost a few hours of my life. And buried at the back of my mind was the certain knowledge that the Colemans were the cause of it.

Bill took me into the guest room facing the cherry orchard and as he opened the window the smell of blossom wafted in on the warm breeze, along with the weak sunshine.

'What a lovely room,' I said, taking in the slightly dated but tasteful décor of the Victoriana vogue. Except for the brass bedstead all the furniture was antique including a beautiful school room cupboard with old brass handles on the drawers at the bottom and glass fronted doors on the book shelves, which almost reached the ceiling.

Bill sat on the bed looking at me while I unpacked. Through the mirror above the dressing table I studied him closely, disregarding the age difference, he and William were as alike as identical twins.

William was not as tall, his frame sturdier. His skin, though smoother with youth was nonetheless weather beaten as opposed to Bill's more cultivated tan. But their eyes were the same.

Kicking off my loafers almost ready to fall asleep where I stood, Bill slid his arm around my waist and pulled down my pencil slim chino skirt.

For a moment I regretted that he was going to make love to me now, when I was so tired.

'Hands up!' he whispered.

I did as he asked without demur, feeling like a rag doll as he pulled the shirt over my head and removed my bra. His eyes caught mine and his face crinkled into a smile. Cupping my breasts in his hands he gently kissed each nipple. Then, reaching behind me he pulled back the duvet, lifted me into bed and tucked me in.

He kissed me so tenderly, my heart ached.

'Sleep tight, my love. God bless,' he whispered, kissing the tip of my nose. 'Don't worry about anything, you're safe here. I'll look after you.'

He was so much like my William that it was difficult to remember that it was Bill.

Closing my eyes before he saw my tears, I snuggled down the bed.

When I awoke it was dark, but the bed side lamp was lit, casting a cosy glow. Bill must have switched it on for me so I wouldn't be frightened in a strange room.

Getting up, I noticed the towelling dressing gown hanging over the brass bed post, he must have brought that too. The faint scent of him clung to the fabric.

I slipped it on and was filled with a sense of well being.

I soaked in a long hot bath; basically I was in good shape and my powers of recuperation were tip top, I thought, peering at myself in the steamed up mirror, its blurry reflection easier for me to handle.

My face was swollen and one eye was puffed and red but the laughter lines were still not deep enough to call wrinkles. My hair, copper red and curly, was my crowning glory, so everyone said. Me, I wished it was straight and fashionable. I pulled it over the small shaved spot to hide the stitches on my crown. And wearing only a thong and bra I tied Bill's robe tightly around my waist and ventured nervously downstairs.

Bill rushed out of the kitchen to greet me. 'Hello, petal. Feeling better now?' he asked, putting his arm round my shoulder and leading me to the table. 'You look fantastic.'

My heart did its usual hand stand when he smiled.

Cassidy bounded up to meet me, yelping an excited greeting.

'What a welcome. I love it,' I said, sniffing like a Bisto kid to hide my pleasure. 'That smells good, I could eat the proverbial horse between two mattresses.'

Albert turned from his cooking and grinned. 'Sorry. Horse is orf!' he said, as he served out a delicious coq au vin.

After the meal we took coffee into the lounge.

'What happened last night?' Albert asked quietly.

Bill frowned, trying to warn him off the subject.

'I don't know,' I said.

'Start at the end, what is the last thing you remember doing?'

'Cassidy wouldn't go into the house with me.' I remembered that much.

My dog couldn't take the reproach in my voice and jumped inelegantly onto my lap. I made a fuss of him till he felt better.

'Maybe I should take more notice of you, my little love. Your sense of danger is stronger than mine.'

'His instinct for survival might have saved you,' Albert said.

He was right of course.

'Either I fell down the cellar steps,' I mused, feeling my sore head, ' or someone hit me and knocked me out.'

Albert, sitting beside me on the settee, reached over and patted my knee.

'But where were you?' Bill asked, leaning forward in the easy chair. 'I searched your house from top to bottom. There wasn't a sign of you anywhere,' he said.

I shook my head, rubbing the space between my eyes in concentration.

'Don't force it love,' Bill whispered, 'It'll come back when you are ready to face it.'

I felt that this was merely an interlude before real life continued. A little light relief.

The image of a dank cellar flashed in front of my eyes and in the background was the ominous scrape of bricks and mortar.

Thankfully the phone interrupted, quelling the feeling of claustrophobia that was ready to surge into a panic attack.

Bill rushed to answer it before I could tell him it was for me. He paused at the door to blow me a kiss.

'I was right, Rowena, he's definitely smitten,' Albert said, shaking his head. 'As I said, it was always too late.'

Tears welled in my eyes at his concern, 'I know, Albert,' I whispered, leaning over to kiss his cheek.

Bill came in, embarrassed and flustered.

'I'm so sorry, Rowena. I forgot to let your family know where you are. That was Mel, Justin has called him, he and Debra are frantic with worry.

'I'll phone them now,' I said, ashamed of my oversight.

Justin soon relaxed once he knew I was alright. He told me James had phoned him, angry because he couldn't get hold of me.

'Tough!' I said interrupting his flow.

'Don't shoot the messenger, Mum,' he laughed, and told me his father had insisted that I called him to explain.

That rankled more than somewhat.

'Explain what? That he left me at the mercy of homicidal maniacs?' my voice was rising but I was still speaking barely above a whisper, I no longer had any control over my once, well battened down, temper. 'And, because I choose not to be murdered in my bed, he wants me to explain?'

I was shaking with anger, but at least I hadn't shouted "Like a fishwife" as James would have put it. The tone of my voice was deadly. Quiet and articulate, the words spat like venom from my lips as though all the patronising condescension that women have endured for hundreds of years had finally broken down the barriers of my restraint.

Bill came and stood behind me, putting his arm around my shoulders he nuzzled the back of my neck and took the phone from me.

'Justin? You don't know me but I would very much like to remedy that as soon as possible.

Would you and Debra care to come for coffee and cake?'

He had one arm wrapped around me and was gently swaying me side to side, moving the receiver so I could hear.

Justin said they would be round in fifteen minutes.

I was still angry with James but instead of shrugging it off, Bill turned me to face him.

'I'm sorry,' I said. After all, he had done nothing to offend me.

He shook my shoulders gently. ' Never apologise because you are angry at someone's attitude. You are allowed to lose your temper, you know.'

After years of James eroding my self esteem, this concept was completely new to me.

'You mustn't go through life making excuses for ignorance and arrogance. Think what this world would be like if no one got angry and no one protested about the suffering caused by greed or indifference!'

He hugged me to him as we walked down the passage to go back into the lounge.

'I must get dressed,' I said, trying to pull away up stairs, but he held on to me.

'Why?' he asked, raising an amused eyebrow.

He was right of course. If Justin, who wouldn't anyway, thought badly of me because I was wearing a perfectly respectable dressing gown, it would be his problem not mine. It was only my awareness of Bill that gave rise to my false modesty.

'I can see I still have a lot to learn.'

Funnily enough, William would have whole heartedly agreed. For all the straight laced ethics of the time, Rowena Berrysford was strong willed and fiercely independent.

When Justin and Debra arrived they were apprehensive, having heard of my injuries. Bill soon put them at their ease and Albert being there helped, of course. I told them I'd go home as soon as I felt strong enough but they all rounded on me.

'OK. I'll come and spend some time with you first,' I told Justin.

Bill interrupted. 'I assure you Rowena will come to no harm here. I'll look after her,' he said and smiling at me, asked. 'Would you like to show Debra your room?'

Debra followed me upstairs, leaving them to talk about whatever they wanted to discuss in private, I smiled secretly at her, she would find out what it was about from Justin and tell me later.

Just after they left, Albert went home too, leaving us alone.

Bill and I spent the rest of the evening getting to know each other. Talking, touching, laughing. We had the same taste in music, enjoyed the same authors and the same books. Best of all, we had a similar sense of humour and made each other laugh.

Personally, I think humour is the staff of life. I recalled memories of days gone by at Beaumont Hall, when Rowena had talked to William on the subject of art, literature and politics. Both William and Bill championed for the equality of the sexes, but in the seventeenth century, when harsh brutality was the order of the day, such philosophy was even more of a rarity than it is now. Although the first Queen Elizabeth had far more impact on the establishment's acceptance of women than her modern namesake.

Bill had the assurance of a strong man who, with no need to prove his masculinity, could afford to be gentle. Even if I wasn't in love with him, he was someone with whom I could share a deep friendship. That is very important; happiness is almost guaranteed if you are lucky enough to be in love with your best friend.

It was midnight when Bill asked if I'd like to go to bed and suddenly tired, I didn't need a lot of persuading.

He had brought Cassidy's basket and Cass was already fast asleep and snoring as usual.

I undressed and put on a baggy T-shirt...Very sexy, I must say. And unable to resist the temptation of the huge selection of books, took a Poetry Now's Anthology of Verse to browse in case I couldn't sleep and climbed into bed.

There was a light knock on the door.

'Are you decent?' Bill asked, his head popping round. 'Whoops, you are. My timing is definitely off!' He came in carrying a hot water bottle and a steaming mug.

'What is he like?' I grinned. 'That smells good, what is it?' I asked, taking the mug.

'Hot milk, cinnamon, honey and a drop of brandy.'

Like Debs and Justin he must think I needed a hot toddy, I smiled.

He sat on the bed as I sipped it. 'It's heavenly,' I said. 'Thank you.'

'My pleasure,' he smiled and thumbed through the book.

I nodded towards the bookcase 'Are they all yours or did they belong to your wife?'

'Some were Margaret's but mostly mine. I still miss her, she was my friend, and I loved her dearly,' he said. Then told me earnestly. "You would have liked her, you know. We loved each other but weren't in love with a great passion. '

Like James and me, I realised.

Remembering Mistress Keeton in the seventeenth century, I nodded, if Margaret was like her ancestor we would have been friends too.

Bill took the empty mug from my hands and slipped the cuddly hot water bottle in the bottom of the bed. 'Keep your feet warm,' he murmured as he brushed the hair away from my forehead. 'I love you,' he whispered.

I drifted off to sleep thinking of his loving gentleness, which spoke louder than words.

CHAPTER TWENTY EIGHT.

In the morning, feeling quite fit apart from the remnants of a headache, I lay wondering about the immediate future. There was no way that I could spend another night at home on my own. And here? Although madly in love with Bill it was tempered with the strong feeling that he would be in danger if I stayed with him. Why, I had no idea.

Everything seemed so calm and peaceful that I thought my instincts could be wrong. But I needed a place of safety for a while, away from the Colemans.

After a lazy morning pottering in the garden together, the watery sunshine changed into the brilliant warmth of summer; one of the unexpected joy's of British weather. Bill suggested a short drive to Daybrook.

'I want to show you the site of Berrysford House. If you feel up to it?'

'That will be lovely, let's go in my car.'

I drove, pulling up under some trees where the drive used to be.

'You found it without directions, Rowena,' Bill said quietly.

'There isn't much left of the place,' I whispered.

Bill held my hand as he led the way through the tangle of stinging nettles and rose bay willow herbs, towards the remaining foundations of what used to be Berrysford House.

I pulled up a patch of dandelions growing through the broken slab that used to be the door step. Then, seeing the ivy covered stone wall which used to be the cool house, I precariously walked towards it over the yellow ragwort carpet which covered the hall.

The stone arch over the back door was still standing, covered with bindweed's white trumpet shaped flowers. At the end of the open roof, the brick chimney stood, it's skeleton finger marking it's place in the indistinct outline of the house William had built for Rowena.

Part of the cool store and stables were more or less intact, Bill, treading carefully over the threshold of the tiny yard room, helped me in to the empty shell.

It's tiled roof had collapsed long ago, only the heavy joists were left and, open to the seasons they were covered with moss. The marble shelf, built into the wall on stone slabs, was still intact on the end wall and under the layer of thick grime and decaying vegetation I could feel the quarry tiled floor.

Even with the strong sunlight streaming in, the north facing cool store was chilly.

'A perfect example of a seventeenth century refrigerator,' Bill whispered behind me.

I did not see the bare stone walls but the jars and preserves which crowded the shelves, the casks of small beer, firkins of cider, the dame jeannes of my best cherry wines. And on the floor were baskets of apples.

So clear was my memory that I could smell the smoke cured bacon which hung from the ceiling; the bunches of dried mint, thyme and sweet basil.

I blinked and saw the lichen growing on the marble slab where my wines once stood.

'Are you alright, Rowena?'

'Yes, just seeing it as it used to be,' I murmured, swallowing the lump in my throat.

'It has that effect on me too, I can almost smell the apples and bacon.'

He shivered slightly. Bill, I realised, was very sensitive to atmosphere too.

'Come out into the sunshine, my love, it's chilly in here even with the sun shine roof.'

He smiled, and taking my hand, he blazed a path for me through the stinging nettles to the stable where the old stone walls had stood the test of time.

The courtyard was not so overgrown, its hard packed cobbles had held back all but the more rampant weeds.

I gasped with delight when I glanced through the archway. Standing proud in the sunshine was a stone seat, grey with age, it's crumbling pattern of rowan leaves recognisable only to me.

Taking Bill's hand we went over and sat for a while, not quite close enough to touch yet drawn by a shared sense of deja vu, closer than we had ever been.

The air was full of bird song and the sound of humming bees. Cabbage butterflies fluttered around the drooping lilacs, their heady perfume intoxicating. Sharing our experiences without the need for words, we were each lost in memories and dreams.

'The building ran from the tallest elderberry tree to the first lilac over there.' Bill pointed. 'I found the original plans. It was built in the Tudor style, half timbered, with fancy chevron brickwork, elaborate chimneys and pargetted gables.'

His blue eyes shone with enthusiasm as he described Berrysford House perfectly.

'I know it so well I can almost see it,' he smiled.

'Yes,' I sighed, closing my eyes against the sun.

'On a day as warm as this the windows would be open to let in the air; the door was carved oak. The curtains were bronze damask.'

'I can only guess at the pattern on the pargetting...'

'A wreath of Rowan leaves and berries,' I told him.

'Of course. For Rowena Berrysford, the first mistress of the house.'

I nodded absent mindedly, looking at the overgrown tangle of weeds.

'The tall blue flags would be coming into bloom now along the drive,' I whispered, shivering as if walking over my own grave. It was all so dead and gone.

Bill put his arm round my shoulders. 'You're cold love, would you like me to fetch your jacket from the car?'

'Yes, please.'

I needed a moment alone. The world was going in and out of focus...

The house seemed to pulsate with life in the diamond clear air as she sat on the sparkling white stone seat to await William's return from his weekly trip to Nottingham on the squire's business.

The glare of the sun forced her eyes into a squint as she heard the crunch of footsteps on the path, recognising her husband's step before she could identify him. He walked towards her, his back to the sun, Rowena smiled, her heart beating an excited welcome.

William had removed his hat, his shirt bloused into the slim fitting trousers, the gleaming riding boots. Perplexed, she stared at the tanned leather; it appeared dull and greenish.

She looked at him for an explanation but his face was merely a dark shadow against the light. Staring again at his boots, she pressed her back against the cold stone, holding her breath as her eyes insisted that William was wearing green rubber wellingtons...

Bill gently helped me into my jacket and all but carried me back to the car, shushing me, kissing my face, rocking me in his arms as I explained that I was crying with happiness that I had found him again.

We spent the next couple of days closeted in the house together, loving every minute of getting to know one another and falling deeper in love. Yet every night Bill did no more than kiss the tip of my nose, often holding his hands up so not to touch me as we said good night and went to our separate bedrooms.

When I took hold of his hand and tried to pull him into my room, he groaned and shook his head.

'No my love. I want you fit and free of James. Free to love me as I love you. When we make love it will be for ever.'

I was acutely aware that he was in the room next to mine. Tossing and turning as desire made it impossible to sleep, the caress of the cool sheet on my skin was no consolation when my imagination went into overdrive. I masturbated myself in a desperate attempt to put out the fire.

When I remembered the things I had imagined I was embarrassed in the morning, but Bill too was edgy and coloured at our first touch every day.

Needing to take my mind off my tightly suppressed sex drive, I talked Albert into fetching my notes.

Sitting side by side with Bill in his office cum conservatory, with the soft patter of rain on the glass roof, I tried to put my notes in to order.

Not knowing what I would want or need, Albert had brought me the entire contents of my In tray. Though, if I remembered correctly, and my memory was still hazy on some subjects, the work I needed was locked away in my desk drawer. Still, I finished the five thousand word article on "Living with a gang of navvies" and faxed it to Jayne Vincent.

Bill closed the account file on his computer and idly picked up my sketch book.

'These are amazing,' he said. 'Is this one me?'

Curious, I looked over his shoulder. He was studying my drawing of William.

'How did you know what I looked like when I was younger? has Albert been showing you the family album?'

Taking the book from him and flipping page over page my eyes filled with tears. I had drawn dozens of sketches of William. Head and shoulders, full length, dressed and- I felt my colour rising in my cheeks- undressed.

I stared at the lifelike portrait of William which he was scrutinising. Stretched out on our carved four poster bed, arms behind his head, one ankle crossing the other, William was looking directly at me through his thick lashes. Naked and aroused, he lay waiting for me.

A tear splashed onto the page and Bill took the book from my hands.

The twin images wavered for a second between the two men. Bill and William.

'I can't remember drawing these. Oh yes, I recognise my handiwork, my technique, but I can't recall putting pencil to paper. But I vividly remember sketching him from life.'

'William?'

I nodded. 'Your ancestor, William Berrysford.'

'You loved each other very much.'

It was a statement not a question.

'Yes, we did.'

Turning the pages of my sketch book was like looking at newly developed photographs which you could only remember taking when you saw them.

William working on the squire's accounts at Beaumont Hall. On our wedding day. In our garden at Berrysford House. With his twin, Sarah. Holding our baby.

I stifled a sob of anguish; hearing the echo of her chuckle as her father swung her in the air. I felt the warmth of her dimpled fingers clasping tightly around mine.

Bill slipped his arms around me and rocked me in his arms. I turned and studied him closely. His eyes, like William's, were shining with love. And passion.

We kissed with hungry desire and fumbled with each other's clothing, unheeding everything in our haste to feel flesh upon flesh.

The telephone shrilled insistently.

Gasping as if we'd dived into an ice cold pool, Bill and I tore ourselves apart.

He picked up the phone and I took it from him, still looking into his eyes. It was Jayne Vincent. Chirruping her thanks for the article, she chattered away talking money.

Bill tucked in his shirt and walked away from me. Watching him go I too, adjusted my clothing as Jayne babbled on.

She told me there was enormous interest in my proposed follow up to the cluster of leukaemia and miscarriages around Upper Berry, especially if I could substantiate the link to fly tipping.

At the door Bill turned and wriggled his hand in the now classic gesture from the commercial. 'Coffee?' he mouthed.

'Lovely,' I smiled, knowing he was giving me time to collect myself.

As Jayne hung up, Bill returned carrying two mugs.

'Only instant I'm afraid. I thought we needed a quick caffeine boost.'

'Thank you,' I said, not daring to look into his eyes for fear of igniting the spark again. And, I noticed, he was careful not to touch me as he passed me the mug.

It would be wonderful to stay with him, hide away in this highly charged love nest.

For the first time in my life I understood why my mother had moved away. It was so peaceful without the Colemans.

Early Thursday morning Bill took me to the doctor's surgery to have my stitches taken out and, feeling fit and fully recuperated, I made noises about going back home.

'Leave it till Monday,' Bill pleaded. 'We can have a nice relaxing weekend. How about putting on the Ritz and going somewhere posh for dinner? Fancy "Des Clos?"' he asked.

Although this blank space in my head was niggling me I didn't want to know. It could wait.

'Lovely,' I said, giving in as easy as that, my only concession was to go home to fetch something glamorous to wear.

Bill had "something" to do, he told me. It was something that he seemed so excited about, he could hardly wait to get rid me of me.

'Tired of me already? Such is the way of this wicked world!' I joked, flinging the back of my arm over my eyes in true melodramatic fashion.

'It's a surprise, but then again, it might not be.'

'That's very mysterious. I love a mystery, shall I stay and help you solve it?' I started to take off my jacket.

'Oh no you don't,' Bill grinned, propelling me to the door. 'Off you jolly well go!'

Taking Cassidy with me (I never went anywhere without him anymore) we left.

Driving into the courtyard the mere sight of my house filled me with trepidation. It looked cold, empty and desolate. My three legged protector was dubious at first but followed me inside without too much fuss. Trusting his judgement I knew it was safe. For the moment.

I carried him up to my room, careful not to step on the creaky stair, in case the Colemans discovered that I was back.

I packed a silk suit and all the usual accessories; shoes, jewellery, perfume, et cetera.

When it comes down to it we are all nomads at heart.

Carrying Cass and the bag downstairs, I wanted to get away from the place. But first, checking the time, I phoned my mother.

She jabbered on a lot about James, he had gone to the house in Mississauga and promised to keep in touch with her. She gave me his phone number and we said goodbye.

I phoned Susan and gave her an edited version of what had happened and my phone number at Bill's; making her promise to phone me if she needed me for anything.

'OK but look, Mum, I really won't mind if you go to Canada. Take your happiness when you can. If it's there, grab it. If in doubt, don't. It's what you always told us.'

I smiled, listening to her answer to what she imagined to be my problem.

'And don't worry about me or Justin, we can look after ourselves.'

'Thank you, Susan, bless you darling, I'll call you soon.'

Then I phoned Debra. It wasn't that I wanted to keep anything from Bill, but our chats often lasted for near on an hour and I didn't feel right about adding to his phone bill.

'I'm glad you called, I wanted to tell you what Bill said to Justin,' she said.

Fascinated, I listened.

'He told Justin he wouldn't take advantage of the situation but he intended to put up a fight for you.'

'What did Justin say to that?'

'He wished him luck. And told him that although he thought you had never been exactly miserable with James, he didn't think you'd ever been really happy, either.'

Bill and I had talked long and often about me staying with him on a more permanent basis but I shied away from committing myself. There was something that I must do first.

Something that I had to finish before I could get on with my life again. But it was good to know that whatever I chose to do, Debra and Justin would stand beside me.

Then I realised, almost with a shock, that even if I wanted to stay with Bill I would still have to talk to James, he deserved that much. It wasn't any use telling myself that I didn't want to. We all spend our lives doing things we don't want to do and far be it for me to break the habit of a lifetime.

To prove my theory, I phoned James and playing the martyr, told him of my injury's and amnesia. He was worried and concerned but I sensed something was not quite right.

'I have something very important to discuss with you,' I told him.

'Have you any idea what time it is over here?' he asked in such a reasonable tone, I could have strangled him.

'Why?' I asked angrily, 'have you lost your watch?'

I heard his surprised intake of breath.

Pressing my advantage I went for the throat. 'I thought you should know that I'm staying with Bill Weston. Give me a ring when it's convenient for you to talk to me.'

He spluttered unintelligibly and before he could speak I said, 'Goodbye dear,' and hung up.

Glad to get out, I drove back to Tannery Lane and as soon as Cassidy and I walked in, Albert shouted from the kitchen .

'I hope you're hungry? Lunch is almost ready.'

It was good to be home.

Bill, all dusty and dishevelled, came rushing down the stairs.

'Come,' he said, holding out his hand. 'I have something to show you.'

His words echoed in my head, stirring the cobwebs from my rememberings.

'I have a present for you,' he said, brimming with delight.

I followed him as he led me to his bedroom. It was a large room with splendid antique oak furniture and a lovely polished wood floor. The ceiling was rough plastered with exposed beams darkened with age.

The sun was streaming through the open window, voile curtains blowing in the soft breeze.

Bill's eyes shone as he pointed to the object at the foot of the bed.

'Look what I've found,' he said, proudly.

I turned my head and saw his gift.

'I remembered where I'd seen the motif on your locket before. It was on this, which has been in our attic for years.'

He took my hand as we walked to the cradle that William had made for our baby...

Rowena fell to her knees and rocked the beautiful cradle. Fingering the letter "R" which William had lovingly carved on the head piece.

Softly she crooned her daughter's favourite lullaby and gently smoothed her brow. "Mamma's little sweeting," she sang as she tucked an errant curl inside the baby's bonnet.

She pulled the coverlet over the babe, tut tutting as her daughter playfully chuckled and kicked it off again. Smiling serenely she rocked baby Rowena to sleep.

"Oh what a sleepy little babe," she whispered, leaning over to kiss her cheek...

She was startled when William pulled her back.

Forcefully picking her up, he wrapped his arms around her, holding her arms tight. Too tight to move.

"William. Isn't she lovely?" Rowena said, turning to face him.

"Yes, my love. But come away now... Please."

It sounded like William's voice that pleaded with her but it was different somehow.

"Rowena!" he shouted, his tone urgent as his fingers bit into the soft flesh at the top of her arms. "It's me. Bill."

His face was wet with tears. "Please listen to me, darling."

The world about me trembled, William's face blurred and changed into Bill's.

I stared at the strange clothes he was wearing; the jeans, his soft knitted shirt; even the smell of his aftershave intruded into the world of William and my baby.

Disturbed by his insistent voice dragging me away, I strained to get back, my arms aching to pick up Rowena again. To hold her, cuddle her once more. But Bill had wrapped his arms around me in a vice like grip, stopping me, pinning me to his world, his century.

I couldn't bear the pain of never seeing my baby again and fought to free myself, to get back. I struggled to escape but he held me fast.

'No. Don't! ' Bill shouted.

Tears streaming down his face, he pulled me away.

His face swam in and out of focus and stretching behind me, I reached for my child, anxious and frightened.

'My baby.' Frantic now, I arched backwards to reach her, desperate to hold her again.

The sweet smell of her was tangible in the air. But the cradle was empty.

'Rowena, my love,' Bill gripped my shoulders, shaking me, holding me here...

"Please?" she begged, in an attempt to ward off the truth. Every fibre of her being longed to hold her baby again.

The cradle was empty.

She threw back her head in desolation and screamed as she remembered.

It was a scream of heartbreak from a mother in torment, a soul not at rest after centuries of loneliness.

A scream that echoed through the silent years which had denied it far too long.

CHAPTER TWENTY NINE.

The Colemans rode through the dense forest as if the hounds of hell were after them. Each man locked in his own terror of the witch's curse. But the old man's greed got the better of him, his avarice greater than the limited imagination which fuelled his fear.

He led them back to Berrysford House, leaving the sweating horses tethered under the trees, out of sight.

As before, they sneaked into the house through the back door of the cool house and crowded round the embers of the fire to warm themselves, safe in the knowledge that there was no one there except the sleeping babe.

"Come on yo lazy bastards there's work to be done. We must inspect the witch's child for the mark of the devil," Walter snarled. "Till we find proof, the Elders needn't know what's happened here tonight. Best be silent. Agreed?"

Luke grunted "Aye."

Coleman grabbed hold of the whimpering Seth. "I said, Agreed?" he yelled, waking the child with a start.

"Yeah. Yes, agreed."

Seth was dazed, the witch's curse still ringing in his ears.

His fa'ther had no patience, raising his hand he slapped his son hard across the face, cutting his lip and making his eyes water. But he had Seth's attention.

"Speak of this to no one. Never! Silence or I'll break your bleddy neck. Do you understand?"

His hands round Seth's throat he shook him angrily. "Swear to me."

Seth's head was spinning and angry tears spilled down his cheeks.

"I swear, fa'ther... I swear!"

Red in the face, he turned on his heel and went over to the cradle, kicking it viciously. Peering at the baby he stuck his tongue out at her and poked his finger into her chubby stomach, grinning as she screamed.

Fascinated, Seth ran his fingers up and down her thighs, leaving a bright pink trail from his black rimmed raggedy nails as she kicked and yelled in protest.

"Shut the brat up. I'm trying to think,' his fa'ther yelled.

Seth put his hand over her mouth and watched her kick as her face turned blue.

Luke saw what he was doing and shouted at him. "Not like that, you bloody simpleton! Stuff your finger in her mouth, don't try to throttle her."

Baby Rowena sobbed. Coleman walked over to the cradle and studied the child, trying to fathom out a way he could safely abduct her without fear of retribution.

He picked her up and shook her like a rag doll, quietening her cries as she gasped for breath. Then, gripping her in one hand he pulled up her gown and roughly examined her, looking for anything that could be interpreted as a mark of the devil. But the child was unblemished; too pretty. He wondered whether that in itself could be considered a sign of the devil but it was beyond even his powers of persuasion.

Seth wandered to the window, quickly darting into the shadows when he saw a lantern flickering near the stable. "Somebody's coming! Let's ger out of 'ere," he shouted and ran.

Luke followed hastily.

Coleman, frustrated at their wasted journey, stood by the back door and looked round the room. The furniture had the rich patina of age, probably gifts from Beaumont Hall but it was too heavy to carry.

He stuffed two candlesticks in his pocket and a silver tinder box. Then he looked again at the carved wooden box sitting on a high table, a stool drawn up close to study the contents. Had the witch not been sitting there when they came in?

Brass bound and locked, the box might be full of treasure, gold or jewellery, or even...

Walter Coleman's face creased as it broke into an unaccustomed grin. Mayhap the witch kept her spells in it! He picked up Rowena's Bible box and followed his sons.

The baby screamed pitifully.

259

They ran for the cover of the trees, mounting their nervous horses just as the stable lad, young Louis Montegue, carrying the lantern high, hurried towards the house.

Mistress Berrysford had never let her babe cry for so long. She was alone in the house and might need assistance.

Coleman weighed up the young boy. He could go back and beat him to death in a matter of moments and the brat too.

He grinned in anticipation and unbuckled his thick leather belt as he started to turn back to the house with murder on his mind.

Sensing danger, baby Rowena howled.

Coleman stopped when he heard her wailing, as if in his ear. Certain that the child was somehow right behind him, he spun on his heel in fear. Slipping in the mud, he dropped the heavy box onto his foot, the brass corner cutting through to the bone.

His accident not only saved the babe but young Louis Montegue too. Fate had more in mind for the young stable lad than an early grave; his descendants had a part to play in the scheme of things.

Coleman slithered to his feet, shocked by the searing pain in his foot as he hoisted the heavy box onto his horse's back, cursing his sons who had scuttled off without him.

Already his foot had swollen, causing the brittle leather of his boots to split open. A splinter of bone gleamed whitely through the oozing blood. Tears of self pity streamed down his face, for the only person who could have set his foot properly, he'd just hanged at the crossroads.

The baby's cries followed him as he galloped away...

I awoke in a darkened room, the familiar sound of my baby's cries echoing in my ears.

I ached to comfort her.

Bill was dozing in a chair beside the bed and as I muffled a sob he stirred and leaned forward to hold my hand. For a second I was confused, thinking he was William. Only the sound of Cassidy's snoring, assured me that I was back in my own world. But I was in Bill's bed and I couldn't remember how I'd got there, only that I was inordinately pleased to see him, as if we had been apart for a long time.

His words tumbled out too fast to understand but they were full of love. He reached over and switched on the flexi lamp beside the bed and angled it low, away from my eyes.

'Without sounding trite, may I ask what happened?' I did my best to grin.

'You were in a terrible state, love, I had to put you to bed and call the doctor.'

'Thank you. But I'm sure that wasn't necessary.'

He gave you a mild sedative to help you to relax and get some rest.' Bill looked at his watch. 'You've been asleep for nearly ten hours. How do you feel now?'

'Just a little confused.'

'Can you talk about it?' he asked, smoothing a strand of hair away from my face.

My skin tingled at his touch. He held my hand, cradling my arm possessively, as if he wanted to touch more of me. I felt loved, safe and protected.

Memories came flooding back to me.

'The cradle. Rowena's cradle that William had carved for our first born.'

I looked around the room trying to see it in the dim light but it wasn't there.

'Where is it?' I asked, wondering if I'd imagined it all.

'Back in the attic where I found it. I'm sorry, I should have realised that it once belonged to Mistress Berrysford, the motif being the same as your locket,' he whispered hoarsely, his lashes blinking away the tears. 'I wouldn't have hurt you for the world.'

I stroked his hair away from his forehead. 'It wasn't your fault, my love, you weren't to know.' I couldn't bear to see him upset. 'But I'm glad you did, it brought everything together for me. I'd like to look at it properly, if you don't mind?'

Bill pressed my hand to his lips, not realising that he had done the same thing many times, centuries ago.

'It must have been passed down from William's Sarah, generation to generation,' he mused. 'I'll get it for you in the morning, as long as it doesn't upset you,' he said. 'I thought I was going to lose you again.'

I searched his face. 'Again?' I whispered, knowing what he meant but wanting him to say it. Did he realise we'd loved before?

'I can't explain how I feel about you without sounding- well, mad,' his eyes searched the room as though looking for the right words.

'I love you, Rowena. The first time I saw you I was overwhelmed with the desire to... No. The *need* to hold you, kiss you. I loved you too much and too soon for it to be the first time. I feel as if I have always loved you; as if I've been searching for you forever.'

My eyes filled with tears at the thought of his loneliness. Of William, never knowing what had happened to me; where I had gone. Searching for me.

'I've never been one to believe in love at first sight,' Bill told me. 'But the first time we met, all I wanted to do was hold you and never let go.'

He loved me. There was so much to I wanted to say but all I could mumble was, 'Oh, Bill.'

He kissed my hand again, trying to find words that didn't need to be spoken.

'Even if it's only a genetic memory. I believe I was William to your Rowena. Now that I've found you, I want to keep you safe; to make you happy. Come away with me, please. I'll take care of you. I promise.'

Visions of us sailing into the sunset together came into my head, but I was torn between my need to stand on my own two feet and my desire to let Bill sweep me off them.

I shook my head to clear away the weakness in me that wanted to cast Bill in role of the swashbuckling hero. Whatever I had to do I must do alone.

'I have to sort this out for myself, I must find where Rowena Berrysford is buried and get to the bottom of this curse thing.'

Taking his hand and turning it over I kissed his palm.

'It's very tempting but I can't run away. And I won't.'

'I'm just so happy to have found you, Rowena. But.' He took a deep breath and looked away before continuing. 'Even though you are divorced, I get the feeling that you still love James. Alright, so I think he's an insensitive fool. A charming philanderer. But even the nicest women can fall for fools and charmers.'

He thought I was in love with James?

Laughter welled up and spilled over, washing away my lingering resentment at my ex husband's disregard. I had been furious that James had been carrying on with whoever caught his fancy. And embarrassed because our friends knew. With surprise I realised I had always been more resentful than heartbroken.

'James?' I spluttered, holding tight to Bill as he too started to chuckle at the absurdity of his fears.

'Yes, I do love him, but I'm not, nor was I ever, IN love with him. 'I love you, Bill. You do know that, don't you?'

He groaned, the animal sound filled me with longing.

'Bill?' I licked my suddenly dry lips; ' I love you so very much.'

'It's taking every ounce of my self control not to kiss you, Rowena,' he sighed, his eyes dark with desire. 'Please don't laugh but I'm trying to behave like a gentleman. I promised to look after you, not take advantage of you when you're so vulnerable.'

His lips feathered over my closed lids, warming my soul, kindling an ancient fire.

I slipped my hands inside his shirt and caressed his smooth muscled back, my fingers tingling with the electricity between us. There isn't any other way to describe the waves of exquisite tension that sparked through me.

Tilting my head back, I waited to be kissed. But his hands gripped my shoulders and held me away as he stood up.

'Go back to sleep my love,' he said shakily. 'I don't want you to pass out on me again.'

'I don't need sleep,' I said huskily.

His eyes lit up and when he smiled his face lost the tired and anxious look.

'I'll make you a milky drink,' he said, blowing me a kiss as he went out of the room.

I waited, trying to keep awake till he came back, but somehow knowing that, like Santa Claus, he wouldn't come until I was asleep.

Safely wrapped in the warmth of Bill's love I was sure that nothing could hurt me again. Closing my eyes, in the halfway state between sleep and wakefulness, I remembered "our" wedding night...

Rowena and William had sneaked away from Beaumont Hall where Squire Keeton had laid on a feast for them, leaving Sarah and Edward Smithson to make the well planned excuses. They were to spend their first night together a Sarah's house on Brickyard Lane, where a bed chamber had been made ready for them.

The room was dominated by a four poster bed and Rowena stared at it, suppressing a nervous giggle.

William took her hand and led her to the fire. The huge stone fireplace glowed pink with reflections of the blazing fire. He had poured her a glass of Madeira and they toasted each other before he helped her to disrobe.

His long fingers fumbled nervously as he undid the tightly laced russet velvet bodice and the full pleated over skirt split at the front to show off the cream satin under skirt, lavishly embroidered in gold thread and trimmed with gold lace. In a trice it tumbled to the sheepskin rug in front of the aromatic pine log fire.

Kissing her smooth white shoulders with masterly restraint, he removed the friponne, trimmed with matching gold braid.

She shivered as William ran his hands over the silk chemise which clung sensuously to her slim figure. It too, was hastily discarded.

His fingers circled over her breasts, lightly stroking the proud pink tips. His head bent to kiss them, his lips teasing each nipple in turn.

Her skin glowing in the firelight, Rowena blushed nervously. Her face hidden by the bright mass of copper curls, her back arched towards him.

William tilted her chin and his lips claimed hers as he carried her to bed. He made love to her then, arousing the need in her so surely their hearts and bodies seemed to fuse together. As their passion mounted, they consummated their marriage with such pleasure it amazed and exhausted them both.

"Next time will be easier," William assured her. "Tomorrow," he promised, "when the discomfort has subsided, I will take you to raptures you cannot imagine."

How could there be more? She was drunk with the ecstasy of undreamed of delights.

"Next time, my sweet love," she answered, "I will show you how much I love you, by the same wonderful means."

Awakening as the birds were beginning their pre dawn chorus, I moved lazily, feeling for Bill, the dream memory so erotic that I wasn't sure whether we'd made love or not.

His arm reached over me on top of the bedclothes, I could feel the length of his body lying beside me, separated by the duvet.

Turning towards him, an image of William superimposed itself on his features, shimmered and was gone.

I ran my hand over his lean body trying to warm him and was overcome by compassion that Bill had spent the night so cold and uncomfortable, for me.

I wanted to comfort him, to show him how much I loved him. Easing out of the covers I lay next to him. He murmured my name in his sleep as I held him in my arms.

Time stopped, ran backwards.

My memories were so sharp and clear that by comparison my surroundings wavered and changed. Bill's face became William's. My mind went back to our wedding night. And the promise Mistress Berrysford had kept the very next day...

As Rowena's hands ran up and down his lean back, William's muscles tensed, his intake of breath excited her and she held him fast, nuzzling her face into his neck and teasing his ear.

She kissed the hollows in his shoulders, tickling him with her tongue as he had done the night before. The taste of him acted like a love potion and she wanted to feel the hardness of him thrusting deep inside of her.

She looked at William through her lashes, her eyes heavy with sleep. But as her hand caressed his cheek, the softness of youth had matured with the passing of time...

I stared, momentarily perplexed, it was not William whom I held, but Bill. And it was Bill's hands that gently tried to lift me away.

'No, my love,' he said softly.

But I would not be denied my chance to show him how much I loved him. Kneeling astride him and tugging at his shirt, I allowed my nipples to rub against his chest, laying over him, pinning him under me. Bill moaned as my lips ran down his lightly tanned chest while I unfastened his jeans and caressed his manhood.

It was Bill who kissed me, Bill who stiffened as the gentle kiss charged the electricity between us. My skin tingled as he pulled me towards him and we kissed, unable to stop. My fingers trembled as my hands ran over his stomach and his taut muscles clenched at my caress. I scratched him, held him, wanted to keep him with me forever.

William kissed her neck, her shoulders, her breasts. His fingers radiating delicious tremors as they caressed her nipples; hard and jutting to meet his touch, they vied for his attention.

She whimpered and gasped with desire, the faint citrus aroma of his after shave lingering under the warm smell of him, sensuous and arousing.

Aftershave?

'Rowena,' Bill's voice registered only briefly.

I blinked, recognising Givenchy's Insense´. I was being used. Rowena Berrysford was using me, making believe Bill was William. But I could not stop her. Did not want this to end.

I closed my eyes. What did it matter, I loved them both.

It was Bill's mouth which clung to mine, the tip of his tongue teasing its way inside. Leaning over him, I kissed his chest, down his taut stomach and took him into the soft cavern of my mouth. Wanting him. Needing him.

Bill's voice cut through my consciousness.

'Rowena. Please,' he begged, gripping my arms as very near the end of his control, he tried to keep me away. ' It's me Bill, not William. You don't know what you are doing.'

I smothered his protest with my lips, wanting to be a part of him. Wanting him to be a part of me.

'Oh, I do, my love. I do. Make love to me now, Bill. Please.'

He eased out of his clothes, and holding my taut buttocks, arched up to claim me.

The world could have reversed its axis as he entered me, but I would not have noticed. We were together, man to woman, back where we belonged.

In frantic desire I rode him, deep and fast, unable to control my urgent need as I exploded with intense ecstasy.

Still tingling from the shattering climax, without withdrawing, Bill rolled astride me.

We made love then, slowly and sensuously as if we had all the time in the world. I knew his intimate desires as well as he knew mine, each kiss, every wondrous touch, kindled remembered joy as our bodies re discovered each other.

Bill's face wavered and blended into William's as the William of the past merged into the Bill of today.

We soared to a tumultuous climax together.

Bright lights flashed behind my eyes and my limbs went weak in a dreamy faint.

'Rowena, my love, are you alright?' he was rocking me in his arms.

'Wonderful' I whispered.

My senses were reeling, I was intoxicated, higher than the highest drug induced high.

Bill stared at me in wonder, then closing his eyes, he kissed me very gently.

Our love was brand new, like sparkling champagne, yet at the same time centuries old, heady as a vintage wine. I loved him so much I would willingly die for him.

He held me in his arms and as we came down to earth he whispered, as if he had heard me, 'I love you so very much.'

Kissing his forehead I comforted him like a baby. 'I know,' I murmured, my throat tight with emotion. A solitary tear splashed onto his ear and, as if an electric shock had hit him, Bill sat up and took my face between his hands.

'Please don't cry, Rowena. I don't want you to cry ever again. You've cried too much, I want you to be happy, my love.'

'I will be as long as I have you,' I murmured.

'Then you'll always be happy,' Bill vowed.

But deep down we both knew that this magic interlude couldn't last forever.

I had a weird feeling, not fear exactly, more like apprehension mixed with a strange excitement that men would feel before a battle.

Something was going to happen, and soon.

CHAPTER THIRTY.

As if Bill too had felt the chill, he got out of bed, shouldered into his bath robe and kissed my cheek.

'Would you like a cup of tea or coffee?' he asked.

Strange he didn't know which I preferred. 'Coffee please.'

'Stay there, it's too early to get up, my love. I'll be back in five minutes.'

When he returned he was carrying a tray with a cafetiere of fresh coffee, milk and sugar and a plate of chocolate digestive biscuits. 'Sorry I haven't any cream,' he said, but I cut him short.

'I very seldom drink tea and like my coffee strong with milk and no sugar. I'm also very fond of chocolate digestives, milk or plain.'

He sat at the side of the bed and we enjoyed our early morning repast.

'What do you intend to do about the Colemans now that our search has found nothing incriminating?' he asked, only the tension in his eyes betraying how much he cared.

'I haven' t decided yet. But I'm sure we were right, I'll just have to dig a little deeper.'

Something itched at the back of my mind. Something I should remember.

'Maybe when I know what happened after I left you that night, I'll know what to do,' I told him. 'All this seems tied up with Rowena Berrysford; after all, it was her curse that started all this hatred. I think she'll have her way, whatever I do.'

'As long as you remember the living take precedence over the dead.'

I nodded. 'Of course.'

'Are you be sure that Rowena started all this? She may have been just another victim, like you.'

That threw me. 'I hadn't thought of that.'

'Perhaps there was a Rowan far back in the mists of time who started it all,' Bill suggested with inspired intuition. 'After all, Roswell, where Wizard's stone overlooks Arnold, is derived from Ro's well. Rowan' s well would make more sense than Rose well.'

'It would explain Joe's theory about my locket being so old,' I mused, seeing in my mind's eye a bearded red haired Saxon warrior, fighting for his life at Wizard's stone, with a man who looked remarkably like Piers Coleman.

I had no warning as the past burst through my flimsy barriers.

The Wizard, Rowan of the Well, painfully made his way up the hill. Mayhap this night would bring an end to the enmity and jealousy of his half brother, Dacra, the dark one. For if he should win Dacra would be banished from the community and if he lost, all he could hope for was that someone would give refuge to his wife and baby.

He rested for a moment, shifting his round shield as he drew the wolf skin tighter around his shoulders, wishing he could command the weather but this he could not do. He had the gift of healing and was skilled in metal-craft, he could make the finest knifes, brooches and amulets in the kingdom. But more importantly could divine water.

He had won the loyalty of his once nomadic tribe when he divined fresh water during a drought and constructed a Well. This had made him the most powerful Ruler, not only in Snottengham but in all Middil Engle.

Surefooted and silent, he moved towards the Stone. The pain had decreased to a dull ache and the blood no longer flowed where he had pulled the arrow out. An arrow fired by one of Dacra's serfs.

He had been taken off guard, this battle between them should have been fought without the help of any man. Or any weapon. He had not expected such treachery, not even from Dacra. Ahead he could see his deadly rival. Only one of his own blood could have the power to challenge him.

When they confronted each other, it seemed as if the sky darkened as they fought for supremacy.

Jerking myself back into the present before I drifted off into the past, the vision of the two warriors disappeared.

'I've a feeling you're right about Ro's well,' I said, pleased that Bill's mind did not shy away from the unknown or try to ridicule it because it was not the accepted view of things.

'It's easy to imagine an ancient battle fought on that ridge,' Bill agreed. 'Saxons, perhaps.'

I stared at him open mouthed. 'You must have more gypsy blood in your veins than you supposed.'

'Enough for me to know that this isn't just a family feud, it is much older and more powerful. Good against evil.' He looked at me sadly, 'You against the Colemans. I want to help you, Rowena. Remember what happened to Mistress Berrysford.'

I nodded, recalling the experiences of the Rowans and Rowena's. 'Every second generation or so.'

'Or whenever they happen to meet,' Bill added. 'I don't have to be psychic to sense the power around you; and I can almost smell the danger.'

He leaned over to kiss me. 'Stay with me, Rowena. Promise you won't leave me.'

'I have to leave sometime, you know that. But I will always come back,' I said, hating myself for sounding so goddamned reasonable, just like James.

'The only time in my life I have known fear was when I realised that Margaret was dying, and I have the same feeling of helplessness now. I am frightened, Rowena.'

He was trying to make me understand what I knew only too well. Holding me as though he couldn't trust me to stay if he let go.

I comforted him but for a moment, I too was afraid.

'Come with me to meet Mr Jeacock, I've just remembered I have an appointment with him at ten o'clock to do a little research,' I said, changing the subject and leaping out of bed, instantly lightening the mood.

One moment we were anxious that this could not last and the next grateful that we had been given this time together.

Bill got up and stood leaning nonchalantly against the door jamb.

'Don't forget to call Justin before you join me in the shower,' he said suggestively, as he dived for the bathroom.

Tingling with excitement at the prospect, I blew him a kiss and picked up the phone.

I told Justin that everything was fine and when I whispered that I thought Bill was winning his fight for me, I was surprised how relieved he sounded.

'Do you know something that I don't know?' I asked suspiciously.

It came to me in a flash. Obvious as hell.

'Barbara?'

'I'm afraid so,' Justin sighed. 'She went to Canada with Dad. Apparently she was travelling tourist class on the same plane. Ena didn't want to upset you, but he took Barbara there with him and to his new house.'

Of all the nerve! Taking the simpering cow to meet MY mother. I took a deep breath.

'It figures. I'm neither surprised nor upset about it,' I told my stepson but angry tears of disillusionment betrayed me.

I put down the receiver thoughtfully, annoyed that after all these years James could still upset me. Then shrugging my shoulders, I dashed to the bathroom after Bill.

He held my hand as I climbed into the bath tub and stood under the shower with my back towards him. I revelled in the sensation of him lathering me with soap as the fine needles of water sensitised our skin.

'I always wondered why showers featured so heavily in erotica,' Bill whispered, cupping my soapy breasts as he pulled me against his erection.

I moaned as an urgent need flamed through me. I pulled his hands to my pubes and leant forward, grasping the taps, squirming as his fingers took me to the edge.

We made love in desperation, our bodies responding as though afraid that once again we might be torn from each other.

Water slicking our nakedness he thrust into me, his urgent need hard and demanding. Hot water beat our flesh with a frantic tattoo as standing under the shower he entered me from behind. Every nerve ending sizzled, the palms of my hands, the soles of my feet.

I revelled in feeling him inside me and forgot to breathe as the pleasure became so acute it was almost painful. Quick and hard we moved together and for the first time in my life I yelled as I climaxed, feeling him eject inside of me.

'Oh, my love,' Bill whispered as he adjusted the taps to direct water into the bath. 'I don' t know what came over me.'

We kissed long and sweetly; all passion spent.

He kissed my nose and pulling me to my feet, wrapped me in a towel and rubbed me dry. But his hands branded me with desire when they touched my flesh and glancing down I saw he too was aroused.

Holding me at arms length, he grinned sheepishly.

'We've waited too long, Rowena. My little man's greedy for more.'

'Little?' I looked at his manhood and stroked him gently. 'He's far from that, aren't you, my lovely?'

Bill resolutely removed my hand and kissed my fingertips.

'I want you to know that I haven't...er... I haven't had a woman since Margaret.'

I put my finger to his lips, knowing he was about to apologise for not using protection.

'Perhaps you'd like to bathe in private,' he suggested.

Reaching for his robe I cuddled it round me protectively, not wanting to wash him away. Perhaps even now a tiny microcosm of Bill might be rushing to find his Rowena.

A surge of love swept through me, my eyes imprinted every detail of his face on my memory. He could be the father of my unborn child. If destiny didn't cheat us again.

'Please don't look at me like that,' Bill pleaded hoarsely.

'Or?"

'Or I'll have to ravish you again,' he said, his jutting manhood verifying his words.

'Oh no, not again!' I said, slipping the robe from my shoulder as I sashayed to the bedroom. 'Come up and see me sometime, big boy,' I murmured throatily, doing my Mae West impression.

'You've spent too much time watching old movies on TV,' he laughed.

'Every golden oldie on Cable!' I admitted. 'It's my secret vice.'

'Mine too. We can indulge our sad perversion in bed. I have a TV in my room and hundreds of video's...'

Before I could take him up on his offer, Albert shouted up the stairs. 'Coffee's on, and bacon will be cooked in a minute.'

I slipped into my undies, pulled on a peach coloured sweatshirt and zipping up my jeans, as Bill quickly dressed; his shirt clinging to his still damp chest. Trying to look casual, we walked sedately down the stairs.

'I don't have to ask how you are feeling, Rowena,' Albert grinned.

I'm sure that my powers of healing applied to me too and I thanked my lucky stars. And the Rowan's.

Bill went to fetch the cradle down for me whilst Albert and I prepared breakfast.

After we'd eaten, I examined William's craftsmanship closely, it was a beautiful work of art. I polished it until the dark wood gleamed and stood running my fingers over the intricate carving. Bill came up behind me and held my shoulder.

'It's rightfully yours, Rowena.'

I nodded. We could keep it for our child. It was a possibility. One of destiny's multiple options.

'It's quarter to ten, love. Are you ready?'

'Yes, Bill. Lets go.'

Deciding that my car needed an airing, Bill let me drive to Jeacock's office. We took Cassidy with us because he made such a fuss when he discovered we were going out. But the little con man fell asleep as soon as I put the car in gear.

Taut with excitement I introduced Bill to Mr Douglas Jeacock, who remembered Bill through Margaret.

'I used to be your wife's family solicitor before I retired,' Mr Douglas told him, taking us down to the basement hideaway.

He searched through a box file. 'I know it's here, somewhere,' he said, absent mindedly. 'I found it for you the other day.'

Then, opening another file he waved a scroll triumphantly. 'I'd put it with the Keeton's file,' he said, grinning at Bill. 'You'll be interested in this too.'

He showed us the yellowed parchment. A Certificate of Marriage. On her sixteenth birthday in the year of our Lord 1666, Rowena Berrysford's daughter had married the squire's son, Anthony Keeton.

I heard his voice through a tunnel of white noise. Noise which filled my ears, my eyes, my head. Noise from which the only escape was into the past...

Rowena and her aunt Sarah were guests at Beaumont Hall for the duration of the pestilence. She had just returned from her daily journey to the plague stricken village, where she delivered her salves along with provisions from the squire, when the vicar came galloping into the courtyard.

"Fire! Fire! 'Please come quickly," he begged the squire. "The villagers are torching a plague house. Shouting about the Colemans and a robbery."

Rowena's ears pricked up, one of the Colemans had waylaid her and stolen the last of her supplies meant for the fishmonger's widow.

As she ran to the courtyard the tocsin rang out from the bell tower, adding its urgency to the scene.

Squire Keeton shouted orders to his men, most of whom were already mounted, their horses champing at the bit, hooves clattering noisily on the cobble stones.

Anticipating her arrival, Louis Montegue, who had been taken on by the squire and was now the Steward of the Horse, brought her a horse and trap.

Anthony Keeton jumped up beside her and took the reigns.

They needed no directions from the vicar, the noise of the crowd could be heard long before they arrived. They saw the cottage aflame and the rabble throwing burning torches into the broken panes of the tiny window, yelling and jeering.

Rowena climbed from the trap and ran towards the burning building.

"Stop! There are men alive in there!" she shouted, frantically trying to get someone to listen but the villagers stared at her blankly as if they didn't understand what she was saying.

An unkempt, dull eyed, woman pushed past them hefting a thick set boy on her hips, screaming as she carried him closer to the flames.

As if in a dream, a path opened for Rowena to pass and she slowly walked towards them. The boy's black eyes stared vacantly at her, his slack mouth dribbling. She shivered as she studied the child, seeing menace in his cold eyes. He was so like his grandfather.

The world splinted as if she was looking at him through a broken mirror.

"Me mester's in there," his mother yelled. "Luke Coleman. He ain't dead," she cried.

No one paid any attention to her.

Young Rowena lifted her head and stared at the fire, feeling its heat on her face, fascinated by the flames that roared around the dry wooden window frame. She flinched when she saw a figure at the tiny window. No two. Two men were trying to get out through the fierce conflagration. Rowena heard their screams.

Everyone heard. Didn't they?

Perhaps she should mention it to the squire? But the thought flitted out of her mind before she could grasp the concept.

As if seeing through another's eyes, she watched silently as the flames devoured them. Their screaming stopped and there was only the crackle of the fire to accompany the jeering mob.

Rowena stepped back when Coleman's blazing roof collapsed, sending a myriad of red hot sparks shooting into the bright heat of the afternoon.

For some bizarre reason she wished her mother could have been there to see the Colemans burn as their house was razed to the ground.

CHAPTER THIRTY ONE.

My head was in a whirl, crowded with memories of "my" daughter. Once again I knew that my rememberings gave me an insight into their lives and sometimes helped to guide my own.

I was content knowing what she looked like and that she was kind and self sufficient, with amazing powers of healing. I recognised her faults too. Stubborn as the proverbial mule. I knew all this as if remembering someone I knew and loved a long time ago.

I became aware of Bill making our excuses and guiding me out of Jeacock's office.

The sky was overcast and the air oppressive, there was going to be one hell of a thunder storm.

Bill seemed rather preoccupied as he opened the car door for me. As soon as we got in, Cassidy jumped on my lap and I stroked him absent mindedly, grateful for his unstinting affection.

'It's incredible how our fates are continually linked, isn't it?'

'Yes, Rowena. It just proves that we are meant to be together. '

He smiled but his face anxious. 'But now that you've found Rowena's daughter,' he said, as he switched on the engine, 'it's over. Leave it alone now and marry me, please.'

Bill looked so strange I didn't know what to say.

My hesitation prompted him to go on. 'We can pack up and live anywhere you like, as a freelance you are not tied to an office and I've been meaning to expand. I can get in a good manager. What do you say to Scotland, or Wales? South Wales is glorious this time of year, we could drive down for the weekend and have a look round.'

He was rambling, as if he was trying to convince himself that I would do as he asked.

'I can't, Bill. Not yet.'

I massaged my temples, trying to erase the dark curtain hiding my memory. 'There's something I have to do first.'

He looked so hurt that I just had to kiss him better. 'What's happened to upset you?'

'I've a feeling that something terrible is about to happen and I want you to come away with me now. We could be on a plane and out of the country in a matter of hours.'

Something about an airport and getting out of the country itched at my mind.

'Perhaps...' I murmured. 'But what about Albert?'

Bill smiled. 'He would follow us wherever we settled. I know he'd like to move somewhere with a better climate, if only Devon or Cornwall. Please say yes, Rowena. I couldn't go through losing you again. Let's get away, right now.'

My heart was so full of love I almost agreed.

'That would be wonderful but I can't. Maybe later.'

'Not later, Rowena. Now!' he insisted.

'We've waited this long, surely a few more weeks won't matter? Don't worry about me, I'll be alright.' It's funny, I almost believed it when I said it.

When we arrived back at Tannery Lane, dark clouds gathered on the horizon, warning of the storm to come.

I felt bright and sort of brittle, ready for battle to commence.

Albert had just made coffee for us all when we were interrupted by an urgent knocking on the front door. Bill went to open it, curiosity making Albert and I follow close on his heels.

It was the young policeman who had called at my house.

'Mr William Weston?' he asked.

'Yes. What can I do for you, officer?'

'May I come in, sir? I'm afraid I have some bad news.'

My heart fell through my stomach, what now?

'I have to inform you that vandals have broken into your office.' The constable glanced at his notebook, 'on Regent Street.'

Bill looked perplexed. 'How bad is it?'

'Central answered the call, sir. But from what I know of the incident someone on the premises reported a break in. We need you to check if anything's missing.'

'I'll come at once,' Bill said, grabbing his coat.

I took mine from the hall stand. If the Colemans had tried to get at me through Bill, somehow I had to steer the police in the right direction.

'No, Rowena, you stay with Albert. I won't be long.'

A feeling of panic overcame me as Bill told the policeman, 'I'll take my car and follow you.'

'No, Bill. Take mine!' I prayed that he wouldn't argue in front of the police. 'Albert's going to service yours this afternoon.' I said, giving him my car keys.

Bill kissed my cheek and looked at his uncle. 'Would you mind doing what she says?'

'As long as you do the same.'

The police car turned round in the wide drive and slowly drove into the lane. Bill followed sedately and I breathed a sigh of relief.

'I think we'll have that coffee now, Albert, while I tell you what the Colemans have probably done to Bill's car.'

They had no imagination and even if it hadn't worked properly the first time, the same trick was worth repeating. This was not nice at all. The Colemans were forcing my hand. Attacking Bill and putting him in danger was not playing by the rules. What the bastards had done to me and my family was inexcusable but Bill had nothing to do with this.

I sat in the cheerful kitchen, toying with my locket, knowing that I had to make my stand before anyone got seriously hurt.

Even as I thought it, I realised hurt was a euphemism for killed.

Dead...

Bill!

They were attacking Bill and I knew without a doubt that he was walking into their trap. He could be killed. It would look like an accident of course.

Panicking, I stood up and put my hand out. 'Your keys! I need to borrow your van at once. Bill's in danger.'

Albert reached in his pocket and handed them to me. 'God speed,' he said as I rushed away.

Terrified, my foot to the floor I drove after him.

My car was parked outside Bill's office, along with two police cars. I ran in, "seeing" it explode in a ball of fire.

'Fire!' I shouted, thumping on doors as I ran past Bill's office to the end of the hall. 'Fire!' I yelled up the stairway.

Joe's head peeped over the banister.

'Out! Quickly. Get everyone out of the building,' I ordered.

'There's only me in today. I called the police,' he said, skipping down the stairs.

'What's going on here?' A police sergeant asked, coming into the hall from Bill's office.

There was no time to argue. 'Can't you smell the gas?' I asked. 'Get everyone out of here.'

Bill rushed to my side and pulled me towards the door. Joe and the two policemen from Central followed on our heels.

I glanced over my shoulder as the constable and the sergeant stood in the doorway, trying to decide what to do. They appeared to be encased in flames.

'Hurry!' I screamed. 'Run!'

The young constable made up his mind and ran. The sergeant however, slowly ambled down the steps. I pulled away from Bill' s grip and started to run back to get the sergeant out of harm's way. But at that instant the office windows exploded and Bill brought me down with a rugby tackle. We rolled together down the slight hill.

The sergeant was thrown by the blast into the street, landing a hand's breadth away from us.

Flames erupted out of the window and licked their way furiously up the wall and at the same time, fire flared through the doorway, fiercely burning the door frame.

The sergeant got up on all fours, shaking his head dazedly.

Bill reached out and helped him as we staggered to our feet, the heat forcing us all back.

In those few seconds a crowd had gathered but were quickly dispersed by the arrival of a siren wailing police car and the Fire Brigade.

The sergeant, suffering from a skinned face and what looked like a broken wrist, informed the Inspector. 'Gas explosion, sir. Good job I cleared the building in time.'

The young policeman from Arnold made to interrupt with the truth but I took his arm and pulled him away.

'Let him have his moment of glory,' I whispered. And looking the sergeant in the eye, smiled. 'Don't forget the constable. It was he who smelled the gas.'

Bill and I watched as the flames destroyed his office.

'Will the insurance cover it?' I asked.

He looked at me and gently wiped a smudge from my cheek. 'Yes. Fortunately most of my records are copied on hard disk which I keep at home; customers, contractors, et cetera. As I said this morning, I could run the operation from anywhere.'

He wrapped his arms around me and kissed the top of my head. 'You knew what was going to happen, didn't you?'

'Yes,' I muttered into his chest. 'But almost too late.'

The Colemans were striking at me through Bill. Because of me he was in danger.

I had to stop them. Whatever had happened in the past could have no relevance today, could it? If only I could remember.

When we returned to Tannery Lane, angry at the senseless damage, Bill told Albert the official version of a gas leak, while I tried to work out a plan of action, concentrating so hard that for the first time in my life, the ringing of the telephone startled me

I rose to answer it, knowing who was on the line. 'Susan? How nice to hear...'

But she interrupted me with a sob. 'Mum!'

'What's wrong?' Panic rose in my throat squeezing my words.

'It's Alice.'

I was so relieved that she was alright that I didn't know who she was talking about.

'Dr Baker. John's mother,' she wailed.

I went cold and stiff with trepidation. 'Yes?' I squeaked.

'We were all a bit worried because no one had seen her for a while.'

I had.

My mind replayed the scene where Dr Baker was sitting at the table with Colemans out of body apparition trying to force poison down her throat. And I heard his words when I had stopped him. "I've got all the time in the world."

'Then this morning we heard that she is dead.' Susan said. 'Killed when her plane crashed on landing in Portugal.'

Suddenly I remembered. The earliest flight out of East Midlands had been to Portugal. Everything that happened after Bill and I had broken into the lab came flooding back to me.

I held tight to the receiver as waves of horror engulfed me. All those innocent passengers. Coleman had murdered them as surely as he had killed Alice and her son. Just as he meant to kill Bill this afternoon, regardless of anyone who might get caught in the blast.

I chewed my lip anxiously as the implications edged in to the dark recesses of my mind.

Susan was too close to this. Not only had she spoken out in support of John Baker, she was my stepdaughter. I must get her to safety at once. As far from the Colemans as possible.

'Darling, you need to get away from all this for a while,' I said, as calmly as I could. "How would you like to visit your father? As a sort of early birthday present. I'll buy you a couple of plane tickets. Perhaps you'd like to take your new boy friend? What's his name? I asked, hoping he would be strong enough to protect her.

'David Woodbridge,' she said. 'He's from Nottingham too. 'But wouldn't dad object to me taking him along?'

'If he does, you could always stay with your grandmother.'

'Wouldn't she mind?' Susan asked, querulously.

I forced a light hearted giggle. 'My mother? She's the first, last and oldest hippie in town!'

'Beats you then?'

I was relieved to hear Susan laugh. 'Careful,' I said. 'Or I'll make you work your passage!'

'How, by flapping my arms to keep the plane up?'

What had started out to be a wise crack conjured up horrifying pictures.

'I'll reserve two seats on the first flight tomorrow, if I can. Just check the time of departure with Air Canada at Leeds Bradford. That's the closest airport to you, isn't it?'

She sniffed and blew her nose in assent.

'Leave everything to me, darling. The tickets will be waiting for you there.'

She told me she loved me; and I told her to take care, terrified for her safety.

Hanging up I realised this was it. There would be no last minute reprieve. I had to leave this refuge. The real world was waiting, champing at the bit to gallop away with me.

It had been pleasant to escape for a while but I had to go back and fight. Had to stop the Colemans from hurting my loved ones to get at me.

Or hurting anyone who got in the way of their lust for money and power.

First, I would get my notes on Arland and the Scorpion virus to see if I had enough evidence to incriminate Coleman. The letter was long gone; he wouldn't make that mistake again. But I'd keep plugging away at him, bit by bit. Drag it out and keep hitting him low. Throw enough mud until some of it sticks.

Perhaps I could enlist the help of John Baker's girl friend at Friends of the Earth, not that the government took any notice of what they called cranks and loonies or environmental groups. I could almost hear their contemptuous groans as they grimly defended their reactionary candidate.

They would stand by him of course... If he won.

And if he did, God forbid, I would try to trap him, entice him into assaulting me. I shied away at the thought of assault and amended it to bribery. I could handle bribery.

Anxious, Bill came to see if I was alright. 'Rowena?'

'I'm sorry but I've got to go to York,' I said. The lie coming easily to my lips. 'Please understand. I can't stay here any longer, Susan needs me.'

I hated using her as an excuse but I had to fight my own battles and had to do it now. I ran upstairs to pack a change of clothes before I broke down and lost myself forever.

Bill held me tight as if he could physically keep me there. Willing to die in this man's arms, I struggled to escape them.

'Let me come with you. We can tell her you're going to marry me.'

'No, Bill,' I tried to smile. 'I have to handle it on my own.'

He groped around in his pocket and pulled out his silver dollar. 'Toss you for it?'

I remembered the last time he'd said that and realised his coin was weighted. Before he could choose I replied quickly. 'Ok. Heads, I go on my own.'

Defeated, Bill sighed, knowing he'd been rumbled and put the coin away.

'Please don't leave me,' he said quietly.

His words were simple but the emotion in his voice ate at my heart.

'I must. I need to sort things out for Susan.' I had to be firm or everything was lost. The longer I stayed here the more danger he was in.

'You will come back won't you?' he asked.

'Yes I will, as soon as I can. I promise.'

My own misery might be well deserved but I was ashamed at the suffering I was putting him through. 'You're the only man I've ever loved. Ever could love. I'm sorry darling, really sorry, I must go, but,' I managed to grin, 'in the words of Arnie, I'll be back.'

Bill looked defeated. My eyes welled with tears but I blinked them away. To make him understand, I told him part of the truth.

'I have to go, Susan could be in danger. And I must end the curse,' I added.

He stared at me, as if he knew I was smearing the truth with omissions. 'You mustn't live your life for some long dead witch!'

I flinched at the insulting description of Rowena.

'Face it. She must have been a witch. Her curse has lasted for more than three hundred and fifty years. She's been dead for centuries yet she's still dangerous. Rowena Berrysford must have had unbelievable supernatural powers, and is trying to use them through you.'

It was true. I had often felt that she was trying to take me over.

'That's why I've got to learn to control the power myself,' I said. 'My power. I know it's dangerous. I am dangerous!' I stressed.

'That doesn't worry me, my love. Let me come with you.'

'No, it's something I must do alone.'

Bill sighed, dropping his hands to his sides, letting me free.

Mindlessly I folded my clothes and packed them into my suitcase.

'You will come back won't you?' he begged.

I couldn't take his heartbreak. My heartbreak. My endurance was at its lowest ebb.

'Of course,' I said, trying to smile.

Taking a deep breath I stiffened my resolve. I could not, would not, let Coleman win this time. Too much depended on the outcome.

I might not be able to prove that he had killed the Bakers but I had John's papers which might be enough to incriminate him. Topple Coleman before he got a seat in Parliament and stop him exploiting the third world with his venomous products.

Snapping the case shut and before Bill could stop me, I picked up my handbag and rushed from the room and down the stairs, calling for Cassidy.

He ran ahead of me, jumping with excitement while I threw a scarf round my neck and grabbed my waxed jacket from the hall. We were in the Volvo before Bill got out the front door.

I steeled myself not to turn round, watching through the rear view mirror as he jumped into Albert's old van to follow me. It was a simple matter even with my limited mechanical knowledge to flood his carburettor and I knew it would be a couple of minutes before he could start the engine. That would give me enough time to get away.

I drove, miraculously without an accident, to Front Street, tears rolling down my face.

Puzzled, Cassidy laid his head on my lap and pawed at my jeans but I dare not indulge in his comfort or my heart would surely break.

I tried to think logically; like James. If I was going to survive this night with only Cassidy to protect me there were things we needed before the shops closed.

I bought two big torches and a stout bolt in the supermarket. And a tin of dog food, some bread, butter and cheese and a carton of pineapple juice, for sustenance.

At the travel agents I was surprised to discover that one could get on a plane almost as easily as a bus. I phoned Susan and asked if she and David, her boy-friend, could be ready to go tomorrow and she said it was Ok so I booked two seats on tomorrow afternoon's flight; the tickets to be picked up by Susan at the airport.

I hoped to ensure her safety by keeping the Colemans occupied tomorrow and prayed that Canada was out of the reach of their destructive powers. I didn't know what to do next.

The night loomed before me like a venomous Cobra.

I was scared to death. One woman and her three legged dog. I reached out for him. 'Come on, Cassidy my old mate. You're all I've got.'

He cocked his head to one side and gave me a very old fashioned look. Trying not to think about Bill, I drove back home, already missing him so much my palms ached. Now I knew why people clenched their nails into their hands in anguish, it relieved the pain.

It had grown dark without my being aware of it, so switching on the headlights to lighten the gloom of the oncoming storm, I drove in to Beaumont Court.

June and Mel's house was in darkness. No refuge there. I was on my own.

Searching for my keys I heard the crunch of a car on gravel and was trapped in the beams of Piers Coleman's Porsche. Now they knew I was back. But this time I was not an innocent like Mistress Berrysford.

This time I was prepared. Ready to put an end to centuries of mindless violence.

CHAPTER THIRTY TWO.

Opening the door and going into my house made me feel like a lamb going to the slaughter. I tried to switch on the light without stepping across the threshold. Darkness lurked in the living room like a living monster.

'Come on Cassidy, don't get temperamental on me now. I need you.'

He yapped to let me know what he thought of my stupidity, then, my intrepid little hero dashed into the house before me and sniffed around searching for intruders.

'Good boy.' I knew how much his bravado had cost him. He hopped back, his tail wagging furiously.

'Oh, my love, what would I do without you?' I murmured, picking him up and nuzzling his soft fur. 'We're committed now to whatever fate has in store for us,' I told him, snorting ruefully.

'If this was a movie, committed was what I'd recommend for someone about spend the night here alone, with the Colemans lurking in the barn. Thank goodness none of them are called "Freddie" and this isn't Elm Street!'

Cassidy yelped in agreement.

I put him down. 'You're getting too damn sassy,' I said.

Not only that, he was probably right. What was I doing acting as bait without telling anyone where I was?

As if reading my mind, Cassidy jumped up and resting his paws on the side table, nosed the phone.

Should I call Bill? Or Justin? But that would defeat the object. I had come here to keep them out of harm's way.

With Cass close at heel we went through the house, checking the attic access, the windows and switching on all the lights. Hoping I'd feel safer if the place was lit up like a beacon, at least then Mel and June would keep an eye out for me. Just as extra insurance.

Panic was accelerating my heartbeat as the darkness outside mirrored the windows.

When we got back downstairs I picked up the mail and briefly sorted out all the mind boggling junk before dumping it on the table, to read after I'd studied John's notes. It would help to pass the time.

Taking the two bright flashlights I'd bought (in case the fuses blew again) and the bolt to put on the door at the bottom of the stairs, I laid them on the table.

'I'll just get a screwdriver from the tool box in the cellar and put the bolt on first, after all we don't want the bastards to creep up and catch us unawares, do we?'

Cassidy backed away and tried to appear interested in a scrap of paper on the floor.

I opened the cellar door.

My lips formed words, trying to quell the rising panic with a wisecrack. 'Been there; wrote the book,' I croaked, my hand shaking as I reached over and switched on the lights.

Relieved when the bulb didn't blow I crept down the cellar steps, afraid to awaken the nightmares which were hiding there.

Noises in my head... Voices. Piers Coleman... Pictures flashed onto my retina.

'Oh, my God.'

I was violently sick as I remembered what Piers had done to me. My knees were trembling, refusing to help me as I leant heavily against the wall.

The spasm passed and I looked round. The dividing wall was still crumbling. But the hole was missing. It used to have a loose brick where I could see into next door's cellar.

When I spread my hands against the wall cold vibrations shot through my fingers and shivered up my arms.

I squeezed my eyes shut, trying in vain to erase the images which came into my mind.

Cautiously feeling my way along the wall, a loose brick almost crumbled under my fingers. I slowly eased it out. And the wall moved slightly.

The Coleman's must have come in to my house this way and carried me into their cellar. Fighting back a scream I remembered everything...

Darkness closed in on me, squeezing the oxygen from the musty air as I gagged in sick revulsion.

I ran back to the kitchen to wash the image of Piers out of my mind. I wanted to scour myself clean. Scald him from my throat.

My knees gave way and I sat at the dining table with a jolt, remembering that Mistress Berrysford had taken the brunt of the assault; protecting me from the degradation until she could take no more.

Or maybe I imagined it. Blocked the truth from my mind to make it easier to take.

I think not.

Fear dissolved as anger blazed, that they should hurt her again.

'You murdering bastards!'

I picked up one of the torches and by its brilliant beam I went back and removed enough bricks to enter the cellar under their barn.

The beam was unsteady but my fingers were shaking with fury now, not fear. The torch illuminated the stained and torn mattress and the memories filled me with revulsion.

Please, God, it was only the bastard Piers who had molested me. Not George too. I was skating on the edge of sanity now, and took a deep breath to control myself.

Swinging the torch round their cellar I spotlighted the old chemical drums with their eagle logo. The beam wavered as it lit upon the cement set in a lump by the new, half finished wall.

This had almost been my last resting place.

I could still feel the hot candle wax dripping onto my face as George gloated over me.

My stomach churned as I remembered that Sebastian got his kicks from watching Piers' sexual perversion. And George.

Oh God, had he raped me?

Horrific memories threatened to undo me but sucking in cool air through my clenched teeth I remembered what Mistress Berrysford had suffered for me. The thought gave me strength.

What had happened couldn't hurt me, it was all in the past. Finished.

'Good evening, Rowena.'

Startled, I spun on my heels and faced Coleman, his ice blue eyes glinted with derision as he strode towards me. 'I'm delighted to see you again,' he waved a bandaged hand at the unfinished wall. 'Especially in such ideal surroundings.'

The index and middle fingers of his left hand were in plastic finger splints. I was gratified to realise that I had broken them when he was in his out of body manifestation.

Behind him stood Piers and George. They did not seem to be so pleased to see me.

Seb's gold lighter glinted in the beam of my torch as he flicked it and lit the stub of a candle.

'Turn off the torch,' he snapped, 'we don't want to arouse anyone's curiosity, do we?'

'Be dammed if I will,' I said, flashing the bright beam into his pale eyes.

Piers, no longer needing a walking stick, picked up a spade and handed a shovel crusted with blisters of cement, to George. They started towards me, cutting off my escape.

'We have some unfinished business with you,' Piers snarled.

I didn't stand a chance against three of them.

Then I heard Cassidy whining in my cellar.

'Cassidy! Here boy,' I called sharply, hoping he would obey without question.

He jumped through the hole in the dividing wall, bless him, and growled low in his throat when he saw the hated men who had hurt him.

The numbing fear left me as my little dog stood square in the path of the Colemans.

Sebastian muttered, 'Don't just stand there. Get the witch.'

'And the damn dog,' Piers added loudly.

There was no mistaking the bravado in his voice. I had only to shout Boo! And he would run. The only trouble was, invisible fingers were round my throat, choking me. Seb's fingers.

He grinned as he casually leant against the door

'Get the witch! Put a sack over her head so she can't put the evil eye on us again,' George said slyly.

'Yes,' his father smiled approvingly. 'That's how to handle a witch.'

From the other side of the cellar he loosened his hold on my throat.

I coughed and spluttered, thanking providence for his arrogance.

Picking up an empty cement bag George held it in front of himself like a shield. 'You hold her,' he told Piers, 'and I'll bag her,' he said, his eyes glittering in anticipation.

Terror gnawed at my bowels and I wanted to run but thankfully my brave little Cassidy was on guard, growling and snapping at them all.

He tousled at George's legs, keeping him back. Keeping them all back. Keeping me safe. Buying me time to draw on my power.

Concentrating, I prepared for them.

As Piers swung the spade over his shoulder to bring it down on my neck like a scythe, my mind parried the blow.

Mentally I squeezed his arm, forcing it back. Dislocating his shoulder.

Shock and disbelief on his face quickly changed to a grimace of agony. His thin screech ended in a whimper when his eyes rolled back and he dropped to the floor.

One down two to go.

My dog just managed to leap out of the way on his three little legs as the spade fell to the floor with a resounding clang, missing him by inches.

'Cassidy!' I yelled, in control of my vocal chords once more, suddenly frightened for him against these bullies. He was too close to them.

'Here, boy. Quick!'

I ran forward to snatch him but when my fingers caught hold he twisted out of my hands, snarling at George as he held the shovel like a club.

'NO!' I screamed.

As Cassidy sprung, George swung the shovel, catching him in the throat.

The sickening thud of steel on bone splintered my soul.

Time went into slow motion as I watched him twisting through the air, bleeding and broken.

Cassidy fell to the ground like a stone.

George mumbled incomprehensibly and went to kick him as he lay panting on the floor.

Grabbing Piers' spade I held it defensively as I bent to pick up my little hero.

'Get away from him!'

Reaching for my beloved dog I shoved him back with my power.

He whimpered and held his hands up in surrender. Sebastian just looked surprised. Piers groaned as he staggered up.

'Back!'

The force sent them all stumbling backwards as if they'd been shot.

'Stay there, you Bastards!' I spat, holding them like statues.

Tucking the spade under my arm I picked up Cassidy and cradling his limp body, thanked God that there was a faint heartbeat.

Turning on my heel I climbed through the gap in our cellars and taking the stairs two at a time, left the Colemans struggling to move.

Running out of the house I realised that I still had the spade. My arm muscles were gripping it so tightly into my body that the blood had stopped circulating to my fingers.

I threw the damn thing onto the back seat and cradling Cassidy on my knee, I drove, breaking all speed limits, to the vets.

My jeans were wet with his warm blood; I crooned and caressed him, driving with one hand as the other held him protectively.

I tried to heal him by visualising the workings of his body, his bones and arteries, but I was ignorantly stumbling in the dark.

There was something of vital importance that I should remember, something that someone had said that would help me. But my mind was blank.

Tears of frustration rolled down my face and splashed onto my trembling hands. Breathing deeply, I tried to remember what I had read about the gift of healing. But the books didn't tell you how; they just proved that it could be done.

At Mapperley top, I felt his heart fluttering beneath my fingers and heard him rasping for breath. Ice cold fear drenched me as the air rattled in his throat and he jerked and trembled violently.

Screeching the car to a halt, with both hands around his chest I frantically tried to make him better, to force my power into him.

I knew I could heal him; I had just forgotten how.

My fingers were gripping him too tight as I willed him to stop bleeding. For a brief moment I was overjoyed as the flow of blood stemmed. Then I noticed that his heart had stopped beating.

I held my breath.

The silence overwhelmed me.

Panicking I searched for a heartbeat, a sign of life.

Shaking him gently I pleaded with him. 'Cassidy, oh, please don't die. You are all I've got.'

His beautiful eyes stared at me blankly.

'Please, darling, be a good boy and I'll buy you a big box of After Eight mints,' I bribed beguilingly. His favourite, forbidden, bad for his teeth, chocolates.

I waited for him to jump up and lick my face, disappointed and puzzled because there was no reaction. I refused to think of the obvious reason for his lack of response.

'Come on, darling. Please stop fooling about,' I whispered.

Desolate, my mind would not accept the truth.

Cassidy's head lolled unnaturally, the wound in his neck was deep, severed through to the bone. Desperately I tried to hold him together, like a child with a broken doll.

My grief erupted. Racked with anguish, I cried like a baby. Sobbing with terrible loneliness, I didn't care about the passers by who stared curiously into the car.

Rocking him in my arms, my tears mingled with his blood as I held him to my breast.

I was alone now. My brave little dog was dead.

CHAPTER THIRTY THREE.

Cassidy was dead.
It hit me like a punch in the stomach. I doubled up, crossing my arms over my waist and sat rocking, trying to squeeze the pain away. My thoughts were in a turmoil; the sun had disappeared from my life, how could I face each day without him?

'Oh, sweet Jesus, help me, please!' I begged as I sat nursing my beautiful Cassidy, trying to keep him warm, holding on to him as long as I could.

He was my friend, my constant companion.

Tears rolled unheeded down my cheeks as I sat numb with shock. I stared blindly out of the car windscreen; people and traffic milled to and fro, carrying on as if nothing had happened. It was unnatural, inhuman.

The confines of my car crowded in on me, oppressive and claustrophobic as my mind replayed in dreadful slow motion George's powerful swing of the shovel.

I shuddered, hearing again the chilling sound as it crunched into my defenceless three legged dog.

The bastards had murdered him, killed Cassidy.

A scream of rage erupted like a boiling volcano and I wanted revenge.

They would pay for their vicious crime, I vowed, still stroking his broken body.

'Oh yes, they will pay,' I whispered, gently closing his soft brown eyes. 'But first, dear God. First, I must lay you to rest.' My throat constricted, making my words unintelligible.

His resting place should be somewhere beautiful, he deserved that. I immediately thought of Bill's orchard where Buggalugs lay under the cherry trees. But I couldn't go back there or Bill would be caught in the crossfire like Cassidy.

I couldn't bury him in my own garden either. Not near those murdering bastards.

Distraught, I started the car, wiping my face on my sleeve. Not in Beaumont Court.

I drove him instead to the woods where it all began; accompanied by the deep rumble of thunder and cracks of lightning as the storm rolled towards me.

The hedges and skeletal branches of trees were illuminated by my headlights as I sped past, emphasising the nightmare quality of the journey. I would have to bury him myself.

Tears filled my eyes again. I couldn't bear the thought of covering him with the damp earth. But I would never allow anyone else to do it for me. He was my dog. My friend. I would make sure he was comfortable before I left him to his lonely sleep.

Holding him on my lap and stroking his soft fur, sticky with his blood, I sang to him as I drove all the way to the crossroads. He loved it there.

I wished I had the faith to gain comfort from religion. I found myself praying there was a heaven where he could play with all the children while he waited for me. But all the while my mind was going round in circles trying to remember the significance of what someone had once said.

My driving must have gone on automatic because I was jolted to discover that I had arrived at the oak tree without any recollection of the journey. I suppose I was in shock.

I parked the Volvo so that its lights were shining into the trees, casting the old oak tree into bright relief. Pulling off my silk scarf, I wrapped it around my beloved Cassidy. And by the light of the head lamps, I carried him to the edge of the trees and laid him under their shivering canopy.

Not a breath of wind was in the air, only the soft whispering of the trees emphasised the stillness; yet I was no longer afraid.

Holding my grief tightly within, I ached with loneliness and daren't allow myself the luxury of looking at him as he lay there so quiet. Trying to shut out the pain I turned my back and groped for Coleman's spade which I had carelessly thrown in the back of my car.

Cassidy had saved my life. And now he was dead.

I stiffened as the full implications of the Coleman's actions dawned on me. These men were evil, hell bent on killing me and mine. I could just as easily have been grieving the death of Susan in my car. Or Justin; or James. And but for the grace of God, Bill would have been burned to death in his office.

I brushed the tears from my eyes and "saw" an almost living apparition of Cassidy jumping at my feet, sniffing and pawing the ground to help me choose a good place to dig.

In a trance I followed him to the oak tree. Wanting him to lay undisturbed, I dug where he scrabbled. The image of his bright soul slowly faded and I was once again bereft.

Concentrating on the grim work I was thankful for the hard physical labour that made my back ache and my hands blister, it helped to keep my sorrow at bay.

The air smelled of damp leaves and earth with a faint undertone of sulphur. It was charged with energy, yet warm and thick, it was like trying to breathe mud.

Stopping for a second, I looked up at the night sky, waiting for the storm to break and wishing that it would hurry and give some relief. Lightning flashed in the distance and I counted three seconds till the thunder rumbled before I carried on with my sad task.

The spade clinked on some solid object making the digging more difficult but I didn't care. Spitting on the palms of my hands I forced my foot harder on to the blade and turned another clod.

Something glinted in the headlights.

I dug another spade full and stared transfixed as I turned the soil.

Something gleamed in the black earth.

I wiped the sweat from my eyes not believing what I saw in the eerie shadowy light.

There, under the tree was a hand.

I looked at it with awe. Dark yellow bones reached out to me through a tangle of roots. I scrabbled the dirt away from the skeleton.

In the dark night, under the old oak tree, I knew I had found Rowena Berrysford.

They hadn't even bothered to move her, the murdering bastards must have buried her where she fell.

I held the skeletal hand reverently to my breast.

A flash of worry crossed my mind and I wondered if I should move her bones and have her buried in consecrated ground, but was dismissed as I instinctively knew that it was too late for that, she wanted to stay here in familiar surroundings.

Looking up through the branches of the oak tree I saw the fast moving storm clouds as they obscured the moon. Electricity crackled in the purple sky and thunder rolled closer. I thought it a fitting accompaniment to my macabre discovery.

Gently stroking the dirt away from her head I had the feeling that I was attending my own funeral; looking at myself in the grave.

With a shock I recognised the remnants of the crumbling material as it disintegrated under my fingers. It was a finely tucked linen cap, its bow undone. I closed my eyes as I recalled stitching it for my trousseau. I brushed the rotting fragments away, almost believing that she would still be alive if only I were fast enough.

I stopped, startled by a stray curl of bright red hair that was trapped inside a fold of the decaying linen. Carefully I smoothed the earth away from her head and as my tears splashed on her small well shaped skull, a jolt, frightening in it's intensity, ran up my arm as I felt her power.

A searing current ran across my chest as if I'd been struck by lightning. I opened my mouth in a soundless scream as it's force knocked me to the ground.

Unable to breathe, I thought I was having a heart attack as her power merged with mine.

It lasted only a second and I lay on her un hallowed grave, burning with a vibrant energy.

I felt like a warrior, not a witch.

Surely this power could not have come from Rowena Berrysford? She was so naïve and her gift was no greater than my own. But, I realised, it had been untapped, almost virginal.

It was then that I remembered what I had been struggling to recall since Cassidy's death. Too late.

The words were my own, or rather, the child Rowena Beaumont's. She was telling Mistress Milly about the screaming hare caught in Coleman's trap.

"It was broken, but I mended it."

Tears of regret coursed down my cheeks.

'Oh, Cass, I'm so sorry,' I whispered, my throat tight with emotion.

I had been trying too hard. Poor Cassidy, his death was a waste. I could have saved him if I hadn't tried so damned hard. Healing was not a science, nor did it need medical knowledge, a child could do it. But I was a novice with such a lot to learn and no one to teach me.

Staring into the stormy sky I knew that this force was much older than Mistress Berrysford. It had been as much her inheritance as it was mine. And each of us, for different reasons, had rejected the gift.

Lightning illuminated the sky and was reflected in the silver posey ring that was still on Rowena's skeletal finger. "Vous et nul autre..." You and none other, I translated the engraving.

I carefully removed it and noticed there was also an inscription inside. Moving into the car's headlights, I read the words. "Rowena and William Berrysford, united forever. 1648."

Taking it back to her I put it on her ring finger. Holding her hand I wept for her long forgotten death, as I remembered her last hours.

I relived my memories too; dreadful memories of the cellar and those too fresh to bear of my lovely Cassidy.

In the silence of the dark wood, my heart full of bitterness and anger, I vowed vengeance and cried at the waste of Cassidy's life. If only I'd had her knowledge before he'd died.

Lifting his lifeless body and cradling him in my arms I wondered if I could bring him back?

No! I was not Frankenstein. There would be no monster waking from the dead tonight. It was not in my power to restore life, only health and I would use it to the best of my ability.

I laid him in Rowena's arms, clasping her bony fingers around him as I stroked his soft fur for the last time and whispered inarticulate words of endearment to be sure he knew how much I loved him. Then I covered them with my silk scarf. At least he wasn't alone. He didn't like being left on his own.

The thought of the loneliness of death was what I feared most.

'This Rowena will look after you now, my darling,' I murmured.

'I have brought you a companion, Rowena, his name is Cassidy. I beg you to take care of him. He is a good and faithful friend, a brave little dog... A hero...' I was choked up with tears. 'And I love him.'

Perhaps he would be company for her and give her as much loyalty and devotion as he'd given to me.

'Good night and God bless you both. Rest in peace,' I whispered as I buried them.

I said a prayer, thinking it fitting, before I stamped down the earth and threw leaves over their grave; keeping it safe from prying eyes.

My heart heavy with grief I prayed that this would be the end of the violence, the wasted lives saddened me. But even as I prayed I knew that there would be no miracles from heaven, no divine intervention to prevent the madness that was to come.

Lightning lit the scene and I screamed as Rowena's pain knotted my stomach. I fell to the ground gasping as the Colemans, Luke and Walter her down as Seth raped her. I felt the bruising punches as they beat her; the terror as they tied the stinking leather bag over her head and I choked for breath as they pulled the rope round her neck and hanged her.

Desperately I fought for control as her death throes threatened to kill me.

'Stop! I know what happened, Rowena. Why are you torturing me like this? For pity's sake, stop it,' I demanded.

She was punishing me for my lapse into sentimentality, knew that I had been wavering on the point of forgiveness. But I was angry with her too.

'This is not the way to treat a friend who is trying to help you!' I shouted.

The sound of the crack echoed in my ears as her neck broke.

I remembered what Piers did to me in the cellar and what Sebastian had done to John and Alice Baker and all the innocent passengers. What George had done to Cassidy and Buggalugs. Of what the Colemans were doing to the planet.

My eyes narrowed into slits of hatred and white hot fury pounded through my veins.

I could never forgive them. I was only human and such forgiveness belonged to the divine. Let them try to make their peace with their God and I would seek forgiveness from mine. There would be no mercy for the Colemans from me.

Mistress Berrysford had reminded me, sharpening my sorrow into arrows of anger and honing my grief into the cold steel of revenge.

CHAPTER THIRTY FOUR.

Kneeling in the damp earth beneath the tree, the storm raged above me but I paid no heed, feeling the strength of my power. Concentrating, I clasped my hands together, searching for the magic.

Thunder rolled and lightning crackled overhead and as it charged through me I stretched my arms above my head and reached for the heavens.

Every pore of my skin tingled as I absorbed the fragrance of the woods, the pine trees, the musky smell of the damp earth. I was at one with the universe. A surge of exhilaration, and like a cool breath of wind, I rose out of my body and soared over the treetops.

Looking down at myself I was afraid. Afraid that my soul leaving my physical body would mean death.

Slipping back to earth, aware of my body again, I lowered my arms and rested them on my knees, breathing deeply to overcome my panic. But as soon as I realised that I was not dead the initial fear left me. My physical being breathed in, releasing it's hold over me and I rose into the air.

Flying in the storm, tingling with it's electrical energy and free from the shackles of my body, was like swimming in buoyant water. I floated through the air towards the bright lights of Arnold. Calmly, as in a dream in which you are in complete control, I circled and swooped over Wizard's stone at Roswell, revelling in the feeling of freedom. There I saw Rowan and his half brother, fighting for supremacy...

Against all rules, Dacra drew his sword and advanced towards Rowan, who stood his ground, unarmed yet unafraid.

"Beware, begotten son of my father. I have the power of the witches tree from which I take my name and you will find I am not an easy prey."

With a cry of rage Dacra charged, his sword sweeping down in a stroke meant to sever Rowan's arm from his shoulders. But the blade did not fall. It was as if an invisible hand had grasped his wrist.

Rowan's mind forced Dacra's arm back until it snapped. His force surged and he threw him back against the alter.

Dacra rose to his knees, throwing a metaphysical punch to Rowan's wounded shoulder.

It was swept aside and doubled back and it was Dacra who fell gasping.

The metallic smell of blood hung in the air as their wills clashed and sparks flew. Each strike depleted their strength and they became so slow that although they both had the power, they were too exhausted to use it.

Almost in slow motion Dacra took his battle axe from his belt and raised it above his head for a vicious strike but Rowan held it in mid air, giving him time to roll away from it.

Dacra's bulk loomed over Rowan and they swayed in a macabre parody of dance.

Tired and realising he was losing, Dacra grabbed for Rowan's neck, meaning to physically strangle him, bringing the struggle for supremacy down to a camp brawl.

Disgusted, Rowan stepped aside and as he moved he aimed the side of his extended hand into Dacra's throat, felling him like an ox.

"You sicken me, sir! Gather your family together and leave. Now," he demanded.

"I will go, half brother. You have won, this time." Dacra whispered with unconcealed venom as he staggered away. 'But my children and my children's children will remember this night. Some day we will triumph and I shall win!"

He raised his hand as if in farewell and his sword which had lain forgotten in the wet grass, was launched at Rowan's heart.

Angered by the deceit, Rowan plucked it out of the air and held it aloft. The heavy sword glowed with his power as he pointed it at his half brother.

"Dacra of the dark, I cannot allow you to misuse your gift. For five hundred years and more your descendants will only be fit for menial tasks. Such is my anger and my power."

As Dacra crawled away Rowan crossed to the alter and knelt before the stone. Reaching under his tunic he removed his locket, which had been a marriage token from his Lady Amaranth. It was enamelled with a design of Rowans on one side and his initial on the other. Inside was a lock of her silken black hair intertwined with his own fiery red. Rowan tucked the tresses safely into his belt before he placed the keepsake upon the ancient stone.

He cast his spell, engraving strange symbols inside which would be indecipherable for aeons of time, to protect every first born child of his descendants who will bear the name of the Rowan tree.

He hardened the structure of the gold to protect it until the distant future, when she who sees clearly, would end this fight.

Like Bill said, Mistress Berrysford's curse was not the beginning. But it was up to me to end it.

I sought the Colemans at Beaumont Hall.

Without a qualm my astral body entered their luxurious sitting room, the solid walls dissolved as I effortlessly passed through them. Remembering that I'd seen Coleman's out of body image, I remained in hiding, watching from behind the half closed curtains.

The stale tobacco smoke of Piers' cigarettes seemed to permeate my soul.

George held Piers down while his father manipulated his dislocated shoulder. Piers stank of fear and neat gin.

Seething with frustration I wanted to rave at them but I would not dissipate my anger in impotent recriminations. Instead I left the house and sought the alarm system, breathing onto the bulb labelled "Lab Office". The alarm sent them scuttling. Sebastian went to the controls and pressed a button. Immediately the noise changed into an intermittent bleep.

'That's got her! The bitch has broken into my office, she's played right into our hands,' he said. 'We'll tell the police we caught an intruder on the premises; breaking and entering. Accidents can happen to intruders.'

I almost laughed out loud when he studiously locked the lab's automatic doors to prevent me making a quick get away before they arrived.

Sebastian tied a scarf into a makeshift sling for Piers and promptly picked up the soda siphon and squirted the contents into his face. 'Come on, we've got the witch trapped!'

Spluttering, Piers tried to argue. 'But it could be anyone. Kids, or...'

'Don't be stupid. She's spying on us, trying to get something for the bloody articles she writes. We've got her this time.'

Piers grin was sickly. 'Yeah, but...'

His father grabbed his bad arm and started to pull him out of the chair.

'Ok. Ok, I'm coming,' Piers whimpered.

'She's in for a big surprise, isn't she Dad? eh?' George chanted.

'She sure is. But this time use the few brains you've got instead of your brawn. God knows I've taught you enough tricks.'

As they ran to Sebastian's car, I simply rose into the air like a wisp of smoke and soared to their laboratory to wait.

The Colemans rushed to investigate, in the mistaken belief that they had me trapped.

In my heightened state of consciousness the stench of their brutality and their perverted violence left a tangible imprint on the oppressive atmosphere.

Briefly I thought of Bill, his strong presence lingered, wrapping me in his love. But I forced my mind onto narrower channels, the Colemans and their relentless pursuit of me and mine. Of the deadly viruses and carcinogens they were carelessly inflicting on the world. And the murders they had committed to safeguard their image.

Looking round Sebastian's office I noticed that it was tastefully furnished. There was an oak desk with a Victorian paraffin lamp on the top. Not, I noticed with grudging approval, converted to electricity. I glanced at the wick and it ignited into a steady flame.

Just what I needed. The soft glow would hopefully preclude the need for electric light and help to maintain my out of body illusion of substance. But I was not invincible. What if they saw through my little plan?

This was not the time to be defeatist. But I kept thinking it was one against three and they'd had a long time to practice their black art. They probably knew dirty tricks that I had never dreamed of and this was a fight to the death.

Theirs or mine.

Looking for weapons they might use against me, I saw an old wooden trunk standing in the corner, black and scarred with age. I moved to the brass bound box, running my fingers over its intricate pattern of Rowan leaves and berries. My fingers traced the pattern with instant recognition.

Rowena Berrysford's bible box.

Holding my breath I lifted the brass catch. It was broken, the bible box unlocked. I almost didn't look, not wanting to face the possibility that it might be empty. But I had to know.

The black leather was yellowed and musty with age but the King James bible was still there.

Opening the heavy tome I read the dedication on the fly leaf. The same words which were engraved inside my locket.

I recognised Squire Beaumont's fine script and remembered the words, passed on from generation to generation by word of mouth until he had written them in the bible and, fearing his daughter's safety in the time of superstitious zealotry, sealed the locket.

On the following pages was our family tree. And theirs.

I stared; expecting to see written as the last entry, the name of "my" baby, Rowena, astonished to see that the page was almost full.

The last name in it was my own.

They had recorded all my ancestors after Rowena Berrysford. And here and there, when the protagonists had clashed, their involvement in each other's deaths. None had managed to eliminate each other before they had an heir.

A wave of fury swept through me like a flash fire. How dare they?

I tried to calm down as I read my family tree from Rowena Beaumont's birth. In almost unintelligible cramped scrawl I saw

"Wich" written over Rowena Berrysford's name and "Hangd" heavily underlined.

Underneath some of my ancestors names were recorded the violent deaths of the respective Colemans. Walter, Luke and Seth in the seventeenth century was scrawled, "Kil'd by fire."

Some of the Colemans I knew of from my ancestors shared memories. Jessie and Hamm in the first world war, who, according to this, had been shot dead by my great grandfather.

There were a few exceptions. I wondered why Uriah and Zachary's deaths were neither recorded nor attributed to Rowena Knight. There must have been times when they could neither read nor write. The omissions were due entirely to illiteracy.

I realised this was why the Coleman's hated me. They had kept the curse alive with the written details of their ancestors deaths and kept track of my family better than any genealogist.

Coleman had no grandchildren. And he knows I am the last of my line. That's why they'd tried to kill me. That and the fact that I knew enough about their dealings to ruin them.

The bible proved that I was right; the Coleman's had hanged Rowena Berrysford all those years ago. Why did I need proof? Some people, James included, would never believe me, no matter what evidence I had and those I wanted to believe me did, without question.

There would be no excuses now. No need to prove what their ancestors had done. What all the Coleman's had done.

My senses went on alert as their footsteps came in to the building., remembering they outnumbered me three to one.

I stood in the shadow of the bible box as the door was unlocked and cautiously opened.

Sebastian didn't try to hide the look of triumph when he saw me.

'Well, well, we meet again! For the last time,' he added. 'Now you know what sort of murdering bastards your family were,' he said, gesturing towards the opened bible.

'Makes interesting reading, doesn't it?' Piers added.

'This time it's Our turn!' George said gleefully.

'Get her,' Sebastian commanded his sons, but after the last time Piers was cautious and George nervously darting glances at his brother, refused to move without him.

Coleman pushed by them and pointed at the only exit. The door slammed shut, the bolts shooting into place.

I clapped slowly. 'Very impressive,' I said lightly, 'for a children's parlour trick.'

Let him show off; drain his power.

With a mere glance at the overhead lights they exploded with an impressive bang; expending no more energy than flicking a switch. Fine splinters of glass showered down on them, cutting Sebastian's cheek. It had another advantage too; they couldn't put the lights on now.

He brushed the blood away angrily and flashed a dart of electric force at me, scorching the bible box.

While George and Piers scooted behind the filing cabinet, distracting Sebastian's attention, I moved to the shelter of the desk, ducking as another bright blue flash singed the polished oak.

I darted pencils at him like arrows. One sliced through his ear as he ducked too late.

'Is this the limit of your powers?' he sneered derisively.

Clicking his fingers he called 'George.'

Peering round the cabinet, George pointed at me, grinning with delight when the fallen pencils flew back at me.

'Novice tricks that even George can do,' Seb informed me while furniture piled itself in front of the window behind me, fencing me in. Heavy furniture.

It takes ten times more energy to move things by telekinesis than by physical strength, I remembered and wondered how often he could do that before running out of steam.

Now the room was only lit by the soft glow from the lamp and a pale sliver of moonlight coming through the window at the side of the cabinet.

Sebastian was sweating profusely and gasping for breath. Yet he fought on with seemingly unlimited power.

Laser like arrows of ice blue light stabbed the desk, leaving smoking holes, each one nearer its mark... Me.

He was toying with me. Darting another at me, I moved a little too late and yelped as it touched my arm. Trying to hold on to the illusion that I was really here I ducked in the narrow space behind the desk, not realising that it made me a target for Piers and George.

'Got her,' Piers said, as George came out of hiding to watch me get my comeuppance.

My stomach sank as they approached, not knowing who to aim for.

So much for my arrogant attempt to take them all on together. On my own. I should have listened to Bill.

Startling me out of my stupor, he came smashing through the window, behind Piers and George, flooring them both with a flying rugby tackle.

'Get down!' Bill yelled, and Coleman's bolt missed me by inches.

'I thought you might need a bit of muscle,' he grinned. 'Sorry I'm late, I went to your house first.'

As Piers elbowed himself up and pointed at me, Bill kicked him under the jaw. He fell back, out cold.

Bill looked at me and winked. 'Thought I might need my steel toe capped site boots as well. As I said before, we're in this together.' He was punching the lights out of George as he spoke.

'Thank you,' I whispered. He'd probably saved me but by joining the fight he had inadvertently scuppered my plan. Unless I could get him out of here, fast.

Two targets made it easier for Coleman, who kept firing in the hope of hitting one of us.

'Fetch the Police, Bill. Now!' I ordered as a flash singed his hair. 'Use the car phone,' and I whispered as a clincher. 'Call an ambulance too. It's only a nick but I've a feeling these bastards will need one as well.'

He glanced at the barricaded door.

'Go out the way you came in. I'll never be able to climb out of the window quick enough.'

'How will you get out of here then?'

Dammit he was quick. The truth would have to do. Or part of it anyway.

'I'll use my powers to move the furniture,' I told him. 'I can do it, Bill. Honest.'

To distract Coleman and convince Bill I darted pencils at Sebastian like arrows to a dartboard. One stuck in the side of his neck and as he tried to pull it out, another gouged his hand.

'Ok, I believe you. But I'll be back,' Bill grinned as he leapt through the broken window.

He was safe.

'You'll have to do better than that, dear,' Sebastian bared his teeth in the semblance of a grin.

He was right. I had to stop these monsters now. Destroy the formula that would poison the earth; the effects of which would be more far reaching than a nuclear war.

'I could squash you like a bug,' he whispered, levitating his physical body a foot in the air to get a better shot at me.

'Don't bet on it,' I sneered, darting to one side as a bright beam whizzed past my ear.

Without flexing a muscle I glanced at him. 'Down,' I whispered, hardly moving my lips.

He dropped to the floor like a startled puppet with his strings cut.

I stood my ground behind the glare of the Victorian lamp. Concentrating; feeling the glass bowl with my mind; smelling the oily pink paraffin.

As Coleman shot a bolt of fire at me, I parried it with the lamp, throwing it towards him as I soared into the air.

When the power from his fingers touched the lamp, the paraffin imploded with a barely audible whoosh.

Flames leapt as they searched for sustenance, lighting up the room with their insatiable hunger. The open window by the filing cabinet drew them to the air, the frame catching fire immediately, reminding me of Walter Coleman's burning cottage.

The astonished disbelief in Sebastian's eyes when he realised that I wasn't physically there, in some small way repaid me for the anguish he had caused.

Before he could summon his depleted powers he was engulfed in flames.

Screeching, the burning figures ran round looking for a way out. Sealed in their own tomb.

If I believed in the biblical hereafter I'd say the last of the Colemans burned in hell fire; wiped of the face of the earth forever, along with the formulas of their poisonous pesticides and weed killers. Glancing over my shoulder as I swooped back to the crossroads I saw the laboratory was nothing more than a pall of black smoke as the flat roof of the old prefabricated building collapsed, shooting millions of red sparks into the air in a brilliant display of pyrotechnics.

No more Colemans to pollute the world, I told myself triumphantly. But revenge was sickly sweet and only momentary.

I came back to earth too fast. My senses were reeling, I felt like a diver with the bends and shivered with exhaustion. Resting my head against the rough bark of the tree I emptied my stomach, wishing I could vomit up the memory of this dreadful night.

The world tilted about me and I clung to the tree, my throat burning with regurgitated bile.

I had killed the Colemans. Murdered them all.

That I was destined to do so, was no consolation.

The last of them had perished in the fire. There would be no more threat to the world from them, the feud that started with Rowan of the Well and Dacra was over, thank God. But would God ever forgive me?

My arms clenched around my stomach, I rocked back and forth in the chill light of dawn, desolate and alone.

In the distance I heard the wail of a fire engine. The ambulance would follow on its wasted journey. And the Police would want my story. Should I tell them the truth? Would they believe me? I doubt it. And would Bill still love me if I told him everything? For tell him I must. This was no little indiscretion that I could keep to myself.

Oh Bill, to lose you again would be unthinkable. Unbearable. But sooner or later I would have to tell him what I had done. What I had become. A murdering witch.

Was this the price I had to pay for protecting my family from this ancient feud?

I tried to convince myself that everything which had happened to us all had been out of our control.

Remembering my ancestors I relived flashes of their lives like a three dimensional video running on fast forward. Rowena Knight and Montegue, Rowan Harris and Mayhew, Mistress Berrysford and "my" daughter. And the father of us all, Rowan of the Well. Each had contributed to my awakening.

Then I remembered what Bill had said about Mistress Berrysford. "She may have been just another victim. Like you."

'Victim. Like me?' I repeated out loud.

Be dammed if I was going to accept that. There had been too many victims, I thought, shaking my head. But not me. Oh no. Not me, I vowed. Not any more.

Then what the hell was I doing running away from my only chance of happiness? As for the guilt, I would have to learn to live with it. And if I carried some strange power, so be it. I could live with that too.

Every muscle in my body protesting, I lurched down the slope and made my way to my car.

Turning the ignition, soothed by the normality of the car's soft hum I drove out on to the road, and sped back to the laboratory.

I saw Bill's Celica in the dock where we'd parked before, and pulled up alongside.

The fire brigade had arrived and the firemen were dowsing down the last of Coleman's Feed and Fertiliser Company. But where was Bill?

Panicking I called his name. What if he'd gone back into the conflagration to rescue me?

The ambulance drove up, followed by a police car and Bill climbed out of the fire engine's cab to meet them. Then he saw me and whooping with joy we ran to each other.

'I thought you were still in there,' he mumbled into my neck, holding me tight.

'And I thought you'd gone back to help me.'

'Do you need the ambulance?' he asked, looking for my supposed injury.

'No Bill, I'm fine.'

Taking my arm he kept to the shadows as he led me back to the transport dock. 'Do you want to tell the police about the Coleman's?'

'I'd rather not,' I shrugged. 'I doubt if they'd believe me.'

'No need to bother them, then,' he said, kissing me as we stood in the shelter of the loading bay. 'They'll find the bodies. If they ask my opinion, I'll tell them they probably met with a nasty accident when they where burning the evidence of their poisonous products.

'After the articles Jayne's published, they'd believe that,' I nodded. 'But...'

'But me no buts, Rowena. Your car or mine? I think we should get out of here before they get suspicious. Follow me,' he turned to me anxiously. 'You will, won't you?'

'To the ends of the earth,' I smiled. 'But first I have to tell you...'

'No, you don't have to tell me anything, except that you love me. Nothing else matters.'

'I love you.' The three little words said it all.

I loved both the Bill who is now and the William who once was. The differences were only superficial.

We both got into our cars and I followed him to Tannery Lane.

The sky was painted with the technicolour promise of Summer as I drove round the mini roundabout, impatient to be with Bill, back where I belonged. We had both waited far too long; centuries too long.

As I pulled up behind his car we rushed to each other and with his arms around me opened the door.

Rowena had come home. The centuries of waiting was over.

At last, Mistress Berrysford had returned to her William, and I to my Bill. In her own way, she had made sure of that.

THE END.